Siana's War

A novel by Charles McCrone

Paperback: 979-8-9861424-1-8
Ebook: 979-8-9861424-0-1

First paperback edition: May 2022

Cover art by Ian McCrone

Publisher: Forgotten Town Press, Issaquah, WA

cm@charlesmccroneauthor.com

Contents

"We shall not cease from exploration
And the end of all our exploring
Will be to arrive where we started
And know the place for the first time"

—T.S. Eliot

WITHIN

For a fortnight Llwyd Emyr had strolled the subaqueous boardwalk of the Edoi Sea, spending lazy sun-kissed hours anticipating the marvels of Ebon Port and the lands of the Aedolae beyond. He now swam the last mile and stepped from the water, dripping, tasting salt.

But instead of marvels, terror met him, slinking out from the jungle.

Knife-edged tails, held high like a scorpion's, fanning in agitation. Muscled forearms dragging massive bodies through fine white sand. Scarlet eyes, caged in spikes of bone, blazing intelligence and malice.

Llwyd Emyr recognized them at once, shocked they were here, at the very doorstep of the realms.

Coethyphys.

Bred centuries ago to hunt trespassers, trespassers like himself.

To *consume* them.

But these three did not attack. Instead they herded him away from his immediate goal, the village of Orse, and toward a lone pier that jutted out into the choppy sea. Three more Coethyphys blocked the beach beyond.

Llwyd Emyr was soon hedged in by a phalanx of mottled flesh and vicious horns.

With no other options, he mounted the pier, knowing this too was a trap.

A lone figure waited at pier's end, looking out at the nearest island of the archipelago.

As Emyr approached, the figure turned, his motion cultured and indolent. The man's oiled hair fell in black ringlets, and a neat triangular beard hung below a disdainful mouth. He leaned on a walking stick.

"Welcome, sojourner," the man said, quietly.

His eyes hid behind an antique pair of smoky glasses. Emyr felt a chill, as if the man radiated glacial cold.

"Who are you?" Emyr asked.

"Pardon me," the man replied. "I am called Ghislain, and I am far from home. I have come to meet someone special, an anomaly in my *thousand* years of experience." His voice lingered on the word *thousand* with a smile. Emyr's dread deepened. A thousand years ago the Aedolae had established these kingdoms, their lives undiminished by the passing centuries.

"And you are?" Ghislain asked.

Emyr was surprised to find his own voice calm.

"I believe you know, and so do your monsters there. So let us not dissemble."

Ghislain gestured with his walking stick toward the beach end of the pier, where the Coethyphys stood like statues.

"They are not monsters. They are rather elegant, but they are at times *disobedient*. Their long hunger makes them strong-headed. They have been hungry for a long time."

Emyr edged backwards. He was athletic. One long jump to the water below? But he suspected it would not be so easy.

Ghislain removed his glasses and folded them away in a pocket of his richly embroidered black tunic. Emyr gasped. Two oval mirrors had replaced his eyes.

This was an Aedolae, a soul-less being in the shape of a man.

In these mirrors Emyr watched tiny versions of himself back away.

"Come now, *Grey King*," Ghislain said. "You have violated our law. Your life is forfeit."

"You named me sojourner," Emyr argued. "You know what that means. You cannot destroy me. No matter what you do to me, I will return, to savor what your kind have stolen away."

"So you think," Ghislain countered, "for to you this world is a fantasy, a playground for your soul. But to us, bred within its confines, it is the sum of reality and your world nothing but a distant rumor and a shadow. What did your Bard say? *There are more things in heaven and earth, Horatio, Than are dreamt of in your philosophy.*"

"I have heard enough," Emyr spat. "Your kind are thieves."

Emyr reached for his Eterokoni, eight artifacts of power collected in lands outside the Detheros, but Ghislain was faster. His stick cracked against Emyr's outstretched hand.

"I know in your world," Ghislain said, "there is another you anchoring this mirage I see before me. You think this makes you safe? There are other ways between our worlds, more abrupt, more *final*. Soon that *other* Emyr will join you here. And then my 'monsters' will get what they need."

Emyr got to his feet, rubbing his wrist. It felt like Ghislain's blow had broken bones. This Aedolae should—*could*—have no power over the other self he'd left behind. But in his gut he feared it was true.

Next Emyr had the most uncomfortable experience of his life.

He startled awake to a lesser version of himself, to hot breath on his face, flickering light from an old lamp. He saw moss-covered stone, and the dark interior of an ancient tower. The grubby man beside him groaned and lifted Emyr's drugged body from the floor, pitching him forwards and down into utter blackness. The stone of the tower disappeared. There was a deafening vibration. The joints and bones of his body were forcibly stretched and torn. He was spinning down an endless well, and then, with a sickening lurch, he was separated from his physical form. He hovered motionless in the center of the dark, watching the brutalized chaff of his body fall away and disappear.

In a crazed rush of images, his consciousness was driven through a shadowy procession of the places he had explored—the graveyard of Nathnang, the Cliffs of Ivilstuen, the Prismatic Jungle, the floating circle of the Gardens—and rushed deeper, toward his *other* body which staggered at the end of a pier. Drawn by this irresistible magnetism, his soul flew through the Detheros, an arc of ash-choked wasteland and spire-like mountains smooth as glass, five miles deep and a thousand miles long, reliving in seconds the hours of pain and toil and deprivation, the steaming pools of mud, the inky black caverns, the torturous climbs through labyrinthine corridors choked with fetid fogs.

He burst free at the edge of the Edoi Sea, soaring into freshness and light. He passed over the miles of subaqueous boardwalk. From a great height he looked down upon the archipelago beyond. Closer and closer now. His consciousness descended. He spotted the long pier, and then with a crush and a weight, his awareness was pulled into the body standing there.

Ghislain laughed and raised his stick. A signal to shore.

The Coethyphys stepped aside to let something pass, a vast shadow bursting from jungle's edge in an explosion of branches and leaves. With lazy strokes of huge wings it traversed the pier's length and where the tips of its wings struck the railings, wood burst in fragments. Its darkness sucked light from the air. Emyr turned and jumped for the sea, but time ripped and lurched. The Shadow had crossed the remaining space. It seized him as he jumped, crushing him against a wall of vibrating energy. As they lifted into the air, Ghislain laughed below.

"Goodbye, Grey King, may the Feast be well!"

Emyr knew he was lost, that his anchoring self was gone. His entire being now lay in this nightmare's daggered grip. But the Grey King had one last protest. One hand could still reach the grape-like cluster hanging from his belt.

The Eterokon of Destruction.

Pearl-hard, but the lot of them crushed easily in his hand.

He had used just one before and it had leveled a hillside.

As Emyr's hand came open, unnatural silence swallowed all sound.

WITHOUT

October 2003

T he girl awoke, sitting up in bed, hands shaking. A moment before she was dreaming in the Fringe, following the shining ribbon that spooled out from her brother's soul. Though many days behind, she had tracked him to the Prismatic Jungle and spoke there with the Solmikaedis perched upon her Shard. And while they conversed the ribbon had snapped.

She had clutched in vain at its unraveling threads.

Fall sunlight dappled through her window. The old farmhouse was quiet. She was late for school, her father off to work. She had fallen asleep doodling. The sketchbook lay beside her, sporting a fifteen-year-old girl's remarkably accurate self-portrait. Below was scrawled, with curlicues: *Siana*.

Feeling a strange dread, she got up, brushed back her hair and looked out the window. John was gunning his dilapidated truck up the gravel road to his trailer in the driveway. She had missed the school bus. Not that either of her parents would care. Mom would be in her room, staring blankly out the window.

The girl gazed at the photos on her bulletin board, steeling herself against the day with happy memories: her brother Timothy, with the foolish grin he reserved for her, next to his new sports car, Timothy looking silly in a tux for her eighth grade graduation, and her favorite photo at the center—the out of focus Polaroid he'd taken of her, eleven years old, in the glass-walled elevator in Oregon, the day they'd played hide and seek throughout the hotel. And one more: she and Timothy at the beach, the only one that showed them together.

Preoccupied with the emotion of her dream, she had forgotten Timothy was home from college this week. He could give her a ride to school. She ran to his room, her favorite place in the 1904 house. His bed was made as if he hadn't slept in it. Her mind protested: she had seen him the night before. With a deepening confusion, she saw that none of his things were in the room.

She soon found out that by the reckoning of everyone else in the family, her brother had died in a car accident several months before.

THE CASTLE

E llie awoke from unremembered dreams to the sound of houses falling outside her window.

It was a morning like all the others.

Shivering, crossing her thin arms over her dirty linen dress, she stumbled to the grimy window and rubbed her fingers on the glass to clear a place to see. She did this every day, but then each morning the window was begrimed again, with no trace of the pattern her fingers had made.

Low hills marched away from the high window of her sleeping place, stacking up against a misty horizon. The wreckage of uncounted days of falling houses speckled this olive brown landscape: splintered timbers, wide halos of shattered glass. As she watched, another house dropped from the sky, pancaking on hard soil a quarter mile off. Some days the houses fell closer to her window, and the impact would shake the floor.

She wondered, not for the first time, if one would ever strike the castle. *What would happen if it did?*

Ellie left her post at the window and walked slowly to the door, as she had done every other morning she remembered. Her bare feet left footprints in the inch thick dust. But there were no footprints from the night before. About this, like the window, she had long ago ceased to wonder.

She turned the cold brass doorknob and stepped onto the balcony. Today, like most days, she had to shield her eyes from the blazing wall of stained glass to her right, a depiction of a tall female warrior. It threw a riot of colors across the polished floor of the ballroom below. At twilight the ballroom would become host to a mute masquerade of waltzing ghosts should Ellie fail to return to her bedroom in time. But in the morning it was empty save for the cold, unseeing eyes of this woman rendered in a thousand welded fragments of colored glass.

As far back as she remembered, Ellie had awoken daily in her tiny gallery above the ballroom. This procession of similar mornings receded into the dimness of her memory like infinitely echoed reflections in a pair of mirrors. She had no recollection of any place but this immense, silent castle nor of the childhood through which she must have lived to become the young woman trapped here. She knew little about herself: only her name, that her sandy blonde hair was just long enough to grab, and that her face felt to questing fingers like the unblemished skin of youth.

Ellie was lonely, and the loneliness of her world exhausted her. Each day she wandered and found new twists and turns which led nowhere in particular. There was no end to the castle, and no way out. She couldn't remember being anywhere else, but her instinct for freedom was strong—and the view from her bedroom window encouraged it. That there might be no way to pass the castle walls to attain this outside of hills and sky offended her sensibilities. And yet she found no way. She remembered, somewhere in the depths of her mind, the concept of food and drink, yet she had never eaten here, and never felt hungry.

Aside from twilight's ghosts, Ellie had only one companion in this forlorn emptiness: the woman whose icy countenance was captured in rich and varied iconography across the length and breadth of the castle. Warrior, explorer, princess. The entire castle, with its endless arrangement of halls, staircases and storerooms, armories and antechambers, seemed to be a shrine to her.

The themes of the iconography varied widely. Some rooms housed solitary images of a blonde warrior in somber black garb gazing into the distance. One hallway sported a sequence of mosaics showing her finding treasure in haunted locales. Some cast her as beautiful, with long blonde hair braided with flowers. Most showed her as fierce and athletic, engaged in battle with monsters that struck Ellie as horrendously unrealistic.

Ellie's feelings toward the images were mixed. She wondered at the hubris or fawning obsessiveness behind such a shameless tribute as this endless, repetitive picture show. But she found herself addressing the illustrations, for lack of any other company, speaking to them as if this larger-than-life figure were her patron deity, her succor.

Today there was something new on the floor of the ballroom: a book, lying as if casually tossed aside. There had never been a book before. Her heart beat a fevered rhythm. Was this morning different, the first sign of change in the crushing sameness of her life? It was both strange and intoxicating. Her mind immediately raced. The discovery of the book might give her mind a landmark, a fixed event in memory. A day from which, perhaps, she could number all the rest.

She rushed down the staircase, falling and scuffing her knee, and under the gaze of her stained-glass demigoddess gathered the book in her arms. She touched it gingerly as if it might vanish like her footprints in the dust. The book was ancient and scrawling handwriting covered its pages.

She began to read.

My name is Siana.

I am the Princess of Time, the nemesis of these Lords of the Night.

I am the Mistress of the Eterokoni, artifacts from a shadowed age, a forgotten past.

Ellie knew at once who Siana was. Siana must be the woman of the iconography, and this book another part of the castle's fawning tribute.

With fascination and hope, Ellie tore into the narrative. And as she read, Siana shed her distance and assumed a mantle of reality in Ellie's mind.

THE ATTACK ON KADESH

1015th Year of the Detheros

My name is Siana.

I am the Princess of Time, the nemesis of these Lords of the Night.

I am the Mistress of the Eterokoni, artifacts from a shadowed age, a forgotten past.

When I was a child I had another name, but it is no longer a part of me, for I wage war against the Aedolae, usurpers of worlds. No one in a thousand years, save I, has forced them to open battle or destroyed their strongholds, slaying their scions by the hundreds. They fear me, as they have feared no other of my kind.

They even killed me, but I rebuilt myself in the sanctuary of Mercair's World and now I have returned, strength and hatred intact.

It was the third year of my war.

My saboteurs struck against Mihali last fall, an attack that cost the Twins their palace but cost me my life. Now we were assembling in the forest above our stronghold at Forgotten Town, streamers of early morning sun slicing through mist. This time we would strike against the jungle demesne of Kadesh, named for another of the Aedolae. I was not ready to take Cylindrax, not with its icy seas. But I suspected the master of Cylindrax, Ghislain—the most dire of my enemies—was visiting at Kadesh. I had reconnoitered the realm from afar using the Eye, my Eterokon of Sight, and I had seen Ghislain's army of

Glacii, ice titans, flanking the Prismatic Pool beneath Kadesh's palace.

We climbed higher into the forest.

My dark blonde hair hung in long straight waves, a conduit for the moisture of the woods to soak the back of my tunic; the strands about my face braided tight and laced with tiny scarlet feathers—nonetheless four inches in length—that came from around the eyes of Mercair's tremendous guardian birds. Years ago, when I was little more than a child, the Aedolae had lulled me into sensuous complacency in their garden prison, where I had braided my hair with feathers to while away dreamy summer afternoons.

I reclaimed the habit now, in defiant mockery of what they had done to me.

I wore my battle garb, smaller Eterokoni in their belt about my waist and the transparent scabbard of the Glass Sword, the largest Eterokon, strapped across my back. I felt strong. When I arrived at Mercair's haven, fleeing the horrors of my death, my body had been weak and soft in its rebirth, but I had not been idle during my eight weeks there. I had swiftly regained the hardness of those years of travel and warfare that had transformed the child into the warrior.

The skeletal limbs of giant maple and cottonwood, richly tapestried with lichen and moss, rustled in the breeze above my head. I almost failed to spot the more deliberate movement of a creature like an enormous spider, which disengaged itself from a canopy of vine maple and landed with a thud on the gravel path in front of me. It unfurled into an exceedingly tall and gaunt man, with limbs and fingers that resembled the surrounding winter trees. Leathery eyelids swiveled, revealing large eyes with red irises.

"Lady Siana"—he croaked—"let us go to war."

I smiled. Talmei was one of my favorites among the saboteurs, and his people—the Estringites—one of the largest components of my army.

"Talmei." I took his hand, and tendrils burst from the bark-like tips of his fingers, wrapping vine-like around my arms. "It is good to see you at your post."

"Of course, my lady," he said. "I watch the portal unceasing."

To leave Forgotten Town one must find the precise place in the forest where the Kalimba Eterokon's power activates the portal. In every other demesne I could pick my place of egress. Not so with Forgotten Town. I knew the spot well, two stunted evergreens forming a tiny grotto of dry ground, carpeted in fallen needles. My saboteurs crowded in close. We were only a few hundred; we had lost many at Mihali.

Would this be enough?

I had Seen the flame warriors and ice titans of my enemies.

I took the Kalimba down from its necklace. It lay in my hand like a tiny lady's fan, each of its six keys inscribed with a runic symbol. I felt for and held down the button on its back, engaging its power, and then struck the fifth key, inscribed with a circle topped by a cross. A percussive note sounded, at first audible only to me, but growing until its power throbbed like a palpable force. No surprise registered upon the faces of my companions; they had done this many times before. Neikolan, the jet-skinned pirate who was my second in command, grinned and showed white teeth.

The portal opened, a circle framing darkness.

It was early morning in the jungle of Kadesh. We stepped out in the Dark Quarter, at an open plaza where multiple boardwalks met. The Kalimba always took one to this exact point of entry. Multiple moons hung low to the horizon, their light fading before the dim illumination of the sun, which was still unseen behind trees. My saboteurs ranged about me. Many had never been to Kadesh, and their expressions grew tense now that the forest of Forgotten Town was left behind.

When the last saboteur passed I released the button, terminating the Kalimba's power, closing the portal. We quickly arrayed in battle lines, with scouts both fore and aft.

I had already mapped any unfamiliar trails with the Eye. I couldn't predict the time of day we would arrive, for any relationship between the time flows of the demesnes was spurious. So my plan did not rely on the cover of night.

We set off in disciplined silence.

We hurried along our selected path. Fingers of sunlight snaked through the dense wall of verdure to our right and dappled against wooden rails and planks. In fifteen minutes we would split into groups and flank the south side of the Prismatic Pool.

We reached a second nexus, a smaller plaza. From here a multitude of trails branched off to encircle the Prismatic Pool and its boardwalk where a thousand torches burned day or night. I credit my army with their efficiency. Despite my disappearance and absence, despite the brevity of the week's preparations, they moved with skill and alacrity. Most—except those like the Estringites whose physical form made it difficult—had become fine archers. The first part of my plan depended on that.

I found it curious we had met no opposition, for the massing of troops from two realms signified anticipation of my next move. A reaction to Mihali.

Was this lack of opposition now part of *their* plan, a ploy to draw us in?

I divided my forces between the trails, going with the rightmost group. Just shy of the Pool, we took to the trees on either side, creeping up to the boardwalk but staying under the dark eaves of the jungle, arrows knocked and at the ready. When all was set I disengaged myself from my group.

And disappeared from sight. I used another of the Eterokoni: the Gauntlet of Invisibility.

It was a silver glove, an impossibly fine mesh of miniature steel links, exceedingly strong. Upon my hand it shrank to a second, shining flesh. I could still see myself, but as long as I wore it I would be invisible to other eyes.

I strode along the Pool toward Kadesh's palace, where massive bamboo tubes were sunk deep, supporting a complicated latticework of tiers and ramps and buildings. The entire edifice was a marvel of bamboos of different sizes and hues.

All eminently combustible.

Solitary figures strolled upon the decks and terraces of the palace, but I knew from my time as a guest there that few residents would be awake at this early hour. Kadesh was a place of nocturnal revelry and feasting. Nonetheless armies of ice and flame still flanked the palace, standing guard without cease. I had counted on this.

I was two thirds of the way along the boardwalk to the phalanx of motionless Glacii. I was nervous, but my nervousness was untinged by dread and buoyed by excitement. Knowing that no one saw me, friend or foe, I took the leisure to approach the railing of the Pool. A wild mix of brilliant hues swirled at my feet, ever-changing patterns in the strange water. The patterns struck me as a symbol. I would be the harbinger of change. The bringer of a chaos too long forestalled by the iron control of my enemies.

I whispered, for only myself to hear:

"Let it begin."

I drew the Glass Sword and spun. Its fragile blade bisected a quartet of torch-bearing poles.

As the severed torches hissed in the mud at Pool's edge, sinking into viscous water, my archers lit their arrows in the fire of the torches before them. I relished the irony of that. Kadesh's own flame, borne aloft on three hundred soaring missiles, arcing high in the air and raining down on his palace.

There was that strange moment of silence, before the battle begins but after its inevitability is established. A moment of waiting, as the arc of the flaming arrows peaked in the sky.

And then the rush of sound, thuds as the missiles met their target, soon wailing and screams as men and women erupted from windows and doors. The palace exploded with activity. Lines of fire spread out from the arrows, which bristled from the structure like black hairs on a boar's back. Figures tumbled from the walls into the Pool. Within ten seconds, the shimmering field of energy containing the Glacii had winked off, and they began to stir. On this too I had counted.

A second volley of arrows took to the sky. Again that strange moment of waiting, but this time crowded with noise. Again the arrows rained down, this time among Glacii. A few of the Glacii fell. They tore at the burning shafts, rivulets of water streaming from their wounds, but their composure under attack was more machine than human. Those that were unscathed shuffled down the boardwalk in my direction. The Seraphi, Kadesh's burning soldiery, had not yet stirred from their posts. I stepped off the boardwalk and stood beside it, facing the Pool.

My vorpal sword, held out at arm's length, blade parallel to the ground, cleaved six Glacii before they even knew they were engaged. I had never seen them this close: automata carved of ice, features hard to distinguish with their translucency and the glinting sun. But what faces I saw were devoid of expression.

I jumped onto the boardwalk, laying waste with the Glass Sword in all directions. With the Pool and the jungle boxing them in, only two could fit abreast on the trail. The Glacii's sole weapon was a row of metal orbs embedded in their thighs. They couldn't see their enemy and the orbs constituted a poor weapon for close range fighting. Nonetheless by the time I had slashed my way through the first quarter of their ranks they began to make ineffective lobs in my general direction. The orbs were massively heavy and crashed through the planking. This gave me more trouble than the Glacii. Splintered and upended boards made it difficult to move so my position—despite my invisibility—became easier to track. The orbs fell closer.

I heard the thwunk of my archers' third volley of arrows, this time targeting the Seraphi.

I was determined to fell as many Glacii as possible. I cut my way deeper into their midst, strategizing to surround myself with them and block the rain of orbs. Too late. An orb knocked the wind out of my chest and I stumbled off the boardwalk. To hurl these things in such a fashion—the Glacii were tremendously strong.

I had reached the end of this part of my plan. My wrist sported a bracelet of tiny stones, another Eterokon. With a wave of this hand I petrified the remaining ice giants. I had destroyed a third of them but I had hoped for more. A hundred archers were now in plain view at the railings, yelling and brandishing weapons. Just enough to account for the number of arrows fired. We hoped to trick the Aedolae into thinking we were quick and easy prey.

It worked.

The Seraphi had not yet stirred, but the great green eagles of Kadesh took to the air, each carrying a warrior of his personal guard. If the presence of Ghislain's forces was bait, the Aedolae must have judged it time to spring the trap. Or perhaps the catalyst was rage at the destruction our arrows had wreaked. All was chaos around the burning palace. There was little open space between palace and jungle, now choked with a throng of people: women of Kadesh's harem, palace staff and administrators, folk of no use and much trouble in a battle. They spilled into the area the Glacii had occupied, making it a risky and ineffectual field of war. So the Aedolae brought the battle to us.

The palace itself was doomed, for the strange waters of the Pool were of little use in quenching fire. This gave me great satisfaction, to destroy that place of opulence and greed and hedonistic pleasures. Another devastation, like the Twins' compound at Mihali, that I hoped would speak louder than purely military victory.

The eagles flew low across the Pool. Some fell to arrows, shrieking as the Pool swallowed them. As the attackers fanned out, the leftmost eagle passed over me, just clearing the torches. I had intended to run back to my saboteurs but this was too good an opportunity. As it passed I jumped and seized its harness, in a single fluid movement swinging myself up and boxing off the female rider. I had a moment's vision of her surprised face and nimbus of jet black hair, falling.

The eagle didn't seem to notice the change in riders and responded to my directives. I relieved two more eagles of their mounts before the rest reached my archers. The eagles swept in, talons out, while Kadesh's guards struck with wickedly curved swords. An Estringite fell. Neikolan yelled commands. After a brief skirmish, the eagles arced away, regrouping for a fresh attack. I continued to swoop and pick off riders. This created great confusion, as all the guards saw was a rider-less eagle crashing through their midst. I targeted leather harnesses and the exceeding sharpness of the Glass Sword pierced these trappings like paper. To the eagle guards' eyes, unscathed warriors were simply falling off.

I noticed one eagle, more massive than the rest, shadowing my moves. Its handler was Kadesh. I had not expected this, an Aedolae riding with his force.

Nor did I expect him to meet my gaze.

"I see you," he yelled, his pocked face flushed with anger. His eyes were black, all pupil. "Sojourner and your toys. Do you think they make you invincible?" His mount snapped at my eagle's tail feathers.

"They do, Aedolae," I returned. "For I died and here I am."

He raised his immense javelin. I should have guessed his intention. Given his oven-hot blast of hatred, I assumed his target was me.

Instead he speared my eagle.

The javelin pinned its right wing to its body. We were now over jungle south of the Pool. I hadn't been harnessed and was thrown free of the tumbling, shrieking chaos of talon and feather as we crashed through the upper canopy. The translucent scabbard of the Glass Sword caught on a branch, and though the straps holding my shoulders strained and cut into my skin, they stopped my descent.

I was able to free myself and climb down. I fought through dense brush to rejoin my archers at the Pool, passing many who were still hidden. Their expressions communicated that they struggled to hold position while watching their fellows fall in the counterattack. It was time.

I rematerialized beside Neikolan, tucking the Glove in my belt, and whispered my directive.

"Sound the retreat."

ICONS

The book slid from Ellie's fingers and splayed onto the polished marble floor of the ballroom.

She had been crouching in what she now realized was a very uncomfortable position and she struggled with sleeping legs to stand up. The blaze from the stained glass had subsided. Her body felt weak and she was breathing fast. She hardly saw her surroundings, the smooth stone columns, the walls velveted with curtains. Instead, imagery from the book resonated in her mind. She wanted to read more, but she didn't want to go back to her unkempt bed in the tiny room above the ballroom. So she decided to go to a room she knew had benches, her legs tingling with returning blood. She thought about what she had read.

Something convinced her Siana had written it herself—a sense of Siana's personality that cut through the grandiosity of the story. If Siana wrote this book, then it was the most important thing in the castle. Which led back to a question Ellie couldn't answer: Where had the book been until now? She had never seen books, no reading room nor library. All the chests she'd opened had been full of dust. The sudden appearance of a book, now, was another example of the oddness of her abode.

She walked out of the ballroom into the murkiness of the broad hallway beyond, taking the book with her.

The castle was lit by torches that never sputtered out, or by wan illuminations with no apparent source. The light never changed, and only in the gallery and ballroom—with their respective windows—could Ellie ascertain the passage of day outside. Nonetheless during her explorations she sensed twilight and day's end; she felt it in her bones. Her body, frail and exhausted in the mornings, was paralyzed with weakness at dusk and the castle seemed to tempt her to immobility. And she knew from experience that day's end—despite the unchanging light—brought horrible things to life. Faces, presences, things she called ghosts. The only hope lay in hurrying her pained limbs back to the safety of her gallery.

The fear of being trapped abroad at night permeated even her morning explorations. She rarely saw ghosts by day, but it had happened often enough to keep her mind uneasy. Most of the time she felt alone, but in certain rooms she felt watched. She avoided those. Some days she had simply stayed in the gallery, watching rain streak the window panes, watching the houses endlessly, endlessly fall. But the boredom of that was worse. And she greatly desired to find a door out into the world.

Each day her search had grown more difficult, for as she expanded the boundaries of her exploration she could now walk all day and see only places she had already been. No doors to the outside, no end to the flow of halls and rooms. It now took her to the dangerous verge of twilight to pass through all the familiar chambers to find something wholly new.

But today her blaze of excitement pressed all that aside. She retraced familiar steps, bare feet padding noiselessly across marble, stone, smooth wood. The folds of her simple white dress swished about her calves. The utter silence of the various chambers that spread out on all sides like the spokes of a wheel was deafening.

The icons of Siana struck her in a new light, each one now framed by the events of the story. She saw the Glass Sword, held aloft in Siana's gauntleted hands. Now Ellie could name the diminutive thumb piano on its nigh invisible choker: the Kalimba.

What struck her most was that *all* the details of the images jibed completely with the book—despite their wide variety of media—whether painting, tapestry, mosaic, or statue.

She passed into a circular room, low ceilinged and dark. A diffuse white light shone up the walls from some indiscernible source in the carpeted floor. Everything was black: walls, ceiling and carpet, save for paintings spaced evenly along the walls.

Ellie had dubbed it the Vicious Room.

The ballroom's stained-glass Siana was a Greek goddess, expressionless, pallid, her clothes wrought in gem-like color. But in this room Siana was a demoness, teeth bared, eyes wild, hair streaming out behind her to blend with swirling black clouds. The nails that gripped the Glass Sword were painted either red or black, and fire reflected on its gleaming surface. Her arms were bathed in blood.

Even more disturbing were Siana's opponents, and before today Ellie would not look at them. But now she dared, searching for some connection to the story. One was a being with an insect's eyes. Another, a man-shaped pit of shadow ringed with fire, had to be a Seraph.

One painting was brighter, but the quality of the light turned Ellie's stomach. It made her think of a graveyard lit by a spectral moon. Ellie couldn't remember seeing it before. Not only did the painting's uncanny realism surprise her, but also Siana's expression, pinched by anxiety. She couldn't recall any such emotion portrayed elsewhere in the castle. She thought back to the book. Siana was self-assured, confident, powerful, certain of the efficacy of her abilities as she led her campaign against the Aedolae.

Eager to read more, Ellie moved on. She had never liked the spiral staircase that lay beyond. After the enveloping darkness of the Vicious Room it made her feel exposed. At the bottom of staircase an arched doorway led into a small hall, whose opposite wall was broken by a trio of doors. All three opened on a grand room which reminded Ellie of the interior of a cathedral. As she passed at random through the middle door, she wondered why this spacious chamber felt homely and safe, while the smaller room housing the spiral stair felt so unprotected.

Something about this Cathedral Room always calmed her, encouraging her to loll on the dark wood benches and examine the ornate stonework of the Gothic ceiling. Today she was too excited for that; her footsteps left behind a haphazard zigzag in the dust as she roamed the room and studied various icons on pillars and walls. There was a plethora of icons here, though all were small and delicate.

She'd sensed a word on the fringe of her mind, tormenting her, throughout many visits to this place. It finally popped into her consciousness: *church*. She had thought of *cathedral* before, but that was more the mental image of a building seen from outside, archaic, immense. This word had a new sense about it, a dim memory-feeling of religious devotion.

Suddenly impatient with the icons, she selected a bench and sat down to read.

THE TRAVERSE OF STONES

1015th Year of the Detheros

B eginning with Neikolan, my captain, my directive to
retreat passed quietly saboteur to saboteur. Those engaged
at the boardwalk were to turn and flee in stages, so it would
appear to be a rout and not organized intent. Those still hidden
would pass among the trees and filter into the midst of those
fleeing the Pool, hiding from our enemies the true size of our
force. I hoped in the tight view-scape of the jungle this ruse
would hold.

We had already achieved much today: for a start, destroying
Kadesh's palace. Whole sections were collapsing and sliding
into the Pool. But I knew the cost in lives of such successes.
I wanted more. And that more depended on Kadesh—and
Ghislain, who had not yet shown himself—giving chase. The
Twins had declined to pursue us at Mihali, leaving it to their
sister's mindless pets, the Nightwings. I judged that Kadesh was
made of different stuff. By his choice the endgame of my plan
would stand or fall.

My encounter with him in the air would help. It told the
Aedolae I was alive and that I myself (and no lesser minion) led
this assault.

From the end of the boardwalk I watched my warriors
pass. The eagles, under Kadesh's leadership, regrouped and
headed back to the palace. The Glacii began to stir from my
petrifaction. Something glinted in the sun near the Glacii's
original location. This could be Ghislain's mirrored eyes.
Kadesh's eagle landed nearby. The Glacii retreated to the same

spot. There was a time of consultation, but it was not long. The last of my group had disappeared down the trail when they began their pursuit. The eagles took to the air, and the rest of the Aedolae's forces followed on foot. This time led by Seraphi.

Good so far.

An unexpected voice interrupted my observations. A young warrior, her hair hidden beneath her helm and her eyes shadowed by the helm's ornaments, had come up on my right, startling me. I could not place her, despite the familiarity of her voice, for I was distracted by the singular nature of the two beings that stood behind her: Solmikaedes, *Singers*. I had heard Kadesh still imprisoned some of their kind.

"I found them in the woods, my lady," said the young warrior. "They came to me to offer their help." She stepped aside, with an uncommon grace.

"We will help you keep the portal open," one said. Their eyes were riotous purple, set in faces both avian and human. I understood their words, but their throats injected alien musicality into every syllable, as if bells rang faintly behind their speech.

"Without us, you won't be able to align the worlds long enough to achieve your goal," the other explained. I did not question them. They were ancient beings, suffering under Kadesh for years uncountable.

"Thank you," I said and beckoned them to follow. The young warrior nodded. The Solmikaedes unfolded their wings to reveal womanly bodies, their skin luminescent purple. My breath caught at the beauty of their plumage, pink and purple at the surface with hints of rich vermilion below. They did not fly but walked beside the warrior, moving with uncanny fluidity. They did not *appear* to hurry.

Ahead of us my entire troop was now at a dead run. I needed to get to the fore, and fast. Passing up the Singers, I touched the curved black Torc at my throat and leapt. As my feet left the ground, they changed, toes and arches spreading and lengthening. The transformation moved up through my body, wings unfurling from my back.

The Torc was the first Eterokon I had ever employed; its shapechanging power had gotten me past the Detheros and into the Aedolae's kingdom years ago.

Eagles shrieked behind us. The running forms of my saboteurs passed under me. I reached the plaza, slightly ahead of the Estringites. So much had transpired since we greeted the dawn here. I transformed back. The air was soon black with arrows as my archers reached the plaza and turned to meet the challenge of our foes.

I reached for the Kalimba, releasing it from my neck, and held down the concealed button at its back. My forces were not yet gathered but this time it wouldn't matter. I struck the second key on its face, with its twin symbols representing Iakovos and Ilanit, King and Queen of Mihali. Stylized sun and crescent moon. A low note rang out, throbbing in the air, shaking the earth below our feet. The note for Mihali.

The portal opened on a panorama of night sky.

Between the demesnes of Kadesh and Mihali lay a passage, an intermediary worldscape. I had been through several times before, finding this route between Kadesh and Mihali most useful in spying. But I had never liked the feel of it.

Mercair called it the Traverse of Stones.

More often than not, night reigned there, and it did so now. The juxtaposition of two worlds always unsettled my stomach. I felt the overlapping of realities in my bones, a sense that would go away once I was safely ensconced in the new world. This time I'd have to sit with the sensation longer, holding the doorway open. I kept my finger on the tiny button at the Kalimba's back.

As the note finally died away, it was taken up from the far end of the plaza—in a Solmikaedis' voice. The vibration of her voice was a different thing entirely, thrumming through my body as a shuddering bliss, pushing away the disquieting sensation of overlapping worlds.

Her sister spoke, soft words that somehow cut through the massiveness of that vibration.

"We will hold it for you. Go, lead your people."

The second Singer now raised her voice, joining the note an octave higher, surrounding it with trills and ornaments. The sheer beauty of it held even the vanguard of our enemy at bay. The Solmikaedes' ability to command admiration knew no boundaries of loyalties.

"Let's go," I said to Neikolan. "Help me watch for the cairns."

And we plunged into a place of nightmare.

PURPOSE

S he hadn't read long but a wave of nausea assaulted her. Ellie let the book drop onto the hard wood of the bench and lay down. Her vision spun and her head throbbed. *What is going on?* Ellie thought. *I am just reading.*

She knew how to read, yet had no memory of doing it before today. Her mind was both energized and exhausted at the same time. She wanted to delve into the next part of the story. But when she opened the book and tried to focus her eyes, the nausea returned. She would have to take a longer break. But she *would* read more. She decided she would walk the castle in the meantime, making her daily circuit of the rooms she knew.

She stood up, cautiously. She approached the altar in the middle of the room, and to her own surprise found herself kneeling before it. A small oval icon of Siana with closed eyes and rich lashes hung on the altar, her lips full and sensuous. The Kalimba was visible about her neck. There was a nimbus of light about her head, as if backlit by an unseen sun. Ellie found herself whispering.

"Siana, my Mistress" she implored, reaching deep for words, her need blending with her new sense of things. "I am alone, and I want to get out."

She had thought to say more, but her voice escaped her. Only silence answered. She raised her head.

And jumped back, for the icon had changed.

The painted Siana had opened her eyes, and stared right at Ellie. There was no consciousness behind the stare, but the unexpected change sent chills through her. Siana's eyes were a stunning, almost transparent blue. The richness of the color was unmatched in any other portrait.

The remainder of the day the castle seemed brighter. Ellie fancied that light from those crystal blue eyes flooded all the rooms, emanating from the Cathedral Room and moving through all the galleries of the castle. Perhaps the castle was Siana's home, and some pressing business kept her long away. Might she soon return, to find Ellie and free her? Such fantasies fluttered through her brain as she walked, but she tried to turn her attention to analyzing everything in light of her new knowledge.

Many images showed Siana's marvelous belt, with its many pouches and straps for her artifacts of strange power, the Eterokoni. While descending a shallow staircase at midday, Ellie spotted for the first time a sequence of tiles set into the outside of the railings. Black or white and only three inches across, she had seen them before simply as ornamentation.

One showed a ring of tiny circles; it must be the Bracelet. The next showed the Eye, the Eterokon of Sight. She analyzed each in turn, finding five along one railing (Sword, Kalimba, Torc, Bracelet and Eye) and four along the other. One of the four was the Glove, which she recognized. The other three she did not. Was one an intricate drawing of a mechanical beetle? The second was a disc sporting a raised fin, perhaps an ancient clock. The third was star-like, also intricate. She retraced the story in her mind, shifting her weight from foot to foot. No, Siana hadn't mentioned these items. Ellie did not remember them from any other icon. Surely they must be Eterokoni, grouped here with the familiar ones in this catalog-like arrangement. She moved on.

After this staircase she took more notice of the castle architecture, seeking for more clues like the tiles. Throughout the castle, dust of varying depth coated every level surface, but there were no cobwebs. This was another instinctively odd feature.

Then she began to wonder about the origin of her "instincts", when she had no recollection of anything but the castle. She possessed sundry ideas, terms and tidbits of knowledge, but all were divorced from any concrete source in memory. For instance, she understood the concept of parents, but had no memory of hers.

The euphoria of the Cathedral Room faded, and the silence of the place became oppressive once again. As she pondered instincts—and parents—a new perception struck her with force: in none, absolutely *none*, of the portrayals of Siana were her companions shown. What of Talmei? Neikolan? This struck Ellie as tragic and unjust. To have one's battles, and one's enemies commemorated, but never one's friends. She sympathized with her mute mistress. Siana was alone in this place, abandoned and alone just like her.

As the day waned, Ellie's rapt examinations and musings darkened into frustration. She had never felt so alive as she had this day, dredged by an exhausting series of thoughts and emotions. She became aware that what had kept her wandering, all this time, was the hope of finding more books. Or better still a library. But she found only places she had already seen.

True, she had been able to intelligently consider many things today. The Sky Room whose frescoes of azure cloud-strewn sky showed in their distance a floating island. The Copper Landing whose burnished floor held a most curious motif: concentric circles made of miniscule chips of colored glass. She had stepped over their sequence of haunted green, brilliant orange, sapphire, emerald, sun-yellow, and amethyst myriad times without caring, but today she *noticed*.

But not another book.

With heavy heart, she turned back. She must. The hour grew late. Her body sensed it.

It never occurred to Ellie to run. She always walked at the same indolent pace, almost a dawdle, even today with her more excited mental state. Going quicker would have helped her to reach new rooms, to expand the range of her search, but she never thought to push her body so. In the past, only her growing assurance in navigating the maze of rooms had enabled her to see more each day, before each day came to an end.

Today she had spent too much time lingering and observing, and hadn't even reached the boundary of her prior knowledge. *That is no way to find a library.* Only the desire to learn more about her Siana, painfully poignant, remained. Now that her strength and will flagged, the orphaned desire wore out her brain.

The day's clarity was slipping.

A darkness in tone reigned over the chambers of the castle as she returned to the Cathedral Room. There was no perceptible change in light when she stared at a given spot. But her peripheral vision clouded with shadows, shadows that disappeared when she turned her head to confront them. And these shadows, however evanescent, crowded her soul.

In the Cathedral Room she checked the altar icon. The image had downcast eyes, as it had before. Had she, in her foolish excitement, simply imagined the wide-open blue eyes? She wanted to kneel again, to force the change. But something in that willfulness struck her as sacrilegious.

Ellie was exhausted. But she did something surprising. Rather than rush back to her bedroom, she decided to sit and finish the book—which still lay on the bench where she'd left it, before her "break" from reading had ended up occupying an entire day. She reasoned with herself that she was close to the ballroom and could flee home should the shadows grow too threatening.

Perhaps she wanted to read positioned in a proper seat with the book comfortably in her lap. Perhaps she waited for the altar icon to change. Perhaps she was afraid the book would disappear overnight as arbitrarily as it had arrived. It was a bit of all these things. In any case it was a small act of bravery, and a sign of things to come. The story had begun to work its change.

THE FIELD OF STARS

1015th Year of the Detheros

C old air washed over us, bracing after the growing jungle heat. To our right the baleful eye of a moon cast hesitant light. That moon was always in that position, just above a never seen horizon, a horizon whose location was only manifest as the place where the stars ended. And such stars! As if little distance or atmosphere isolated them, they twinkled endlessly and eerily over this scene, and something about them unsettled. They cast no useful light, and their arrangement in the sky suggested a pattern, a pattern to make the skin crawl. I could never quite grasp it, and always ended up turning my eyes aside. But the need to find this pattern, somehow resolve it—or negate it—was an ever-present weight on one's mind in this place. A temptation to look again, and again. I had once found here a skeleton of human shape, sitting upright in a nook of stones. I wondered if he had succumbed, and gazed and gazed until the flesh had wasted on his bones and the breath had left his lungs.

Before us a staircase of flattened boulders led between rows of giant stone daggers. Each step was a hundred feet wide; my entire force could mass on this tremendous staircase at once. The stones hung as if suspended on unseen strings. Complete blackness showed between and below them. Day or night, there was no ground to see. I had dropped pebbles from the staircase in the past, but they never struck bottom, falling from sound and view as if swallowed by quicksand. A single misstep on the Traverse would mean death or oblivion.

The first section was easy. Neikolan and I walked side by side, and my people followed, up the staircase to the first landing. There were only a few dangerous gaps between the stones and the boulders were level. Still I disliked the place. The daggers cast baleful shadows of moonlight across our path, and I always had the sense they were watching. That they would destroy me, if they could. Today was no different. Their disdain was palpable.

"Hurry," I yelled. "We must be within the Labyrinth!"

To my surprise, the portal was still visible, a rip in the black tapestry of this world, the harsh light of Kadesh bleeding into stygian dark. I could still hear the voices of the Solmikaedes, the low note that throbbed with no need for a breath, the high notes that wove intricacies above, below and around it. Had they hidden in the fringe of the jungle or had they disappeared into the Song? Either way, the Aedolae's forces did not disturb them but rushed through the portal, filling the lower steps of the staircase and the air above it. Javelins soared, and with cries some of my men and women fell. The Glacii come through, crowding the steps. Kadesh's voice rang out and the eagles were the first to give chase up the stairs. I plunged through the cleft in the wall of rock before me and led my people into the Labyrinth.

The light from Kadesh's demesne, already made wan by the suffocating dark of the Traverse, disappeared. The portal had closed. Our enemies were trapped with us in a netherworld from which I was the only means of escape.

Within the Labyrinth I felt trapped as well.

I had never encountered another living thing here, but every shadow harbored menace. There was never quite enough light to discern whether the shadows were empty. In the deep silence I sensed a high faint tinkling, as if I could hear the stars. I drove my attention forward, for to lose the cairns was sure death. The first cairn was thirty feet ahead, perched atop a rocky crag in a pool of moonlight. The labyrinth's path was a patchwork of small stones, with yawning abyss between. Flat faced standing stones, twice my height, formed an irregular wall on both sides, broken by intersections with other paths. I forced myself to lead decisively and make room for the press of troops behind. We could at best move four abreast here and I did not want the pursuers to trap us wholesale against the far wall of the maze.

I do not know who placed the cairns, tiny stacks of flat stones. But they do lead true, and not a one is ever missing. Given the Traverse's tangible malice, it surprises me its spirit hasn't shrugged off the cairns and thrown them into the Void, eliminating such an incongruous friendliness. Perhaps they were placed here by some powerful sojourner in the uncharted past. But whoever their author, I blessed them that day. Led by the cairns, our front line soon reached the Field of Stars.

Neikolan and I emerged from the Labyrinth through an arch cloven in its far wall. Ahead of us was a sketchy mosaic of stone discs, scattered across a vast sea of stars. Only the largest of these discs would be a comfortable perch; the smallest would only support a passing footstep. As many were three or more feet apart, they would force us into a lethal game of stepping stones across the void.

But such was our path.

At my command, the army fanned out as wide as the second landing here allowed and we all commenced the game. Faint sounds of battle rang behind, where the rearguard of my saboteurs was holding off the forefront of the enemy at the top of the stairs. I again noticed the young female soldier, moving between the stones on my right with great precision. Again, that nagging sense of familiarity.

I had warned my people of what came next. Midway across the Field of Stars, the mosaic of stepping stones began to bend sharply upward. Gravity began to tug and pull us in a new direction. The first time I had experienced this, I had been paralyzed with fear, thinking if I moved to the next stone—a bit higher up and angled—I would fall backward and lose my footing. Only a fatalistic streak had saved me from inertia. I discovered that by an aberration in the gravity of this dark place one could always jump from stone to stone as if both were level—while all the same seeing and sensing the curvature of the

Field. Feeling the tug of gravity at one's back when standing, but unaffected by it while jumping.

I saw fear in the closest faces. The young warrior had been the first to follow my lead. I should have been able to see her nose and mouth beneath the helm, but I could only see her eyes.

The sense of curvature and imminent falling worsened for about ten jumps, then without warning gravity righted and we were standing on the level at the far end of the Field. Before us was the third landing, a panoply of broad, flat and irregularly shaped stones crested by slender standing stones. Like empty masts of petrified ghost ships, they cast needle-thin shadows in the hollow white moonlight.

Glancing back, my eyes met a strange sight. The Field of Stars, a wide parabola of tiny white stones, was level in front of us but then curved upward. At the top of this parabola was the ceiling of the Labyrinth, now completely perpendicular to us. What had felt level at the time now hung high in midair.

I must credit Kadesh and his guards. While the rest of the Aedolae's forces navigated the Labyrinth he led his eagles across the empty blackness above Labyrinth and Field. Flying through the shift in gravity must have been disconcerting, but on they came, shouting and hoisting their javelins. The brilliant green feathers and the bright raiment of the guards struck a bizarre contrast with the unearthly chiaroscuro of the Traverse.

There were skirmishes as my warriors still crossing the Field attacked eagles passing overhead. Some, pierced by javelins, fell between the stones, their cries swallowed up by nothingness.

Kadesh clearly targeted me now. Harrying my forces in the Field of Stars would have been more strategic; with their precarious footing on the stones his advantage was immense. But instead his eagles made straight for the third landing.

There was brightness at the top end of the field: the Seraphi had begun to cross. Well and good. And Kadesh's lust for my death gave the remainder of my people safe crossing.

The eagles were upon us. I dared not use the petrifaction Bracelet; the scene was too chaotic. My saboteurs would have to prove their mettle in battle. Some had participated in the attack on Mihali, but many had spent their time in my Brigandrie harrying the enemy with stealth, or from a distance; less of it in open battle. Much of today had been strategy and retreat and cleverness. Now for the fighting, for which they had trained.

"Focus on dismounting them. Cut the harnesses, or slay the eagles over the void," Neikolan ordered. Battle lines formed. I drew on the Glove and disappeared.

As the eagles swooped in talons first, I transformed my hands and feet into a gecko's pads and climbed the nearest stone needle. Soon I perched at the very top. I drew the Glass Sword and waited.

I beheaded the first eagle that flew by, cut a wing from the second, and then Kadesh was onto me. I jumped onto a third eagle, dispatching its rider, and landed my mount in the middle of the fray below. The melee was bitter. Most of the Kadesh's guards were grounded now, scimitars flashing in the moonlight. They were greatly outnumbered, but far better skilled.

One guard crumpled under a massive boulder hurled by an Estringite. The shadows, intensified by the press of people, made discernment difficult. I rematerialized. None could stand against me, for the Glass Sword cut through both weapons and flesh. Despite their impressive swordsmanship and their taunting cries, this contingent of the enemy was doomed.

I engaged a tall blonde amazon with a giant broadsword. To my surprise her weapon did not shatter beneath the blows of my Eterokon. So: a chance at true sword-craft. I was confident, for my sparring with Alt in Mercair's World had renewed my abilities. But this blonde giant was a challenge, not only skilled but strong and tall.

A red glow filled the Field. Seraphi coming. Time for the critical resolution of my plan. I needed to get away from this blonde guardswoman before it was too late.

Several things happened at once. With a whoosh of wings and shocking fire an eagle's talons ripped through my back. I was pitched forwards by the impact of the collision. The amazon's broadsword, in a powerful two handed swing, clashed on stone inches from my head. Then she fell with arrows in her chest and face.

Kadesh laughed as he swung his eagle up and away from where he had attacked me from behind.

I forced myself to my knees, feeling blood sheet my backside.

I grabbed the fallen amazon's sword and flung it at his retreating form with all my might.

It spun several times in the air and sunk itself deep in the body of his mount.

The eagle shrieked, pitched Kadesh off its back, and fell into the void. He had been above the Field by the time the sword had struck, and had to seize the rim of a stepping stone to avoid joining the eagle in oblivion. With evident pain he drew himself up. He was about seven stones from the landing. Several nearby archers knocked arrows and took aim.

"Hold," I breathed. "Let him see the final destruction." This was ideal, that he have a ringside seat for the final act of my plan. I got up and turned to face the Field. In the blackness of the Traverse, the Seraphi were visible only as outlines, several hundred human-shaped silhouettes of fire. They were armed with their customary weapons, unusual weapons that were part two ended sword and part two ended whip, gripped in the middle and held perpendicular to the body. Each end was a snake of fire, one moment a gleaming blade, the next a whip.

In regular battle we would have stood no chance against half that number.

Now was the perfect time.

I raised my arm; the small stones on my wrist glimmered in the wan light. I summoned their power, focusing my mind on drawing forth more of that power than ever before. And then I released it in a silent wave, a ripple in the backdrop of night.

As it struck the front lines of the Seraphi, the black shadows of their bodies materialized out of thin air, coalescing into grey forms of men and women. Their nimbuses of fire sputtered and were quelled. And to my great excitement, not only the

Seraphi's bodies turned to stone, but the lines of petrifaction moved down their arms to encase the weapons in their hands, spreading the length of their whips, turning flame to stone. The weight of their petrified whips, far broader than their height, was perfect to unbalance the statues. They pitched and plummeted into the void by the dozen. So much for my concern about the petrifaction wearing off.

My goal in drawing Kadesh's minions into this nightmare place was dismantling his army for good. I was succeeding beyond my wildest hopes. We would not have to brave the Field of Stars a second time, to topple the petrified enemy. The wave of petrifaction rippled through the Field, bending to follow the twist in gravity, and the entire host of Seraphi fell.

And then it struck the Glacii behind them, at the far end of the Field. Ice titans lost their translucence and darkened into stone. Not all of these fell, but no matter. We would be gone before they awakened. Once I closed the portal they would wander the Traverse forever, until whatever power animated them failed.

Kadesh's expression contorted in horror and rage. The last of his celebrated defenders dropped soundlessly into the void, and save for the distant statues of Ghislain's Glacii, the Field of Stars was empty.

"Shoot him," I said, impregnating those two simple words with six years of hatred. I hadn't counted on slaying an Aedolae. No one had killed an Aedolae. This would be the first time, the unprecedented and unanticipated end to our triumph.

A host of bows rang, and Kadesh's body shuddered under the impact of twenty black arrows. He sank to his knees on the stone. Pity he did not fall. I would have to go do it myself.

A voice, poignantly familiar, interrupted.

"Siah, you're bleeding so much!" There is only one person who calls me by that nickname. I never expected her here.

It was Paris.

Paris, the dancer I'd stolen away from Kadesh's court. Paris, my dear friend and oasis in the travails of war.

Paris. My complication and my entanglement.

I spun about, shocked. I thought she was back in Forgotten Town, with those minority of us not suited to be combatants. She had always stayed behind.

But she was here. The helm of the young warrior who had shadowed me much of the day clattered from her hand. As she ran toward me waves of long brunette hair streamed free. Her face was veiled, but her grey eyes were deep wells of concern and pain as she collapsed against me. I folded my arms around her back, and raised my lips to kiss her brow. She dared not return the embrace for her fear of my wounds.

"I was so scared," she breathed, that musical voice. She too had wounds, though none deep, along both arms.

"Paris, why?" I asked, as she stepped around to examine my back. I drew her back to face me. "It's not as bad as it looks. But why?"

"Because I am silly and foolish," she said at first, eyes downcast, but added: "No! Because I thought you were gone forever, last time. Because I've hardly seen you since you returned and denied my heart. Because if something were to happen to you again, I'd want to be there, at least to be with you. Because I belong with you. All those reasons." I had always accused Paris of dividing every subject into a myriad pieces.

Paris liked to talk.

I didn't know what to say. I was terrified for her safety. I had put her at terrible risk, drawn her, who had refused to carry a dagger the night I secreted her out of Kadesh, into this bloody melee. I remembered something that my resurrected mind had forgotten: a phantasm of Paris had accosted me in Ampizand before I died

"How long before you kill me too?" it had said, without any of my friend's sweetness. I remembered the other ghosts, shades of other companions and allies whose lives my war had cost. And now she was here, with none of that ghostly accusation. Only wide eyes full of love, foolish love.

"It's OK," I said, trying to manufacture a reassurance I did not feel. "I'm just glad I didn't lose you here. How did you find the Solmikaedes?"

"They found me. They sensed I was there and got free in the wreck of the palace."

They taught Paris to sing in her youth, before Kadesh got word of their friendship and locked them away. But there was no more time for questions, nor time to send Paris to Talmei, where she would be safer.

A nagging feeling drew my attention back to Kadesh.

Slaying an Aedolae was not so easy.

Kadesh was straining to his feet, body still bristling with arrows. A haze of fire grew about him. My archers fired again. Their missiles whistled through the air, and stopped a yard off, unable to penetrate the growing nimbus of power around Kadesh's body, sticking to it as if sunk into clay. And then his fire grew and devoured the wood of the arrows.

We could not kill him. We would have to trap him here with the Glacii. Escaping quickly.

"Draw near!" I shouted, and took down the Kalimba. I could feel Paris' body beside me, staying close, her fingers tucked beneath my belt. I engaged the Kalimba and struck the sun and moon key again, sounding the note for Mihali. Here at the third landing we could complete the passage. A wall of light opened behind the landing. The azure sky of a Mihalian afternoon. Ten rope bridges led from the landing—through the opening portal—to the cliffs of the massive sky island of that demesne.

"To the bridges, hurry," Neikolan cried as he led the charge. The company split into prearranged groups. I held the portal and backed slowly across the landing. I would not have the Singers' help. I kept my eyes on Kadesh.

I had not seen the true power of an Aedolae revealed before, and I was immediately sure I did not want to see it again. I learned a new respect for their power that day. Enormous wings with no substance but scarlet energy unfurled from Kadesh's back. His body grew threefold in size. A grotesquerie of horns sprouted around his black topknot. His human face dangled from the lengthening prehensile neck of a lizard. And the arrows projecting from his expanding body rearranged themselves to become wicked black spines along his flanks.

I had to know: I took a bow and an arrow from the quiver of a fallen warrior and shot it at Kadesh's face. It sank into the wrinkled scarlet skin of his pate. Then the arrow plowed uncannily through the flesh of his head, the skin parting in ripples like the wake of a ship. It straightened itself up and hardened into a new black horn.

This did not bode well.

My forces were through the portal, and the bridges swayed and creaked beneath their weight. I shaded my eyes against the light and took Paris' hand.

"Let's go."

We turned to run. Kadesh's transformation was complete and the huge thing he had become, half dragon, half man, launched itself from the stepping stone that barely contained its bulk. His wings whumped lazily behind us. We reached one of the bridges and I released the portal. But not in time. The bizarre suspended head, grimacing, burst through, followed by reptilian body. The portal closed on his newly formed tail with silent finality, whacking off its end in a spray of blood. This downed him, onto the line of stones supporting the bridges. The darkness of the Traverse vanished behind him, replaced with the gorgeous blue sky-scape of Mihali, miles of sky laced with puffy white clouds as far as the eye could see. Only the last few stones of the landing remained, cut off from their fellows in the Traverse, hanging over miles of empty sky. And the dragon that was Kadesh thrashed in pain on those stones, decorating them with his blood.

Paris and I were halfway across the bridge when I heard cries of consternation from my army. The bridges sagged beneath our weight and it was hard to see what was going on above us. I glanced back. With the same corporeal plasticity that had absorbed my arrow, Kadesh's severed tail end had sealed and hardened into an armored club. His wings spread. And then his voice, still the same, rang out:

"Did you think we were so easy to kill, sojourner? And I see that, adding to your impressive list of wrongdoings against me, you have in your possession something that is mine."

"She is not yours," I yelled back, "and she never was. I do not 'possess' her. She is by my side by her own free choice."

That was for sure.

Kadesh flapped his wings and lifted off. I didn't know if I possessed a weapon that would work against him now.

We reached the cliff just before Kadesh reached us. I had time to see the cause of my people's cries: the plains of the sky island were black with Achthroi, an army thirty times our number, more Achthroi than I had ever seen. Iaakovos and Ilanit, the Twin Aedolae of this realm, headed the army. Five great sky ships, sails billowing, hovered above the host, their prows mounted with giant colored spheres of glass, *weapons*. And a flash of tiny mirrors on the forecastle of one ship spoke of Ghislain's presence here.

It was impossible. There wasn't time for Ghislain to come here. The Aedol Via between Mihali and Kadesh was months of travel. We had taken the passage. I had seen him at Kadesh, the same mirrored eyes flashing in the sunlight. And how could he know our destination? The shortcuts of the Kalimba were my knowledge and mine alone. Nothing made any sense. My mind reeled.

Sunlight glinted off the giant spheres, great winches tugged by a legion of jet skinned men to focus it, rotating the spheres to aim. White-hot beams were striking us, igniting clothing and flesh.

As I stared at the incomprehensible scene before me, Kadesh seized Paris from my side, dragon claws sinking into her shoulders. Her cries whipped up into the air; the force of his wings knocked me aside. I reacted far too late, hands clutching emptiness. Kadesh, with Paris dangling and kicking her feet, sailed low over my army, following the cliff edge, completing the swooping curve that had brought him past and so quickly out of reach. The agony of hearing her pain surged through me. Kadesh had begun to bank, to rendezvous with one of the ships, when Talmei swung both arms and dealt him a fearsome blow. An Estringite's thin and wiry limbs are far stronger than they look. In this case strong enough to throw Kadesh to the left, out beyond the cliffs, and into a tumble. His legs struck one of the suspended bridges, and the bony protrusions of his hide snapped the bridge in two.

In the force of the collision he relaxed his grip on Paris.

She fell screaming.

Her limbs flailed and grasped at the trailing end of severed rope. She hung over immeasurable miles of nothingness. I watched in horror; the moment froze.

I was surrounded by screams as I turned to reach for the dangling remains of the bridge. The ten foot beams of light carved corridors of death through my people. I heard Iakovos and Ilanit order the Achthroi to advance. But it was sound echoing down a long tunnel, sound heard in a dream.

There was only Paris, struggling to reach the rope with her other hand, to keep herself from falling, falling, falling...

DISCOVERY

The book fell from her grasp. She picked it up, hands trembling, seeking more. There was only the moldering back cover, a deep green board empty of words and images.

How could it end like that?

Ellie still saw Paris clutching the severed strands of the bridge. Was she going to die? Did Siana perish too, caught between dragon-Kadesh and the invincible forces of the other Aedolae?

Am I in Siana's tomb? Ellie thought, *in an immense museum commemorating the dead?*

That would explain the endless iconography. Perhaps Siana had perished many years ago, and her legend had grown, engendering this kind of tribute. The woman she had been reading about could indubitably fuel a legend.

Her mind was clearer but her body remained exhausted. At least she had finished the book. That had been her goal, and she had risked the terrors of the night to do it.

She left the Cathedral Room, muscles aching, clutching the precious book, taking the middle door as was her wont. With her mind still on the story she did not notice at first the tremendous change; the blackness that yawned to her left did not at first distinguish itself from the peripheral shadows of dusk.

Then she realized the small archway leading to the staircase room framed pitch black, lit with small pinpricks of starlight.

The horror of that inky nothingness drew her like a moth to a flame.

She went to it, stunned, seeing where the floor vanished, ragged at its edge as if cut by some jagged instrument. She peered into the void, and fancied she could see some shadowed version of the spiral staircase up to the Vicious Room, its bottom ending in midair. The room that lay between arch and stair was for all effective purposes gone.

She had never seen this kind of darkness anywhere within the castle; certainly not here. She had always lain down to sleep while dusky twilight still reigned. She had always awakened at full day, and never during the night. But she *remembered* true night, and she remembered stars. Why and how this memory of night had been grafted, unexpectedly, and in terrifying realism, onto the route of her daily return was beyond her understanding.

But what else did it remind her of? Oh, yes, the Field of Stars from the story.

Her wondering was overcome by a rush of panic. There were redundancies in the routes she knew through the castle, places where multiple doors or hallways intersected, led to the same place. Not here. She knew no other way back to her ballroom and gallery. If this room was gone, she was stranded. Stranded with the nighttime of the castle closing in, with her body feeling wrecked. Why was she so weak? She had never wondered before. She had always been this way.

What would she do?

Her mind raced, logic overshadowed by terror. She crumpled to the rim of the blackness, doubled over, weeping. For a while, she heaved with sobs, forehead pressed against the cool stone. And then a stray observation stilled her. She could not remember crying before.

A tiny laugh escaped her throat. The novelty of this day! To hope, to pray, to weep. Experiencing her fear in force, and surviving it cheered her. She remained, still Ellie, in its wake. She stood up and turned her back on the arch.

Well, she thought, if I'm going to be stuck out here, I am going to make something out of it. I'm going to explore further than I've been able to go before.

Her resolve carried her exhausted body back through all the rooms she had visited that day. The light in the castle stayed constant, despite the nagging sense of encroaching dark. As if she could sense, here in the bowels of the castle, the weight of the dark outside, where surely the sun had gone to bed. But though the light had not changed, the soundscape had.

Where stillness, deadness, a waiting silence were the rule of the daytime, now whisperings, rustlings, creakings assailed her from all sides. Never in the same room with her, always from a room adjacent or distant, snaps and booms that echoed through intervening chambers. Despite her resolve, her throat tightened with each noise. Such noises had always been the harbinger of night, things she heard behind her as she retreated through the last of the rooms to her quiet gallery where they never intruded. Now she was surrounded, the noises coming at her from all sides, their makers unseen. A random piece of information popped into her head: as buildings cooled at night, their materials changed shape and clicked and groaned. Maybe that was it. But the air in the castle was no cooler on her skin. It was never cold and never warm, always the perfect match for her threadbare linen dress. Now as ever.

The frequency of the noises increased.

She entered a broad circular room where she had deliberated and turned back several days ago. A balcony framed the room, and under its shade it was darker than most places in the castle. There were no other exits on the ground level. She paused, stymied, until she recalled that a ladder on the far wall led up to a hole in the balcony floor. The balcony had a low railing and a series of steep tiers like an old playhouse. She could see multiple exits from the balcony. She had never taken the ladder before, for climbing the ladder into a whole new set of rooms had felt like a commitment time would not allow.

But tonight she might as well.

Still the ladder gave her pause.

She wavered at the bottom. Then a terrific groan sounded from the sitting room behind, where the door still hung open, as if one of the room's huge gilt chairs were dragged rudely across the floor with a squeal. Ellie hurried up the rungs.

She emerged through the trapdoor and tumbled onto the balcony floor. Her heart was racing, from unaccustomed exertion and fear at the tremendous noise, the loudest sound she had ever heard in the castle. She forced herself to peer over the lip of the balcony. She was surprised to see a fire burning in the sitting room's formerly empty hearth. It crackled with cheerful noise but its unprecedented appearance terrified. What unseen thing had lit the fire and pulled up a chair to enjoy? She wanted to go back and see, even imagined the fire's pleasant warmth, but she did not dare.

Keeping herself out of view, she half crawled, half stumbled to a random choice of exit from the balcony. Beyond was a narrow armory, suits of armor on small daises flanking both walls. It was darker within; Ellie must have reached a part of the castle where the light was truly failing. Her bare feet waded through thick dust. The heavy door swung shut behind her, slamming. The reverberation shook the floor and was enough to topple one of the knights off his stand. The clamor was too much for Ellie's frayed nerves, and she dashed madly forward, while the metallic crash rang off the walls and assaulted her from all sides. At the far end of the armory was an arched opening into a high and broad chamber. Ellie raced through, swooning, and collapsed senseless.

• • • ● • ● • • •

She woke up to something warm upon her cheek. She lay on her side on a cold surface. Rolling onto her back, she opened her eyes. Above was a high vaulted ceiling with ribbons of gothic stonework. Sunlight from a small circular skylight set in the apex of this ceiling nearly blinded her; its warmth had awakened her. She rolled back to her side and looked around. The room resembled the Cathedral Room near her gallery, for she lay at the end of an aisle between rows of dark wood benches. She remembered these were called "pews". Her body was sore from sleeping on hard marble.

Usually she had little sense of dreaming during her nights, and what little she recalled was fragmentary and dim. But this morning, she recalled vivid dreams. Right before awaking her sleeping mind had been repeating a phrase. *What was it*? Oh yes: "Siana Princess of Time, Siana Princess of Time", a litany chanted over and over. And there had been a revolving kaleidoscope of images, not taken from the walls but kindled by her imagination from the book:

Siana hoisting the Glass Sword aloft for a death dealing stroke.

Siana's white skin and blonde hair framed by the blackness of the Field of Stars. Siana's crystal blue eyes.

Siana walking through the Forest above Forgotten Town, in Ellie's dream no longer accompanied by the Estringite, tall and tree-ish, but alone, her black garments shining like jet and her hair falling in gorgeous waves, adorned with brilliant feathers.

Siana the Deathless.

As she remembered the images, something incongruous nagged the edges of her consciousness but she shrugged it away.

She stood up and stretched, less refreshed than usual. She realized she did not have the book; in her fear she had left it outside the Cathedral Room.

How long had she been out? It must be long after morning. Her heart exulted. She was alive, and she had spent the night away from the safety of her gallery. What she had feared had not destroyed her. She remembered the firelight, the groaning, the mad dash along the armory, the terror. But the simple fact of her survival eclipsed all these. She was starting the day in a chamber she had never seen. What might she discover? Might she at last find an exit? In this bright and cheerful room, drenched in unexpected sunlight, all her fears were dim and impotent.

Before her was a stone basin, so close she might have struck her head against it when she swooned. And inside was water!

Water: a new marvel in a string of novelties. The book, the firelight, sunshine. She had not realized the depth of her thirst until now. She extended a finger and touched. Ripples danced across the crystalline surface, and dappled sunlight sparkled in its depths. Holding her hair back with both hands she bent forward with dry lips. As she drank, coolness pervaded her body.

Next she was gulping and then she jumped in. The buoyancy of the water lifted her dress and the exquisite sensation of the water rushed along her legs. She had never felt anything so delicious. She devolved into wild playful thrashing, as she threw water on her arms and face and stung her eyes. She cupped water in her hands and drenched her tangled hair. She was not satisfied until she had soaked every inch. She did not realize at first the novelty of her own laughter, bouncing off the walls.

She lay for a long time with her head propped on the stone rim, contentment pervading her being. She surveyed her hands, her long fingers. She stroked the flesh of her arms, examining her body with a new curiosity. She ran her fingertips, nails longs and ragged, along her thighs and calves, the unaccustomed touch stirring her skin to new wakefulness. She looked at her legs and arms. She was very thin. Had she ever been different? She didn't know. She felt her ribs beneath the clinging second skin of her waterlogged dress. The fabric of the dress was riddled with many small holes.

She stood up, water streaming. She ran her hands along her jutting hipbones, and up her body, passing over the softness of her breasts. She tried to smooth and untangle her shoulder length hair. She wrung out the bottom of her dress and gingerly stepped out. The floor was slippery, another new feeling.

The other Cathedral Room had an altar. This one had a statue of Siana. The raised daises holding them were identical. The sunlight had passed over the basin and was now inching toward the statue as the sun rose higher. Ellie stepped through it, a flush of warmth, and walked to the dais. The litany returned to her mind: "Siana, Princess of Time." This is how Siana had introduced herself in the book.

That was the nagging thought: What did "Princess of Time" mean? Nothing in the book explained.

As if in answer, her eyes alit on what lay at the statue's feet: a circle a yard across with a fan shaped protrusion. From some subconscious font of experience she recognized it as a sundial. The gnomon did not cast a shadow yet, for the sunlight would only strike it briefly during the day. The object reminded her of one of the tiles along the railing yesterday, an Eterokon that she could not name.

Time. Sundial. Eterokon. They must be connected. But why hadn't Siana mentioned it?

She knelt beside of the dais, running her fingers over the rough stone. It and the Siana statue were carved of a single piece; Siana's stone toes rested on its edge. The statue's lifeless gaze supplicated the far distance. Its arms were outstretched and the upturned palms joined together to form a flat surface.

And there rested another book!

Again Ellie's heart leapt. With reverent gentleness and barely contained excitement she stepped onto the sundial and retrieved it. Like the other book it was old and moldering; this one was deep grey, both front and back boards. On the cover was a clock face with minute and hour increments but no hands. Inside was the same handwriting. She carried it to a nearby bench. Rivulets of water still streamed from her dress and body, but she ignored her wetness for the room was warm.

She began on the first page.

THE PASSAGE OF THE MOON

1.5 years before the Attack on Kadesh

I found the fifth of the Eterokoni while passing from Kadesh. I was alone. Yesterday I left Forgotten Town, passed through the Forest, and came into Kadesh's realm. My eventual goal was to return to Ebon Port to speak to Bierce. I was frustrated and needed information only he could provide. I could have gone a different way, but I chose to pass through Kadesh.

Why? I had spent a year and a half exploring avenues of access provided by the Kalimba, usually alone. Telling myself I didn't want to put anyone else at risk, but knowing in my heart the real reason was a determination to test my own mettle, unbuttressed by any aid. I wanted necessity to draw my strength to the surface.

And that is what necessity had done.

I hadn't explored many passages between the demesnes and Ebon Port, but returning to Bierce presented an opportunity. The Kalimba's portals often led to an intermediary worldscape, a *passage*. I was determined to know them all. To travel them both directions so I would know both ways out, the points of translation.

To challenge the Aedolae I needed every tool.

Pressing the circle and cross I found myself in a jungle at midnight. A trio of moons hung low in the sky. I was standing on dry wood planking, a boardwalk, fashioned of the same jungle hardwoods surrounding me in the moonlight. I recognized the scene from my first tour of the Aedol Via, two and a half years ago. I was in the Dark Quarter, devoid of the otherwise ubiquitous torchlight of Kadesh. I had been a guest at Kadesh's palace.

As I wandered that night my mind ran over the events of those two and a half years. At the start of those years I was a child, with some sharp wits, but few powers at my disposal: only the Torc and the Eterokon of Tongues. Later I found how to use the Kalimba and this discovery gave focus to my anger. The Kalimba changed wandering to exploration, freeing me from the singularity of the Aedol Road.

And my anger had sharpened into a desire for vengeance.

Two years ago I had left Bierce behind, taking passage aboard a Glowship, fleeing Ebon Port. The Glowship had been assaulted near Mihali, attacked by the same pirates who now were part of my company. During the attack, driven to desperation, I had abandoned my companion and used the Kalimba to escape. Neikolan, captain of the pirates, had been close enough to pursue me through the portal to Forgotten Town. In the Forest above the Town, the Forest that would someday boundary our mutual home, Neikolan and I had found ourselves in a battle of wits instead. My threat to leave him there, trapped forever, won me that contest. Eighteen months later, he was my second in command and I *his* captain. In the time in between, after I had returned him to his island home near Mihali, I had grown indeed, mastering the powers of the four Eterokoni I possessed. In our second battle, I bested him not in words but in prowess.

Passages and demesnes. Despite their strategic advantage most passages—like demesnes—were perilous. One thing bothered me about the Forest and Forgotten Town. All of the other keys on the Kalimba corresponded to domains of the Aedolae. Yet there was no Aedolae for this key, with its half-moon, circle and cross. Bierce had been no help on this subject. Why did this key lead to the empty town, and not a typical Aedolae stronghold? Instead it was a place free of peril. A refuge.

In the operation of the Kalimba Forgotten Town was a final destination like a demesne; just like other demesnes, I could leave Forgotten Town by striking the key for any other world. But Forgotten Town was unique in that this operation could only be done at the precise point in the woods where one first entered it. This specificity made it more like a passage.

Such were my thoughts as I wandered, coming to the Prismatic Pool and its encircling boardwalk. Across the Pool was the palace, a massive domicile whose bamboo walls housed many of the realm's people and hosted a majority of the realm's business. I had stayed there as Kadesh's guest, but I would not be welcome now, unveiled as Siana, enemy of all his kind. Time to move. I'd done my habitual reconnaissance.

Turning my back on the palace to face dark jungle, I activated the Kalimba.

There was a thunderclap and then a subsonic rumble. I was thrown off my feet. With a hissing sound deeper darkness enveloped me. I had never experienced this kind of transition before.

And then stillness.

Rough gravel mixed with mud bit into the flesh of my face. I pushed myself part way up. I lay on a hillside amid low scrubby vegetation, on a rude path that wound down the hill below and out into a flat garden space. The sky was dark, empty of stars and full of roiling clouds backlit with wan phosphorescence from a hidden moon. The hillside was dark but in the garden below tall plants with thistle heads glowed with spectral light, each pod-head an eerie green torch. A chill breeze whispered across the scene, waving the thistle torches. Shadows capered across the ground.

A line of spindly trees crowned the hill far above, their upper branches like undulating fingers against the sky. Uphill the trail on which I lay led there. Lights twinkled in the gloom between the trees, sparkling and fiery compared to the wan illumination of the garden, bobbing left to right—lanterns carried by an unseen procession. A faint sound accompanied, the sound of chains drawn across stone. Something about the lights and sound, the whole scene, radiated menace.

I drew on the Glove, the Eterokon of Invisibility.

Its effect, here, was not expected.

I was immediately besieged by a cloud of huge moths, coming out of nowhere as if spontaneously generated by the brush. The smallest were as big as my hand, the biggest several times that, and they flitted mindlessly about me as if I were an attracting light, slapping the skin of my exposed face and hands. I could feel the feathery chalk of their wings. That was annoying enough but it was the faces, half-glimpsed, that I could not bear. On their undersides were petite faces, uncannily human, with vacant eyes and oddly incongruent grimaces. Like people whose minds have been split in two, one part wiped clean and the other subconsciously ruing the change. I have never seen such an expression anywhere else.

Their onslaught forced me down the trail, gracelessly and noisily, to the garden. I beat back the moths with flailing hands but they were too many and too stupid to heed my smacking. I could no longer stand it and took off the Glove. Instantly they were gone.

Well, that settles that.

I glanced back up the long slope. The lights still bobbed along its crest, but the grating noise and the feeling of menace were gone.

I reminded myself there was no necessary correlation between one's sense of danger and actual danger.

Unfortunately.

The garden was a circle framed by trees. Interlocking walking paths laced between beds of night blooming flowers, the torch thistles, and other large plants. Most reached above my head, making it difficult to see ahead. In the weird light of the torch pods, I had more the impression of graveyard than garden. Either way it looked regularly tended. *By what?* I wondered. I wasn't sure I wanted to meet the answer.

When first in a passage one has no idea of the other end, the place where the Kalimba can be activated again and a second portal leads to the originally selected demesne. I knew I didn't want to go anywhere near the yellow lights, so I plied the garden's trails instead, keeping as straight a line forwards as the curvature of the paths allowed. I was thankful the chill breeze died down, for I was uncomfortably cold.

In the periphery of my vision, on all sides, something moved, bone white.

I melted into the shade of a stand of grasses. From the shadow of the encircling trees, albescent white figures were moving into the garden, vaguely humanoid torsos supported on six impossibly spindly limbs with multiple joints. The figures picked their way amid the plantings, hovering like giant spiders, glowing with captured moonlight, tending the plants with vestigial forearms attached to their bellies. I crouched down and wiggled my way deeper into the grass. My rustling noises sounded quite loud to me, but they gave no indication they heard. I watched from my hiding place, for an exceedingly long time, while the spider beings examined each part of the garden, moving toward the center. A spindly leg crunched down on the gravel in front of me, two inches in diameter and hardly strong enough to support such a being's weight in a logical world. The foot was crablike. The torso was lowered closer down and I got the chance to inspect it close up. The shape and size of the body was human, but beneath the pallid, tightly stretched skin, the pattern of the bones was all wrong, as if human skin was pulled across a crustacean carapace, seam and plates visible beneath. And the head, which drew uncomfortably close to examine me—it had no features at all, no ears, no ears, no nose, no mouth. Its face was a hairless orb. I bore its sightless proximity in silence. It must have been satisfied that I was growing well, for it raised up on its filament legs and stalked off. Soon after, a slight darkening in the air suggested the beings had receded back into the forest, taking their glow with them. Apparently that was gardening for the day. I was relieved.

I left my hiding spot and continued, gravel crunching beneath my soles. The yellow lights above were also gone. A sense of complete solitude washed over me, and not a comfortable sense. It was the sense that I was alone in the night, doomed to haunt forever regions of darkness and emptiness, never again to see the light of the sun, or to hear a spoken word. Though I could not see beyond the garden's protecting wood, my mind pictured endless night gardens, ruins of abandoned houses decaying in gloom, trails through shadowed woods, stagnant rivers that were glistening wounds across a black landscape as they reflected the dim light of an overcast sky. These images assaulted my selfhood, threatening to strip my persona until I walked a zombie through the night, apprehending only the horror of my own emptiness.

I knew, without doubt, that this place knew no day.

A desperate urge to be free welled up in me and I ran for the opposite side of the garden, careless. Just then the clouds split to reveal a gibbous moon. This was no moon of the ordinary night sky. I could swear it swiveled in the heavens like an eye turning in a vast black face, fixing its gaze on my ant-like non-entity in the landscape below. As it swiveled subsonic rumble shook the ground. I dashed forwards, finding an opening in the trees where one of the garden trails continued on. The eye of the moon turned to follow me, and again the whole scene rumbled with its motion, as if the moon was fixed in the sky but in its effort to move, it jostled and shifted the entire world around it.

The trail was flat, wide enough for a carriage, with an overhanging arch of trees. The moon cast a long corridor of wan light ahead of me into the gloom; at the end of that corridor the land rose. I ran, stumbling against a barely seen litter of branches. The moon peeked through the trees, cleaving the heavens in its hunt for me, casting beams of lights like groping hands.

This is not possible, I thought, but then laughed aloud.

Who was I to say, seeing what I had seen, doing what I had done, what was impossible?

The moon dipped lower, its light brighter, the face of a malevolent giant peering into a dollhouse, seeking me in the shadows. I shrunk from its beams into the darkness at the edge of the avenue, my progress impeded by my attempt to stay out of its light.

I wasn't getting anywhere at this rate.

I had about decided to challenge the moon—my first melee with a heavenly sphere—when I had the distinct feeling of being watched. The avenue led up and the trail and the wood stopped ahead and the land dropped away. The moon came to rest at this place, hanging directly in the center of the path, framed on either side by the last stand of trees. And silhouetted in that moonlight was a tall figure in flowing robes.

Watching me.

What the hell, I thought sourly, and walked toward it.

The moon shifted behind it, rocking the scene, giving the impression—humorous in another context—of trying to peek over the figure's shoulders. The figure raised one gloved hand and immediately the moon froze in the sky. The air rippled, and a grinding inertia clamped down on my body, upon the whole scene. The light dimmed and the moon receded into the distant heavens, emptied of animation.

A dead cold rock.

Who was this person, to command the moon?

A cold red eye dominated his forehead. The high mantle of his cloak hid his neck, hid any mouth, and showed only a pair of slits in the center of his flat face for a nose. He was half again the height of a man. His figure was invisible beneath the billowing cape and moonlight silhouetted his form.

"Aren't we clever," his hissing whisper pierced the air, "to come here, a sojourner? Let me welcome you."

He raised his gloved and clubbed hand again and everything disappeared—replaced by a scene where we sat opposite one another at a circular stone table. A wide plain stretched into dim greyness on all sides. The moon still shone, but far overhead. At the center of the craggy stone surface was placed a single object, a small sundial, 3 inches across.

An Eterokon.

He motioned with his hand. A glass appeared in front of each of us, filled with dark red liquid. I could see nothing of his face save the slitted nostrils and the single baleful eye, inhuman in the extreme. He stood rigidly upright. He gestured toward my drink.

I didn't touch it.

"Who are you?" I demanded.

"If I told you," he hissed back, "would you tell me who *you* are?"

I didn't answer. My body was tight with apprehension. I sat sidewise in my chair.

"As I thought," he observed. "You ask what you deign not to reveal about yourself. Your kind are rude. But it is of no matter." He was silent. I took the Kalimba down from its necklace.

There was a weird thrumming in my mind. Perhaps this table marked the translation point out? If this creature knew this, why would he bring me here?

"Ah, now I see," he said. "The mystery of this sojourner revealed. None has come here before, save for this girl with her Kalimba." I bristled at his condescension and instantly felt I had erred. I had assumed him to be some local denizen of this nightmare place. I now suspected he was something more. He had brought me to this table to reveal who I was.

"My brothers have failed again to safeguard their realm. You know, they would destroy those things if they could"—he pointed at the Kalimba—"but they cannot, and are pathetically inept about keeping them out of the hands of such as you."

I was about to portal my way out of his company, but now sick curiosity stayed me. "Your brothers are the Aedolae?"

"Brothers, masters, enemies, depends on perspective." He gestured dismissively.

The cyclopean eye. His mention of the Aedolae. I knew what he was. I had read about the priests of the Coethyphys in the Library of the Ancients.

He continued, "They harbor a great hatred for your kind, but I do not share it. I find your kind rather useful. Take it." He nodded stiffly toward the Eterokon of Time. I knew its name but not its function.

"Why would you give it to me? Why is it here?"

"So many questions, little sweet." His voice dropped to a darker whisper. I felt hypnotized as he walked slowly toward me. He pawed at the mantle of his cloak, a grotesque mockery of grace, and I saw either side of his face was mantled in horns, horns that twisted back on themselves and dug into the flesh of his cheeks. In each of these cages of bone another red eye flashed.

"I give it to you for many reasons," he said, and he reached out his right hand to stroke my paralyzed face. This hand was ungloved, and three taloned fingers ran through strands of my hair, falling to linger on my shoulder, then down my side, as if he was tasting me through his touch. This was no sensual lust, only a more visceral desire. "One reason is I know you have means to escape, so I cannot harm you. The second is that with this thing you will do much damage to the Aedolae, and this both amuses and intrigues me. And last because giving it to you matters nothing. I will have you in the end all the same; it is the thing for which you were made."

His hand moved back to my face, tracing the fullness of my lower lip. I shuddered, struggling against the binding of his spell.

I bit his finger.

It was like biting a corpse. There was no blood, and his flesh was soft and mushy beneath the roughness of his skin. I spat and jumped up, repulsion freeing my limbs. Days later I would shudder recalling his words of imminent ownership, his scaly touch. I was so sickened by this being that I considered leaving the Eterokon there to spite him. But my desire for the Eterokoni was too great. I reached forward, gracelessly, and seized it.

A throaty chuckle escaped him.

"So sweet, you are," he whispered, apparently unconcerned about my bite. "Mark my words, little sojourner, we will see each other again."

I activated the Kalimba and watched with relief as that sepulchral place faded away. Fresh seaside breeze filled my nostrils and revived me.

That is how I found the Eterokon of Time.

And I have no idea how to use it.

THE TIME ROOM

E llie closed the book, and lay it gently on the bench beside her. The sunlight had crept far along the floor, closer to the statue. Her dress was no longer soaked, only damp. Nightmare images from the book whirled in her mind, and her eyes hardly focused on the room around her, seeing instead Siana's mad flight from the moon. It was strange to reflect on such images, here in a tranquil sun-bathed chamber.

Ellie had wondered why Siana called herself "Princess of Time". In describing her acquisition of the Sundial Eterokon, the second book gave a partial explanation. But Ellie was confused. This book referred to a time before Siana's attack on Kadesh. Which meant that Siana possessed the Eterokon of Time when she led that attack, but either its powers were not useful to her in that battle (which seemed unlikely) or she still had not yet mastered them.

None of this squared with Siana introducing herself as the Princess of Time.

So....if Siana died after the end of the Kadesh narrative, she would have perished before ever gaining the Sundial's power.

Which meant that she *must* have survived so she could gain it later—to earn her self-granted title.

Ellie knew she was grasping at threads, arguing based on things she did not know. But the sense that Siana still lived wouldn't leave her. She might simply be believing what gave her hope, what she wanted to be true, but it didn't feel like wishful thinking. It felt real.

Ellie rose from the bench, eager to continue her quest. This time she resolved to keep the book with her. She wondered if the other volume still lay on the floor where she had left it, a foolish oversight. That she had discovered two books, consistent with each other, telling of events from a larger story, and written in the same handwriting, buttressed her conviction that there must be more somewhere. She determined to take advantage of this unprecedented day and explore!

She walked toward the statue, holding the precious gray book flat against her chest. The sun had reached the foot of the statue and was striking the stone sundial. It cast a thin needle of shadow down the side of the dais to a place where an unusual regularity in the veins of the marble floor formed a boxy pattern. She fell to one knee and saw that the finger of shadow terminated at a thumb-shaped indentation. She set down the book and placed her thumb in the hollow. She could feel a little opening under the marble flooring. She was able to lift up, and out, the section of the floor framed by the box, revealing a hiding place beneath the stone. She was surprised how quickly and automatically she had acted, as if the whole procedure had been eminently obvious.

The floor of this hiding place was a mix of grey scree and dirt. Another sundial lay there, wrought of brass. This one was diminutive after the aspect of the Eterokoni in the images. The realization bludgeoned her.

This wasn't another icon. This dusty, hidden thing *was* the Eterokon of Time.

She sat back on her heels, reeling as this new piece of Siana's world confronted. This wasn't a picture or an account in a book, but something Siana had touched and held. The way the morning had unfolded: her question, then the answering appearance of a second book, and the way the book had occupied her until sunlight struck the sundial and revealed this spot. The coincidence was uncanny.

She cupped her hands about the Eterokon. Who had hidden it here? What need drove Siana to be separated from this thing, her namesake? Would she return for it? Was this place not a tomb but a museum for the Eterokoni? But if so, why would one be hidden? Should she leave it hidden, or carry it with her? The questions dazzled.

Her threadbare dress had no pockets. In the end she hid both the book and the Eterokon in the hollow and replaced the stone. She had always been able to retrace her steps in the castle. She would be able to find this chamber again.

Ellie spent the next few hours exploring the rooms adjacent to the Time Room (for this is what she named it). The rooms were unremarkable. But in this portion of the castle there was a greater sense of light, unexplained by any windows or skylights. Pausing midafternoon, she wondered about her plans for the night. She doubted she could retreat to her gallery in time. She was loathe to give up her quest, and certainly not for an uncertain chance at safe return. She had no guarantee the way wouldn't still be blocked. She resolved to sleep in the Time Room. Hadn't she already spent one night, unscathed? Buttressed by this confidence she continued her search for more books.

She scanned the iconography, the walls, the lush ornamentations of the architecture with an increasing intensity. More of Siana's belongings might be here, hidden. She also hunted for images showing Siana using the Sundial, clues to whether she indeed had lived to command its powers. But Ellie did not see it in play anywhere, though she did occasionally see it strapped to Siana's belt. She remembered the change that had overcome the image on the altar of the Cathedral Room. In a similar fashion, would she now see the Sundial represented in pictures back in the familiar portion of the castle? She wondered.

As the day waned, her explorations, intoxicating at first, continued to turn up nothing, and became tiresome. Her mind strayed back to the events of the second book. Something about the mysterious being of the moon passage disturbed her. The dire malevolence that clung to him in the book radiated into her mind. It emanated into the room about her. She was eager for the safety of the Time Room, and turned around.

On cue, the nighttime rustlings and creakings started up around her, an unseen and toneless orchestra tuning up.

She thought on the second book as she walked back. Its eeriness struck her imagination deeper than the battles of the first. The newest picture in the Vicious Room came to mind: Surely it portrayed the moon passage, lit with uncanny light, Siana uncharacteristically ill at ease. She had found that strange yesterday. But today she sympathized: *Siana, I would have felt the same if I had been there.*

The same way I feel here.

The synchronicity struck her. The same sense of dread mystery, of not seeing what lay hidden around the corner in the next bend of moonlit trail, the sense of wandering endlessly, an amnesic phantom spirit. Siana's jeopardy had been more concrete in the battles at Kadesh and Mihali. But the ghostly world of the second book struck unsettled Ellie's imagination more. It made the growing sense of night more oppressive than ever. She was grateful when she reached the Time Room, glimpsing through the eye of the skylight a flat grey sky above. She lay on the same bench, and stilled her haunted mind by running over the details of the places she had seen, confirming to herself the map she'd been making in her mind. It was an old strategy to avoid becoming hopelessly lost in the past in the castle's twists and turns; she'd never had a way to write things down.

She wished she was in a bed and not on a hard bench. Her mind strayed between waking and sleeping in a way that was unusual. *That must be because I'm here and not in my gallery.* Occasional noises from outside the room would jolt her from sleep. In a more wakeful moment, feeling insecure, she went to the hiding place and dug out the sundial and book, taking them back to the bench. She absently fingered the stringy material hanging from the book's binding and turned the little sundial over and over in her hands. Sleep finally claimed her.

THE MISTS CLEAR

E llie awoke a few hours later; the shadows in the Time
Room had deepened and the skylight framed inky black.
She had the sense something had disturbed her sleep. The
silence was strange. She did not recall ever being awake in the
castle at full night. Perhaps the silence was normal.

Behind the statue and its cloaked features was a sharp-edged
shadow, humanoid in shape, that filled the considerable height
of the wall. Its limbs splayed out in bizarre contortion and its
head, turned to the side, was lined with a crest of diminutive
triangular horns. Ellie's body stiffened in apprehension.
Nothing that had been in the Time Room by day would cast
such a shadow; this something must have entered. Straining her
ears for the slightest sound, she slowly raised her head above the
back of the bench and scanned the room in all directions.

Nothing to explain the shadow.

Her eyes completed their circuit of the room and returned
to the far wall. The reptilian shadow was still there, joined by
two others, similarly contorted. One had three visible limbs, the
other had two limbs but an abnormal number of joints. As she
watched in horror, giant shadow men winked on on all four
walls, a procession of malformed shapes, no two alike but all
akin in grotesquerie. Several were skeletal, with eyeholes in their
shadow heads.

This is not possible. She saw no source for the shadow
procession anywhere in the room.

Why is that phrase familiar? Ellie wondered.

Siana had said the same thing about the moon.

Ellie reached for the book and pressed it tightly to her body. Her other hand closed on the Eterokon.

And then the shadows began to move.

The motion was miniscule at first, like shudders cast by dancing firelight. Maybe it was her nervous imagination. But the jerky shudders magnified. The nature of the movement was more disturbing than the figures' shapes. They were like puppets shaken by a palsied hand. She pushed herself into the triangular hollow where the back panel and the seat of the pew met, willing herself into nonentity, praying that the shadows would just leave her alone.

She had thought herself safe here!

She put down the Eterokon and covered her face, peeking through gaps in her fingers. The figures were moving in a clockwise rotation around the walls. For an insufferably long time the mad parade gyrated, with her its trembling nucleus. The sense that their dance was weaving a spell about her, an impenetrable net, grew intolerable. To her own surprise, she got to her feet.

"Go away!" she bellowed, her arms ramrod straight, fists clenched. The strength of her voice shocked her. As the echoes died away, the shadows froze and faded into nothingness.

She collapsed.

She got up a few minutes later, noticing smears of blood on the marble where her hands, bleeding from her own nails, had struck the floor. The shadows' obedience was too much to digest. Her lungs ached with the force of her scream and her body felt completely wasted. She went back to the bench and fell dead asleep.

That night she dreamt again, with sparkling clarity. In her dream it was first morning she woke up in the castle. She knew this beyond any shadow of doubt. She had never been able to resurrect this day in her memory before.

She dreamt of a narrow room, floor coated in dust, a new place. She had never been here. She struggled to explain how she had gotten there. Nothing. She tried to remember the prior day. Nothing. Remembering her past was like trying to capture a dream upon awakening, all its details tantalizingly out of reach. And then, she tried to remember her name, and found with horror she could not. There had been a moment of clarity and will, but within minutes it slipped, replaced by a thunderstorm of bewilderment.

She stood. Her body felt bruised. The light in the room was as dim as her mind. She did not recognize the simple threadbare dress she was wearing. It was not hers; it felt wrong. She collapsed back onto the low bed. She was afraid to move toward the door and its brass doorknob. *I have to stay here. Only here am I safe. I cannot leave.* She did not know where these thoughts came from. They did not feel like her own.

• • • ●• ● • ••

The days passed, perhaps a week, inside the gallery she dared not leave. Sitting crouched, holding her knees to her chest, not cold, not warm on the dirty bed, staring at the doorknob, fearing that something might come in. Studying the featureless room to no avail. There was molding where the walls met the floor, a flat ceiling, no other furniture or objects. Every color a faded green. Her eyes sought patterns in the peeling of the paint. She sat and rocked herself, not eating or drinking, sleeping all night and sometimes much of the day.

She was no one, and nothing would ever change.

The smallest of changes happened. Her body, still weak, recovered from its bruises. The slightest bit of will was resurrected in her mind, a tiny phoenix taking flight from an field of ash and devastation. Her thoughts emerged from the tangle of confusion to wonder again at her name. She strained her mind for a whole day, and found she was Ellie. She was sure of that.

And sure of nothing else in the whole world.

She thought on her name for a whole second week, but nothing more came to her. Her mind was exhausted. She slept another week. And then, emboldened by her discovery of her name, she finally tried the door—

—And first saw the stained-glass image of the goddess. The goddess was Siana, but in the dream she was still nameless. After her dim weeks in the tiny gallery, Ellie was astonished at the painful brilliance of the light, the sparkling colors. In Ellie's dream, this brilliance grew, until the room's outline faded and only color remained.

Before the dream ended, she stood outside—outside!—in a field of summer flowers, and she could feel wind and sun upon her face. She was naked, with dry grass rasping against her calves and thighs.

And then light and color ebbed and darkness overtook her.

Morning sun flooded the Time Room. Her second morning here, and she had survived. The Eterokon was beside her on the bench, the book on the floor. She laid them to rest in the hiding place. Her dream came back to her with total clarity.

How much time separated today from the last day in the dream? Several weeks must have gone by, for she'd had time to gradually test her own limits and explore so much of the castle. Perhaps months, or even years. Enough time to have no concrete memory of the events in the dream. But she was now utterly confident about one thing: *there was a first day*. A first day of imprisonment. She had been a grown woman when it happened. She had been somewhere else before.

She felt her face. Her skin was young and smooth. If years had passed, there had not been many.

Imprisonment. She hadn't called it that before.

She remembered the wind on her naked skin. Her mind retained many words and instincts despite its forgetfulness, from another place where she had known and experienced all sorts of things. She knew there was a thing called childhood. In what world had she spent hers?

"You know what you need, Ellie," she said aloud, speaking out loud a new habit. "You need to sit and have a good think. You haven't had a good, clear think for a long time." She felt uncommonly fresh this morning. Confident that thinking would do her good. The gradual dissipation of the mist in her mind must have begun with the finding of her name and led, ever so gradually, to today.

"But first, a bath."

She repeated yesterday's frolic in the basin, this time with more grace. She drank deeply, picturing the water flowing beyond her stomach to saturate all the nooks and crannies of her body. She didn't think to take off her dress; it had been a part of her, as long as she could remember.

She decided the basin was as good a place as any for thinking, reluctant to leave. The urgency to explore more before night did not press her today. *I survived last night's horrors, didn't I? I dispelled them.*

Her thoughts returned to the idea of childhood. She had grown up somewhere else. She lacked memories, but she had knowledge, so she should be able to reconstruct that world from facts. A random list formed in her mind:

1. I both ate and drank, and normally—though apparently not here—people drink and eat with regularity.
2. I know about the church, pews and altars, and they are holy, deserving of respect.
3. Things like Siana's enemies didn't live in that world, because before I read the books those images here struck me as strange and preposterous; like myths or stories; but the things Siana says in her books ring true for me, not like stories.
4. I must have read books before. After all, I remember myths, and I remember how to read.
5. I know the idea of male and female, and I am a woman. I know what Siana means when she talks of men and women. *OK, Ellie, that's too basic to be useful.*
6. She knew that she'd had parents, that people had parents.

7. She knew that the castle was unusual. There should be spider webs. Her footprints in the dust shouldn't disappear by themselves over night. The patterns her fingers traced on dirty glass shouldn't disappear overnight.

The last point derailed her list-making.

Siana spoke of a myriad worlds, Kadesh, Mihali, Cylindrax, and the places between them. They each had different climes, weather, and inhabitants, despite their seeming proximity. The time of day was inconsistent between them. The whole concept struck her as both normal and abnormal at the same time. Does Siana's tale make sense only because I have read other stories, other myths? This seemed a pretty good answer. I don't think I come from Siana's kind of world.

Nor do I come from the kind of world in which this castle is possible.

This jived with the whole trajectory of her recent ruminations. Nonetheless it was a revelation, a culmination of those thoughts.

I don't belong here, and I am sure of that.

But what help was that? It didn't guarantee she wouldn't remain trapped. She tucked her list away in her mind. Enough thinking—it is time to get up and move. *I don't belong here, but here I am.* "Knowledge is power"—the quote surfaced from some unplumbed depth. So more knowledge she would seek.

THE LIBRARY

After finding the first two books in two days, Ellie's expectations had been great. On her third day, the disappointment was severe. Her mastery over the shadows had filled that day with a sense of inevitability. But she ended up going to sleep in the Time Room empty-handed.

The following three days piqued her desire to a fevered pitch. She imagined finding another book, held aloft by a new statue of her mistress, or laying forgotten on a polished wood floor.

Her anticipation was so high that when she discovered the library on her sixth day away from her gallery, it overwhelmed her psyche and she knelt, mute, in its doorway.

Its entrance was a double door, each side eight feet square and four-paneled. Outside that door a wide balcony joined a broad foyer via two ornate wooden stairs. A chandelier with a hundred lit candles was a glowing sun high in the vaulted ceiling of the foyer, casting rich orange light. The series of rooms leading to the foyer had been this same style, elaborately dressed in cherry, mahogany, and ebony, not stone or marble like so many other places in the castle, both beautiful and intimate. These rooms were uncommonly bright, with candles rather than torches, the shadows less harsh. But the most striking detail was the absence of dust; every surface gleamed as if polished by a legion of servants.

The disappearance of the ubiquitous dust had sharpened Ellie's anticipation. She had searched this complex of rooms, which presented a dizzying array of options, for the better part of a day until coming to this foyer. Her legs had shook as she climbed the left-hand stair.

Twin doorknobs shone in the candlelight, wrought in the shape of swans taking flight. The metal was cold beneath her fingers. The door swung easily on its balanced, oiled hinge. The room within was large and dim; a second story wrapped around the entire perimeter of the room, and overhung the far half. In the shadows, Ellie could see the room was chock full of books with old and weathered covers. Every wall had bookshelves, with little break between them, and a grid of low shelves crowded the center of the room. All of the castle's many rooms were empty compared to this. This room felt *full*, and its fullness assailed her senses, like a warm breath exhaling from its interior.

At last Ellie rose and stepped inside. In a semicircular reception area not much wider than the doorframe, a tiny jeweled light shone from a side table, casting a warm circle of light onto a plush chair. A book lay open, face down, on the side table as if someone had just been reading it. Behind the chair a wrought iron railing separated this sitting area from the room behind it. On either side gently inclining ramps led up to the main part of the library; the railing filled the space between them. She picked up the book on the side table. The deep green of its binding was identical to the first book she had found. She turned it over. She recognized the paragraph at once:

Neikolan and I emerged from the Labyrinth through an arch cloven in the far wall. Ahead of us was a sketchy mosaic of stone discs, scattered across a vast sea of stars.

It was the same book. Ellie put it down as if it were hot to the touch. How on earth had it gotten here? Her eyes swept about nervously.

Something else struck her odd. The lamp on the side table was electric.

She had only seen torches—or candles—within the castle. Yet this electric light seemed entirely commonplace. She came from a place with electricity.

Both forms of light fit with her sensibilities. Hmm.

She ducked her head under the side table, tracing the line of the electrical cord until it disappeared behind the chair. She sat down in the plush chair, searched the light for its switch, and flicked it. The sitting area was thrown into shadow. She didn't like that, so she flicked it back on. Gold flashed on either side of the open doorway.

A pair of statues flanked the inside of the library's doors. She got up to examine them, pushing the other part of the door open to admit more candlelight. She was surprised that neither represented Siana. This felt significant.

That would not be the library's last revelation.

The right statue depicted a gentleman, dapper in an old fashioned hat, one hand raised as if proffering her his arm. Over his other forearm was crooked a cane. His expression, cast in solid gold, seemed kindly to her and his lips, framed by a neat mustache and goatee, were pursed in a slight smile.

The left one was the same height and the same workmanship, but it depicted a radically different being. Orb-like, many faceted eyes crowned a face both avian and insectoid. In place of a cane, this statue held a carven staff whose weighty head lay against its high cheekbones. It resembled an Egyptian deity, that strange combination of human and animal she remembered from some book in her past. She didn't enjoy the appearance of this statue, but it was different than Siana's opponents in the Vicious Room paintings. The bird-man was cold, regal, powerful; but not evil, she decided, though she could not pinpoint why.

Her attention returned to the books. The day was waning. She had to pick a few to take back to the Time Room. She wondered if she could get back by nightfall. Her repudiation of the shadowy figures emboldened her, but nonetheless she was loathe to spend the night anywhere else. But she had to make a cursory exploration of the whole library before she returned.

She strolled the lower level first, examining books from random shelves. None had titles or words upon their covers; a few had simple designs; all the covers were heavy board in somber colors, frayed at the edges. All the books were written in the same hand, though with their immense number that seemed impossible. The light in the library was annoyingly dim; perhaps she would have to bring in a candle next time.

She had never thought to move a source of light before.

Something drew her to the upper level, so she took the delicate twisting staircase up. Here the upward glow of the electrical lamp helped, and there were fewer shelves, with broad patches of bare wall between. The walls hosted unusual bas reliefs of Siana's face in anguish, a deeper torment than portrayed in the spectral painting in the Vicious Room. The raw intensity of these images pierced Ellie. The Princess lacked her usual grandiosity and grace. These were Siana buffeted, limbs akimbo, against the walls by a hurricane wind, squashed in two dimensions.

She tore her eyes from the bas reliefs to study the shelves. She needed to divine the arrangement of the books. Without titles or labels, the task daunted. She sighed and walked to one end, starting with a lone shelf. She assumed all these books were penned by Siana; all must be part of the story of her life. So to fill in the gaps in her knowledge, she need only to pick the right books.

To her surprise, all the books on this shelf, equally weathered, were blank. She moved to the next shelf and selected a random book. She skimmed the first couple pages. Siana described leaving the seashore retreat of Mercair's World to return to her saboteurs. Ellie decided this book must be immediately prior to the first book she had read. She replaced it on the shelf and was about to select another volume when she heard a crashing sound through the open doorway. It sounded several rooms away; her blood froze. A desire to flee—and the familiar terror of impending night—shook her.

She raced down the stair, bare foot slipping on one of the lower steps. She half fell the remaining distance, bruising her ankle. At random she seized a trio of books from different shelves as she rushed for the door.

The foyer below the balcony was empty. The castle was silent. Somewhat calmed, she considering resuming her appraisal of the library.

With three books in her arms prudence won out.

"Enough reading for a day," she thought, and left. Careful to add to her mental map as she retraced her steps, she returned to the Time Room, invigorated by her discovery. Her arms ached from the unaccustomed weight of the books, but she welcomed this fatigue as a chance to build her strength. The walk back was so quick and the castle so quiet that she chided herself for her sudden panic. Nonetheless, the prize in her arms consoled her. Three books! At last!

The Time Room was dim and peaceful, the eye of the skylight grey with dusk.

She went to her familiar bench, under the gaze of the statue of her liege. At this time of day normally she would sleep. But she was too excited for that, and settled down to read. She selected a book with a red cover at random. The familiar handwriting greeted her and she began.

EBON PORT

Five years before the Attack on Kadesh

The glow of the hidden moon haloed the tree-line of a nearby island as I climbed from the water and hoisted myself up the pier. The webbing between my fingers, already beginning to recede, made my progress noisy and indiscrete. The mermaid's tail was of no use either, but as I perched on the pier's twisted and fractured end, dripping copious amounts of seawater onto old planking, I was relieved to see my tail split into human legs.

My transformation, even in this strange world, was too much for a jet-skinned youth night-fishing in the bay. He cried out in shock, his cry too loud in the dead quiet of midnight, and ran down the length of the pier. I swore under my breath. I had studied the pier for a long time, as I bobbed in the water, and judged it deserted. It stood apart from all other piers and docks of the nearby marina, and looked as if some wayward ship had decimated its seaward end not too far in the past.

I hadn't counted on Ebon's villagers having skin the same hue as the deeps of the night. The boy wore wine-red shorts, but the bulk of his form had been camouflaged. I hoped his cry would go unnoticed.

Changing with the Torc was murder on my clothes. Ending up naked when returning to human form tended to discourage its use. But I had decided I would rather begin my sojourn in the lands of the Aedolae naked than drown in the churning currents of the bay.

Completing my transformation from mermaid to girl, I hurried toward the beach, streaming water, wearing only the two necklaced Eterokoni at my throat.

I was here on a mission of reconnaissance. At first I had despaired, when the man known in these worlds as Llwyd Emyr—my brother Timothy—had disappeared. He hadn't known I was tailing him, but the silver cord spooling out from his *animus* had snapped in my presence, and he had vanished from two worlds.

I was afraid of entering this inimical kingdom, but my heart refused to forsake him. I don't know if my intense love—-my *need*—for him, or my pigheadedness, compelled me more. Regardless, I had mastered my fear and arrived here at Ebon Port, the first stronghold of the Aedolae.

I had little idea what to expect. I knew only a few things about the land beyond the Detheros, either things from my brother's journal or hints from my conversation with the Solmikaedis in the Fringe.

There was no movement or sound among the tall silhouettes of ships and fishing craft at the docks. As I reached the sand, the full moon emerged from behind trees and scattered silver across the bay, frosting the rigging of the ships. I noticed the jungle bordering the narrow crescent beach had been disturbed, many trees broken and splintered. Opportunistic shrubs and grasses grew where violence had opened jungle to sun. Catching a flash of white amid the brush, I poked around and found a tremendous skull with a sapling growing through one eyehole. Horns half as long as my arm protruded from either side of the nasal openings. There were three eyeholes in all. I couldn't find other bones to match; perhaps salvaged by villagers or scavenging animals?

I thought of the lumbering forms I'd seen in the tunnels below the Detheros and shuddered.

I threaded through driftwood toward the docks. What was I here to achieve? I had no concrete plan. But it is the province of youth to take action. I was determined to get my brother back. I must not have looked like much, navigating the dunes at night. A lone waif with sandy blonde hair, spiky from my defiant hacking of the flower threaded tresses I had grown during my time in the Gardens. The knife I used lay at the bottom of a cliff far above the Detheros. I had no weapons now, only the wickedly carved Torc of black metal at my throat, and the tiny bejeweled Kalimba on its fine thread below. The first was an artifact of formidable power. The second I had no idea how to use, but suspected it to be the same. In the Gardens Mercair had explained to me that each of the kalimba's keys, with their tiny engraved symbols, represented one of the Aedolae's worlds.

A teenage girl, with only two Eterokoni to her name.

Mercair told me it was the Aedolae who trapped me in the Gardens for a year, dulling my restless mind and forestalling my progress toward the Detheros. So, lone waif or no, they had taken notice of me. And, lone waif or no, I had come through—or rather under—their great Barrier.

The full moon was over the main island now, making it bright with moon shadows. I had reached the docks. Of inhabitants I had only seen the boy, but I was nervous. I had heard of the guises of the Aedolae but I knew nothing about the appearance of their minions. The rustic dwellings dotting the hills, visible now in the moonlight, seemed the humble abodes of fishermen; if not human men and women, nonetheless beings who desired lives of simple contentment. I could not imagine these folk as scions of the Aedolae.

But still...

A broad avenue, littered haphazardly with stepping stones, led from the docks up to the first buildings. A strange thing began to happen. As if signaling the dominion of night over the busy activity of day, the avenue narrowed, filling in with small gnarled trees that grew in minutes out of the dusty soil. Grand flowers unfurled from the ground, their circular heads like sunflowers of a ghostly pallor.

In minutes, the broad avenue became a mere path an arm-span wide, winding through an impromptu forest.

Something about this unexpected transformation drew me from my hiding place in the shadows. I took it as a sign: I alone trod this street of night blooming flowers, my form a pale dream within the mantle of night. As I followed the curve of the path without fear, figures emerged from the riot of vegetation and flanked the trail, maidens and lads in diaphanous robes. Their cupped hands held lighted orbs that cast no shadows. Their eyes were downcast under lustrous lashes and they spoke no word. By the time I reached each new figure, it had assumed the stillness of a statue, but its flesh was warm to my touch. Behind me, their procession formed a serpent of lights winding down to the docks.

The trees thinned and the trail opened into a cobbled street. At trail's end two last figures faced me: a girl with long curly tresses on my left, a spiky haired young man on my right. Their eyes were not hooded like the others, but appraised me. Their expressions were mild.

I approached. They wore dark matching skirts but their chests were bare, even the man's smooth and hairless. Their skin shone as if oiled, and upon each of their bellies an elaborate tattoo of a clock face showed midnight. To my shock the tattooed second hands moved across their skin. As I approached, the girl assumed an expression of fear or anxiety, and turned her eyes from me, but the young man continued to regard me steadily.

"Welcome, Princess of Time," he said.

My eyes narrowed. He knew the moniker by which a thirteen-year-old girl had christened her daydream self.

"A prophecy, perhaps?" he added, with a tone more mischievous than amused, and gestured to his companion. I followed the gesture, and saw that the clock hands on the girl's tattoo had disappeared; only the twelve carets around the face of the clock dial remained. Her face was still turned away.

I glanced back at the young man; his clock face showed a stroke past midnight. A leather-bound book had appeared in his hand during the interval of my distraction: my brother's journal, exactly as it appeared in the waking world. Its dreamworld analogue had vanished the day the silver thread snapped. Since then, I had not been able to resurrect it in my dreams, where I needed it most.

I worried that he would taunt me with it, or destroy it. Instead he handed it to me.

"Something you will need, Princess of Time. Let this gift remind you that knowledge is more valuable than many strikes of a dagger," he said, as if alluding to the daggers arranged around my slumbering form an immeasurable distance far away, back in the waking world.

I took the journal from his hand. The youth beckoned again to the girl, who now held neatly folded garments. I set down the journal and dressed, finding the garments a perfect match for my mission and my mood: close fitting black tunic, tight about my breasts, black breeches ending high on the ankle, sturdy well-treaded shoes like low boots. A wide stiff belt with an assortment of clasps and tiny pockets. Vambraces for my lower arms buttressed with steel panels. A rugged knapsack for my back. A looser fitting vest with a fine mesh of tiny metal rings. Despite the young man's comment, small daggers nestled in sheath pockets at both thighs. Soon dressed, and with the journal safely tucked away, I thanked the pair profusely.

"You are welcome," the man said. "Help may come when you least expect it."

And with those words, they spun on their heels gracefully, assuming the mute and incognizant stance of their fellows. I stood between them now, on the edge of the street. I examined their clock tattoos. Time had resumed on the girl's clock. As I watched, the minute hand unexpectedly accelerated, whipping around the dial. The hours of the night flashed by as I stood, paralyzed. What magic was this? Dawn lightened the sky before I could tear my eyes from her.

As a rainbow of color lightened the horizon beyond the docks, I watched an eerie reversal of the midnight scene along the avenue. The figures disappeared into the trees with graceful indolence, the night blooming flowers closed, the trees grew backwards. The piles of earth displaced by their preternatural growth were sucked back into the dusty ground of the street. The winding path was a fishermen's arcade once more.

Released from the spell, I reacted instinctively to the surrounding clamor of voices. The streets had filled with figures. I shrank against a building to my left, as a jet-skinned woman pushed a wheelbarrow into the street from the uphill side of the village. Within a minute, many others had joined her, going about the business of the day. A band of sunlight caught me from behind, throwing my ruddy shadow onto the cobbles. Fearing imminent discovery, I touched the Torc at my throat, changed my fingers to a gecko's pads, scaled the building's stone wall and gained the thatched roof in an instant.

I proceeded to fall through the thatch into the abandoned upper story of a warehouse, making quite a ruckus.

I had to laugh despite my anxiety.

I crawled to an unpaned window and looked down on the street. A few men gestured toward my hiding place, but their expressions showed no great concern. I sighed in relief and studied them. All of their features were the same polished jet as their skin: lips, fingernails, the irises and the surrounding conjunctivas of their eyes. Only their teeth flashed white, and bright white at that. In their black mouths this gave them a predatory look despite the human cast of their faces.

Moving from upper story to upper story to survey the village from multiple hiding places was easy—for a girl who had shapechanged her way through the steaming mud, blasted rock and deep darkness of the Detheros. The only inhabitants of Ebon Part seemed to be these black-skinned men. I assumed this island also harbored at least one Aedolae, likely its lord. I did not want to encounter him.

My thoughts always led back to my brother, a dark obsession. His journal mentioned nothing past the Edoi Sea. Perhaps in a single night's dreams he had passed this place and encountered misfortune somewhere else? Why was he missing—dead—in the waking world? My gut felt he was alive.

Or was that my heart?

Neither his journal nor the other strange books in his collection explained the least bit of what was going on. Despite popular sentiment, I knew we could die in dreams. But nothing mentioned a dreamer vanishing from the waking world against his will, or the world closing about his memory like a wound without a scar. I'd lost my brother, then I'd lost my mom, driven to suicide by Timothy's fate and my father's infidelity.

My father. That selfish hippie. That fucked up man.

My thoughts were interrupted by a sound that had grown steadily in volume: the howls of some person taunted by a jeering crowd. I was in a cleft between two chimneys on the roof of an inn. I crawled to the gutters. A young man with unkempt hair stood with his back to me in the middle of the street, scanning in a harried way for a place to escape. My whole body tensed. His skin was white. I lost sight of him as a group of jet-skinned youth emerged from a side street and encircled him. I could not understand their language. The hounded man appeared to lack a faculty for speech; his strangled cries rang out like the squeals of a pig. He flailed at his tormentors, who were cool and easy in their stance. Other men and women stood in storefronts, watching the scene. I noticed now that a few others were also not jet-skinned. And then the hounded man lunged at one of his attackers and turned his face toward me.

It was the face of my brother.

Wild-eyed, bronzed and bearded, I still knew him.

As I leapt from the roof, the power of the Torc coursed through my body and dragon wings burst from my back (ruining yet another set of clothes). My fingernails lengthened to talons. As I landed in the fray, the wind from my wings swept back onlookers and I slashed left and right, finding purchase in flesh. With cries of terror or pain, everyone scattered.

Save my brother.

As my wings retreated into the tattered remnants of my tunic and vest and my claws vanished, I knelt beside my brother, fallen to his knees in the dirt. Tears stung my eyes as I gathered him in my arms.

"Timothy, it's me," I whispered.

But his arms failed to clasp me in response. His eyes didn't register me. He mumbled and fell back on his bottom, glancing about distractedly. A couple of his tormentors peeked around buildings.

"Timothy," I pleaded, with a sinking emptiness in my breast, "it's your sister, don't you know me?" But the trembling, mumbling thing resembling my brother just sat there and absently picked at his beard. He took no notice.

I tried to settle the torn fabric of my tunic over my body. My mouth hung open. Thought and emotion raced, competing, through my mind. Was this worse than finding him dead, finding this shell of a man? I studied the worn and sordid condition of his clothes, the filthiness and unkempt appearance of his hair and skin, the wasted muscles, the soiled condition of his pants. I knew, with a sick feeling, that my brother's mind must have been lost for a long time.

I stood up from my crouching position and screamed in defiance, daggers flashing in both hands. Peering faces disappeared behind timber and stone.

"Come back here, I'll kill you all, dream phantoms," I hissed at them. My eyes scanned the now-empty town with wild defiance.

"My lady?" a soft voice said at my backside, inches away. I spun, daggers passing through the air where my supplicant's stomach should be. But the man had side-stepped with preternatural agility. He was white-skinned. Long black hair, partially braided, framed a face oriental in cast, finely featured, and—I noticed—very beautiful.

"My lady, you do yourself no good acting like that." His voice was gentle, despite the fact I could have torn a hole in his belly and still brandished daggers. "There is something you should know."

"Who are you?" I demanded, in low tones.

"My name is Daevon, and I am from your world," he answered, pushing the tips of my daggers downward with the end of a staff. "I came here with my master Ambrose many, many dream-spans ago. But what you should know is that *that-*"—he motioned with his staff toward the pitiful man lying in the shade of the inn with closed eyes—"is not your brother."

I sputtered in protest but he cut me off.

"It is a *xemenos*, so Ambrose says, and he knows many things about the perplexities of the dreamworlds. It is a shade, or fragment, of a dreamer. But not the dreamer himself."

Conflicting emotions swept through me, exhausting after the grief and rage I had experienced in so short a time.

"How does your master...know?" I stammered.

"Well, we don't *know*," Daevon replied, "but my master is wise. Like you, he passed the Detheros, and beyond that, he found a way to leave the world and cheat his own mortality, to live here forever. He has maintained his estates here and explored much of this demesne without the Aedolae's interference. And besides which," he added grimly, "he has kept both himself and me from being eaten."

I wondered at that, but did not ask. My brain was busy with other things.

Instead I asked, "So if this is not my brother, where *is* he?"

"I don't know; I have not seen him in this realm," said Daevon. "But I have exerted much effort these eighteen months keeping this xemenos from drowning in the bay or falling over cliffs—"

"Then why weren't you protecting him now?" I accused. I remembered my brother's—the *xemenos'*—howls of confusion and distress.

Daevon's face was sheepish. "Well, I had seen you up there"—he gestured toward the rooftops—"and I had the intuition this might flush you out—"

"You used my brother as bait!" I cried, boxing him in the chest, causing the tattered remains of my tunic and vest to slip down my body.

"My lady, I told you: he is not your brother, and he came to no harm. And you were more than capable at scattering the mob. You did so with applaudable drama." As I gathered the split panels of my shirt about my breasts, he added with wry humor, "You won't do much good with your hands holding up your clothes. We should go; it won't be long before these youths master their fear and decide to test your mettle. We can fetch you clothes from my master's abode."

As it turned out, Daevon fetched me something far more significant.

THE AEDOL VIA

We left the village and its small circle of civilization carved from jungle. I tied the panels of my shirt to the strip of cloth still looped around my neck. Daevon assured me the xemenos would be safe for a while; the townsfolk and the ruffians would be more concerned with gossip and seeking further sight of me. As we rushed along rough and narrow paths, mostly forced to move single file, it was difficult to maintain our conversation. We were climbing above the coastline the opposite direction from the docks, and Daevon took a bewildering number of turns. Through occasional gaps in the verdure, I saw the beach narrow and become sheer cliffs. For a while we walked the open top of one cliff; the drop to the sea below was precipitous.

"Eighteen months ago," Daevon was saying, "the xemenos appeared at Orse. Earlier the same week I spotted Coethyphys on the northeast side of the island—"

"What are those?" I asked.

"Dreamflesh eaters. I'd never seen Coethyphys at Ebon Port before." Timothy's journal had mentioned such creatures. Daevon continued. "The next day something took out half the marina and carved a semicircle out of the jungle beachside with huge destructive force—"

"Then this carbon copy of my brother appears," I interrupted again.

Daevon held up one hand. "Whoa, miss."

"Would a Coethyphys head be about this big?" I spread my arms.

"Yes, why?" Daevon's eyes narrowed.

"Because there is a skull in the woods by that lone pier."

Daevon nodded. "All these things indicated the presence of a dreamer. After many long years free of such anxiety, Ambrose and I worried. But with familiarity the worry faded as all worries do. No further reappearance of Coethyphys—perhaps killed by the same force that destroyed the ships and trees. No trouble with the Aedolae. Just the menial task of safeguarding a simpleton's life, free of any larger drama." Daevon laughed, somewhat uneasily. "But now you appear, and put a face to the puzzle."

"Sorry," I offered.

"I think is time you tell me who you and your brother are."

We had come to a high promontory, bathed in morning sun. To the southeast, a fleet of black-sailed ships were disappearing into distant haze. These, I would soon learn, were Orsian traders, headed to far lands on their biennial tour. Closer in, islands of a myriad shapes and sizes filled the archipelago of the inner Edoi Sea. We paused, letting the stiff breeze cool our bodies, slick with sweat from the fast pace Daevon set amid the close air of the jungle.

Standing there, I decided to trust this handsome man from the waking world, *my* world, and I told him my name, my self-chosen title. And I told him about Timothy, and my mission.

Daevon's expression grew increasingly intent.

"There is no trace of your brother in the waking world?" Daevon asked. His eyes showed his struggle to accept this. I nodded. "I have never heard such a thing. There is only one way a dreamer can leave the waking world: by their own free choice. As Ambrose and I did in 1914." Daevon smiled at my subsequent expression. "Does my beautiful young companion think she is talking to a phantom of the past? Why, what year is it now?"

"2005," I answered. "A lot has changed."

"I imagine." Daevon laughed. He had called me beautiful. Did he believe that, or was he being polite? "Your brother's disappearance is so unprecedented it has me at a loss. I had hoped your story would explain more." He paused, scanning the brightness of the ocean, and I could tell he sought a way to frame the issue so he *could* be of help.

"Let us retrace what happened to your brother," Daevon continued. "We know the Coethyphys were here. Coethyphys are rarely seen. Their heyday was centuries ago, when they had thousands of dreamers as prey. Now they are secretive, few in number, their ways sundered from the ways of their creators. From your story, your brother was no fool, nor complacent. He wouldn't have stayed long in one place. He would have moved on, to explore the stolen beauties the Solmikaedis promised him. If your brother was their intended prey, and they came here to intercept him, they must have been forewarned of his coming."

"Does the xemenos mean he died?"

Daevon's compassionate expression let me both like and trust him the more.

"I don't think it is like that. A xemenos is not a ghost. As Ambrose explained it to me, it is the product of dream disruption. The dream body is a different thing than a waking world body, susceptible to different kinds of insult. Perhaps your brother died. But other kinds of trauma, not fatal, could have made this thing." Daevon saw my frown and continued. "Besides if your brother died, he would just wake up. A dreamer's death is not a fatal event. It wouldn't explain him disappearing from the waking world. My hypothesis is the moment you saw the ribbon snap Timothy came *fully* Within."

This jived with my understanding of dreams. I was not the typical teenager.

"Ambrose and I," Daevon went on, "have safeguarded the xemenos' life, hoping for more information. I will continue to do so, for he is part of this puzzle. But I must warn you: my master is a hard man, and cares more for his own survival and knowledge than aught else."

"So my brother came Within," I reasoned, "and therefore it looks like he 'died' in my world. But that doesn't mean he survived the Coethyphys attack here. He could be dead everywhere."

Tears began to stand in my eyes, making my words careless and awkward.

"We don't know he encountered the Coethyphys that were here," Daevon replied. "We don't know that the skull you found belongs to one of them. We don't know what destroyed the marina. We may not know much, but ignorance is preferable to false despair. Hold your heart steady, Siana."

"Thank you," I said, touching his arm. "Do the Coethyphys work for the Aedolae?"

"The Coethyphys are not cooperative. The Aedolae were once their handlers, but never their allies. The Aedolae now avoid them, with their desperate need for the Coethyphys' services lying centuries in the past."

We had returned to the jungle and were scrambling down a steep incline, with little opportunity for hand or footholds. At the bottom was a rude shack. A steep wooden staircase led down the cliffs to another long and isolated pier.

"If your brother is Within, you will find him," Daevon said. "The Aedolae have always underestimated us. Their resentment of us blinds them to our power."

"You have been so helpful," I said. I caged my surge of joy, steeling myself against indiscriminate hope. But that hope would stay, tucked away in some corner of my mind, and it would give me strength.

There was a tiny clearing surrounding the shack, boundaried both above and below by cliffs.

"This is the outpost of my friend Jico. He is a bootlegger, and soon the last Orsian ship will sail by and take on that part of its cargo not taxed or sanctioned by the masters of the trade routes.

He is waiting on the pier, but if he comes back up, you can say you are a friend of mine."

"Why, where are you going?" I exclaimed, irritated by the sudden petulance in my voice.

"Uphill to my master's place. I'll come back with the best match of vest and shirt I can find, or at least a needle and thread. I won't be long." With a smile, he hoisted himself up the cliffs via a network of ragged ropes. He laughed as he disappeared. "Wish I could shapechange, so much easier!"

I took in my surroundings. The door to the shack was open and its windows were largely shattered. The room inside resembled a tavern. I surmised there was more to Jico's estate than met the eyes, and the look of abject poverty was purposeful. I contemplated sitting on a barstool to wait, but Daevon's sudden departure rankled me. It did not do to trust too much.

So, after checking that Jico was not near (the grizzle-haired figure was still on the pier gazing out to sea) I hastily removed my clothing. I wouldn't ruin any more of the fine outfit with which the clock figures had gifted me. I found a chest in the corner, empty save for cobwebs, and laid my garments inside.

Then I returned to the clearing, touched the Torc at the hollow of my throat and changed into a tree.

I palpated my bark-encrusted body with the slender branches that now served me for arms; my guise felt convincing. The Torc struggled to get rid of my face, for a slitted mouth, a knobby nose, and my eyes still remained (I almost poked one out with my awkward twiggy fingers). But when I closed my eyes, a sheen of fragile bark folded over them like eyelids, and when Daevon returned—if he did—I would shut my mouth and make that disappear as well.

As fate had it, I used my disguise before that. I heard a rasping breath. Something was scuffling down the steep incline, the same path we had taken. My tree eyes had limited range of vision, so I only saw it once it reached Jico's shack.

It stood a head taller than Daevon, grotesque in form. We don't realize how much we take symmetry for granted until we see a humanoid figure without any. Its arms attached to its torso at different heights, they differed in length, and they had a differing number of joints. Its orb-like, insectoid eyes—four in number—were placed randomly about its craggy face, and even its mouth was set on a tilt. Its gait—for its legs were equally disproportionate—was painful to watch as it meandered through the front room of the shack. But despite its hideous awkwardness, I could not pity it. It was seeking something, with a malevolent gleam in its eyes.

My mind's instincts are often sharper in dreams, and I knew that *something* was me.

It studied the cliff face up which Daevon had scrambled. It glanced toward the pier. It studied the path along which we—and it—had come, seeming perplexed. It didn't have much of a nose, but it raised its nostrils as if scenting the air.

And then it moved slowly and deliberately toward me. I narrowed my eyes and mouth to slits as its horrible face inched closer. I could feel its breath, which rattled in its chest, as it made a slow circuit of my tree-self. Its face crinkled tighter in what I assumed was confusion. It stepped back, gnarled, scaly fingers opening and closing. A clicking noise rose from its throat. Even its naked hide was a mismatch, furred in places, hard and reptilian in others. It made a second tour of the shack and was returning to me when metal clanked above my head.

It staggered backward, pushed by the force of the silver bolt now lodged in its shoulder. Gears grinded noisily behind me, and a rain of dirt clods fell through my leaves. As the thing clicked loudly in pain and rage, a second bolt whizzed across the clearing, narrowly missing its face, knocked off axis by my branches. The thing tore at the shining missile lodged in its body with clumsy talons and dragged itself uphill and back toward Orse.

As I changed form I fell into Daevon's arms, as he alit from the ropes behind me.

"Useful thing, glad I brought that," he said, throwing down the crossbow to better support my weight. He stood me on my feet and frowned at the scarlet trickle down my arm. The second bolt had grazed me.

"A bleeding dryad."

He smiled.

I liked him all over again, smiling back.

I was immensely grateful that the insect man accounted for my shapechanging, and I wouldn't have to explain my suspicion. Daevon had come back, good as his word. He had not betrayed me. Hard as my life in the waking world had been, I was not immune to the redemptive quality of sudden infatuation. Daevon looked my brother's age, and no doubt I was just a young girl to him. But as I stepped out of his arms, I blushed from head to toe. I was entirely naked before him, and he was happily appraising the subtle curves with which nature had endowed my seventeen-year-old frame.

It is indicative of my positive feeling for him that I managed another weak smile.

"God damn Torc," I muttered and rushed, gracelessly, for the shack.

"Here try this on," he said a minute later, throwing a bundle through the doorway. A folded shirt, a bit too large, and of softer material than the ruined one. But at least it was black.

"What was that thing?" I yelled.

"An Achthron. They live in caverns at the apex of the island. I'm surprised to see one here. If one spots you, all of them will know, including the ones up there with Him."

"I'm dressed now," I yelled. Daevon came in and sat on a stool. He set to repairing my mailed vest, using a small sewing kit. He worked deftly and soon I was donning it, my outfit once again complete. I spread my arms for him with a stupid grin, which he returned with graceful affection. His gaze rose from my outfit to my neckline.

"The Eterokoni." He studied them. "I would guess the Torc is the shapechanger, but what of the tiny instrument?"

I fingered the Kalimba. "Mercair told me that each key represented a different world. He said finding it was a mark of my power. But he didn't tell me what it does. I wished I had asked; nothing in my brother's books says."

"The worlds would be Ebon Port," Daevon mused, peering at the tiny symbols engraved on the keys. "Mihali, Zoorn, Kadesh, and Cylindrax. The symbol for Ebon Port is this, for Bierce saw it in the Spaerodont's lair." He pointed at the character closest to my right shoulder, a U laying on its side, joined to a cross. "So the keys must run in order of the Aedol Via, the great road through their demesnes." (I remembered the Aedol Via from Timothy's journal.) "But there is an extra key. Hmm. Who is this Mercair?"

"Right outside the Detheros I got trapped in a recurring dreamscape, and for long time I forgot who I was. I was there for a year of dreams before Mercair came to my rescue. He was dressed a gentleman of, say, the early 1900s—your time period. But I was dazed, I asked him nothing about himself. I was like a drowning girl, simply grasping the hand of my rescuer. When I left that dream, I left him behind."

"These things will be of great interest to Ambrose. I wish you could meet him, but he is off exploring in the Summer Isles. In his absence, I decided to bring you another thing." He withdrew from his pocket a four pointed star carved from a single cherry-red gem. He affixed it by its slender chain to one of the hooks of my belt, settling it into one of the belt's pockets. "It is the Eterokon of Tongues, and the xemenos had it when we first found him. How many Eterokoni did your brother have?"

"His journal says eight."

"Eight"—Daevon whistled—"of the reputed twelve! Your brother is a rare dreamer. This would alarm the Aedolae indeed. But the xemenos had only this one."

"Thank you," I said, as I removed the Star from its pouch and fingered it. It refracted even the shack's dim light amazing ways.

"I thought you would need it," Daevon explained, "and it is yours by right, his sister. My master will deny seeing it this way at first, and be wroth. But I will say that I was overwhelmed by the rare presence of a dreamer, and furthermore my 19th century eyes were overcome by the sight of her feminine charms."

His finely proportioned face split with a grin, which narrowed his dark eyes.

"Well, I thank you," I said, holding my hands in my lap and feeling a bit foolish. "What do you think happened after I saw the ribbon snap?"

"I don't know, but your brother wasn't here long. I would have found him. Siana, I have devised a plan that suits your need," Daevon said with authority. "Continue your search by traveling the Aedol Via, as close to a sure and safe passage the dreamworlds offer. Through the power of the Aedolae, it remains stable and unchanged; it will prevent you becoming lost in random dreamscapes and it will take you through all the demesnes. You can shapechange, and with the Star you have the power of tongues, so you can pose as a native Orsian aboard this last ship. You will find Timothy and return here with the traders when they complete the Via. Then my master can offer both of you whatever help he can."

This was a lot to digest. I appreciated his confidence in my quest.

"How long will the traders' route take?" I asked.

"They will return a year from fall," Daevon said without inflection and stood up. My heart sank. To leave this man—who had given me kindness beyond what I could expect anywhere else in the dreamworlds, a kindness of the sort I had only experienced from my brother in the waking world—leave this man and be gone that many months! Kindness, and gifts, and good advice. Leaving him was crazy. I studied his handsome face, framed by braids. If I had never met him, I would have forged on (blindly!), buttressed by the hardness of my heart. But now my heart was soft within me.

"Could you come with me?" I pleaded, knowing the answer. Without intending it, I had circled my arms about his back. He was very tall. I wished I hadn't destroyed my hair. It had been so long and blonde and beautiful when Mercair found me.

Daevon did not back away, but neither did he indulge the embrace. He held me, close but not tight. He reminded me of Timothy, kind and even, quiet but confident.

"I wish I could, my lady," he said at last, "but I cannot abandon my master. I owe him too much. I have given you what help I can, for now." And then he was lowering his face to mine, placing a kiss upon my surprised mouth, short but not chaste.

"Live, succeed, and return to me," Daevon said.

The promised ship—the ship of Daevon's plan—must now have docked at Jico's; many feet clattered on the planking below. I peered through the dirty windows and saw a black-sailed ship of ebony wood.

"Quick!" Daevon exclaimed, "become one of the jet-skinned!" And so I did, in the sudden rush acceding to his plan without the objections I otherwise would have raised. My arms and legs were now a deeper black than my clothing, carved from black marble.

"Leave your teeth white." Daevon laughed and I adjusted that. "There you are: Siana to the last feature, but dipped in black paint." His laughter trailed off as a trio of Orsians pounded into the room, Jico in tow.

"Follow my lead," Daevon whispered.

Jico was human, Arabesque. I would learn not all men and women of the dreamworld are like the Orsians. Many resemble people from the waking world, though often with some exotic or unusual aspect. But they are products of the dreamworld still, having no commerce with our world, and not like us in many ways.

That night found me aboard the Orsian vessel, as the illicit cargo was stashed in secret places behind the legitimate goods that would be traded more ostensibly in the bazaars of the demesnes. It had all happened so fast. I felt very alone despite a day full of negotiation and conversation in a new tongue. Daevon convinced all parties (though I figured Jico only partially) that I was a native Orsian closeted in Ambrose's estate as a servant and protégé since my pubescence. I would now fulfill my promise as Ambrose's adept by gathering information for him along the Aedol Via. They accepted this explanation, by virtue of their association with Jico, and in turn Jico's association with Daevon and his master.

Fortunate.

Even more masterful was Daevon negotiating away the cost of my keep aboard their vessel with hints at my special knowledge and military prowess.

This was one of many things worrying me, as I drowsed in lantern-lit darkness in my tiny cabin below ship, my pallet gently rocking as the docked ship bobbed in the water. I wondered what they would expect of me. I had shown little ship-craft so far; I had set both male and female sailors to raucous laughter with my ignorance as we sailed from Jico's pier to the main docks. Luckily, Daevon's story of my closeting accounted for that ignorance, for all Orsians are people of the sea, traders and fishermen. But I would learn. I had much to learn. I knew so little about where I was going. Timothy had only hints and rumors gleaned from his books and what various entities in the Fringe had told him. I had his journal. But in truth only the barest information had passed the Detheros for a thousand years. I would go where so few dreamers had ever gone, into the strongholds of the Aedolae.

The Aedolae, who had imprisoned me in the Gardens and took away the freedom of my nights—the only solace in my waking life.

Dawn came early, sunlight in a cloudless sky. The morning spring air was chill with a memory of winter, but warmed quickly. If I had been less distracted, I would have wondered at the strangeness of the ship, its plethora of strange equipment and devices that no sailing craft of the waking world would need. By midmorning we had set sail, striking eastwards into the blinding white corridor the sun cast upon the waves. I stood at the rail, feeling guilty, but assured by my new shipmates that staying out of their way was best until I learned more.

We passed through the Summer Isles, an uncanny ocean oasis, where the water was so still and pristine I could see the shadow of the boat on the floor of the sea. These isles were small and low. Some sported impossibly tall and slender trees, whose branches met overhead to form a leafy cathedral roof for our passage. Some sported no vegetation save a close cropped grass, like green disks that floated on the water's surface. The quality of the sunlight was different in the isles, white and pure, sparkling magnificently wherever it caught a drop of moisture on leaf or bark. Though the Orsians are typically garrulous, no one spoke during this passage. I was enraptured, and my heart sank when we returned to the noise and flapping wind of the open sea. I went to the rear of the ship, and watched the Isles gradually disappear, feeling like my soul had been left behind. I envied Daevon's master, Ambrose, his exploration of them.

These isles, like so, so many things, had been sundered from humankind by the Aedolae.

We hoisted the full panoply of our sails, left the last of the archipelago of the Edoi Sea behind, and made for open ocean.

REVELATIONS

S he closed the book. Deep night had settled in the Time Room. The account was far older than any she had read; Siana's ignorance of the Kalimba's function established that. Ellie's head was a jumble of images and words. Timothy. The Gardens. The Detheros. The xemenos. Achthroi.

Her mind lit upon the most significant thing of all: dreams.

All this time she had been reading about dreams. Siana's explorations of what Daevon had called the dreamworlds. Ellie felt the rug had been pulled out from under her mind. Why hadn't the other two books mentioned this?

Imminent conclusions began striking Ellie with piercing force. She sat bolt upright in the pew.

If these books are accounts of dreams, of the dream persona of a woman from the waking world, then chances are this castle isn't anywhere in the waking world.

This castle is a dream shrine to a dream warrior.

This castle is a dream, and I, Ellie, am dreaming it.

And I am a dreamer too.

Ellie's mind recoiled from this last conclusion. The account was clear: to Siana, the world of the Aedolae was the world of dreams, but to the men of Orse it was *the* World, their world, and not a dream at all. So perhaps she was *not* a dreamer, but instead like the Orsians. The concept made her head spin. For wasn't she trapped here, boundaried by these walls? She never woke up, out of this dream into that other world, the waking world of her liege. She even fell asleep here, dreaming dreams within dreams. Her experience of the castle had been *everything*, as long as she could remember.

Her initial euphoria faded, and she felt imprisoned all over again.

But then Ellie remembered the list she had made during her bath. She had concluded she didn't come from the kind of world in which Siana's adventures happened. She had reached that conclusion honestly, without reading this last book, without her current desire for that conclusion to be true overmastering her reason. There was no reasonable doubt.

She, like Siana, was not from the world of dreams.

But why don't I wake up?

She spent a painful half hour blundering around in the twilight, trying to wake herself up. But no amount of pinching, yelling, willpower or ploughing her frail body into obstacles was sufficient to the task. Her mind stubbornly refused to wake up, to give any indication it was not already fully awake. She returned to her pew defeated.

Careful thinking got me this far. I better stop trying to commit dreamworld suicide and have another Think.

Timothy.

Siana had a brother, who preceded her into the world of the Aedolae. He had another name for himself, what was it? *Emyr.* Siana's anger in the first two books suddenly made a good deal more sense. It was personal. Much more than the fleeting reference to Kadesh's possession of Paris. She had been separated from her brother.

The Aedolae had created the Detheros to block dreamers. Timothy had broken through and then disappeared. This older book demonstrated that Timothy was the original reason for Siana's foray into their worlds. So why didn't the first two books mention him? Was he indeed lost to her, so only her vendetta against the Aedolae remained?

Princess of Time.

Was Siana even alive?

Ellie's mind returned to the old question. She had reasoned the existence of the moniker meant Siana survived the battle with dragon-Kadesh and earned the title later. But this book revealed Princess of Time was a name she gave herself, before she'd earned it, daydreaming as a young girl. Ellie's mental assurance that her liege was alive quavered under this new information. But the feeling in her gut hadn't changed.

Was that feeling just foolish hope?

Ellie was eager to read more. She knew it was late, but she had to know more. She had to know if Timothy had been found, if Siana had survived her confrontation with the massed forces of the Aedolae at Mihali.

Another thing struck her. Both of the statues in the library had a counterpart in the book she'd just read. The statue on the right had to be Mercair:

I was there for a year of dreams before Mercair came to my rescue. He was dressed a gentleman of, say, the early 1900s.

That was interesting. Ellie hadn't seen a positive figure from Siana's saga portrayed in the castle before.

And the other statue was an Achthron.

Or was it?

Siana had found the Achthron abhorrent. This statue had not struck Ellie with a similar abhorrence. Then she remembered the procession of malignant shadows on the walls of the Time Room. *Those* were Achthroi. She recalled the grotesqueries of their form, the mal-proportioned flailing limbs. Siana's account jived with that, gave her the same feeling. So what then was the second statue in the library?

Her mind was tired with emotion, tired with reason. But not too tired to select, at random, a second book from her pile.

MIHALI

Five years before the Attack on Kadesh

Mihali.
Sky island. Placed amongst the clouds of the sky with no apparent means of support.

A crust of sun-blasted plains lands. Valleys a vertical mile in height, with no floor but empty air, piercing the roughly circular perimeter of the island. We approached the floating island from far below, our sailing craft long since pulled aloft from the ocean by giant balloons deployed from within the hull. I remembered our approach, the island eclipsing the sun and framed in a nimbus of white light, the radiating zigzag of the valleys making Mihali resemble an ancient rendering of the sun in bronze.

Mihali. Dock-towns concealed in the shadows of those vertical valleys, buildings perched on precarious outcroppings or nailed into the scraggly pines growing from folds in the cliffs. Rope ladders and bridges forming a spider web of connections between buildings and docks. Dockmen and -women who scuttled along like spiders, oblivious to the floorless abyss below. All framed, above, below and without, by an endless azure sky.

The docks were held aloft by some power of the Aedolae of this place, the twin sovereigns Iakovos and Ilanit. Perhaps that same power suspended the island itself in the aether of the sky. The docks floated some yards from the cliffs, placed in wider valleys so that ships could reach them. Many of the walls between the valleys were narrow enough to be pierced by short passageways hewn through the rock, so the docks led easily to other clefts, narrow and dim but filled with traders and dock-town denizens, thronging with activity.

Mihali. Not only dock-towns, but City: grand City of the high plateau, dominating plains lands and rocky deserts. White walls five hundred feet high, impregnable and serene in the still hot air. A city of grandiose stonework, buildings and walkways fashioned either from stones of rich jet or cool ivory. The quarries of such rock are a mystery, for the native stone of Mihali is rough, pale, and crumbly, utterly lacking the City's sublimity.

Behind this City's high walls is the greatest market of the dreamworlds, and in Mihali the power of the Aedolae has the greatest profit for the business of men, and seems the least corrupted by evil and arrogance.

I spent two weeks within those walls, conducting the business of my shipmates, selling and haggling, replenishing stores, seeking for rare things to command value in Kadesh and Cylindrax. No one spoke much of that other demesne through which we must pass, Zoorn, but the evidence was everywhere; not a day passed in the market without some adept of the Zoorn cult preaching its doctrine of eternal suffering. I had not found the City of Mihali threatening save for these madmen lacerating their skin with barbed jewelry, with their necklaced icons of men and women transfixed by spikes. We all avoided them as best we could.

After two weeks in the City, I had achieved absolutely nothing.

Every day I learned so much about these worlds, precious knowledge a dreamer outside the Detheros would give much to possess. But I didn't find that which I sought: evidence of my brother.

During the month we sailed to the edge of the Edoi Sea, and then into sky beyond, I spent evenings in my cabin rereading his journal, reflecting on my too brief conversation with Daevon at Ebon Port. Trying to forge some stratagem. I felt pathetically limited. My only tools were the Eterokoni. I possessed three, and was using two of these every minute to maintain my disguise, but the third was still of no use. I needed to understand it.

Mercair had spoken of worlds; Daevon had matched these to the demesnes of the Aedol Via, but the Kalimba possessed an extraneous key. Resolving this mystery was another item on my travel agenda. Bierce had seen the symbol for Ebon Port—the first key—in the lair of its Aedolae. So I desired a closer look at the Aedolae of each realm.

I had failed in Mihali on all counts.

Not for lack of power. An Orsian could not penetrate the palace of Iaakovos and Ilanit. But I had the Torc, and I should have used it to that end. I was too scared and I am ashamed to recall this. Recent years have purged me of such weakness.

I was also afraid to ruin my disguise. I had been a jet skinned girl for over a month. Quarters were close in the City and opportunities to slip away close to nonexistent. I was busy learning a tradeswoman's skills—and keeping my ignorance from revealing itself in fatal proportions. The Eterokon of Tongues gave me a facility with languages that the Orsians increasingly put to work. Busy translating the speech of a bewildering variety of dreamworld folk (the Orsians assured me this resulted in their best cargo in years) I let the days tick by and my doubts cement into inaction.

Tomorrow we would be leaving.

We had left the City at daybreak, taking the wide tunnel under the scorched and dangerous desert. We were guarded front and behind by a small company of mercenaries hired in the City, our goods pulled in rented wagons by the famed zebracorns of Mihali, striped and well-muscled. The sun ticked off the hours far above, unseen, while we plied the timeless dark, down ramps and through galleries carved from the living rock. Even the "newer" galleries had already formed stalactites and stalagmites. Occasionally, we passed up a Mihalian busy keeping the procession of torches alight.

By late afternoon we were back at the docks, trading lightly and busily transferring goods to our ship, which had floated idly on its tethers during our weeks away, its grand white balloon shifting in the subtle breeze of the deep ravines. The sun had left the island surface by the time we paid our mercenaries and sent them back with empty wagons. Now the sun hung in the void on a level with us, setting aglow the ragged silhouettes of the valley entrance. They say the sun never sets on dock-town, for there is no horizon for it to dip behind. It only sinks lower and further into the void below until a murky twilight envelops everything.

The Orsians' last night at Mihali is a tradition of revelry. I found myself in the midst of a grand feast. Our inn combined small cabins perched along the cliff face with larger spaces carved into the rock behind. We ate in a banquet room sixty feet square. The high ceiling still showed the strokes of the workmen who had hewn it. Three walls were stone, but the fourth, to my left, was a pair of enormous wooden shutters, currently folded back such that a floorless void began ten feet from my table. Across that void (two hundred feet of open air) a network of ladders on the opposite cliff face jiggled with human life.

None of this unsettled our hosts, nor the Orsians intent with the merriment bought by their trading profits. I was poor company that night, my mind overshadowed by failure and imminent departure, and fortunately my fellows chalked it up to my youth. In the City, my Orsian shipmates had been sober businessmen, but this night permitted a grand exception. Some of the men eyed me in an unprecedented way; all of us women had been treated chastely on our journey.

Their lascivious looks now both surprised and unnerved me.

One man in the room eyed me a different way. He was the Master of the Docks, in his late forties or so. He had overseen the whole of our business at the cliffs with a gentle confidence, and I noted he was accorded a deep respect by all, dockmen, -women and outsiders alike. Even those who had haggled most fiercely did not cross, challenge or belittle him.

He reminded me of my brother.

He glanced at me; perhaps my sobriety singled me out. He smiled, as if he understood. I had noticed him consume, for a slender man, a prodigious amount of delicacies, and he even now dug into another grand helping.

I was distracted by an Orsian woman proffering me dreamworld liqueur. To my embarrassment, she had noticed our exchange of glances.

"You'll have no luck bedding that one," she whispered. "You're comely enough, but he is unassailable by female charms."

I'd had no such thing in mind.

The woman said no more and walked off, a dockman's arm about her waist. I glanced around in panic. The imbibing of liquor was devolving into lubricious pairings, as prospective lovers slipped away to the cabins of the inn. I was young and totally unready for such a thing. My mind was full of my quest.

And now the memory of Daevon.

The sun left the room. The dockmaster was alone at his table, sipping lightly from a flagon of emerald wine. I got up, and walked to him, keeping my eyes straight ahead and willing confidence into my stride. The others would think me ignorant, or desirous to succeed where other women had failed. Or both. I didn't really care.

I didn't have in mind what they thought.

What *was* my thought? Perhaps he reminded me of Timothy. Perhaps I sensed he would provide answers. Escaping the attentions of the remaining men was also a good catalyst.

To my surprise, he rose, and by the time I reached him, he stood offering me his arm. I heard gasps behind me.

The Master of the Docks led me from the room.

He didn't say a word or look at me until we had walked, without haste, all the way to his chambers. We passed a single guard in the narrow hallway approaching his abode, fiercely countenanced and well-armed, who surveyed me coolly. The dockmaster acknowledged him with a nod.

The Master's chambers were hollowed out from a knife's edge of rock separating the valley in which we were docked from the next, comprised of six or seven single-roomed floors. The view was astounding, for every wall save the rock behind was windows, 270 degrees of glass looking back down both valleys and out into the haze of sky where the dimming sun retreated into far aether.

He led me to the highest room and beckoned me to sit in a plush chair mantled in long black and white feathers. He sat down opposite me in a similar chair; his face was framed in sunlight and hard to see.

"Welcome," he said. "My name is Faisanne."

I hadn't known his name.

"I am Jaena," I said quietly, confused by the whole incident so far. He sipped on a tall glass of clear liquid, and leaned back. His shirt spread open where a few buttons were undone. Something hanging about his neck gleamed in the sunlight.

An effigy of Zoorn, a naked girl impaled in several directions by slender spikes passing clear through her body.

My heart froze and I clutched the arms of the chair. Faisanne showed dismay at my posture, until he realized I bristled at the icon. He unclasped the effigy from his chest and placed it in plain view on the low table between us. The graceful form of the girl balanced on the surface of the table, and she looked like she was dancing a ballet despite the horrendous piercing of her body. The workmanship was exquisitely beautiful, far more beautiful than those carried by mad adepts I had seen in the City.

"Indeed, young Jaena," Faisanne said, his voice low and toneless, "you are in my power here. I can imagine why you would be afraid. But do not be. My motivations were pity and curiosity, not seduction or harm. To be truthful, you remind me of someone, someone dear." His tone had warmed. I raised my face from my transfixed appraisal of the icon and caught his eyes. There seemed no menace there.

"I did not come by this icon by the usual route, and I claim no kinship with Zoorn's flagellants. Nonetheless it is dear to me, in a way more authentic than zealotry. Look around." He pointed at the octet of silver icons placed or mounted at each corner of the room, all pierced humanoids, varying in gender and shape. "This room is warded, like all my chambers, by the power of Daphne. She herself placed them here."

"Who is Daphne?"

"She is the Aedolae of Zoorn."

What!?

Was this man, who reminded me of my brother, a scion of the Aedolae?

"I am sorry," he breathed into the silence. "I have dismayed you again. Jaena, I am no lover of the Aedolae, and though it is treasonous I will admit that. And I make this admission in a chamber she herself has shriven. I may be a servant of the Aedolae; all Mihalians carrying out the business of the Twins are. But this Daphne, Dark Queen, she is *my* servant, for the story of my life bent her to my will. But tell me, what is your quarrel with the Aedolae, your fear?"

He asks so easily. He who has entertained an Aedolae in this very room.

For reasons I cannot explain, I told him. And in that telling gave him my real name.

"You are," Faisanne said, when I was finished telling far more than I first intended, "what the myths call a *sojourner*. I'd always doubted the concept—that this, my world, is simultaneously a sojourner's dreamworld. It never made sense. But here you are, confirming this. No matter what, I'd never doubted that sojourners were something special, something unique amid the magnificence and potencies of the demesnes. How comes a sojourner to look like an Orsian?"

In answer, I touched the Torc and transformed.

Back into the blonde freckle-faced teenager I had almost forgotten.

"Ah," Faisanne breathed. He appeared tired; his body slumped in the chair. "And that is?"

"An Eterokon," I answered. "Apparently the bane of the Aedolae." I smiled.

"Remain like this," he said, "if I am to help you. Your real self is a disguise now."

"Help me?" My voice surely betrayed both my hope and my skepticism. Despite it all, I wanted to trust this man. Since leaving Daevon, I'd been of little use on my own. I had yet to learn my own strength; I still depended on strangers to achieve my ends. How long, before my good fortune ran out? Until my intuition about whom to trust led me astray?

"What is the goal you failed to achieve in Mihali?" Faisanne asked.

"To find my brother, or an Eterokon, or to learn something useful about the Twins and their powers."

Faisanne acknowledged this, musing. "I bear the Aedolae no love. Even the Twins can be cruel masters. But you must promise that if I help you, you will bring the Twins no harm. I understand—if living soul does—the motivation of love. Because of your love for your brother I will help you. But for you to understand the kind of help I offer, I need to tell a story, the same story I told Daphne. And there is time for my story, before that help arrives."

So as twilight filled the ravines and quieted the press of human activity along their lengths, Faisanne told me his tale.

THE DOCKMASTER'S STORY

I t began thirty years ago, when we began to build the tunnels to the docks.

Being on the tunnel crew was my first job. The Twins were eager to establish a less risky approach to the City, for during much of the year winds made sailing overland to the City foolhardy. Caravans ran afoul of deep ravines, and were vulnerable to predation. The job was easier than expected for we found many natural caverns to utilize in our route. Ahead of schedule we finished the main tunnel and all seemed well. At that time I still lived in the City with my family.

Nine months later, when I was almost twenty, the trouble began. City dwellers were found dead in their beds. Many young Mihalians simply disappeared. Survivors whispered of shadowy figures that invaded their homes by night and crouched above them, sapping their energy. They came to be called Soul Eaters, and fearful rumors spread. Iakovos and Ilanit sent soldiers into the tunnels but they could do nothing to stop the rush of spectral forms.

One soldier received a message for Iaakovos and Ilanit. The unseen speaker explained that the scourge of the Soul Eaters was her retaliation for the Twins' violation of her underground sanctuary; their tunneling was an offense and the vilest hubris.

A reasonable young man, I was naturally disinterested in the rumors. I thought them a superstitious explanation for plague. The preposterous tale of an unseen Voice in the dark added to this conviction. Besides, all this happened to Other People.

The tales became reality for me one furnace-hot night the following summer. I would soon leave my family for a position at the docks. I remember casting aside my sweaty sheets, and walking to the open window. Few lights are kept burning in Mihali at night, so only the blue-white radiance of the moon, low on the horizon to my left, illuminated the street below. It was deathly quiet, only the occasional sigh of wind, or the barking of a dog far off. I stood at the window for a while, frustrated that I could not sleep. I fancied I caught some movement in the periphery of my vision. My mind went at once to thoughts of Soul Eaters, whether I believed in them or not. And indeed something left the shadow between two buildings across the street and crossed to my side. Something roughly human in form, but reflecting moonlight like water. It disappeared from my view under the overhang of the window sill.

Then a hundred whispers filled the block. Light glimmered off a great host of the same kind of creature. Passing in and out of alleys, crossing the street in both directions, leaving the far end of the street to fan out into the plaza beyond.

Windows in most of the City have no panes, and it is difficult to close the shutters that we use to block out sandstorms. Nonetheless, I reached for them. But I was interrupted by my uncle groaning in the chambers above. I rushed out of my room and into the stairwell, bounding up the crumbling stone steps. My uncle stirred in his bed but he did not seem distressed. Relieved, I turned to descend.

The iron gate to the street at the bottom of the stair hung open. Something stood on the landing beside the open door of my room, dimly luminescent. I had always imagined a ghost would look like this. It did not move or look up. The figure became more defined, the clear form of a woman coalescing out of the dark. Perhaps it was a woman all along, seeking refuge from the terror of the Soul Eaters, and my fear had created the vision of a ghost.

I rushed down the stair to her succor. To my surprise, she was entirely unclothed. She turned her head, slowly, distractedly, toward me. I had judged her a woman, but in truth she was a girl, her figure slight and her body hairless. Her bosom heaved and her blue eyes were wild. Her face was framed by a mass of strawberry blonde curls. She was breathtakingly beautiful. Both her naked loveliness and her evident distress pierced my heart. I took a step toward her, offering my hand.

Then I realized my mistake.

She shrank back, eyes narrowing, lips curling back in a menacing hiss. Her mouth was full of gleaming white teeth, all sharpened into fangs. I jumped back. Now I noticed the exceeding translucency of her skin, beneath which a blue network of veins ran with inhuman clarity. None of the warm pink of blood and human life.

She was a Soul Eater.

I could have shrunk in terror, or tried, in vain, to attack. I could have yelled out to wake my family. But I am stubborn, and don't like to be wrong. I refused to forsake my initial impression of her as young and scared. Soul Eater or not, I had seen what I had seen.

When I backed off, she closed her mouth. Her chest still heaved. She might be a Soul Eater, but she breathed, she was alive. I decided to talk to her.

"I am called Faisanne. I know I am supposed to be afraid of you, well I am, but you are afraid too. Why?"

Her eyes narrowed. She looked as if she strained to hear a human voice.

"Afraid," she repeated, her voice empty, pitched low. I could see the fangs behind her beautifully shaped lips.

"What is your name?" I asked. It was a strange question to ask such a creature. But it fit my instinct that despite what she was, she was also a young woman distressed.

She was silent a bit, puckering up her face.

"It was Mercedes," she said. Her voice was less empty.

"Was?" I asked.

"I haven't heard my name in a long time," she said. She glanced to her left and right, scanning the stairs in both directions, looking out to the street. Nervous.

"Come," I said, with foolish bravery. "Come in, if you are uncomfortable." To this day, I marvel that I *invited* a Soul Eater into my bedroom. She looked genuinely perplexed. I risked offering my hand again. This time she took it. Her skin was cool, but not cold, smooth and soft. She came inside and stood uneasily to the right of the window, where she could not be seen from the street.

"What are you called now?" I asked, standing by the foot of my bed.

"I am called nothing. I am nothing," she said. "I am hungry."

It was a statement of fact. I changed the subject.

"Can I call you Mercedes?"

For the first time she met my gaze, and held it. Her blue eyes were deep pools, and out of that depth, something was rising to meet me.

"Yes, I will be your Mercedes," she said simply, with a throaty tinge of lust.

And then she faded, until the lines in the masonry behind her shone through her skin. With a rush of wind and glint of light, she was gone.

"Is she the one I reminded you of?" I asked Faisanne.

"Yes," he replied. "It is your youth, and your eyes."

"Succubae, incubi," I said. "There are stories in my world. Did you ever see her again?"

"I did," he replied.

She returned the next night.

I was asleep when her fingers brushed my cheek. I sat up in bed.

"Say my name," she said, her voice low and tremulous. She pulled the covers down from me and sat on my thighs. Her gaze was direct, unshielded, searching my face.

"Mercedes," I said. What had I gotten myself into.

"Say it again," she demanded, and I did.

She was silent, then her body shook with sobs. I realized she was crying. Tears coursed down her pale cheeks, as her lips parted to show her fangs. She fell against my chest, tumbling us down. It is a strange memory to cherish, making love to a Soul Eater, but it is my most precious memory, that first night with Mercedes. Like any memory of the beginning of love, the first surrender.

I have told very few, Siana, of any of this.

She stayed with me long that night, letting me hold her, her flesh feeling ever warmer beneath my touch. Words were few between us, but significant, as she tried excitedly to remember things about herself, the girl she had once been. It became obvious what had become of the young Mihalians who had disappeared. Mercedes remembered turning fifteen, but after she was taken, her life was a shadow, and she would not talk about it. But her memories, her excitement, validated my first impression of her—and the concern I had shown.

The third night she came she was angry. Her voice dissolved into hisses and growls.

"I am a monster, and you made me remember who I am. Why? Why did you not leave me ignorant?" She paced about the room, taller than I remembered. "You have taken from me the pleasure of my feeding, the only pleasure I had. Do you know how many men I have slain?" She clenched her fists in anger, her sharp nails pierced the flesh of her palms, and a sallow blue blood dripped from the holes. Tears welled in her eyes, tears blended with fire. "I had to leave you last night, all our words and touching, all those memories, and then I had to suck the life from a man's chest to slake the need of my damned soul. I wish I could die." And she stormed from the room.

I did not see her again for a long time.

I moved down to the docks. Surreptitiously, I became an expert on succubae—we have that word too—gathering books, reading late into the night. I uncovered a little known truth: the Twins were once a Trinity. Iakovos and Ilanit had a dark sister, whom they drove into the underworld, and who I suspect is the patroness of the Soul Eaters. But none of my reading explained how I, a simple dock hand, could free Mercedes from the demon life to which this dark sister had fated her. I wondered if Mercedes would come return, or if the fleeting memory of her girlhood had been lost again in the horrors of her life.

But the following summer she did return, this time at dock-town. I had been reading late by candlelight. With a whisper she materialized in front of me.

"I am sorry," she said, as if her quarrel with me had only been the day before. "I have thought hard and long and torturously, for it is hard to think with a monster's mind, and I have decided that you were a saint to be kind to me, and that I prefer being a monster who knows who she is." And then she kissed me, making no attempt to close her lips or hide her fangs. My love for her was hopelessly confirmed. And she has been my beloved ever since, coming every night without fail these twenty eight years. That night was the first night she fed on me, and I have sustained her life all those years with my own.

• • • • • • • • • • •

How does that work?"

Faisanne laughed at my puzzled face.

"A succubus gathers her energy," Faisanne answered, "by draining a person's life force. She can place her hands on me, or withdraw it with a kiss. It is painful, and it was hard in the beginning to trust her to restrain herself, to not fully satisfy her hunger. Mercedes and I live an exhausted half-life, sharing the vitality of a single being. I eat voraciously (as you have seen) but it is still hard for both of us.

"But I was determined to free her from murder and self-recrimination. It was easy for Mercedes to agree to surviving half starved. The hard part was freeing her from her mistress, for the Soul Eaters were the Voice's revenge. Removing Mercedes from her service was not going to be welcomed."

"That is where Daphne comes in," I said.

He laughed. "Exactly so. I turned one Aedolae against another. I didn't plan it. But once every ten years or so, Daphne comes to Mihali, seeking new disciples. I was in the City on business and devotees of Zoorn were making a grand procession through the streets, with the usual self-inflicted injuries, blood on naked skin. A young woman was held aloft in a cage, impaled with slender javelins, carefully placed so that she still breathed. Chants of 'We accept our misery, O Queen' and 'Ecstasy in suffering', all that kind of thing. This time I saw Daphne herself, a few feet behind the cage, robed in black. Daphne is both beautiful and unnervingly inhuman. Her eyes flashed diamonds. There are jewels set into the flesh of her arms in runic patterns. Her proportions are not quite right, too long and narrow. And as she approached my position, the march of her entourage stopped."

"Why?" I asked. Faisanne laughed.

"Because I had yelled out, louder than the adulations of her crowd."

"What did you say?" I breathed.

"'Greatest Daphne, I suffer deeper than any man!' or something to that effect," Faisanne replied. "Daphne beckoned her litter to be lowered to the ground. She came, towering over me, and I am a tall man. 'What claim do you have to suffering, unbloodied Mihalian?' Daphne said. My love for Mercedes and my terrible need to satisfy her, to answer her, drove me past the paralysis in my voice.

"'Great Queen Daphne. What is the greatest suffering? Is it of body, or of soul? It is the suffering of love!'

"'Hold this man!' she said and left me in the none too gentle grip of one of her soldiers. That night, in a Zoorn cult stronghold in the City, she came and spoke with me alone, save for the company of that one guard.

"'Your answer was good, given nobly under duress. Fear is of the body, but anguish is of the soul. It is anguish that most interests me. Tell me, Mihalian, the nature of your claim.'

"Daphne listened to our tale without interrupting, pacing about the small, darkened room like a tiger about to spring. When I finished, she was quiet for a lifetime of moments.

"*'You have chosen the way of Zoorn, Faisanne'*, she whispered at last, *'for surely you know a succubus is immortally damned and you will die before you are free of this love. There are many who serve me, but their embrace of suffering and pain, however intense, fades as they tire of the ecstasies of youth and grow into the weariness of maturity. But you have bound yourself for a lifetime. Yours, Mihalian, will be one of the Great Stories of suffering. I care nothing for love, for it does not interest me. But I do care that my Dark Sister does not interrupt the flow of your story. So I will help you. Go to your home and await me there.'*

"The next night Daphne came to these very rooms and set her spells of protection upon Mercedes and me. Her icons remain at each corner of my rooms, weaving a net of her power about us. And Mercedes and I each wear an icon about our neck. Daphne's protection must be clear to the Exiled One, for she has never harried Mercedes nor sought to reclaim her. But I still fear her malice, which must be great toward us.

"Thanks to the unlikely intervention of Daphne, Mercedes and I have been free, these long years, to play out the story of our love. I had thought, at first, Daphne would ridicule my plea. But with each passing year, I learn more of her wisdom. For the little things, like fighting the specter of exhaustion to eke out another moment with my beloved, become more torturous over time. And poor Mercedes; by day, her soul is a wraith drowsing in subterranean haunts, and by night she is trapped in this tiny apartment to live out all the hours of her waking life."

MERCEDES

As Faisanne finished, I was thinking about Daphne. He believed Daphne was only motivated by her credo of suffering, but I doubted somehow she was entirely unmoved by the love at the heart of his story. If so, it was interesting an Aedolae would show compassion.

I filed away that observation for future utility.

"I'm sure you have divined the identity of my help"—Faisanne rose from his chair—"and she is here. Stay. I need to explain your presence."

There was a footfall in the room below. Faisanne disappeared through a trapdoor. A wooden ladder rested against the open edge. I supposed a dockman didn't need stairs in his home.

In the now deeply shadowed room, the figurine of the impaled girl shone faintly.

A woman's voice rose in momentary anger in the hushed conversation below. A few minutes later the end of the ladder swayed with movement. Faisanne's head popped through. His down-stretched arm escorted a teenage girl into the room.

Faisanne lit a lamp set in an alcove. It cast shadows across Mercedes' face, as breathtakingly exquisite as he described. She smiled at me shyly in a tight-lipped way. She wore a simple sky blue gown and appeared a girl of thirteen summers or so, little more. She leaned against Faisanne, both arms wrapped around his right arm. Her strawberry-blonde hair fell in gorgeous curls across her shoulders and past her waist. She did not seem upset now.

"Welcome, sojourner," she said quietly, releasing Faisanne, and curtseyed. She looked more Faisanne's daughter than his lover. Other than a gravity in her voice and bearing, she obviously had not aged a day since their first meeting. This was what Daphne had meant by her immortality.

Another aspect of their curse.

"We don't have a lot of time," Mercedes said, "to get you to the Palace and back by sunrise. I need a few moments with Faisanne, then you and I will go." As she spoke, low and measured, I saw the flash of fangs in her mouth. A strange contrast.

They went below. Presumably so she could feed.

I shuddered.

The three of us soon left Faisanne's chambers, and Mercedes dematerialized into shadow. I remained my normal white-skinned self, per the dockmaster's recommendation. The Zoorn guard betrayed no emotion as we passed. Few were abroad at that time of night to wonder at the rarity of Faisanne's female companionship. There was also a modest guard at this end of the tunnel to the City, and Faisanne waved us through. As soon as a bend in the tunnel took us out of the guards' sight, he sent me on alone.

"I will wait for you here, else the guards will be suspicious. Mercedes will meet you ahead." And indeed she did. She flowed out of shadow onto a wide stair bathed in torchlight.

"How can we get there in time?" I asked. It must be almost midnight.

"Faisanne said you can shapeshift. Besides, I know shortcuts. Pick something fearsome and fast. I guarantee you can't outpace me." She wriggled out of her gown. "Clothes slow me down. Yours too."

Her body beneath the gown was as childlike as Faisanne's description, but now that we had left him, her stance and eyes were feral. She scanned the darkness between circles of torchlight.

An effigy of Zoorn, the very match of Faisanne's, lay against her naked bosom.

I became a huge wolf.

"That will do, but get rid of the teats," Mercedes said. I elongated my neck to scan my underside. My breasts were bizarre covered in fur. Mercedes laughed and I blushed, if wolves can blush. I corrected the oversight.

The following two hours were a race through nightmare and shadow. I could barely see Mercedes as her form blurred into translucence and flowed like moonlight through the subterranean maze. I couldn't see much else either, even with the Torc, for we soon left the main tunnel carved by man and detoured into darker, older places carved by water and wind. Yawning fissures necessitated powerful jumps with my hind legs, and in other places I changed into something gecko-like to climb sheer cliffs to unseen inky heights.

Mercedes merely flowed up such obstacles like a backwards waterfall.

We spoke little, save for an occasional word or admonition from my guide. Still I knew she grew nervous as we neared the City. She paused at the entrances to caverns and scanned them carefully, slowing our crazed pace. In some of these caverns, a torch had been left burning.

We descended a crumbling stair, constructed in some prehistory of this world, to a circular space like the bottom of a well. The rock walls were slick with trickling moisture. Open doorways led out to rudely hewn passageways. Mercedes reached the last stair about ten steps ahead of me. There was a rushing wind and a blur of white whirling motion.

She was surrounded by a menacing, taunting circle of half-materialized figures.

"It is the traitoress, the lover of daylight flesh," an incubus with wild curly hair hissed at her, "come to pay a visit to her forgotten brothers and sisters."

An incredible change waxed across Mercedes as she spun round, trying to keep all of them in her sight. They were eight or so, incubi and succubae. Mercedes' lips parted to show a fearsome mouthful of fangs, growing in length and number as

I watched. She slashed out with black nails that became talons. Blood flashed in the confused mix of ghostly forms below, sprays of both blue and red. Mercedes was everywhere at once, streamers of hair flying.

"Help me," she hissed. I had watched for too long, staring in shock. Her face was crisscrossed with bloody weals.

I shifted into a werewolf with a quadruple pair of taloned arms, and leapt into their midst. My flailing arms passed through some forms with resistance, as if cleaving water, and clobbered full into others as they materialized to attack, flinging them against the dark, wet walls. Bones snapped. They hadn't noticed me before, and my sudden appearance and ferocity scattered them. With a rush of wind, the chamber was empty. Mercedes wouldn't stop to consider her wounds, but hurried us on.

"Quickly now, before they return with more." Her voice quavered. "We were hoping I wouldn't encounter them. Don't worry, I will be fine. I bleed but it takes far more to do me lasting damage."

Nonetheless, she looked terrible.

We pressed on, and came to the underside of the Palace. She materialized in a neglected crypt she explained was directly below the throne room of the Twins. Her ragged wounds had already faded to dim lines.

Something in the darkness caught my eye. Two rusted metal poles propped against a trunk. Each sported a weighty icon, immediately familiar from their tiny analogues upon the second key of the Kalimba: one a circle with a dot at its center, and the other a sweeping crescent. On the Kalimba they were entwined, a sun and a moon. Finding these massive representations here in the palace of the Twins fit my observations. The first key represented Ebon Port, and the second key must represent Mihali. The keys of the Kalimba were paralleling the course of the Aedol Via through the demesnes, as Daevon thought. But why were Mihali's icons neglected, gathering dust and rust in the bowels of the palace?

Not for the last time, I wondered: what is the Kalimba *for* ? It must have some deeper purpose than being a visual record of arcane symbology.

"I can take you wherever you want to go," Mercedes said. I asked if we could see the Twins. I thought Mercedes might balk at that.

She didn't.

She led me from the crypt and along a bewildering network of passages, stairwells, and galleries. She was barely visible in the darkness; now that speed didn't matter, I resumed my Orsian appearance, thinking jet skin would best hide me. We encountered no one. Light through an open arch signified our arrival above the throne room.

Beyond the arch was a wide balcony framing an enormous oval chamber. Goliath columns supported a dimly seen ceiling, and the marble floor gleamed with the omnipresent pattern of black and white squares. Even at this late hour, the throne room was not empty; the Twins occupied their thrones and a lone supplicant stood before them, dwarfed by the immensity of the place. His shadow lay long across the patterned floor. We padded along the balcony, keeping hidden, to get closer.

Even right above them hearing was hard. The supplicant, hidden by a stiff, high-cowled cape, spoke low and the whisper of his voice was an impenetrable tangle of echoes by the time it reached us forty feet above. Iakovos was jet skinned like an Orsian, bearded, barrel-chested. Ilanit, his sister, was not Caucasian white, but porcelain white, with delicate features. I was surprised to see no guard; perhaps all were outside the chamber. We had crept in through an open and unguarded doorway. I marveled at Mercedes' skill.

I wondered if I could kill them.

The naiveté of that thought amuses me now. I did not have the power then. I wonder if I have it now.

No such doubt stilled my hand. Rather, it was uncertainty. I knew the Aedolae had shut out dreamers from the deep worlds of night. I knew they imprisoned me against my will in the

Gardens and stole my memory. But I didn't know my brother's fate, beyond the guesses Daevon and I exchanged. I needed to know more, and measured against this, killing the first Aedolae I encountered seemed ill-advised.

A rich baritone voice broke through the tangled whispers—Iakovos, speaking for the first time: *"Torc of the Starmen."*

"I've got to get down there," I whispered in frustration.

"You need to use your imagination." She smiled her tight-lipped smile and became a breeze that left the balcony.

On a candelabra to Ilanit's right perched a flock of crow-like birds, a Queen's pets.

The wind that was Mercedes scattered several into the air. She had given me my chance.

As the birds resettled, jostling and pecking, I was among them, jockeying for position. I now had a ringside view.

The Twins' supplicant spoke again, "Indeed, my Master said it was the Torc. He bade me book passage with the Orsians and bring you this news."

"You have done well," Iakovos said. "I apologize for the initial coolness of our reception." Iakovos was a Greek god, curly-headed and muscled, massive arms gripping the flat arms of his seat. A fan of white stripes radiated across each black cheek; these seemed not cosmetic, but pigmentation in his flesh. "Come closer, and tell us more about this woman."

As the supplicant moved in the light, I recognized him: one of the white-skinned men at Orse, who had witnessed my rescue of the xemenos. The Torc he spoke of was even now transforming me into a bird. I had not heard of "Starmen"; but perhaps the animate skeleton from which I purloined the Torc was one. The supplicant had seen more than I hoped, for he gave them an excellent description of my appearance.

Both before and after my transformation. Damn.

I had assumed for the past six weeks my arrival within the Detheros was secret. No longer. I didn't know how my Orsian disguise, tested against the Aedolae's powers, would hold.

"Leave us now," Ilanit spoke, gentle but firm. "You will be rewarded and your needs attended. Your information will be passed to all the demesnes. Speak yourself no further word of it." A man with the bearing of a majordomo but the weaponry and garb of a ninja entered my field of vision from an unseen entrance. His step was utterly silent on the marble floor as he came to the dais to receive Ilanit's instructions. Both this man and the traveler bowed as they left the Twins' presence.

Iakovos turned to his sister. His simple linen shirt did not lessen the power of his presence. "These news are grave. We have neglected the Detheros for too long. When was a sojourner last seen in Mihali?"

"354," Ilanit mused. "I have never been comfortable with Ebon under the control of that Abomination—"

"The Spaerodont," the King corrected, "but I agree. It should not have been allowed control over the crucial gateway. If Ebon Port were our domain—or Ghislain's—defenses would be in place. This sojourner would have been marked and detained. But she could be anywhere now."

A lot of good the Twins' power had done them spotting me here. I laughed, and my laugh came out a caw.

Famous last words. (Famous last caw?)

Ilanit stared at the candelabra with a curious expression. She was beautiful, with a very full upper lip and smaller lower lip granting her a petulant aspect. Her face radiated stripes like her brother's, but in black. Elsewise, her albino face blended seamlessly into the silk of her thick hair, pure white.

She stood and walked idly toward my perch. "I do not relish it, but I fear we must call a Council."

"I do not miss the Councils," Iakovos grumbled. "Kadesh is depraved. Ghislain is mad. Daphne is cruel. Only you and I, Sister, have fulfilled the charge of our kind."

I had thought of the Aedolae as a unified front, almost as one Being. This was most illuminating.

"We have done so, Brother."

Ilanit's voice was distracted, but the attention in her icy blue eyes—eye so fair as to almost lack color—was sharp. Those eyes singled me out. Her voluminous sleeve fell from her white arm as she offered me a finger to on which to perch. I shuffled on to it, not daring to disobey.

"But at what cost? What will the banishment of Isabiel our Sister cost before we are done?" She held me a few inches from her lips, perched helplessly on her index finger, staring at me with narrowed eyes. Behind us, Iakovos grumbled again. Ilanit began a slow circuit of the dais, stroking my feathers. Her unblemished face was impossibly young for a thousand years of life.

"Do not taunt me with that," Iakovos exhaled. "Attend to the matter at hand. Must we call a Council? Cannot Mihali stop this invader, when her path leads along the Via, past our very doors?"

"Do you abhor them so? You would avoid them lest they remind you of how we were fashioned, Isabiel, you and I?"

"Enough!" Iakovos boomed.

Ilanit relented. "I accede to your wisdom, Brother, Architect of Order. We will do what is in our power first. If we can give account of the sojourner's destruction, it will buttress our standing in their eyes. For I dread any Council as much as you."

And then her tone changed.

"What is the voice of the Vinna?" she queried the King.

He looked perplexed. "Why would you ask? You know the Vinna bird has no song, no voice at all."

"Did you not hear this very bird," she explained, turning herself—and me—toward him, "speak a few moments ago?"

How immense my ignorance! The power of the Torc could not save me from my own foolishness.

Perhaps I must try to kill them after all.

Mercedes spared me that attempt.

A horrific ululation rang out beyond the throne room. I hope to never hear a man yell that way again. The King leapt to his feet with a lion's grandeur. A scuffling commotion echoed through the throne room as a door slammed open. I launched myself from Ilanit's finger. The Vinna on the candelabra scattered. In the confusion Ilanit did not see the one bird that flew over the balcony and disappeared.

I had learned much, and we could not have stayed longer. Mercedes had known my peril, and attacked and drained the life force of a guard. We were back in the crypt before the commotion settled behind us. We raced back to the docks against the coming of day, driven by my fear of what had almost happened, driven by Mercedes' fear of the incubi and succubae finding her again.

During the long trip through Zoorn to Kadesh I would ponder what I overheard, weighing it against my brother's journal. Building in my mind and heart the foundation of my strategy.

As dawn frosted the pines above the docks, Mercedes and I stood again at the end of the tunnel. The hours of the night had felt a lifetime. We were a strange pair, wolf and wraith transforming to women scarcely past the years of their childhood. And what kind of childhood had I had?

Mercedes was sad and serene, young and grim, all at the same time. I do not remember what I said—beyond my expressions of gratitude. But I remember her words:

"You have cost me a night with my beloved, the only content in my life. I do not rue you that, or Faisanne his generosity. I ask only that you remember us. I did not understand power when I was fifteen. I do not like what I am, Siana, but I have grown to appreciate my power. I see power in you, and I predict it will grow strong, very strong, with time. I ask that someday you use your power to help Faisanne and me.

"Slowly and surely we run out of time. He calls me his bride, but time is driving a wedge between us, as it ages his body and leaves mine untouched. Some day he will lack the strength to feed me, to live his double life, and I will lose him forever.

"I have spent the whole of my time with him within the walls of his home. Never to stand beside him at festivals, never to feel the sun on my sun, never to be his wife in the eyes of those who know, love and respect him. I do not grow old with him. I cannot bear it, Siana, I cannot bear it. Help us, someday, if you can."

And then Faisanne was back. They kissed with passion and then Mercedes melted into shadow.

He seemed refreshed. He escorted me past the tunnel guards' puzzled expressions. We hurried to his apartments.

The twilight had lifted from dock-town when I bade him goodbye, resumed my Orsian appearance, and passed his Zoorn guard.

My heart and mind were both full to bursting.

The Orsians congratulated me on my conquest with jeers and fanfare. The seduction of stalwart Faisanne was an event of epic proportions. I shrugged it off, feeling any acknowledgement would be a betrayal of Mercedes. My sleepless night provided a ready excuse for my curtness.

Such is the ship-craft of the Orsians that even in their hung-over state, they worked in the cold with nimbleness and efficiency, stowing our accoutrements and rigging the great balloons. I was even less use than usual.

They poled us out from the dock and propelled us along the bottomless ravine, thrusting against both sides. Soon we were in the open air where fierce sunlight blazed over the edge of Mihali.

Clouds formed an unbroken carpet of white miles below.

I often wondered how the Orsians navigated such a featureless expanse. But navigate they did, flawlessly, until weeks later we left the blue tapestry of the sky and descended into the turgid seas of Zoorn. The Aedol Via became a maze of shallow canals between low mud hills, brown and grey, opening into the famed Graveyard of Lost Ships. Next through the Veil to the nightscape of Zoorn.

A passage into dread.

But that first morning, I didn't think about any of these things. My heart was full with Mercedes and Faisanne, the sadness of their love. Despite its tragedy, they were together.

Two, where I was only one. Even surrounded by the Orsian sailors I was alone. I longed for someone to know my heart, to love me as I was.

On to Zoorn.

DREAMS WITHIN A DREAM

Ellie finished the Mihali account deep in the night. As she drowsed on the bench, Siana's loneliness and her own loneliness twined into a single raw emotion that escorted her into the world of sleep. She then had another dream within a dream, remembered vividly when she awoke in the Time Room the next morning.

• • • ● • ● • ● • •

Ellie hovered above a fog-strewn landscape at night. She passed over slumbering forest and meadows that exhaled mist, crossing a rural highway and descending toward an old house. She was moonlight, washing into a second story bedroom placed tight against the eaves. The light of her body illuminated jumbled illustrations on the wall.

At their center was a single notebook page, wide wavy handwriting declaring "Siana, Time Princess". A hasty sketch of a young woman, ninja-like, filled the rest of the page. The page was a sacred nucleus surrounded by a cloud of drawings done on an amusing variety of media. From post-it notes to restaurant placemats, these drawings comprised a complete mandala of alternate selfhood, the daydream persona of a teenage girl in bas relief. One scrap of paper at the lower left corner proclaimed in a looser, sloppier hand: "To leave the world I hate."

Beyond this mandala lay the girl herself, the dreamer. No longer content with daydreams, her body was surrounded by a dark nimbus.

At the edges of a queen mattress set upon the floor, four daggers pointed inward, toward the sleeping form of a seventeen-year-old girl. No blankets adorned her; instead her slender figure was a rough facsimile of her alter ego upon the wall—as best her limited means would allow. Ragged bracers upon her arms and legs, a stiff brown vest over a tight-fitting black T, military utility belt over black leather miniskirt. The door was locked, to prevent her family from seeing her costume. She knew, like icons directing the inner gaze of a Byzantine ascetic, that these things were merely symbols of her real self. But within the world of dreams she would be transformed.

In the softening light of the watching moon, her face was younger than her years, her anguish gone in the reprieve of sleep. But her eyes moved under closed lids, her mind waking to dream.

Ellie saw now through Siana's eyes.

Siana was winding her way through the scattered trail of sixteen months of dreaming, back to where the prior night's dreams had ended. It had taken her three nights to penetrate the subterranean horror of the Detheros, and now her soul retraced that horror in fast time. She steeled her consciousness to ignore the lumbering menaces fringing the edges of her vision. With a gasp, her dreaming mind burst forth into the shallows of the Edoi Sea. Last night she had dreamt of a sun-drenched Edoi, but to her surprise, the Sea was cloaked tonight in starry black.

Rushing toward her dreambody, Siana levitated above the water, moving toward the beginning of the Aedolae's realm. She could not see the famed boardwalk of the Edoi below the surface of the water. Her eyes were dazzled by a vast semicircle of stars, bright in the absence of the moon, their number vastly greater than the heavens of the waking world. No islands, nor waves, nor sailing craft marred the glassy mirror of the sea.

On the horizon was a glow. She couldn't tell whether it moved, or if she moved toward it. Perhaps both. It waxed into a glowing disk, lit like graveyard fungi, and passed below her feet. Then another glow, bright and broad. It cast a brilliant orange oval of light onto the water, obscuring the stars.

In rapid succession, four more great ovals proceeded below her—sapphire, emerald, sun-yellow, amethyst. In the dream she turned her gaze behind, where the discs receded and appeared to curl up into the heavens. There they formed a single image, a rainbow of interlocking colors stretching from zenith to far horizon. The image burned into her memory.

In the last moments before gaining Ebon Port, her dreaming mind lost itself and became still.

• • • ● ● • ● ● • •

E llie awoke to sunlight. It struck the sundial at the foot of the statue. So it must be later than her first morning in the Time Room. She felt drugged. She remembered the dream, which burst into her mind wholesale. She rubbed her eyes and sat up.

The three books sat beside her, the second still open face down on the bench. It must have dropped from her fingers when she fell asleep. Her body hurt all over from slamming herself around.

When she'd tried to wake up from the dream in which, apparently, she was still living.

One more book. She was eager to read. The second book, the story of Mihali and Mercedes, had fascinated her but told nothing about Timothy or Siana's fate. She fingered the third book as she reflected on the strangeness of her dream. The details were so pure that she could easily the place the dream in Siana's chronology: Siana as a young girl first penetrating the Detheros and reaching Ebon Port—right before the events of the first book she'd read from the library yesterday.

Ellie doubted her own imagination could have conjured the vividness of the dream. Was the castle somehow transmitting more of Siana's story to her?

She retraced the dream's events, ending with the colored ovals. What did that remind her of? Oh yes, the circles in the floor of the Landing. The order of the colors were the same. *The castle is projecting these details into my mind, just as it embodies them in its own shape and structure.*

The sunlight in the Time Room had passed the statue and sundial now, and the hidden cache of book and Eterokon beneath. Ellie felt more awake. She crossed to the statue, sitting down at its feet. Then she opened the last book and began.

THE SORCERY OF THE ICE

3.5 years before the Attack on Kadesh

My anxiety had been rising since Kadesh.

It didn't help that my shipmates were agitated, and growing more so.

The passage through Zoorn had been uncanny. The desert passage had been perilous. We had taken it as a lone ship—the inventiveness of this dream folk amazing me again as our ship became a wheeled sand skimmer. Leaving the desert, we had banded together with three other craft and splashed down into a river that appeared with the strangeness of dreams out of nowhere.

I was glad to be done with sand.

As a group of four Orsian ships we plied the broad river passage through a blasted wasteland where it grew ever more cold. I was huddled in furs as I stood at the prow of the ship and squinted my eyes against the gelid wind ghosting off the flatlands to my left. The sun was a white orb that barely crested the horizon each day, occupying a tiny gap between earth and an otherwise overcast sky. The Orsians would not speak of the reason for their dread, other than vague references to Chaotics—wild men of the tundra—and certain indigenous beasts. They said in a week we would be in the waters of the Cylindrax Sea. I scanned the tundra ceaselessly but saw nothing of danger so I had plenty of time, at first, to think.

Remembering the sneaking glimpse I had of Daphne—who matched Faisanne's descriptions.

Remembering the plinth beside Zoorn's nightmare road, hoary and crumbling, where a symbol was engraved: a circle atop a cross. The fourth key on my Kalimba, leaving the third a mystery.

On our way out of the Veil, a party of inspectors, aided by two Achthroi, had boarded our craft and analyzed it top to bottom. I tried to bear their regard steadily and was grateful they posed me no questions. They were huge men, swathed in shadow, with bloodshot eyes, heavy brows and rotten teeth. The Achthroi behaved like the one at Jico's, sniffing more than looking; I feared their surveillance the most. We were let go without incident, but the feeling persisted that they had been searching for me, for they passed over our cargo and did not ask for the customary bribes.

Kadesh had been better. We had reveled through the nights and slept through the days; hidden in moonlight and torchlight I felt more safe than Zoorn. Next to Zoorn, Kadesh was a place of brilliance and merriment.

And then desert, which persisted so long I lost my desperation to be free of choking dust and windborne sand, gritting inside my clothing despite my best efforts to keep it out. We spent several terrifying storms shrouded in scarves and goggles, our muscles straining to keep us upright and on course.

Through months of travel, the feeling that I was marked, pursued, did not abate. Measured against the sum of my anxiety, the knowledge gained on my tour with the Orsians was a paltry thing. I had gained in nerve and stealth since Mihali. But I had not gained the power Mercedes had forecast, the power I so greatly desired.

I was impatient.

Twice great forms paralleled our course in the desert storms. My fellows discounted this as a mirage of the storms, a typical thing. Why were these huge forms—which I was sure I had seen—of no concern to them, when the empty tundra filled them with dread? By the end of our second day on the river, the emptiness had lulled me into a rare ataraxis. I drowsed in my furs.

A cry from the lookout, a lad named Benjamine, changed all that:

"Halt ship!"

An officer scurried up the ropes, and then a few minutes later returned to engage the captain in low and animated conversation. The ship was steered toward the starboard side of the broad river. The other three craft followed and drew close, observations and orders yelled between the decks. Rumor spread quickly.

Coethyphys had been sighted on the port side.

Daevon and I had discussed Coethyphys with such level-headed ease. But back then I was a foolish dreamer who had never seen them, hailing from a world where such monsters were only story.

We rounded a curve in the river, and the Coethyphys were visible to all. Seven, eight, maybe ten, on a high ridge, black against setting sun. The ruddy light behind them obscured their color, but the shape was obvious enough. Serpentine. Spider limbs jutting at right angles from the torso, triangular heads framed in horns. Silhouetted in fire.

They were utterly still. Watching.

If I had thought the Orsians apprehensive before, it was nothing to the five days that followed. Coethyphys represented the direst straits of a dreamworld denizen. The sailors spoke in whispers, if they spoke at all. The wide expanse of water separating us from the Coethyphys was little consolation. Not for the last time, I wondered if my presence risked all their lives. Perhaps I should leave, strike out across the tundra on my own. But I was terrified. I could not contemplate striking out in the middle of nowhere by myself.

The Coethyphys followed us. We didn't see them move, hidden behind the ridge that was our constant companion to larboard. But they would be at the next portion of the ridge, watching. Only to disappear and crest again. Something about this stealth, the fact that we never saw them move, was unnerving.

The cold intensified exponentially. Frost clung to my Orsian eyebrows and settled in the black ringlets of my hair. The sun dimmed to a condemned moon shining through evanescent haze. The clouds congealed overhead into thick rows of serrated darkness. Snow began to fall on the sixth day, making the decks slippery. Benjamine, who had taken a liking to me for we two were the youngest on board, said we would soon pass the delta into the Cylindrax Sea, leaving our watchers behind.

It wasn't to be so easy.

The seventh morning of our river passage dawned bleak and windy. A lazy snow still fell and the clouds ahead were black. I shimmied up to the lookout with Benjamine, noticing his helpful but over-solicitous touch. The river downstream fragmented into numerous waterways separated by small islands of frozen earth. We would strive to stay in the center of this delta, traveling with the main flow of water. Even from our vantage point at the top of the mast, the Coethyphys were nowhere in sight. A rising and brutally cold wind soon forced our descent.

The sun struggled to rise and illuminate the landscape on our left. The first hour of the day we sailed in silence. And then crisis struck.

We rounded a stiff curve. Before fragmenting into delta, the river narrowed to a point. We would pass through this notch in a quarter hour, where the land on either side flattened to meet the river and the ubiquitous ridge to our left vanished at last. The other three ships had pulled ahead during the night and we heard their shouts of dismay first.

The Coethyphys held the pass against us, their mottled flesh a wall of patchwork colors: heliotrope, eggplant, mud brown, green the hue of decaying vegetation. A huge group, thirty or more. They waited along the left bank of the notch.

There was no doubt of their intention.

The men of Orse had travelled the Aedol Via for generations, and they adhered to tradition. They stuck to the classic route of the Via in the face of uncertainties—such as the trackless aether of Mihali—that would daunt any mariner of the waking world. But their terror of the Coethyphys conquered tradition. With oars, sails and anchors, all four ships struggled to impede their forward motion in the rapid and narrowing current of the river, and succeeded in gathering in the middle of the river so the captains could converse. Maps unfurled on decks.

I saw the proposed escape route on paper first, before I espied to starboard a small break in the tundra, even smaller than the notch, an alternate exodus of river water to the scattered ways of the delta. It had never been explored, but our captain argued it must lead to the same sea. In all things the Orsians were efficient, and so was their divergence from tradition. Within minutes we had entered this small, deep river-way. All sight of the Coethyphys was left mercifully behind.

Snow fell in earnest and the black clouds unleashed a blizzard. Helmsmen cursed as they struggled to keep us in the center of an unknown, narrow and fast moving river. Snow piled on deck. The wind buffeted us fiercely, its unpredictable surges tossing us against equipment, the masts and one another. This waterway followed a more torturous course than the known route, for we plied its twists and turns for an hour, winding back into the landscape, and still did not reach the sea.

Without warning the banks receded and we were propelled into a wide bay. There was no detectable current and once our momentum had spent itself, our progress slowed to a halt. Through the driving snow the other ships were only silhouettes, drifting in a semicircle beyond us. The surrounding water was the color of slate.

The wind stilled, with uncanny abruptness.

Next was a weird luminosity below the surface of the bay—subaqueous floodlights. To this day, I do not know what they were or how they connected to what happened next, only that they preceded it. Such is the strangeness of dreams. I rushed to the railing. I was surprised to see the bottom of the bay, illuminated by the wan light, perhaps a mere twenty feet below our hull.

Then two things happened at the same time. The floodlights went out. A deafening thunder crack emanated from the water.

The entire bay froze over.

A sheet of glassy ice, reflecting the grey cloudscape above. Even in the worlds of the Aedolae my mind recoiled at this impossibility.

"Drop the plows!" the captain shouted. These were huge triangles of mirror bright metal, standard equipment on an Orsian craft. Men and women scurried and with a grinding of hand-winched machinery the massive plows lowered toward the ice. On closer inspection, I noticed a few veins of open water survived, especially around the ships—as if our presence in the water had foiled the eldritch freeze.

A cry went up even as I saw them. Coethyphys, an uncountable number, on the shore of the bay to our larboard side. Individual Coethyphys detached themselves from the group and heaved their heavy bodies onto the ice. With grotesque undulations they moved toward us.

To where the ice was rendering us immobile targets.

We would have perished for sure had not the wind come to our aid, blowing with renewed ferocity toward shore. We raised our sails, rowers strained and cursed at the oars, and the cunningly designed ice breakers splintered us a narrow passage back toward the river mouth, barely visible in the snow. Without the plows we would have been trapped.

Our ship was fortunate to have lagged behind the others; the ice was more complete further out to sea, and those ships struggled to cut a passage. The distance between us and them widened. A complement of Coethyphys detached themselves from the throng undulating toward the other three ships and made for us. Orsian spear-throwers arranged themselves at the rail, fear obvious in their faces. I lacked strength to hurl the great spears, so I took a bow.

"Aim for the legs, cripple them, pin their legs to the ice," our weapons master shouted. The Coethyphys' sole means of propulsion was their powerful forelegs; they had no other limbs, only a snake-like torso behind. Their symmetry was bizarre, wrong, as if their form defied proper obedience to laws of gravity.

Black Orsian spears whistled through the air. One struck the lead Coethyphys in the neck, slamming its heavy head down on the ice with an audible thud. It screamed and tore at the wood shaft with its talons, bloodying its neck and breaking off the spear at the skin.

It kept coming.

Other spears found their marks in Coethyphys forelegs, hobbling their progress. I took aim at the leading beast, focusing on the middle one of its three scarlet eyes, the only one not caged in bone. My arrow hit its mark; the beast dropped. I had time to smile—for a moment.

The river mouth was a hundred yards away. The ice here was only floating chunks. As we jetted out from the field of ice we picked up speed, even against the outflowing current of the stream. Our pursuers were stalled by open water. At the lip of the ice they stood and thrashed their tails. The ice below one gave way and it flailed at the edge of the shelf as the weight of its body sucked it down.

Behind our pursuing Coethyphys the other three craft were indeed trapped. The passage we had carved was glossing over with new ice and the other dark veins of water had disappeared, frozen through. Through gaps in the wind-driven snow I could see Coethyphys massed about each boat, the ends of their long tails raised like scorpions, hewing at the hulls. One ship broke open like a nut, and Orsians spilled onto the surface of the bay. Masts toppled. Even at this distance, and through the wind, I could hear the screams and the splintering wood.

We reentered the river-way, high banks to either side. In the concentrated current, our progress slowed. No Coethyphys harassed us from the right. And then came the floodlights again,

shining ahead and behind, below the enraged surface of the
river. A sick feeling pervaded my being. I knew what this meant.
They shone for a minute and then the same cracking thunder.

The river began to freeze.

Water this deep and fast could never freeze. But nevertheless
the choppy surface congealed into shining planks. Tense
minutes passed. The icing over was too slow, too incomplete, to
incapacitate our plows. We broke through.

And then our new attackers were upon us.

Not Coethyphys, but something I had never heard of. They
were invisible until the first howling menace launched itself
from the starboard bank of the river and crashed onto the ice
a hundred feet away. I saw long streamers of orange fur, a lurid
orange unlike the fur of any waking world animal. A radiant
orb-like eye was set in a feline face.

A host of others followed: lithe jungle cats the size of
warhorses gliding down from the craggy river bank on bat's
wings. Shards of ice fractured and were thrown up in crashing
showers as they landed and struggled to stall their momentum.
One cat skidded, its claws etching a crazed parabola in the
surface of the ice, before disappearing into dark water. The
weight of another cat broke off a wedge of ice, and it rode that
piece like a surfboard, stopped only by the side of our ship,
where the ice smashed out several protruding oars.

The cats were smart. Seeing their fellow ride the ice, the rest
endeavored to engineer the same trick, with fair success. We were
surrounded by a snarling fury of winged beasts and the river ice
thickened around our stalled progress. The cats each had only
a single eye, and several of those eyes began to glow an intense
scarlet. A second later, globes of energy burst from these eyes
and pounded the ship with destruction.

Men yelled, pieces of the railing exploded around me, a
mast groaned and split. A fulminant blast of snow obscured
everything. I drew my bow but couldn't see any target. I was
conscious of Benjamine at my side. The ship shook beneath me
as more globes broke through the hull. Spearmen threw into

the blinding whiteness and some found their marks, for the cats hissed with pain.

And then the cats leapt on board. One landed mid-ship with a thump, pinning a woman to the deck. It turned toward Benjamine and me. We were no match for two thousand pounds of screaming feline, so we grabbed ropes and furiously climbed. It leapt toward us, but fell back, deflated. A spear, thrown from behind, transfixed its head.

"I still have my bow," I yelled through the gale. "I can get a better shot up above."

So we kept climbing. We were up fifty feet when the second cat struck. By ill chance its jump carried it full force into the mast from which we hung, snapping it in two. With sickening vertigo I was hurled through the air, spinning and tumbling, one foot tangled in the thrashing ropes. I landed on the ice and something cushioned my fall.

I rolled over and found that it was Benjamine.

Not only I, but the shattered mast had landed on him. His eyes stared, frozen in the shock of his final emotion. The ice shelf groaned beneath us and tilted, cloven by the mast. I struggled with stiff fingers to untangle my foot and got free in time to roll away and watch both my friend and the massive timber slide down into darkness.

I fought to get to my feet. The ship was barely visible in the maelstrom but it was not far. I was surrounded by the cats. Anger and grief at death, Benjamine's death, the death of so many sailors back in the bay, flooded me. If I could barely see the ship, those on board couldn't see me. Time to do something useful. I touched the Torc at my throat.

Shapechanging doesn't automatically impart the attributes of the form I take. This time it did. I became a winged cat, but bigger, equipped with a fully functional radiating eye. I blasted the nearest cat into a smoking wreck of fur. In an instant the rest formed a vicious circle around me. The treachery of one of their own kind did not faze them.

I lunged, slashing with my talons, forcing them back, blasting with my eye. In that craze of motion, I decided to one-up them. I grew a second eye and blasted in two directions.

Though their claws tore into me, they couldn't stand against my strength or my rage. My decimation of their numbers gave the Orsians a chance. They resumed rowing while the spearmen, less overwhelmed, dispatched the remaining beasts. I had saved not only my own life, but the entire ship.

New problem.

They were pulling away, making their way upriver, and I wasn't onboard. If I returned to Orsian form, out here on the ice, they would be never see or hear me. I had a second to decide, before they left the ice for moving water.

I marshalled the power of my feline legs and ran wildly across the ice. Leaping from floe to floe, I gained on the ship. At the edge of the ice field, I crouched and sprang, flying toward the ship, cresting the ruined railing. I smashed onto—and through—the roof of the captain's cabin. But not before an Orsian dagger, thrown as I flew overhead, pierced my right leg.

I woke up in a pile of broken timbers. I had changed back to Jaena not Siana. The Orsian sailors stared at me with wide eyes. My body bled from a myriad talon wounds and the dagger projected from the muscle of my right calf.

I was also naked, black skin gleaming with melting snowflakes.

Damn Torc.

I could not speak coherently. The story I concocted later (*I had been hurled onto the ice by a cat, my clothes torn beyond use, and I had seized the hair of another, clinging to him during his mad attack on the ship*) might have worked had there been a cat in the wreckage of the cabin. As there was no cat, the incident marked the end of my felicitous relationship with the Orsians.

It didn't help that Benjamine—whose parents were on board—was dead. The Orsians couldn't discount my story, and they didn't know what sorcery to accuse me of. But they wanted to accuse me of something, and in their indecision they confined me below deck and promised to take me before the powers at Cylindrax. Great. A private audience with Ghislain, and in chains. Not my preferred way to gather intelligence.

The traders were devastated. Despite their preparedness and skill—which had saved them—the violence of the attack was unprecedented. The mood as we fought our way upriver and out to the Cylindrax Sea was one of shock and apprehension. All were amazed at their survival. And amazed that no Coethyphys blocked our passage when we returned to the notch; in fact that was the last I saw of the Coethyphys for a long, long time.

The cats had done no critical damage to the hull, for all of the holes blasted were far above the waterline. But the vessel was impaired in other ways (masts and sails) vexing to a crew about to traverse a perilous arctic sea. As we sailed, the rigors of repair work gradually thawed the rigor mortis of shock.

I had my own healing to do. In neither waking or dreaming world had I ever suffered such harm. The dagger had struck me in a fortunate place, but nonetheless I still limped a bit when we reached Cylindrax a fortnight later. My other wounds were superficial but many and painful. Being deprived of the sailors' company, trapped below with little to distract me, made the pain harder.

THE XEMENOS

The only time I saw the light of day, through all the trip to Cylindrax, was a singular and strange incident halfway through our passage of the Sea. One dawn while I was drowsing in my bunk the ship slowed and an uncommon clamor filtered down to my ears. It was cold and damp in the hold and once awakened I couldn't fall asleep again. So I lay still and listened to the ship bump and grind against something, and sailors climb up and down the ladders.

A half hour later I heard footfalls in the cramped corridor outside my prison.

"The captain wants you, hurry and dress," a sailor barked. Minutes later, swathed in furs, I blinked against the wan grey light and looked over the railing at a chunk of ice several times the length of the ship but too flat to look a proper iceberg. At its far end was a sloppily constructed igloo. At the foot of the ladders the captain and a few other men surrounded a strange figure.

Like us, he was swathed in furs, but next to the Orsians' rugged resplendence he was pure barbarian. His clothes were careless, and his beard was wild and tangled. His face was hidden beneath a hood, but the beard that showed was not the black of an Orsian's but frost-flecked brunette. He and the Orsians gestured back and forth but clearly the conversation had not proceeded to understanding.

"He hailed the ship," my summoner explained. "We heard tales from the last Tour that a madman lived here on the ice—"

"Where *no one* lives," a nearby woman interjected.

"—so the captain stopped for him," my summoner continued, "but we can't make heads nor tails of him. Crazy, I say. Don't know how he has survived out here alone. But the Captain called for you, translator, for it seems Master Bierce taught you every language there is to know. So get."

I descended with pain in my still healing leg. The ice-coated guide rope was shockingly cold. The semicircle of mariners parted at my approach. The madman raised his head. His skin, though hard to see but for the massive beard and the frost, was white.

"Hello," I said in a dozen languages. The Star gave me skill with tongues, but not diplomacy. I didn't know what else to say. The man stared. His expression was familiar. I felt, against all reason, I had seen him before.

Then he spoke. "Will you take me with you?"

At first I didn't understand the words. I had been speaking Orsian, and a score of other tongues, for a year and a half. My mind turned a somersault and realized he had spoken English.

"Will you take me with you?" he asked again.

"I don't know, it is not my ship to command," I managed to say. "Tell me who you are."

One of the sailors gasped, seeing we conversed. The captain nodded, giving me leave to continue, his expression a guarded mix of pleasure and suspicion.

"I do not know my name," the man answered me.

I had to be talking to a dreamer. I limped closer. His hood fell away in a gust of wind. Piercing blue eyes emerged from a mantle of matted hair. The face, the expression, everything was so familiar...

The face of the xemenos at Ebon Port.

The face of my brother.

I restrained myself from shouting his name, throwing myself in his arms. He wouldn't know me as an ebony-skinned girl with black ringlets and night-dark eyes. I had to get him alone so I could transform.

"Ask him how he got here," the captain implored.

I didn't have to ask.

"I was in the air." The madman's voice was hollow, softer than before. "There was pain, a thousand sharp pains, and I was carried here and dropped... "

I attempted to translate this vacant explanation, while this doppelganger of my brother mumbled to himself. A sick feeling rose in my stomach. The captain looked annoyed.

"What is his name, where did he come from?" the captain pressed. I told him the man could not recall his name.

"My captain wants to know where you came from," I asked the man. I wanted to know too. Despite the resemblance, this was not the xemenos from Ebon Port; even with the weirdness of dreams I didn't think that possible. Daevon had promised to guard him.

Could *this* dazed creature instead be my brother?

"I came from a land far away," he began again, struggling to hold my gaze, studying his feet instead. As if memory was painful. "I came to an island, a boardwalk, and then the man with mirrors in his eyes was there and he struck me. There was an explosion and I was flying, high, high...."

He looked up at me and implored again: "Take me with you."

I reached out for his hand, I couldn't help it. I studied my elegant fingers, carved of glossy jet, against the hoary roughness of his palm.

I turned and told the captain the man was confused, unable to give a coherent account of himself but in need of our help. The captain stepped aside to consult with his officers. Here was my chance. I spun the man away from the others. I touched the Torc and let my face revert to its natural form: Siana.

No reaction.

I took his bearded face in my hands and forced his wandering gaze to see me. Crystal blue eyes—just like mine—regarded me with diffident confusion.

"Timothy, it's your sister," I said, a heaviness deflating my words. "Don't you recognize me...?"

But he was the same as before.

The submissiveness of this feral man, letting a strange little girl seize his face and direct his gaze. What had they done to him?

My heart sank, confounded.

And then the smallest narrowing of the eyes, a spark of something in his face. He seemed to regard me for the first time.

"There is something you must have," he said, his voice still hollow, but the words were definite. "Come." He motioned toward his ice-hewn hovel.

"He wants to show me something. He is very afraid, I think. Let me go with him, he wouldn't harm me. I will come right back," I begged the captain. He waved me on, resuming his conversation with the others.

I wondered if I would find the ship gone when I returned, the Orsians unloading a problem instead of picking up another.

The arctic wind and slap of the waves swallowed all other sounds. The man pulled aside the thick hide that served as door and ushered me within his tiny igloo abode. Another hide served as both floor and bed; there was little else. A turquoise light suffused the interior, glowing between the ice blocks that formed the walls. My companion knelt at the far end and scrabbled at the base of the wall with a piece of bone. I waited.

He returned with a delicate bracelet, from which depended by other fine chains a score of tiny mottled stones, polished to a lustrous hue. I knew it from Timothy's journal.

The Eterokon of Petrifaction. The man did not accompany the gift with further words, but fumbled to place it about my ebony wrist.

Tears ran down my cheeks, unbidden. I stooped to kiss his brow.

"You know who I am," I whispered. "I know you know."

He stood, the decisiveness gone from his haggard countenance now that his simple mission was accomplished.

"I was carried, over deserts, there was a moon in the sky." He continued his story as if no other thing had passed between us, as if fated to forever tell the tale of his ruin. "I watched myself drop to the ground, falling in the sand. And then I fell, fell to the ice. And then I watched myself far above in the sky, crushed against the blackness, watched myself fly away over the sea..."

"What did you say?" I demanded. My ardor scared him. He shrank from me. "No, no, please, please come here." I extended my hand again, and without thinking, my hair went blonde and my skin whitened. I cradled his head against my bosom. "It is OK. I am your sister, your favorite sister. Tell me again what you said."

"The beasts, the eaters, they were there with the man with the mirrors in his gaze, they weren't supposed to be there," he gabbled. His voice was broken.

"Tell me about when you were dropped here, when you watched—"

"I lay on the ice and cursed him," the man answered, more lucidly, "but I don't remember his name. And I watched myself in the sky, like a mirror, and the thing that carried me before, it carried me into the distance until I couldn't see me anymore. I lost myself and I don't know my name." He wept in earnest. I had never seen my brother cry. Even in this broken facsimile of a man it was painful to see.

For facsimile he was. I was sure now. In the waking world this story of seeing himself at a distance would be madness, an impossibility. If I hadn't met the xemenos at Ebon it would be madness to me as well. But I knew of such things now. This was not my brother, but *another* xemenos. It had shared my brother's consciousness until it fell away from him and then it had watched some *thing* carry my brother further away. But where had that thing taken him? Bierce said a xemenos was a form of dream trauma. What violence had this thing done to Timothy, that it created more than one of these copies?

My mind raced, so many conjectures, so many thoughts.

"How many times did you watch yourself fall?" I asked.

"I saw myself fall below the moon. And I saw myself fall in a jungle and there were torches. And I saw myself fall in a desert. And then I fell, to live on the ice forever..."

So five xemeni, I counted, at least. For he hadn't mentioned the one at Ebon Port. And more could have fallen after this one was splintered from my brother.

The hide rustled behind me. A sailor, sent to fetch me. My instincts are quick, or I would have appeared blonde.

"We leave. The captain will not take this madman," he informed me brusquely.

I stood slowly. The machinery of my mind still whirled. Torn between prudence and compassion for this pleading thing that was my brother and yet not, I had to conclude leaving him here was as good a course as any. In the waking world, no hermit could survive in a place like this, but this xemenos had. Despite his suffering he would continue to survive. Besides, I was in no position to cross the captain. I hardened my heart to go.

I turned back to the xemenos.

"We cannot take you, not now. But I will come back for you."

I hoped I could keep that promise.

Back on the ship, I wheedled from the Orsians a half hour reprieve from my prison, by insisting they show me where we were on the map. I told them Master Bierce would find a way to help the man. They shook their heads at my presumed naiveté, but I got the information I needed.

Once back in the hold, I turned the resplendent Bracelet over and over in my hands. I read my brother's journal. My leg hurt. I was cold. I was a prisoner. But I had gained power, power that rested in my ebony palm, sparkling in the lantern light. My brother had had eight Eterokoni. Now I had four, including two he'd never possessed.

Another aspect of my quest was unfolding. I could gain power by recovering the Eterokoni. And now I knew how: when Timothy's soul splintered, the xemeni had taken his Eterokoni as well as his form. The quest to find these shadow men now loomed as large as the quest to find Timothy. For I needed their Eterokoni to both elude and confront the Aedolae.

Twelve were rumored to exist. Timothy had had eight. I had four and xemeni might have Timothy's remaining six. If

I recovered those, I would have ten, surpassing my brother's mark.

What I didn't realize, then, was possession was only part of the story. Being able to use them was the other. I knew so little then.

Mercair told me the Aedolae knew of my explorations and imprisoned me in the Gardens. From Mihali, I knew the Aedolae were no longer a unified front in their governance, but divided by suspicion. The ice xemenos mentioned a man with mirrors in his gaze. This fit the Orsians' description of Ghislain, for whose realm we sailed. So had Ghislain been at Ebon with the Coethyphys, complicit in my brother's fate? If so, he likely acted independent of the other Aedolae's authority. His realm was next on the Orsians' tour. This was my chance to discover critical information that had eluded me so far.

It made me nervous as hell.

Nine days later we reached Cylindrax and my association with the Orsians, with whom I had traveled for a year and a half of dreams, came to an abrupt end.

I was allowed on deck for the approach to Cylindrax. We had sailed all day through a dense bank of fog, when it parted to reveal the largest constructed thing I had ever seen.

At first I thought the sun's white blaze reflected off a wall of ice. But my adjusting eyes distinguished a building. A building the size of a mountain and the color of a glacier. It was a perfect square and this made its size disturbing, for the only things we are accustomed to seeing on that scale have the soothing irregularity of nature.

The surrounding sea had a glassy tranquility, undisturbed by wave or ice. The gelid air was bracing but the sun was glorious on my face. After our grey, ice-choked passage, this sea was vividly beautiful.

Save for the eerie emotion that mile-high faceless cube stirred in my soul.

Gleaming white docks, boardwalks and pavilions fanned out along the near side of the cube, and arched avenues cut into the bottom of its near face connected its interior to the docks. The cube's blinding façade had no other break save for a slight tracery of gridded pattern beneath. Each square of that grid must have been several hundred feet across.

Around the docks a barrier of metal poles projected from the sea. Topping each was a huge symbol: a cross above a half circle. This matched the sixth (and last) key on the Kalimba at my throat. Below these symbols the poles sported a twisted fantasy of blades and spikes, which filled the space between them—a scintillating forest of nightmare trees growing from a placid sea.

Iakovos said the master of this place, Ghislain, was mad.

The only gap in the barrier of the poles was an amphitheater with a seawater floor. Its roof was a tubular metal grid of horizontal scaffolding. Compared to the other worlds within the Detheros, this place had an alien cast, fashioned of glass and strange mirrored metals not found in the waking world.

We appeared to be making for the amphitheater. Only later did I wonder what wind could fill our sails yet leave the glassy sea undisturbed.

The unnerving cubic building—which was Cylindrax City—filled more and more of my vision. Dark birds wheeled about its far off heights. Its facelessness was hypnotic, drawing my eye to trace and retrace its edges and gridded substructure. And then, with a flash, its entire surface came alive.

The face of the cube was coloring a deep blue, and in the middle of that immensity was a tiny boat, seen from far above. The boat's V-shaped wake cut the tranquil sea into sparkling ribbons. Mesmerized by this mile-wide image, I watched the boat grow larger, until it filled the screen. For a screen is precisely what the cube had become, a massive screen depicting the scene of our approach.

Something glinted off our starboard bow, pulling my attention from Cylindrax. It reminded me of a Japanese beetle, iridescent purple and black, though wrought of metal and bigger than my head. I crouched instinctively. It buzzed up with a metallic whir, regarding me with conical metal eyes. Its dark pupils were holes into an abyss.

Behind it, a grainy four-thousand foot image of my Orsian self, crouching, was projected onto the screen. The beetle lost interest in me and buzzed off to cast images of my fellows onto the side of Cylindrax.

We arrived at the canal through the amphitheater. The beetle-like thing whirred off and was lost against the scenery. Sharp-edged shadows cast by the tubular ceiling crisscrossed our deck and the bright water ahead. Most of the amphitheater's rows of bleachers were empty, but the place was so enormous that the minority of seats occupied still added up to several thousand spectators watching our approach. I saw Estringites for the first time. More Orsians. Winged men and women of an unsavory mien. Brown-skinned men with staves carved from bones of goliath sea creatures. And row upon row, closest to us, were the Glacii, the ice soldiers of that demesne, motionless. One might have thought them statues. But something about their placement made me think otherwise. As we sailed in, every eye was trained on us. A different chill than the air traveled the length of my body. Ahead impossibly delicate causeways curved from the amphitheater to tiny openings in the cube a hundred feet above the docks. Along these causeways ant-sized figures strolled. With the quiet vigilance of these spectators, the legions of Glacii and the barrier of spiked poles I felt more negative about Cylindrax than any place I had been. Not a good place to be brought as a prisoner.

I wondered if we were all prisoners here.

Night didn't come to Cylindrax at the expected time. We had been docked for what felt a day but when I was brought above the sun still blazed high in the unchanging sky.

At our final arrival, I had been sent below, while the officers conducted business with the marshals of the docks. No one told me anything. But an Orsian woman, Tayla, had come below to fetch me at last, with a wrapped bundle. Inside was a scarlet mask: wire frame and velvet fabric stretched between.

"You are going with us to the balls," she informed me, looking uncomfortable. She had once been friendly. "The captain wanted to leave you here under guard but the rule is that all personnel must come within, and there is no returning to the docks until we depart. They would not bend the rules."

"What is the mask for?" I asked.

"We wear masks in Cylindrax. It is a precaution. Old sailors tell of times when such precautions were not taken, and the weirdness of Cylindrax caused much travail."

"What kind of travail?"

"Visitors became mirrormen, each reflecting the face of the other. Or some became faceless. Cylindrax is a place of illusion. Be careful not to lose yourself, Jaena. Know the masks of those nearest to you and be not deceived." With that she lowered her own mask over her face. I did the same. We climbed the ladder into the unexpected sun.

A mask was not all I wore. I was brought into Cylindrax in chains.

GHISLAIN

T he chains, small links but thick, shackled my arms and tied me to two burly Orsian men. They rasped against the polished surface of the docks as we walked. Everything else was so quiet that I felt ostentatious. My guardsmen were equally annoyed, clear from the set of their mouths beneath their ivory masks. They had hoped for more than guarding me.

The architecture of the place dwarfed us. Everything in Cylindrax was built on an seemingly purposelessly cyclopean scale and built for a quantity of inhabitants it lacked. I felt small as the dark line of our procession crossed the empty and unnaturally polished pavilion. The arch that swallowed us up was a hundred feet high.

All the edges and lines of the place were sharp enough to have been cut by lasers.

We traveled an hour along a bewildering series of passages, galleries, stairways and ramps, up and into the heart of the giant building. The path we trod was unlit but never dark, for the walls were translucent and light came at us from other rooms, far or near. It was as if I wandered a Christmas snowstorm, seeing the candy-colored light of decorated houses through the veil of the storm. Interruptions in the light told of figures moving against them, but nothing was distinct, no silhouettes. Even the floors and ceilings were translucent, so we saw blurred forms moving above and below. Occasionally walls and balustrades were so transparent we stumbled against them. Other times they shone like glass and reflected our parade of colored masks. Our guide was a lone Cylindraxian, impeccably dressed with honey-colored skin. How this place had been constructed was beyond me. I had seen no more fantastic dreamworld wonder.

We entered a large oval chamber, well occupied and ringed with high balconies. Throughout our passage there had been a murmur of noise, as indistinct as the figures in the fog, but now the sound was rich and defined. This was the ball, a feast for our special group of Orsians who brought rare things to Cylindrax. (Here the illicit nature of some parts of our cargo were more openly acknowledged and discussed.) The revelers at the ball were as varied as the folk of the amphitheater. Many wore masks, masks as unlike in style as the dreamworld species that wore them. There was feasting, many of the delicacies appearing to me none too wholesome. The music was the first I'd heard since Kadesh, at first pleasing to the ears but increasingly bothersome with the same eerie quality as the lights in the passages. Whenever one paid it attention, the strains of the melodies grew fuzzy and far away. When one paid attention to other things, the music grew loud and intrusive and grasped at the mind, only to evanesce again.

The Orsians participated with delight but to my eye not without an undercurrent of apprehension. Women were shy about leaving the company of their mates; the whole group clung together. The native people of Cylindrax resembled our guide, their manners more elegant than the folk of Zoorn or Mihali. They spoke a soft and musical language that dripped condescension. Even as they hosted with impeccable grace, I thought they treated the Orsians as quaint peculiarities. And to my eye the Cylindraxians strove to draw us apart and scatter us throughout the crowds.

My guards accompanied me grudgingly, allowing me food and drink, sober and vigilant in their task. Hours passed and I had grown drowsy and bored when my fortunes changed dramatically.

A man appeared on one of the balconies. Everyone turned to acknowledge him. He was tall, with shoulder length black hair, and a neat triangular beard. His eyes were hidden behind a pair of glasses with dark lenses. His walking stick drew my gaze, translucent and flashing a tremendous ruby. He raised his arms to the crowd and laughed, jovial but with undercurrents of ice. On his shoulder perched the mechanical beetle from our approach.

The beetle flew into the crowd, hovering a few feet above us. The enveloping circular wall of the chamber became a screen, with the beetle's eyes projecting each of us in massive proportion across it. The crowd took delight in seeing themselves, and soon most heads were turned upwards.

The beetle hovered closer and projected the faces of my fellow Orsians onto the wall. Tayla with her distinctive mask. But her eyes, amplified, squinted with concern. She was frowning. Concerned murmurs in the Orsian language rippled through the crowd. The beetle had shifted its form mid-flight, taking the aspect of a mechanized owl. It swiveled its eyes toward the guard on my left. His huge face on the wall was the same as ever: grumpy. The wall's scene panned from the guard and followed the length of grey chain that bound him to a young girl.

A girl in a scarlet mask, with white skin and dark-blonde hair falling to her shoulders.

I didn't immediately register. Neither did my guards, watching the anomaly on the wall unfold. But slowly they turned their shocked attention to the girl between them. No longer an Orsian. The owl buzzed in closer, throwing a wide-eyed image of masked Siana onto the wall.

My gaze was drawn to the man at the balcony. He had taken off his glasses and in the light of the blazing chandeliers his eyes flashed mirrors.

The man of the ice xemenos' tale.

Ghislain, the Aedolae of this place. An Aedolae who perhaps had reforged a bond with the Coethyphys.

I imagined how I must appear to him: a blonde youth flanked by Orsians. Had he heard the report from Mihali? I guessed so from the tensing of his hands on the railing, the urgency in his stance.

I panicked. I yanked at the chains binding me to my unnerved guards, who had drawn their cutlasses. Something rattled at my wrist. I had forgotten that I wore the Bracelet of the xemenos. It had slid from under my sleeves and now clinked against the shackle on my wrist.

A wave of power froze everyone within twenty feet. I tugged at my chains, now brittle stone, and they snapped at the guards' wrists. I flailed them about me in a wild arc, shattering the links to pieces. The revelers surrounding me were ash-grey stone. No time to contemplate my new powers. I sprang for the nearest exit.

The way I took was an upward winding ramp. I heard a great commotion at my back, and closer the whirr of mechanical wings. The owl. At the top of the ramp I spared a glance back. I wouldn't be able to outrun the thing; it was upon me. So I braced myself against the wall and boxed it with my foot.

I caught it by surprise. It clattered and spun down the ramp with satisfying drama. I resumed my flight, finding myself in a long corridor with a row of identical doors. I took the rightmost, furthest from the ball. I closed the door behind me.

Inside a tremendous staircase spiraled through the midst of a vertiginous arrangement of translucent cubic rooms, stacked like a child's blocks. Within the cubes black figures moved against jeweled lights. The stair was shadowed, more so as I climbed.

I ascended for a very long time. Life with the Orsians had toughened me, but nonetheless this stair winded me. My leg hurt. I must have climbed twenty stories before I paused to catch my breath. In a mile-high building, twenty stories didn't count for much. I was lost and in extreme peril.

Not a great combination.

I kept climbing.

After the same distance again, the stair ended without warning, passing through a hole in the floor of a bizarre room. I say room. The room's ceiling was six inches above my head. It had no visible walls. Feeble white light emanated from the floor but succumbed to shadow. I stood on a huge stage in the middle of an enormous dim spotlight—with the ceiling pressing down on my head.

It was claustrophobic.

In such a place, how could I track my movement? I contemplated going back down and decided against it. What if I kept the portal to the staircase just in sight, and walked a circle around it? I would gain another fifty feet of visibility and not lose my bearings. I might spot a wall or exit.

My strategy failed. There was only more shadow. I couldn't tell whether I'd completed a full circuit. An irrational fear rose in me: *there were no walls*. If I left the stairwell behind I would wander here in dreams forever. I teetered in indecision.

Until I saw it.

The effect anywhere would have been chilling, but in this stark white place doubly so. A crooked black head poked out from the portal. Cock-eyed antennae swiveled. A misshapen hand gripped the edge of the opening. It began to pull itself up.

It did not resemble the ones I had seen but I knew it instantly: Achthron. As a rule Achthroi differ, sharing only a penchant for grotesque deformity and a blend of insectoid and reptilian features. I remembered the sniffing and hoped its eyes weren't as good as mine.

Quietly I backed away, into that limitless dark. I wasn't sure whether keeping it in sight was smart or stupid, but decided on the latter. I wandered aimlessly for ten minutes or so when the ceiling vanished up into a vast emptiness lit by a spider web of dim light, like illuminated cracks in a distant roof. I wandered for a few more minutes. No sign or sound of the Achthron. I came to a curving shaft of metal, that spun down from the darkness and ended a few feet above the ground, a catwalk of sorts, with good tread and a barely walkable incline. It had no visible means of support. I hoisted myself up and began a nerve-wracking ascent. I have good balance but as the radiance of the floor receded and the catwalk whorled upwards in a mad spiral, I was sick with vertiginous fear.

When I could no longer see the floor the catwalk passed another, which curved by underneath. Soon it was so dark I could barely distinguish the path in front of me from open air. Then I was in the middle of a wild jumble of causeways, on all sides above and below, curving and zigzagging through dark space. The diffuse glow from the cracks told of far walls and ceiling. None of the other catwalks was close enough for a jump so I stayed my course, trying to keep my heart from bursting through my chest, taking deep breaths to keep my feet steady. At last all the other causeways were below me and the glowing lines drew near.

My catwalk ended in open air.

Ahead of me, light outlined a door in an otherwise unseen wall. Why did the catwalk end here, six feet from its ostensible goal?

Six feet is not far to jump. But it felt so with no floor in sight, and no guarantee the door would open.

Something clicked below me. On a different catwalk the Achthron crawled, down on all fours and sniffing.

I backed up as far as the incline allowed, and made a good run. I touched the Torc at my throat. No use; it still failed. Only my normal muscles propelled me over black nothingness. Time slowed to allow me to contemplate the death of my dreamself. When one deep dreams, this is no easier to contemplate than waking world death.

The door gave way to my shoulder, not without some pain, and I was through. It slammed against the wall with a boom terrifyingly loud after the long silence of the climb.

I rubbed my shoulder and leg and contemplated why the Torc no longer worked in Cylindrax. It was not a conscious decree of the Aedolae; he reacted to my presence only after I changed. I had never heard of Eterokoni failing. I had much to learn.

I didn't lie there long. An Achthron still chased me and I hadn't exactly been discrete. I stood up. I was surrounded by ten stories of wrap-around balconies, and was instantly reminded of the interior foyer of a large office building at night. An artificial waterfall gurgled down a diminutive stone mountain, splashing into a kidney-bean-shaped pool. A glass-walled elevator was docked on this floor, cables and machinery filling the open shaft above it.

Something achingly familiar, shocking here in Ghislain's realm.

This was the hotel in Oregon where Timothy had taken the Polaroid of me, seven years ago. In this very same elevator.

What the *fuck* was going on? Every detail in the expansive lobby was right.

Instinctively, I walked toward the elevator, thinking of that photograph, my foolish grin.

A noise broke my reverie. I crouched and peered around the elevator shaft. Behind a row of potted palms were dark shapes, low to the ground. Antennae quivered between the fronds.

More than one.

With my leg and an useless Torc, I was no match for them. So I pushed the glowing green UP button, as good an idea as any. The stainless steel doors of the elevator sighed open. Inside was red velvet carpeting, wood paneling and a glass wall overlooking the palm trees and waterfall. As the door closed, black forms lunged across the courtyard. I scanned the buttons, seeing floors 1-12 and a 13th button that read G. Must be that silly superstition about naming floors 13, so they named it something else. In any case, G was the highest. I pressed it.

As the elevator slid upward, an Achthron threw itself against the glass. I glimpsed three eyes and a slitted mouth. The glass held fast and the smashed face slid down and out of view. One more thump, then only the elevator's silvery noise. Floors raced past and I approached the glass ceiling of the hotel. The shaft passed through it.

Blinding sunlight. Through the window glass a half mile of featureless and perfectly level surface. I knew at once: this was the top of Cylindrax, the very roof, even though reason protested I could not have come that far. The elevator doors popped open.

Ghislain stood there, hands resting on the ruby head of his walking stick.

"G" stood for Ghislain. Stupid me. A clever touch, that one detail deviating from the norm.

My eyes scoured the panel for the "Door Close" button. I pressed it but my hand passed through fading metal. There was no elevator. Only me, squinting in the sun, and acres of flat nothingness at the top of the world.

And the man with mirrors for eyes.

"I had to rescue you from all that nonsense below," Ghislain spoke, voice low and rich, but cold all the same. He offered his arm. "Would you care to join me in my evening walk?"

My mind went back to the Gardens: Mercair coming into my bower and offering his arm the same way. Yet Mercair had been there to rescue me.

I stood, uncertain.

"As you wish, Siana," Ghislain said, "but must we stand here facing off? It is so vulgar."

"How do you know my name?"

"Who is it that hosted you with such resplendence in the Gardens? In your naiveté you failed to hide your dream-name in the shallows of the Fringe."

"*You* imprisoned me! *You* took away all my memories!" My hands shook with anger.

"I did nothing to your *real* self. I only neutralized you when you trespassed in places you had no right to be. That is *my* right, dreaming girl. It surprises me you dare come here, where your freedom is again forfeit."

In this way, Ghislain confirmed my speculations and named himself my jailor; it had never been the Aedolae *en masse*. Not surprising, if he had also confronted Timothy, with Coethyphys in tow.

With that in mind, I demanded, "What did you do to my brother?"

Perhaps he would tell me, thinking me without hope in his thrall.

Ghislain answered with a sardonic grin. "Llwyd Emyr? I did no violence to him."

"Don't be coy. You were there. Some power took him two years ago, carried him through the sky."

Ghislain raised his walking stick and tapped its ruby head against my chest, punctuating each of his subsequent points. "I don't doubt that you know. You have proven more intelligent" (*tap*) "and more persistent" (*tap*) "than I have expected. No other dreamer has come to Cylindrax for hundreds of years. The *Grey* family has quite a pedigree."

He saw my eyes widen. "I know that name too. Your brother's subterfuge was as weak as yours; he used the Welsh word for grey. Were it up to my ineffectual compatriots your brother would have caused serious trouble. But I dealt with your brother, and there is nothing to prevent me from dealing with you."

Instinctively I touched the Torc, with little hope it would work. To my surprise it did, and wings began to unfurl from my back.

Ghislain chuckled. "You thought it was only the failure of the Torc that tipped the odds in my favor? You have always been in my power and the Torc changes *nothing*."

The air rippled.

• • • ● • ● • • •

I was clad in rags and my hands were stretched and tied painfully to the wooden stake that ran along my spine. An ill-shaven man in a long black garment held fire to the straw. His voice was Ghislain's.

"Whose power formed these worlds, gave structure to your dreams, kept the chaos of nightmare at bay?" the man who was Ghislain, and yet not, spat. Behind his archaic glasses flames reflected off his eyes. The crowd at his back, clad in somber grey, were clouds reflecting a sullen heaven. They chanted: "Burn her, burn her, burn the witch!" Tongues of flame from the burning straw licked at the pale flesh of my exposed ankles. I tried to pull my feet away.

Defying the fire, the man drew close, sticks breaking beneath his feet.

"How dare you go against me? How dare you defy the Law with your sorceries?" he said. I thrashed against my bonds. No prior experience of pain, awake or dreaming, compared. I swooned, falling into the reprieve of unconsciousness. And still he leered, blackened teeth, but not burning...

· · · ● · ● · · ·

I regained consciousness on a velvet sofa, fluffed pillow behind my head. A massive mahogany desk dominated my field of vision. The pain was gone. Slatted wood blinds let in a filtered spring sunlight and the sounds of birds.

"Tell me about your symptoms, the paralysis in your leg," a fatherly voice spoke from behind the desk. I did not trust something in the voice.

I jockeyed myself partially upright, finding myself in a stiff and uncomfortable dress with ridiculous petticoats. The speaker was silhouetted in the sun, his face hard to see. My right leg did hurt and I reached down to rub it. As I bent, I could hardly breathe what with the restraint of my corset.

"Doctor, I don't remember much," I stammered. My brain was as hazy as the partially glimpsed spring afternoon beyond the office window. The doctor scratched notes with a pencil and murmured.

"You suffer from a hysterical amnesia. The prognosis is not good when the disease has progressed this far. Are you feeling distressed?" He stood and reached for a vial on a shelf.

"I am, because I don't remember seeing you before."

My mouth moved but I was disconnected from the words, as if I watched myself in a movie.

"A pity," he said to himself, "this utter waste of the young ladies of our day." And then to me: "Here, this should help you relax." Light glinted off the formidable needle and this snapped me to my senses. I jumped up and almost tripped on my dress.

"Ah," he said, and his voice became an unexpected sneer, "the paralysis has left." Sunlight flashed against something else. He had taken off his glasses to read the increments on the reservoir of the needle, and his eyes glowed silver.

I grabbed a gilded bust off the end-table and threw it at his head.

His form was mist and it smashed out the window instead.

The shards reformed into a stained-glass illustration of Jesus' temptation in the wilderness.

· · · ●·●· · ·

I had been watching early morning sun gradually fill the picture with bejeweled luminance. I tucked a coiled strand of my long blonde hair back into my habit. I was too young to be here, my figure hidden beneath severe black clothes that betrayed nothing of youth save the freshness of my face. I was scared of the world but joyful at the quiet masonry and low voices of this place.

There was a footfall behind. I turned to find a man, not a priest or monk, pacing the rough stone tiles. He was in shadow, but his merchant's clothes were obvious, neat and trim with fiery red accents. At seeing his walking stick, topped with a blood colored stone and a sign of black magic, my heart froze. He had come for me. I couldn't remember a thing about my life, only that I had come to the abbey to escape something, *someone*, and this was he.

"You thought you could do without me, Mary"—his voice was low and even—"they always do. Everyone imagines a world where their dreams, their whims, are satisfied—without me. Light without darkness. Freedom without power and punishment."

He drew closer, and pointed with his walking stick at Jesus, poised on a high cliff, tempted by the Devil to throw himself down.

"See! Your Christ, he needed a betrayer, and he needed a power to crucify him. Your religion celebrates God's willingness to sacrifice his Son, but He couldn't have done it without me."

My eyes went wild. This man had confessed he was the Devil. I turned to run, blonde hair flying free, and slipped on the marble floor of the transept. My right calf hurt. The man walked toward me, his pace indolent.

"Come now, Mary, you need not be afraid. How you have demonized me!"

His words made no sense. I struggled to stand, but my leg gave way again. Without conscious thought, my hand went to my throat, to the token there, sharply edged. I had no memory of it, but it sent a tingling feeling through my body. White light radiated from my skin; I began to levitate off the ground. Had I been a sorceress, and this man a warlock? Had he come to expose my fraudulent bid at sanctity?

I spun, and feathers, brilliant white, brushed my face. I flew toward the frescoed ceiling and a gold-ringed skylight. Or was I somehow an angel? I could not comprehend.

As I crashed through the skylight, the man cursed below. I was sucked through earth, my body parting concrete, and then expelled with a whoosh out and onto the hard pavement of a city.

• • • ●•●•● • • •

A beastly hot summer assailed my senses. My hair was in pigtails and I wore thongs on my feet, a pink tank top and black shorts. A crashing wave of youth with banners and painted faces surrounded me, and we coursed down streets which shimmered from the heat. I had been marching for an hour, but my head was abruptly woozy and my leg hurt. I ploughed on for a few minutes, but it became clear I couldn't walk further. Disappointment swept over me. I had been waiting for this protest for months!

Sputtering a curse, I broke from the group and made for the sidewalk.

"Jacqueline!" shouted my friend Katie, but she was swept away by the crowd. A few minutes later, an eerie quiet reigned. I was parched. The storefront nearby was a café. Perhaps I could get a drink, then limp after them at my own pace. I might still arrive at the demonstration before it ended.

I went in.

Inside was even quieter. Sunlight struggled to penetrate the uncommonly dusty windows. No one staffed the cafe's counters. It appeared I'd stepped into the 50s. I glanced about, perplexed. A lone gentleman sat at a table by the window.

"Have a seat, miss," he said. I was about to protest being called "miss," but the words died in my mouth. I sat obediently on the edge of a chair opposite him, wiping my brow.

"You were part of that group?" he asked. He was dressed in an overly formal fashion, perhaps forty years of age. He was handsome, in a European sort of way, but his eyes were hidden behind tinted sunglasses.

"Yes," I sighed, "but not anymore. My leg started hurting."

"They're all idiots," he said flatly. I gaped.

"What?" I managed to spit out.

"It is so easy to criticize corporations and governments when you know nothing of the difficulties of running a world," the man said, with an overly dramatic weariness. A tone engineered to suck me into an argument.

"There will be no world if those companies keep at it," I couldn't help saying, but then changed the subject. "Does anyone work here?" I merely wanted something to drink.

"Where is *here*?" the man asked nonchalantly. I was really irritated now. He had gone from right-wing nutcase to total nutcase.

"Look outside, *Siana*," he hissed. I began to protest that my name was Jacqueline but those words died in my mouth too. I walked to the door and threw it open. An arctic wind ripped into me and blew the paper placemats off the tables. It was like daggers of ice through my skimpy attire. The open door framed a flat polar nothingness that dropped off into brilliant blue sky.

The surface of Cylindrax.

• • • • •• • •• • • •

II Come back in," Ghislain said, "you'll freeze in an instant."

I considered leaving and slamming the door in his face, but decided better. What difference would it make?

"Okay," I conceded, my mind full of whirling memories, the past hour of shifting dreamscapes he had conjured.

I sat down across from Ghislain again. Apparently I would confront my doom not as Siana, Princess of Time, but Jacqueline, twenty-first century hippie. I surveyed my face in the cafe's mirrors. At least it was *my* face the pigtails framed.

A soda had appeared in front of each of us. I considered tossing it in his face, but I couldn't bring myself to use a soft drink as a weapon against the Aedolae.

"You win," I said. "I'm impressed. You are more powerful than a lowly dreaming *girl*. So what do you want?"

"I want your kind to stay where we put you: Outside the Detheros, no longer weaving your foolish dreams into the fabric of our grandeur."

"What right do you have to keep us from dreaming?"

"It is not a right," he said, "but a necessity. How easily you come here, all of what?—*eighteen* years of age—and pass judgment on me. I have lived a millennium. Your petty thoughts, evaluating my kind, simply should not be thought. *You* have no right. And yet you persist in thinking them. Hence my necessity. What would happen should you achieve your aims? If you had your way would you destroy me, destroy Kadesh, destroy Daphne?"

"I came here for Timothy," I countered.

"I know your heart is darker than that," Ghislain replied, "but you dare not follow such darkness."

"I might," I said.

"You are too ignorant to know the repercussions of such power. So it is with Jacqueline, whose memory I borrowed: she has no idea the chaos her blind utopia would wreak."

"Timothy is my right," I said. My hands shook in my lap.

Anger. Fear.

Both.

"*Timothy*," Ghislain said, "another trespasser, another criminal. You both abandoned your rights at the gate to our kingdoms. You had your world but you weren't content in it, nothing but a pathetic depressive unable to claim your power in the world of your birth. So you come to *my* world. Unlike you, I am content in my world. And I will be more content once you are gone."

Despite the malice of his last sentence, Ghislain's tone never changed, still matter of fact, congenial. But his words bored holes in my brain. I felt as woozy as Jacqueline in the sun.

But still.

"Where is my brother?" I asked.

Ghislain continued as if I hadn't spoken, "You asked what I want. Instead I will tell you what I will *do* with you, Siana,

Princess of Time, now that you are utterly and irrevocably in my power."

A clattering noise behind the counter interrupted Ghislain's diatribe. I jumped. He rose from his seat for the first time. As he turned his eyes rightward, desperation drove me toward the last item in my arsenal. I took the Kalimba from about my neck and settled it in my lap. Ghislain had let me use the Torc when I left the elevator but I had no illusion that he would let me use it again. He hadn't mentioned or noticed the Kalimba.

Too bad I had no idea what it did.

The mysterious noise was explained by the mechanical beetle/owl scraping onto the counter, upsetting a glass container which rolled and scattered straws onto the floor. Currently a Japanese beetle in aspect, it whirred over to Ghislain's outstretched arm. It had survived my kick, evincing no damage to its iridescent exterior or its substructure of clicking gears and sliding mechanisms.

"You have met my Ikonos before." Ghislain turned back. "I will show you further of his talents." I watched in wonder as the Ikonos transformed again, its exoskeleton dividing, recombining, sliding over and under other pieces to create its avian aspect. It hooted, a train whistle sound.

"He not only projects what is, but can see what will be. What remains for you now in the dreamworlds? The Orsians gave you passage, but think you can return to them now?"

The dusty windows of the café became images. Gears spun and clicked inside the Ikonos. Orsian villagers, as I remembered them from my few days at Ebon Port. Ships sailing into port, jet-skinned traders spilling out and climbing from wharf to tavern. Men and women gossiped in streets and storefronts, and the Ikonos projected above them a spectral representation of their thoughts: me blonde and shackled at the ball, my pale blue eyes visible despite the mask. This image grafted back onto my history with the Orsians, as stories spread and the White Witch became quick legend: the witch who spoke in daemon tongues and conversed with madmen. Who divided into multiple personas and attacked the ships as a horde of cyclopean orange-furred cats, who aided the dreaded Coethyphys. Never mind I had stood with the Orsians through the Coethyphys' attack. This fact, in the world the Ikonos projected, was quickly forgotten.

These things hadn't happened yet; Ghislain was trying to make me desperate. And in this, he erred. For I felt desperate enough already. Instead I would take the Ikonos' story as helpful warning.

I am not a good actress, but I feigned disbelief and distress.

The scene shifted, to a Council of the Aedolae, where Iakovos and Ilanit gathered with Kadesh in their zebra-pattern halls. A procession of the Zoorn cult, much as I imagined it from Faisanne's story, approached the Mihalian throne, with Daphne at its head. A square cage of gleaming metal bars, borne by a score of men harbored my naked body, transfixed by spikes and held aloft by them at the center of the cage.

I wanted Ghislain to think I could no longer bear to watch, that he was breaking me down. So I cast my eyes downward. In truth, I wanted to look at the Kalimba in my lap, for my finger had found a tiny button on the back, behind a fold in the wood. Somehow I had never found it before, but either fate or dire need revealed it.

I pressed it. I felt a throbbing, a vibration below audible pitch. I studied the Kalimba's keys: Ebon Port and Mihali. Zoorn, Kadesh, and Cylindrax. And in between these groups, the unknown key, its symbol a circle flanked by a semicircle and cross.

The windows had grown dark, neither images nor sun.

"Before I show you more, I will pose you a bargain," he said, "for your refusal will amuse me. If I kill you now, your dreamself will be sent across the Detheros. If you promise not to return then I will release you from my power."

"What a bargain, I get to die."

"Next to the alternative," Ghislain said, "it is. What do you imagine happened to your Timothy?"

"I don't know; you haven't told me. I will answer your bargain, but tell me first: does he live?"

"He does."

"Then my response to your bargain is no. For I will not forsake him."

"Then you are a fool. Refusing me will not save him either."

"Then so be it." I pressed the mystery key on the Kalimba. I had nothing to lose.

I don't know what I expected to happen. The function of the Kalimba seems obvious in retrospect. Then I acted only on instinct, selecting the only key that had no association with an Aedolae's demesne.

The subsonic throbbing grew until it filled all the room.

Behind Ghislain a window opened in the wall of the café, showing a leaf-strewn gravel road meandering between tall maples. The window's edge glimmered with a sharp white light. Even as I sat transfixed, this edge began to contract.

I was letting my salvation disappear. I stood, hiding the tiny Eterokon in my cupped hands, not releasing the button and key. Feeling the portal's exhalation of cool mist, Ghislain turned.

I shifted the Kalimba into one hand, moving my thumb onto the key, and decked him with a chair.

The continuation of the chair's trajectory knocked Ghislain's Ikonos aside. I dashed across the intervening space and threw myself at the cafe wall.

I fell into another world, an early winter morning. The portal shrunk behind me. I slipped on leaves, Jacqueline's thongs functionally useless. The café disappeared and the wood stretched in all directions. I never saw Ghislain's reaction.

Something glinted in the sunlight, a diamond on a bed of leaves. The beak of the Ikonos, sheared off by the closing portal as it gave futile chase.

The magnitude of what had happened settled in my brain and I began to laugh, kissing the Kalimba and placing it about my neck. What later became commonplace was then a brilliant and beauteous thing: to translate from world to world, to leave danger a immeasurable distance behind. To escape and stupefy my enemies. Ah, the glory. I had power unique amongst all the creatures of the dreamworlds.

My breath sparkled in the sunlight. My bare toes were ice. I walked hurriedly along the tree-shrouded path. An hour later I descended for the first time into Forgotten Town.

THE PARSON

E llie placed the book on the sculpted sundial. It must be afternoon. She'd never sat through a whole day before; she had always wandered. The book was the longest book so far and had completely absorbed her attention. She rubbed her eyes and stood up shakily. Her bruises hurt, but the feeling was bracing, invigorating. Could she still reach the library today? She wanted to know where Siana had gone after Forgotten Town. The holes in Siana's storyline were still so immense.

The sunlight had left. The statue above her didn't resemble the young woman she was getting to know. She piled all three books in a neat stack at the end of the bench. She thought of taking them with her, but decided not to. She left the Time Room, and to her surprise soon found herself jogging along. She was going faster than a slow walk for the first time, without conscious intention. She would reach the library for sure. It felt good, despite the pain of her bruises.

Until she missed the higher threshold lip of the Squares Room.

She called it the Squares Room because its floor was diagonal squares of emerald and black tile. The center of the room was a dais of white-flecked black marble, ten feet across. But today she didn't even see it. She had been looking across the room and into the long hall beyond, thinking of the library. The higher threshold of the room caught her foot and sent her pitching forward onto hard tile. She fell in a crumpled heap, slamming onto her right shoulder. She rolled onto her back and groaned.

A rustling noise yanked her bolt upright.

Someone sat on the dais, face turned away.

This was no ghost. Hidden by a dark cloak, the figure was bent over arranging items on the dark marble, oblivious to her crashing fall. It was the first time she had seen someone else within the castle—in fact, the first time in her dim memory she had seen anyone at all. What should she do? She was both terrified and elated by this unexpected company. She decided on caution. She stood quietly and stole out of the room.

Other doorways opened on the Squares Room. She found one from which the figure's face was visible and peered around the frame. Her heart fell. The young man's light beard was reddish. The cowl of his cloak fell away from a head of reddish blonde hair. He was studying his meticulous array of flowers and plants.

Her disappointment revealed how much she had unconsciously hoped for Siana, or some other character from the books. This man was neither. But nonetheless he was the first real person she could recall seeing. And he seemed unthreatening. His face was bathed in light, but there was no sunlight to account for this. He rearranged the bundles of twigs and flowers with a slow methodology that was calming to watch. She couldn't take her eyes from him, but she didn't know what more to do.

"You can come sit with me," he said, without looking up. "I know you are there."

She thought of Ghislain offering his arm to Siana atop Cylindrax. According to Siana's account the Aedolae was gentlemanly. Yet sinister. Could Ellie trust anyone in this world of dreams?

She walked, shy in her threadbare dress. He glanced up and smiled.

"Why is a young thing like you wandering around the heath, and what's more, without shoes?" he said with genuine concern. Despite his obvious youth (she judged him no more than thirty), his hair was already thinning. He had a broad nose and sharp dark eyes.

"What do you mean by heath?" Ellie said. Her voice croaked and sounded funny to her ears, rusty and broken. It didn't seem to belong to her.

The man squinted his left eye, a mannerism she found in the ensuing conversation to be a habit when he was considering things. He stood up and brushed dirt, fresh brown dirt, off his cloak. He wore sturdy sandals that enclosed his toes and wove up his legs to disappear under his cloak.

"If you aren't familiar with the word 'heath,' we could call it a moor, though it's really the wrong kind of soil for that." He threw his arms wide.

"But it's a castle," Ellie croaked, utterly confused. She stared at the variegated collection of vegetable matter at the man's feet. Where had it come from? And the fresh dirt?

"A castle?" the man squinted again, cocking his head. "You mean the ruins?"

"No!"—the testiness in her own voice surprised her—"I mean right here, the walls, the floor, the marble thing you're sitting on. Don't tease me!" Tears welled in her eyes. Why was he doing this to her? She had thought to trust him.

The man sighed.

"I'm not teasing you." He reached into his cloak and withdrew a hunk of bread. Ellie's eyes widened. He patted the marble next to him. "You do look hungry. I have more than enough bread to share."

She sat down, forsaking conversation to greedily devour pieces of bread he passed to her. Memories of food flooded her mind as she ate. After she ate every morsel, and he ate none, she blushed at her rapaciousness. The folds of her thin dress had accumulated a fair reservoir of crumbs.

"When was the last time you ate?" he asked her.

"I can't remember."

"What is your name?"

"Ellie."

"Nice to meet you, Ellie."

He offered his hand. She held it, feeling his calloused fingers, studying the dirt embedded beneath his nails, before she remembered to shake it.

"I'm Parson Graham. So tell me, Ellie, what are we sitting on?"

"It's a big circle, made of marble, a raised platform," she explained.

"Okay," he said in a measured tone. "What do you see around us?"

"I see a tiled floor, green and black tiles, and four walls, and there are six open doorways in and out of this room."

"I see," he mused. He scanned the room. "We have a conundrum, because I see us on a flat stone in the middle of the heath. Where you see doors I see standing stones, the last weathered remnants of a long forgotten building. I saw you running between them before you came to me."

Ellie knew the castle was a strange, but this was too much!

"Reason tells me," said the Parson, as if Reason were an old friend of his, "that you are insane, or hallucinating from starvation. But She also tells me that we never know the truth until we test things. I've found the world is often stranger than our expectations. So rather than arguing about the inconsistency of what we each see, let us test things out."

"Okay," Ellie said tentatively, still amazed that she was talking with another person, that she had eaten food. She didn't know what he meant.

The Parson stepped off the platform and crossed the room.

"Have I reached the wall yet?" he asked.

"Almost," Ellie replied, beginning to grasp his strategy.

"OK, tell me when."

She did, and then watched, shocked, as he proceeded to walk through the wall. A tightening circle of stone swallowed his back. Then he was gone.

"What did you see?" he yelled from the next room.

"You walked through the wall."

His face and chest emerged from the stone. "Well, we've established that what you see is not real to me and places no limitations on my behavior. It is very tempting to conclude you are crazy. And yet, we must make a further test." He returned and took her hand, leading her toward the same wall. He laced his fingers in hers.

"Tell me when we're about to strike it," the Parson instructed.

"Now," Ellie said. He paused then forced their intertwined hands forward.

She yelled as her fist struck the wall. His fingers slipped, carried by the momentum. They didn't stop until his arm was buried to the elbow in stone. She stepped back, knuckles smarting, feeling annoyed.

He circled behind her. He cupped his body around hers and moved her toward the wall.

"Close your eyes."

She obeyed, still trusting him, against her nervous system's better judgment.

A few seconds later, cold stone flattened her breasts and belly. The Parson kept pushing her until she was uncomfortably smashed.

"Ow!" she pleaded. He withdrew his weight. She turned to face him.

To her annoyance, he was grinning.

"I'm sorry," he explained, "but clarity is always worth a little pain."

"My pain!" she spurted.

"I'm glad you have a little spunk," he said. "You were pretty washed at first. We know now that you aren't insane or hallucinatory. I'm a strong man, and you are a slender and I dare say emaciated young woman. There is no way you could have resisted my pushing; a real wall was stopping you. With your eyes closed you didn't know exactly when or where to resist. Reason demands, despite the seeming illogic, that for you this castle is very real. This fact of the castle's existence, now that we have established it, explains other things."

"Like what?" Ellie asked. She sensed that this man might be an ally, perhaps even a friend, a thought which stirred her insides like the taste of food.

"Like the fact that your skin is dim and grey, despite the beautiful sunshine that is striking my face. Or that you stand in that dress, not acting cold, but it is approaching winter. It would explain the book that I found here, perfectly dry despite the rain."

"You found a book?!" she exclaimed.

"Yes, about the adventures of one *Siana*," he said. "I had to carry it a ways before finding a comfortable place to sit and read. It was a strange story, about things of which I have only heard rumors."

"Did it talk about Kadesh and the Traverse of Stones?" Ellie blurted out.

"It did." So the Parson had returned the book back to the library. But how had it gotten to the ballroom before?

Ellie spent the next several hours strolling between the Time Room and the library, talking with Parson Graham. His pace was reflective, even slower than she usually walked. Every so often he would and pull a sprig or flower from the floor. With amazement she would watch it materialize in his hands. They discussed the castle architecture as Ellie saw it; a few things corresponded to ruins the Parson saw, but most did not. Every so often they would lose each other as the Parson walked through a wall and Ellie struggled to rejoin him. He asked many questions and Ellie's heart glowed in the light of his attention.

Her courage waxed and she edged the conversation toward the subject of escape.

"If I followed you to the edge of the heath, or back to your village, perhaps I would be out of the castle and free," she suggested as they stood in the antechamber below the library landing.

"Perhaps," the Parson said, studying a long root recently pulled up. "But it seems equally likely that a wall that I cannot see would separate you from your freedom."

"But if it were the last wall, maybe some men from your village could come out and break through it," Ellie whined, feeling defeated.

"We can't attack what we can't see." The Parson met her gaze. His eyes were a gentle brown. "I know you are impatient, and rightly so. But what we have here is a *mysterium*. It is a puzzle to be solved by our reasoning powers, *not* by brute force. You need to regard Time as your friend and not an Enemy. Time is on your side."

Ellie squinched her face in disapproval.

The Parson stretched out one upturned palm. A splatter of water struck it and ran off his wrist.

"It is beginning to rain. I know you are tired, confused, afraid. But I think your *mysterium* is beginning to unravel. For example, I come here several times a week and yet you have never seen me before, nor I you. I think the worlds we inhabit are growing closer together. Be patient and do not rush the process of unraveling. I think you need to know much more before you get free."

As she watched, a driving rain enveloped him. He pulled up his cowl. It was bizarre, seeing rain splash against him and pool on the polished wood floor—but only seeing the drops after they made contact with his cloak.

"I have to go," he shouted against the storm, which she could not hear. "I just saw lightning flash on the horizon and this is no place to be in a thunderstorm. My wife will be worried already."

Turbulent emotion ran through her. She resisted the urge to seize his hands.

"Please, please come back!"

"I will come tomorrow!" he hollered, "and I will bring more food than bread. I will do everything I can to see you through this mystery!" He pulled his hood tight around his head. "Be thankful you are dry," he added with a laugh.

He fished in his pockets.

"By the way," he said, placing a dark something, cold metal, in her hand, "I found this a week ago. Perhaps it will be of use."

He closed her hand around it and turned to leave. A random thought struck her.

"Have you ever seen the falling houses?" she yelled.

"No, no falling houses."

He had disappeared through the wall. She opened her hand.

In her palm, begrimed with rain and rust, lay a giant metal key.

Back in the library, everything was the same: the statues, the little sitting area, the electric light with the first book she'd read lying beside it. Tomorrow she would begin another search: for what the key opened. But tonight (she could tell night was near) she wanted another book. Time was "on her side". She determined to be more systematic, to read the books in order if she could. She contemplated seeking the beginning of the narrative, or at trying to fill in the holes between the last three books.

I won't be that systematic, Ellie thought, *but I won't race ahead to the ending either. I'll make sure to find the book after her escape from Ghislain.*

That was harder than she expected. She tried to remember where she seized the three books the night before. She read fragments of paragraphs from various books and resisted getting sucked into any of them. There was a loose arrangement to the colors of the bindings, which led her eventually to the proper shelf. But it had no gaps where a book had been withdrawn. One book from this shelf described Siana wandering through a hedge maze in an empty, sunlit world. That wasn't right. On the shelf above she found a book about Siana leaving Ebon Port with Daevon. Well, that was too far forward in the storyline. At last she found a book that began:

I was still wearing Jacqueline's outfit when I returned to Ebon Port.

"Close enough," Ellie said out loud. She took the book and headed back to the Time Room and her bench.

WITH BIERCE

3.5 years before the Attack on Kadesh

I was still wearing Jacqueline's outfit when I returned to Ebon Port. One of the straps on the tank top had come loose and the thongs had long since disintegrated on the gravel road in and out of Forgotten Town. I didn't look like the Princess of anything.

I could have been in worse shape. Wandering the Town's empty streets was peaceful and stilled the terror of my meeting with Ghislain. And then the Archaic Garden was nothing but lazy sun-drenched afternoons, silence broken only by the buzzing of giant bees. But long solitude had begun to wear on me, as did the feeling of being lost.

I had gone back to the place in the woods where I had first entered the realm of Forgotten Town. Pressing the key for Ebon Port—using the Kalimba for the second time—I had expected to be translated there. Instead I found myself in an unfamiliar place: on a broad pavilion, its stones cracked by the passage of time.

Acres of gardens circumscribed this pavilion, comprised of a dazzling panoply of flowers, miniature trees and sculpted hedges—and statues whose features were worn to facelessness. Despite its stonework's hoary age, the Archaic Garden betrayed signs of careful tending, though I saw no gardeners during my indeterminable stay there. I explored all of it, finding it roughly oval in shape and surrounded by a tall wood. When I tried to pass through the trees into the murky darkness beyond, I found myself instantly spun about and coming back into the Garden.

There was no way out.

I contemplated returning to Forgotten Town but my resolve slipped as I sunbathed day after day on antediluvian benches. I worried I would lose myself here like I had in the floating Gardens of the Aedolae before. I pressed the key for Ebon Port again, to no avail. I positioned myself in the exact spot I entered the garden; getting out of the forest above Forgotten Town had required as much. But still the key for Ebon did nothing. I thought of pressing a different key but was too frightened. I wanted to get back to Daevon.

My way out ended up being the maze that lay within a square of exquisitely trimmed hedges. One day I found and passed through a small gap in these hedges. The labyrinth inside was vastly larger than the outside perimeter. I had nothing to lose so I wandered in the maze for what felt like a day, while the sun above never shifted its position. At last I came to a nexus at the center of the maze. With the inexplicable and sometimes elusive intuition of dreams, I knew I had found the way out—that using the Kalimba here would lead me to Ebon Port.

My first experience *between* worlds—with what I came to call Passages—had come to an end. Later I learned each passage had two points where one could enter or exit, depending on one's direction of travel—very specific, and sometimes very hard to find.

My finger hesitated over the key for Ebon Port. I was leaving a place of safety for imminent danger, returning where the story of my sorceries might jeopardize my life.

"Fuck Ghislain," I said out loud. "He won't scare me into choosing to stay here, another prison of ease and comfort." I struck the key.

Never did a portal open in a more convenient place. I had been afraid I would be dumped on the main street of Orse, or perhaps in the lair of the Spaerodont. Instead I found myself on a wooden terrace overhanging a courtyard. It was deep night, the heavens spangled with stars, the air cool and calm. A figure stood at one end of the terrace, stirring the coals of a brazier. I froze. He turned toward me, the faint orange light illuminating his features.

I recognized him at once.

"Daevon!" I cried.

"You have returned," he said, in my language of the waking world. He seemed not in the least surprised. What did it take to faze this man? "That is good, my lady." He was dressed in a linen shirt and trousers, and his black hair was braided about his face. He was exactly as I remembered. He crossed the terrace to me.

"You have grown up," he smiled, gently cupping my chin and tilting my face toward his own. "Still in one piece. Was my advice sound?" He led me to a bench tossed with embroidered pillows. I sat and he knelt facing me.

"It was good advice," I affirmed, but I couldn't begin to sum up my myriad adventures. "I learned many things and I got myself in a large degree of trouble. But everything I learn raises another question."

"Well, this is a good house for the answering of questions," he said as he looked me over. "Perhaps now you have a better idea what questions to ask." He had discovered the scar on my leg from the sailor's knife and ran his finger along it. "Was this part of the trouble?"

"Let's say in the last eighteen months I met a succubus, infiltrated the Palace of the Twins, eluded Achthroi at the Veil of Zoorn, got chased through frozen wastes by Coethyphys, got stabbed in the leg, met another xemenos in the Cylindrax Sea, met Ghislain in person, and figured out how to use the Kalimba."

"There's an eventful agenda," Daevon laughed. I found myself staring at his finely shaped face and lips. "Enough to exhaust a young lady."

He sat down next to me, placing his arm behind me on the crown of the bench. His persistence in referring to me as a lady—and his tone in general—betrayed more than a small measure of antiquated chauvinism. From what little I knew of the time period in our world he'd left behind, I could expect as much.

Discrepant with this decorum was his sitting two inches from me and running strands of my now long blonde hair between his fingers. That, I surmised, was roguish behavior.

"It was frightening more than exhausting," I said.

"Nothing to be frightened of, little Siana," he said, with a diminutive I wouldn't have accepted from anyone else. "This is about the safest place there is. In the morning, you shall meet my master, for he has already retired, and then there will be time for questions and discussions. I was about to go to bed myself. You must be very tired."

I wasn't, but he just smiled and scooped me up in his arms.

Consequently I first entered Master Bierce's house like a bride carried across the threshold.

So far my experiences within the Detheros had lacked the gauzy unreality of common dreams; instead they had been sharp, brilliant and—save for the power of the Eterokoni—entirely out of my mental control. But if I hadn't know that Daevon was a real man, a dreamer like myself, I would have thought this night, shrouded in starlit shadow, was such a dream. A dream conjured by the heart of a girl who had always longed for requited love.

He carried me down dark hallways to a small bedroom whose window opened on a steep precipice of jungle trees and a pschent of velvet night sky. He lit me upon my feet and I noticed, owing to the broken strap, Jacqueline's tank top had slipped and bared my left breast.

"Let me get you more suitable night clothes," Daevon said. "We have had female servants in the past." He had seen my nakedness and politely turned his eyes aside, without any show of embarrassment. Even-tempered in all things, as was his wont.

"No, don't," I said, touching his hand. He turned back and met my gaze. We each sought something in the other's eyes. And found it. He bent to kiss me, one strong hand placed gently behind my shoulders. It was our second kiss, this time not chaste and not short.

"Your hair has grown so beautiful," he said, stroking it where it splayed across my nipple.

All my life, I had never felt beautiful, only thin and awkward. I had argued with my full lips and large eyes in the mirror, thinking my features overbearing. But tonight I wanted this man, and tonight—in fact, for the whole of my stay at Bierce's—he treated me as if I were beautiful. I don't know if I ever came to believe it, but for now it was more than enough.

I slipped the other strap off my shoulder and the top fell to my waist. Daevon took me in his arms a second time and laid me on the bed, which received my body with divine softness. And then he enveloped me in his arms and I knew nothing but pleasure until sleep claimed me in the deep hours of the night.

The twittering of birds woke me late in the morning. The hot jungle sun traced squares of light on the bedcovers. I lay limbs akimbo, tangled in the sheets, so blessedly peaceful that I had no idea where I was and didn't care. I felt like I was back at home, awaking in the farmhouse, thinking I had missed the bus again. But then I realized the room was all wrong, and memories of our tryst crept into my blissful head. I sat up.

I wore a simple white nightgown. Oh yes, Daevon had put it on me, explaining the night would grow cold. At some point he'd left the room.

I left the room and walked down the hall, retracing Daevon's steps from the night before. I passed a number of closed doors and then found myself in the front of the house, a spacious quartet of intercommunicating rooms full of late morning sun. A bewildering collection of books, maps, artifacts and other curiosities were strewn across shelves and low tables. Bierce's dreamworld house was splendid, its Victorian-era architecture infused with innovations and beauties only possible in the world of dreams. Wraparound windows gave a panoramic view of the archipelago. In the sparkling water, far off, even now the Orsian craft returned from their long tour.

I would have been on one of those ships.

I jockeyed between two telescopes to an open doorway. Here was the terrace where I had met Daevon. Wooden steps led down to the courtyard. Birds of brilliant plumage hopped from benches to tables and scurried about; the air was full of their songs. Chrome flashed in the sunlight, for between the low stone wall of the courtyard and the press of jungle verdure stood a fence of slim rods topped with flattened metal discs.

Still in my dreamy haze, I picked my way down the stairs. Despite Daevon's admonition of coming winter, the day felt warm on my bare arms and legs. Next to the busyness of the birds, the two men in the courtyard were very still. I didn't notice them until I reached the bottom stair.

Daevon sat at ease on the right, and smiled broadly at me. The man on his left was overdressed for the weather. He glared at me from under bushy brows. His lush hair was curly but greying and I surprised myself by finding him exceedingly handsome. But his handsomeness was Daevon's polar opposite, stridently masculine and lacking Daevon's graceful beauty. Even sitting still, his posture radiated energy and imminent motion. And then he spoke, addressing his manservant.

"*What*, Mr. Endou," he said in a low but commanding tone, edged with irritation, "is *that*?"

"*That*," Daevon replied, clearly immune to his master's tone, "is our savior of the dreamworlds, Siana, Princess of Time."

"Pshaw," Bierce said, and returned his attention to the gaily hued birds, who crowded him fearlessly and took morsels of bread from his hand.

"Siana," Daevon said, "I introduce my master, Mr. Ambrose Bierce, Civil War hero, journalist and Prattler extraordinaire, lexicographer for the Devil, and victor over the scourge of mortality." He motioned toward Bierce with a sweeping gesture.

Bierce merely harrumphed.

I bit back laughter.

"Daevon, prepare our tea, and while you are at it, see that our guest is properly dressed." He gestured dismissively in my general direction. I imagined how I appeared to Bierce: a disheveled blonde rubbing sleep out of her unfocused eyes, bony knees poking out of a flimsy nightdress. Not a great first impression to make on a man of the Victorian age.

Daevon led me up the stairs with a smile, his touch light and sensual. A half hour later we returned with tea—and a different Siana. My hair was combed and tied back with a satin ribbon, and my body fully covered (and unpleasantly hot) in a heavy velvet dress. Now that I presented as a proper lady, Ambrose stood up and bowed stiffly.

"I am pleased to make your acquaintance, Miss..." He expected my last name.

"Um," I replied, feeling stupid, "it's just Siana." Bierce's eyebrows wrinkled, but he nodded.

"Pleased to meet you, Miss Siana," he concluded and sat down, returning to the map he had been perusing. Daevon filled the silence by serving me tea. Around Bierce all the small and silly awkwardnesses I had ever felt in the presence of perceived authority— principals, ministers, or whatnot—coagulated into a singular discomfort. He radiated the dignified confidence and brusque, masculine superiority of an earlier time.

The silence stretched for ten minutes, oppressively quiet save for the occasional twittering of birds still nearby. I would have loved to talk with Daevon, but sensed that wasn't appropriate either. Finally I could stand it no longer and surmised any tidbit of idle curiosity was a good place to start.

"Mr. Bierce," I said, hating the smallness of my own voice, "what are the rods in your fence for?"

He glanced up. "They are our first line of defense. When they sense the approach of hostile creatures they glow green, Achthroi or whatever else. Then we retreat to the house and augment the creatures' bodily composition with airborne metal. Most have learned to leave us alone."

"Here," Daevon said, placing a metal trinket in my hand, a diminutive facsimile of the discs atop the fence. "It will alert to you to the presence of Achthroi, wherever you are." I slipped it into a dress pocket.

Daevon turned to Bierce. "Master, you are not exactly playing the host today. This young lady comes from a future time in America. Perhaps, despite what I am confident is the enduring magnificence of your reputation, she knows little of your exploits. You are an engaging storyteller and it would benefit her to hear more about her host, and how we came here."

"I would love to," I said meekly.

Damn!

I was even sitting up straight, with my hands folded ladylike in my lap. Was there a feminine cultural subconscious that produced this kind of behavior, activated by the right attire and the right company?

Bierce preceded to speak at length, rarely meeting my gaze, or even looking my way. He was a strange blend of poise, power, and veiled discomfiture at my presence. But he *was* a good storyteller, and I learned a lot as the day passed into afternoon. About his military service, his long career as a newspaperman, about the corruptions—as he perceived them—of the society and government of his day. Uttered by a less capable speaker, Bierce's long monologue would have grown tiresome, grating on a teenager's ears. But waiting for his next witty or irreverent vignette kept me entertained for hours. And besides I had been a bookish child.

As the afternoon waned, it became obvious Bierce would happily fill more than one day's time with his stories. And he did. I spent hours in the courtyard over the next few days, hearing far too little about the world inside the Detheros. My timidity around Bierce, his artful domination of our time together, and his skill as a speaker kept me from pressing my own agenda. Then for many hours afterwards he would retreat, silently, into his own pursuits, toying with his instruments and maps, or reading by the fire Daevon stoked each dusk. Bierce so totally disregarded me during those times that I would have been lost as to how to conduct myself in the house without Daevon's steady presence beside me.

Bierce needed someone like Daevon to mediate his personality to rest of the world.

On the seventh day, I summoned the courage to interrupt Bierce midstream.

"You haven't told me how you and Daevon came to the world of dreams."

The three of us stood on the terrace, surveying the Sea. A cold breeze filtered my hair. Bierce stared at me with an inscrutable expression, then deigned to acknowledge my interruption.

"We found a portal in Mexico, a place once monitored by the Watchers in Silence. Through that portal, we passed bodily into the Fringe. We followed the threads of my old dream memories, for I have always dreamt ardently, even when I would have preferred not to. Those threads led us, in time, close to the Detheros, where the reputation of the Aedolae has escaped the barrier around their lands. I had heard rumors of glories missing from the Fringe, which seemed to me dim, chaotic, empty. We reckoned those glories lay further Within. So like your brother, we determined to pass the Detheros, to not be shut out by these Lords of the Night. And so we did."

Remembering my ghoulish passage through the Detheros, I felt, for the first time, a kinship with Bierce, a sense of common experience placing him, Daevon and me—of all the legions of humankind—in the same small company.

A company of which my brother was the only other living member.

"Isn't it risky to come totally Within?" I asked. "You have no waking world body in which you can reawaken."

"Of course," Bierce answered, "but I was an old man, tired of the world, even tired of myself. I had nothing more to lose. In this world, I have found ample compensation for the risk: if not eternal youth, a sort of eternal late adulthood." He laughed heartily. "Here I've had many years of contemplation and relative peace, wonders beyond any prior dreaming. It is Daevon who took the greater risk with more to lose."

"I wouldn't say that," Daevon broke in. "My adopted country was in turmoil. Bierce's offer of eternal employment in an exotic land was too good to refuse. I extinguished my waking self at the apex of my youth, so herein I get to enjoy the same forever."

I guessed this was a subject of past teasing. Bierce must have hoped the world of dreams would restore him to greater youth.

That moment sparkles in my memory. Ambrose and Daevon grinning, and the soul of razor-edged Bierce unveiled for an instant in the sun.

The moment didn't last. At nightfall, Bierce departed for Orse and then was away for a long month of exploration in the Summer Isles. At first I took his exit personally, thinking it connected to my brash interruption, but Daevon assured me not. Bierce examined the constellations for signs that such journeys would be fruitful, and the time was opportune. Normally Daevon would have accompanied Bierce on such a trek. I felt bad about that too, but Daevon quickly dissuaded me, using arguments other than words.

That long month sealed me as a woman. By day, Daevon shared mysteries from Bierce's researches and estate, and taught me sword-craft and martial arts. I threw myself into these physical pursuits with great abandon, soaking up his instruction, taking pride as my slender frame gained noticeable muscles. Our sparring by day (Daevon encouraged me to be ruthless) and our lovemaking by night formed a creative circle, each giving energy to the other. I was exhausted, I was blissful, I was loved, and I was beginning to feel both grown up and powerful.

He was a splendid teacher and I had fallen for him hopelessly.

Early in the month I inquired about the xemenos, wondering why I had not seen him around the estate. Daevon explained he lived with a sympathetic village woman who got some useful service out of him. That was enough for me; I did not want to repeat the pain of seeing a xemenos again.

When Ambrose returned, I was displaced as mistress of the house, my newfound rhythms blasted away by his forceful presence. With Daevon I could wake up and traipse about the kitchen naked, kissing him in the morning sun, rewarded with his magnanimous smiles. With Ambrose it was back to velvet dresses and tea.

The Summer Isles were usually a balm to Bierce's gruff personality. This time the trip did not go well. On Bierce's first few days back were several long colloquies from which I was excluded, with silence and dark looks in between.

The dark looks came from Bierce's discovery of both aspects of what Daevon and I had been doing to pass the time.

A few days after, his mood dissipated and Bierce began to talk to me again. But the tone hadn't changed. I was a lady, and he was entertaining and impressing me. I heard more of his story, but we never got around to talking about the Aedolae, the xemeni or any of the matters pressing my mind.

There came an evening when I couldn't take it anymore.

Twilight was earlier as the winter solstice approached, and snow drifted lazily down out of a darkening grey sky. I protested it shouldn't snow in the jungle, to which Daevon replied that my memories of December and my presence were influencing the weather. Bierce followed by asking whether it snowed in Washington in the waking world.

His question was a magnet for all my bottled frustrations.

"How would I know?" I snapped. "I dream to escape that world. I can't and won't think about it while I'm here. I hate that world, it is grey and dead like the sky. I'm not here on vacation, Mr. Bierce. I'm here to get my brother back and kick the Aedolae's collective ass."

Bierce stood at once, with bristling eyebrows and mustache, his body rigid with fury. But I didn't stay to see—or hear—more. I stomped off as unladylike as possible, and fled down one of forest trails to a little hollow carved out of jungle, where there was a different viewpoint of the great Edoi Sea.

Daevon was beside me in moments, touching my arm. It was cold away from the house and its coal-fed braziers.

I shrugged his hand away and turned on him hissing.

"You said this was a good house for questions. Well, it isn't. We're just having one endless fucking tea party."

Daevon grinned. I couldn't, even in that moment, hate him for it.

"So how do you *really* feel about it?" he laughed.

"Like I'm female wallpaper for the eyes—or ah, ah, an estrogen-endowed backdrop for monologues!"

"Unfortunately that's my master's default opinion of women."

"I thought *you* were chauvinistic!"

"Me!?" Daevon looked both shocked and amused. In fact, speechless, which was rare. Snow was collecting on the neckline of my dress and trickling beneath as it melted.

"I've been working on him," Daevon said at last, "in your favor. As best I can. It's been harder than I expected; I was never privy to how Bierce interacted with young women of his day. And I took the initiative to train you myself, to the best of my abilities."

"I know, I know," I reassured, "and I am grateful. But I need more than training. I need information."

"He has answered some of your questions," Daevon offered, but I could tell he misdoubted the comment even as he made it.

"Barely," I said. "He doesn't see me as any kind of equal or ally. He's not confiding in me. This isn't getting me anywhere. What do I do?"

Daevon put his arm around me. "Right now, come in for dinner before you freeze." Bierce's servant gently led me back.

What I did began that night as I undressed. And it led, in time, to a many unforeseen consequences.

Including Paris.

Daevon left me in my bedroom and went to join Bierce in quiet conference by the fire. I was relieved to get my dress off, despite the cold. No electricity here. Some impulse led me to the mirror. I surveyed myself in the light of the gas lamp. Shadows slumbered in the hollows of my body, and gathered about the Eterokoni around my neck, the tiny Kalimba and the curved black Torc. My eyes fixed on the Torc even as my mind lit upon an idea.

Usually the Torc transformed me in moments of duress or anger into otherworldly forms modeled by my immediate surroundings, like the cyclopean orange cats or the black-skinned Orsians. But that night before the mirror, the Torc responded in small, measured increments to the calculated intention of my thoughts.

I did my hair first, watching it recede into my head until I had short bangs, my ears showed, and there was fuzz on the back of my neck. Next I shrunk and drained my lips of color, and sharpened the contours of my nose. I shortened my eyelashes.

My eyes strayed down my body. My breasts, not big to begin with, disappeared into my chest, my nipples contracted. Waist widened, hips shrank, until the slight hourglass of my figure was gone.

My mirror-reflection twin smiled back at me with a wicked gleam in his eyes.

LICH OF A STARMAN

S leeping in the world of dreams is a strange affair. Mostly I do not remember having dreams within dreams. Sometimes I don't sleep but my spirit is liberated from my dreambody the same way it is freed from my waking world body to pass Within. Thus liberated, my mind wanders in a confused semblance of that part of the dreamworld in which I have fallen into a second sleep. But when I do remember dreams within dreams, they are vivid and portentous.

All three things happened that night.

After my time at the mirror, I fell exhausted into bed. I slept soundly for a while but as grey light stole in the window, I heard voices in the house, and I remember looking in on Ambrose and Daevon in the front room, though they did not react to my presence. They peered through the various telescopic instruments and pointed at something, a black shape winging about the island. Bierce sounded worried.

And then I was back in bed, dreaming dreams within dreams. This is what I saw.

• • • • ● • ● • • •

A dismembered skeleton freed itself from the alpine rock face that had been its crypt. It knit itself back together. I watched in horror as one hand reached for a leg bone and placed it in the socket of the pelvis. It had only half a skull, with ruby colored stones as eyes, one floating within the eye socket, one floating outside the bone where the skull was gone. The stones gleamed brighter than the sun. Its grin of shattered teeth was wider than a human mouth. One bony finger gestured wildly at my throat, at the Torc I had stolen. It had wings too, bones so narrow they were filaments, the wingspan immense.

The skeleton seized its other femur and hurled it like a boomerang. It smacked me in the stomach, tumbling me from my perch. I desperately grabbed for purchase on the stone, two fingers held, then slipped. I plummeted.

As I fell, glancing off the rock face of the pinnacle, knocked into open air, my mind fixated on the skeleton's wings, sketching onto that framework of bones leathery reptilian wings, grey-green skin. Then, recoiling at such ugliness, I drew massive feathers instead, gorgeously arrayed. There was an uncomfortable prickling at my back and an explosion of color at the periphery of my vision.

I had grown wings.

Arresting my fall, I beat my wings, turned about in mid-air, and alit safely on the ground. My tunic fluttered loosely about my chest, split and ruined by the massive appendages that had grown from my back. I tore it free.

· · · ● ● · ● ● · · ·

I sensed I was awakened by some noise no longer present. The house was silent now, and unexpected sunlight streamed through the window. I remembered my dream at once: a real memory of my discovery of the Torc, high above the Gardens from which Mercair had rescued me, floating above the Detheros.

That dream was of the first day I used the power of an Eterokon. My first transformation.

And to my surprise, last night's transformation—my mirror-twin brother—still stared back at me from the mirror.

To complement my new masculine appearance, I rummaged in Daevon's closets, patching together an outfit from a combination of his gear and the less demure outfits he had sewed me while Bierce was away. I was soon arrayed in my preferred black: stiff pants and a close-fitting shirt and vest that would not distract in a melee. There were no waves of blonde hair to tie back this morning.

I collected a few of the weapons with which Daevon and I had practiced. I determined to make a stunning introduction of my new mien to my chauvinistic master. I was about to head to the courtyard to find my host, when my quiet morning was blasted out of recognition.

From the hallway near the kitchen I watched the ocean-facing plate-glass windows explode. Something airborne, huge and black, tore through the front room and threw me aside in a maelstrom of objects and papers. I struck my head on a bookshelf and I must have blacked out, for I woke later to stillness and silence.

I brushed glass and dust from my black clothing and stood up. The windows were destroyed and a ragged line torn through the roof. A lazy breeze rustled strewn papers.

The metal poles surrounding the house glowed bright green. Sign of a hostile intruder.

Where were my hosts?

I grabbed a stout pole from Daevon's collection, strapped a scabbarded sword across my back and picked my way to the terrace. The courtyard was empty; one chair was overturned.

A clang of steel from the cliffs above the house.

Within the guarded perimeter of his sensor poles, Bierce maintains several garden spaces, claimed from jungle and flattened into wide earth shelves. I knew the way. I started up the path beside the house, noticing several trees had been shattered or sheared off. Had all this been perpetrated by the same thing Daevon and Ambrose had watched through the telescope at dawn?

Daevon shouted, something unintelligible, then groaned in pain. I raced up the last section of the path, a narrow stair of stepping stones. A line of trees hid the fight from view until I burst into its midst.

Bierce was backed against jungle's edge, waving a sword. Daevon lay crumpled in a heap beside him, surrounded by a litter of thrown daggers and abandoned nunchuks. I saw no blood but he didn't stir. And between me and the two men was a carbon copy of the opponent in my dream. Hearing me it turned its head.

The ruby eyes of a Starman's lich surveyed me with cold fire. The mouth of the shattered skull, hideously both humanoid and reptilian, split in a toothy grin. Bierce, seizing the opportunity of its distraction, rushed forward and slashed at its skeletal wings. One wing fell in an osseous rain. One of its hands was already gone.

I knew from experience none of this would slow it down. Memories of my fight with the Starman flooded my mind, the endless blows I dealt it in mid-air and its equally endless reconstruction of its own body, while I suffered more and more bruises and wounds.

It turned back to Bierce. I leapt forward, with the Torc adding superhuman spring to my jump. I plowed into its chest with the pole held before me and smashed it in two, passing straight through its broad ribcage. I rolled clear as the two halves of the skeleton tumbled down. The garden space was already demolished. My roll and subsequent spring to my feet had brought me even with Bierce. I spared a glance his direction.

"Who are you?!" Bierce demanded. His tone mixed outrage and relief.

"Don't you know?"

As he gazed into my eyes—still crystal blue—his face opened with recognition. I smiled back cunningly.

Back to work, and none too soon.

The top half of the skeleton sat in the middle of the garden like a scarecrow, severed spine now a pole rammed into the ground. It grinned and hurled its dismembered femurs at us. Bierce deflected one with his sword and staggered backwards. The other knocked me down. Its bones were heavy, quite effective weapons.

"What did you steal from it?" I cursed and got to my feet.

"Nothing I am inclined to return," Bierce said, "and nothing for which the dead have need."

I rushed the lich where it sat. Tiny wing bones summoned by the magnetism of their master glanced off me. I smacked off its arms at the shoulders, but its legs were already reforming on the ground.

"Toss the bones into the jungle," I yelled at Bierce. "Slow it down." Bierce immediately acquiesced, seeking out and flinging bones. I was impressed. My status had gone up a notch.

I tried to pin the unattached legs to the ground but they were too strong. One managed a well-placed kick that sent me sprawling.

"It's not going to give up!" I yelled at Bierce. "You'll have to return what you took."

"And give up a secret I have sought for years?" he replied breathlessly.

"Well then, we have only one chance."

"What?"

"Pull out its eyes."

Mercair had yelled me the same words of advice from the perimeter trail of the Gardens, a tiny figure far below.

The armless lich was back on its feet.

"RETURN THE TABLETS," its tongue-less mouth bellowed. I was taken aback. The last one had never spoken.

"Now you've got it worked up," I said to Bierce. "Here catch!"

I brought both my weapons down in the vicinity of its head. My placement was lucky. The skull came loose and rolled to the ground. I tossed it to Bierce.

The remainder of the skeleton would be doubly dangerous now. The wings flailed violently, and the wind from their strokes threatened to knock me off my feet. The arms, now reattached, groped viciously in all directions, bony fingers threatening to pierce me. I danced about to elude its blind mania, punching off stray bones and trying to chop off its feet.

Meanwhile Bierce struggled with the skull thrashing in his arms. He yanked out one ruby eye, but the remaining ruby was adequate to the task of animating the skull and skeleton. The chattering jaw seized Bierce by the hand and chomped off one finger, a finger Bierce is missing to this day. He screamed, and the skull bounced free.

On the ground, the skull traced a winding but resolute path back to its body.

"Do I have to do everything myself?" I shouted, knowing I was being juvenile and cruel, but feeling justified by my treatment at Bierce's hands.

Time to do something dramatic.

My mind remembered my transformation into a tree at Jico's outpost and willed my skin to the thickness of bark and my body to the heaviness of wood. With my heavy left hand I struck the thrashing Starman and stopped it in its tracks. I then hurled my full weight upon it, smashing it to the ground.

I had learned a thing or two since the Gardens.

The skull flew at me, but my wooden fist passed through and transfixed it on my arm. The shattered jaw chomped to no avail.

I plucked out the remaining jewel where it hovered in the empty eye socket and ground it beneath my feet. I let the lifeless skull slide off my arm.

It was done.

Bierce kept his feet, staunching the blood from his lost finger against his stomach. I approached him slowly, letting my body return. My hair lengthened until it flowed blonde behind me, and my breasts grew beneath my shirt. When I reached Bierce I was no longer his male rescuer, but the woman he had never really seen before.

"The Tablets," I said, "are on me, and don't you forget it."

"Apparently," he breathed heavily, "I have been a fool, Miss Siana. A damned fool."

• • • ●•● ● •• •

C hristmas was long past, and the remnants of my miraculous snow lay in drifts on the terrace and courtyard. Bierce and I had talked long and late again, while Daevon occupied himself reading a battered copy of Bierce's famous dictionary, interrupting us to read aloud what he deemed the more hilarious entries.

"—and in that dream I finally knew what the horse said," Bierce was saying.

"Listen to this one," Daevon interrupted from beside the fire. "*Maiden, noun: A young person of the unfair sex addicted to clewless conduct and views that madden to crime. The genus has a wide geographical distribution, being found wherever sought and deplored wherever found. The maiden is not altogether unpleasing to the eye—*"

"Enough," Bierce barked, jumping from his chair and taking the book from Daevon's hands. "Haven't you read the one that describes the author? *Lexicographer, noun: A pestilent fellow who, under the pretense of recording some particular stage in the development of a language, does what he can to arrest its growth, stiffen its flexibility and mechanize its methods.*"

Daevon rolled his eyes. Bierce flipped to a page.

"Ah," Bierce said, "here's one. *Loquacity, noun: A disorder which renders the sufferer unable to curb his tongue when you wish to talk.* Here's another. *Laziness, noun: Unwarranted repose of manner in a person of low degree.* Why don't you get more logs for the fire?"

He closed the book and threw it back in Daevon's lap. Daevon admitted defeat and went to fetch the wood.

I pulled the blanket tighter around my legs as Bierce and I resumed our conversation. I was dressed in my fighting outfit from the melee with the Starman, and Daevon had braided my hair tight to my head, collecting the braids in a ribbon at the back of my neck. I hadn't reenacted my transformation into a man, but I had been careful to keep my appearance as masculine and military as possible, attempting to divorce my image from the velvet-clad maiden of Bierce's courtyard soliloquies.

Bierce, even still, could not accept me as an equal. If there was such a thing as an equal in his mental landscape, Daevon was the only one. Everyone else was an opponent or an inferior. My particular rank of inferior, however, had evolved. Bierce now treated me as a protégée, and I preferred that to being female wallpaper. As a protégée, I had spent many hours by the fire and in the instrument room, learning from Bierce in patient, measured steps the sum of his knowledge, from both Without and Within. He was an excellent teacher, now that his heart was set to the task.

Tonight we were speaking of dreams.

"As I was saying," Bierce said, "that morning I finally understood the horse's words."

"You never understood them before?"

"I'd had this dream on a recurring basis all my life," Bierce answered. "The same wood, the same red moon shining low through the mists, the same landscape of cultivated fields and strange houses scattered through the mist. The same milk-white horse. And every dream the horse, to my horror, comes to me and speaks. I know it is English, yet I cannot process the words. And then I wake. All my life I felt that the consistency of this dream—in both its composition and its ubiquity—carried great import. But I could never grasp that import, or whether it was malevolent or benignant. Years ago I wrote about this dream prophetically, *'Perhaps some morning I shall understand—and return no more to this our world'*. I must confess, I went to Mexico with no clear idea what I sought. But I had a sense. And that premonition was fulfilled when after a long life of dreaming, and of dreaming this particular dream, the dream concluded for the first time. The horse spoke and I understood what he said. He told me about the portal in the Copper Canyon that brought us here. He was my Charon, ferrying my soul Across when, at last, it was time for me to go. I wasn't able to understand his words until I was fully done with the world."

"You are a real life Randolph Carter!" I exclaimed.

"Who is that?" Bierce wrinkled his formidable brows.

"H. P. Lovecraft's main protagonist. I stole my brother's Lovecraft anthologies when my mother wasn't looking. She told me it would give me bad dreams, which in retrospect is pretty funny. Anyway, you would like his work."

"Lovecraft?!" Bierce was incredulous. "The vexatiously verbose writer of letters to the editor?"

"Well, he isn't remembered for *that*," I countered. "He's considered the master of supernatural fiction now. Of course, there's Tolkien too."

"Who?"

"Let's not get into that."

Daevon had returned and stoked the fire.

I continued. "In one Lovecraft story, Randolph Carter dreams his way back into his childhood and disappears from the present of the waking world. In another, Carter journeys through the dreamworld in search of the gods. Amazing stories. Though Lovecraft didn't know about the Aedolae. You remind me of Carter because you have done the same, but for real. You did it before Lovecraft wrote his tales, and he never knew!"

My appeal to Bierce's vanity settled him.

"So who or what was the horse?" I asked.

"I have no idea," Bierce returned, "but I don't think he was a figment of my mind. Perhaps a shapechanger from Within. I have never found Herein that mist-filled scene but I did dream of the graveyard of Nathnang in great and accurate detail when I was a young man. We passed through it on our journey here, and every detail was the same."

"You used that in your story about Carcosa," Daevon observed.

"Back then you had no intimations about the Aedolae?" I asked. Bierce shook his head. "How do you feel about them now? They're your landlords, from a certain perspective."

"I haven't seen the others, but the Spaerodont is a damned annoyance. He broods over the Library of the Ancients and makes my research difficult. If the others leave me alone, I'm happy to ignore them and continue my business."

"But it's only a matter of time," I argued. I was pressing a sore point, but one too important to sidestep any longer. "Ghislain intercepted my brother at Ebon Port, somehow he has Coethyphys—or at least a few of them—on a leash, and he doesn't want us here. You are just sitting around waiting for the axe to fall."

"You can't take them down," Bierce contended. "They are too powerful."

"I can," I said. "I can and I will."

The crackles of the fire filled Bierce's silence.

"You saw what I did to the Starman," I pressed. "You are a gifted dreamer, Mr. Bierce, and you have discovered great knowledge. But something different was entrusted to my brother and me: the Eterokoni. You and Daevon both admit Timothy possessed an unprecedented number. You have seen what I can do with a few, and I intend to recover the rest. I intend to use them as they were meant to be used. As weapons—as *the* Weapon—against those who intend us harm. Do you disagree the Aedolae deserve this?"

My question was honest. Bierce knew far more than Timothy or me about the wonders the Aedolae had usurped. Part of me still doubted—and therefore wanted a watertight philosophical justification for the campaign to come. Perhaps some echo of Ghislain's condemnation lingered in my heart.

"No, I don't disagree." Bierce sounded uncharacteristically tired. "But this vendetta will change you. Right now you are a young woman, a dreamer. Do you want to become a vigilante?"

"I want justice," I replied.

"Justice is a word," Bierce retorted. "It lives in the minds of men until the battle starts. War is not justice, it is butchery."

I tried a different tack. "I have heard your story. You never let any kind of corruption go unchallenged during your lifetime."

"She's got you there," Daevon laughed.

Bierce looked annoyed. I was pressing my luck, pushing Bierce past our new roles of teacher and protégée, roles with which he was obviously comfortable. But I was young, and disdainful of Bierce's comfort.

"You've been here for decades and you've done nothing about them!" I scowled, with a not so military petulance. I read Daevon's resulting expression as: *I backed you up but give it a rest.*

"I'm retired," Bierce grumbled, without his typical ire.

"And I'm a fiery young blonde ready to kick Ghislain's butt."

"And I, Miss Siana," Bierce finished, studying the fire instead of me, "am just one old man."

THE ARRIVAL OF THE GAU

W inter passed to spring.
       In February I turned nineteen in the waking world.
I continued to revel in Daevon's instruction in combat. I was
joyous, my mind afire with new knowledge and the laying of
plans, plans conveniently divorced from their future enactment.
I became guilty of the same comfort I criticized in my host. I
purged such guilt by arguing I was learning so much I could not
possibly afford to leave. And besides, there was no sign that the
Aedolae knew I was there.

Bierce did not answer or address my accusations again.
However he grew more focused in his teaching. He would lift no
hand against the Aedolae, but he expanded our curriculum to
include topics of a military nature. He willingly let his academic
and pedagogical zeal overshadow my military intentions.

That way he could wax poetic, without his disdain for war's
lack of principle painting him a hypocrite.

• • • • • • • • • • •

O ne early morning I couldn't sleep and found Bierce
       reading a book from the waking world.
He put it down at once when I entered the room. This was
not typical.

I sat and pulled a blanket around my legs.

"Many empires and tyrants have assumed superior military prowess guarantees invulnerability, an assumption proven wrong on the field of battle time and again," Bierce expounded, as if continuing a conversation we'd already begun, "but unlike in stories, it is not the superior morality of an underdog that triumphs against empire. History is happy to smash such vanity and leave evil in power. Rather, the underdog's cleverness, his *strategy*, succeeds while his opponents drowse in arrogance. You must exploit this.

"Analyze the lay of the land, the field of battle, and determine those things, however few, that lie in your favor, and anticipate your most dreadful disadvantages. No specific engagement yet lies before you. But the principle is the same."

Here a more Socratic teacher might have asked me to lay out my advantages and disadvantages. But Bierce was no Socrates. He was happy to lay them out while I listened.

"The biggest advantage is that you can't, in the end, be killed. Your dreamflesh is a creation of your dreaming soul and its extinction leaves you intact. But that advantage is coupled with your disadvantage. For once you are killed Within, your dreambody is cast outside and you have to pass the Detheros again. If that crossing was hard before, in the wake of a confrontation with the Aedolae it would be far harder. You would return to find the whole battlefield arrayed against you.

"Your next advantage is your *de facto* invisibility. For months, the Aedolae haven't found you here. And the Eterokoni enable you to be a guerilla warrior, striking and disappearing. We need to hold onto that advantage as long as possible."

I ventured to interrupt, mildly, "Can we discuss each point before you lay out the next?" Bierce nodded. "What can we do about that first disadvantage?"

Bierce was quiet for a minute.

"There may be an answer. Things I have read suggest dreamflesh can be anchored to a particular location. Then, if the dreambody dies, the soul can rebuild the dreambody in that place. Deana the Semprite is said to have done this, many centuries ago, so when she left the world and came to the *Land Beyond the Bed*, she not only—"

I snickered and Bierce paused to glower. The quaint term was from his writings, he had used it before in conversation, and every time I thought it was damn funny. I'm sure he thought I should have outgrown the reaction by now.

"OK, OK," I said, hiding my smile behind my hand. "What is a Semprite?"

"Like Daevon and me, Deana came bodily Within, but she also achieved functional invincibility in the dreamworlds. She was killed many times by the Aedolae but her soul always found new expression."

"So where the hell is she now, when we need her?"

"That is an excellent question," Bierce said. "I have never met a Semprite."

"How did she do it?"

"She stole something from the Coethyphys."

"But you don't know what."

"No."

"And you don't know where the Coethyphys are either." I frowned.

"Remember," Bierce explained, "that the Aedolae are not gods. They didn't fashion their worlds *ex nihilo*. It is closer to the truth to say that they superimposed their worlds on top of what was already there. There are older places that lay just outside the Aedol Via, lawless and haunted. The Coethyphys, when they escaped Aedolae control, found plenty of lairs in which to hide."

I broke in, "Bottom line: I need to find whatever Deana stole."

"Not an easy task."

"If I could find the Coethyphys I could also find Timothy."

"Why do you say?" Bierce raised an eyebrow.

"Ghislain and Coethyphys were both there when my brother was taken. Ghislain didn't give me the impression he held

Timothy at Cylindrax, or he ever had him at all. He likes to keep his hands clean. No, I think the Coethyphys have my brother."

"Ghislain said that he lives? Coethyphys don't keep dreamers as household pets."

"Yes, Ghislain said he is alive."

"And you believe him?"

"Why would he lie? It would profit Ghislain more to say 'Timothy is dead, so get lost pesky dreamer'."

"I can't fathom what is in the self-interest, or self-*satisfaction*, of a being like Ghislain. Chances are his satisfaction lies in your torment. You know," Bierce said, touching my hand, a rare gesture, "what the Coethyphys were bred to do."

"I do."

"I have learned more since you first came to Ebon. I do believe your brother lives, but for a different reason."

"What?"

"The xemeni. A xemenos gets its form from a dreamer—that much I knew before—but it is also sustained by the life force of that dreamer, no matter the geographical separation. If your brother ceased to exist, so would his xemeni. Furthermore, the xemenos and the dreamer must be rejoined." Bierce said. "But the situation is complicated. I do not know what part of your brother lives in the xemeni and what part of him—if you are right—the Coethyphys have. I believe your hope lies in restoration: to save your brother, and bring all his sundered parts—the xemeni—back together."

"There is so much, Ambrose," I said, using his first name in the intimacy of the moment, "we don't know. I traveled with the Orsians to gain knowledge. And you have taught me so much. But is there no end to it? Will I understand what is needful before it is too late? I want to *do* something, not sneak about around collecting information."

"Siana," he returned, "you are on the fast track! I have gathered information for decades. You must be patient."

"But what do we do," I argued, "when despite all you know, you can't resolve my first disadvantage?"

The dawn's first sunbeam slanted across the scarred surface of his broad map table.

"We go to the Library," he said.

• • • ● • ● • • •

F rom both Timothy's journal and the Solmikaedis in the Fringe I knew of the Prism, taken by Kadesh within the Detheros. But there were other examples of Aedolae theft. In the twilight of the past, the Library of the Ancients had stood outside the realm of the Aedolae, tended by a long-forgotten race and drawing into itself the mysteries of a thousand worlds through its magical magnetism. Then the Spaerodont enveloped it and carried it to Ebon Port, thrusting it into the rock face of the dormant volcanoes above Orse, sundering it from those who sought its secrets. Enamored of his theft, he brooded over it like a medieval dragon sleeping on a carpet of pilfered gold.

Much to my disappointment, we didn't go until April, for despite its proximity Bierce had only gone there twice before. He had not relished the experience, and preferred researching in further flung locales, piecing together over years what the Library might have yielded in a day.

Bierce procrastinated until the Orsians were poised to leave their winter harbors for the Aedol Via once again. We hadn't decided if I would take passage with them again. I knew how to use the Kalimba, and disguising myself with the Orsians again would be perilous. But I didn't want to miss an opportunity. So with my time at Orse perhaps coming to an end, we finally undertook our expedition to the Library.

Bierce and I left before dawn. News of some commotion down in Orse drew Daevon away, so he didn't accompany us as planned. The jungle was quiet and the last shadows of night pooled between the trees. The way was strenuous; we climbed to the summit of the island, where it split into a line of rocky crags.

I had never been this far before. Bierce had affixed his warning discs about our wrists, as Achthroi were our biggest risk this side of the Library gate. Bierce had his six shooter and a knapsack of ammunition. I had a stout staff and Daevon's finest blade.

The path soon leveled off. Ahead the jungle verdure thinned and ended at bright sky. We mounted a stony escarpment above an ancient volcanic bowl, now overgrown with mosses, ferns and stunted trees. A jagged ridge flanked either side of the bowl; the leftward ridge glowed with impending dawn. Morning sun touched the treetops to our right.

And ahead of us the Peak of the Spaerodont brooded over the volcanic landscape. Wiry orange-barked trees like madronas grew along its face, willowy trunks forming a latticework of color against basalt boulders.

"Where are the Achthroi's caves?" I whispered.

"On the other sides of these ridges. None open into this valley, but there may be Achthroi about. The Library itself needs no protection; the Spaerodont is deterrent enough. No Orsian has come here for uncounted generations."

An icy thrill ran through me. What were *we* doing here?

"Where is the Library?"

"See the oculi?"

Guided by Bierce's gesture, I noticed flute-like spires, spectral white, many as tall as the trees, thrusting skyward amid the boulders.

"Those," Bierce continued, seeing my puzzled expression, "are part of the Library. The Library is alive. It is an entity, albeit an *architectural* one. Despite the Spaerodont's unyielding grip it struggles against its bonds. He submerged it in darkness, but it puts out oculi—penetrating the rock ceiling of its prison—in order to fill its interior with light."

"And where is the Spaerodont?"

"That is a harder question. Its bodily form is usually, as the occultists would say, *astral*. But all the same it's here. It slumbers, and again I say *usually*, during the days. So we must be out by nightfall."

"That is not encouraging," I said quietly.

"Remember that here you will see wonders few dreamers have seen. Fix your mind on that."

We waited until the sun filled the bowl with light. Bierce scanned the way ahead several times with his spyglass. His strategy was to wait until any Achthroi present at our first approach had time to find us. Better to engage them here, with an easy jungle retreat at our back.

When at last Bierce deemed our passage safe, we threaded our way through the bowl, a twenty minute crossing that felt much longer. After the cover of the jungle, I felt exposed and the twisting path led around blind corners where each time I expected enemies to pounce from behind the misshapen rocks. The air was stagnant and bitter on my tongue.

On the other side our trail gave way to volcanic scree and my shoes kept slipping. The day had grown hot, but nonetheless darkness clung to this side of the bowl and we passed openings in the pocked surface of the Peak that exhaled a tomb's coolness.

A black metal portcullis caged a semicircular opening in the side of the Peak. We had arrived at the gate.

With a self-satisfied smirk Bierce produced from his knapsack a giant key, carved from chalcedony. Finger to his lips, he motioned silence and turned the key in a lock to one side of the Gate. A tiny door opened in the immensity of that black metal cage. It swung aside silently.

We entered a grotto hewn from the living rock, overhung with ferns and littered with loose stone. Gleaming statues lay broken on the floor, cast from their pedestals. Each was of peerless workmanship, carved from onyx, marble, or single pieces of cyclopean ivory to represent beautiful creatures of the past, some hominid in form, some feathered. Their wreck was clearly deliberate, noses and arms shorn, faces disfigured. Their resplendence captivated me, magnified by their ill treatment to a grand and tragic sadness.

To the left rear was an aperture in the stone, just wide enough for us to pass abreast. The hallway beyond was a striking contrast: gloss-white and perfectly square, its walls perfectly smooth. On the left thick but clear panes of glass opened onto the bowl. This hall was full of morning sun.

And then we were inside the Library.

Grey darkness, as if the sunlight could not pass this point. A fan-shaped stair arced down to an expansive gallery. I hesitated but Bierce took my hand. The walls below were thronged with closed doors. A further row of doors lined the balcony above. No stair led to these.

A dome of lustrous white stone formed the ceiling, cracked in places and showed the black basalt of the Peak. A spectral white light illuminated the Library, dim and seeming to emanate from the white stone itself.

One moment the gallery was empty. Then a woman stood before us, several heads taller than Bierce and dressed in a flowing robe washed by the spectral light.

"Who is that?" I whispered, heart pounding.

"That is a Librarian," Bierce returned loudly, appearing to relish my discomfiture.

The woman glided toward us, no feet visible amid the swish of her garment. Her eyes were large and their outside corners slanted down. Her elongated face reminded of Daphne's but without cruelty. Her mouth was small and flower-like, with exceedingly full lips. Her whole appearance shimmered, like sunlight on waves.

"What do you seek, Master Bierce?" she asked, pursing the petals of her lips.

"The Coethyphys," he answered forcefully. The Librarian's high forehead wrinkled.

"Their room, even here, is dark with the shadow of their evil," she replied. "Are you sure, Master?"

"I am sure," he replied. The woman had not acknowledged my presence.

"I will have Mistress Zia guide you," she said. From amid the billowing folds of her robe, a small creature, also shimmering, fluttered on cherubic wings to hover in the air before us.

Her black hair was gathered in pigtails and bound with cords dangling flashing rubies. Her eyes were also preternaturally large and the irises glowed violet. Like the Librarian, the surface of her skin rippled like cool water, yet she was a splash of color against the Librarian's spectral white. She smiled.

Zia giggled a cherub's laugh, apparently unbothered by Bierce's intended purpose, and waved us forward with her pudgy hand. Her scarlet blouse and skirt were richly brocaded.

I shook my head in disbelief and whispered to Bierce, "Even if you had said the Library was inhabited, I wouldn't have expected *that*."

Zia was not my only surprise that day.

The Library seemed, at first, to have no books. Instead knowledge from the distant dreamworld past was gathered in every other conceivable form. Statuary. Relics. Tapestry. Items reminding of the Eterokoni, lining niches in the walls. Mosaics. Painted ceilings. Strange machinery. Raised on pedestals, devices resembling vehicles. A regular alternation of deep shadow and sunlight filtered and refracted down the oculi. The silence was broken only by Zia's occasional giggle (she never spoke) and our footfalls through ancient dust. Some rooms had been shattered by stalactites or stalagmites, forcing us on awkward detours.

Bierce said these were acts of aggression by the Spaerodont, attempts to pin the Library in place.

The Library had many levels, with many balconies and diminutive half floors beginning partway up the walls. We took a bewildering array of staircases until I had no idea if we were above or below the level where we started. I doubted I could trace my way back. In enemy territory, this struck me as a liability but Bierce appeared at ease.

Until Zia produced a skeleton key from the folds of her brocaded garment and opened an odd door on our left. It was at most four feet high. and set three feet above the floor in a featureless sweep of hallway. No seam had been visible until Zia engaged the key. Bierce raised a bushy eyebrow.

Getting through was awkward. A dark, short ramp led us upwards.

I gasped.

The corridor beyond was cyclopean in scale, flanked by Romanesque columns. Six to a side statues of white marble, eighty feet in height, dwarfed us. I knew them immediately, for the first on my left was Ghislain.

Here his face was empty, stone eyes hidden behind stone. I didn't know the statue opposite, a robed humanoid with both insectoid and avian features. The next pair were Iakovos and Ilanit, facing off, followed by Daphne and Kadesh, and the workmanship was utterly realistic. The next six were unfamiliar. One was fanged and slavering, striking me somehow as female. This one must be Iakovos and Ilanit's dark cousin Isabiel. Opposite her, shapeless and horrible, was—perhaps—the Spaerodont. The next four possessed an angelic beauty, unlike my impressions of the Aedolae. I must have been wrinkling my forehead in puzzlement for Bierce answered my thought.

"Legend says there were more Aedolae in the past," Bierce explained, "but several were murdered by their kin for opposing the ousting of dreamers. These"—he pointed at the angelic beings—"are likely some of them."

"One key on the Kalimba leads to Forgotten Town," I mused. "Could one of these have created that world before she was murdered?"

"A possibility," Bierce answered, "though I've always assumed that a demesne draws its power, its stability from a living Aedolae."

"Maybe it won't be Forgotten Town next time I push the key, if its Aedolae is dead."

"Also a good conjecture," Bierce replied.

Hours had already passed, and Zia's impatience with our talking was obvious. We moved on, descending.

We descended about six stories, via a series of ramps and stairs, arriving at a dark atrium whose black marble floor was littered with fragments of volcanic rock. Its warmth contrasted uncomfortably with the coolness of the rest of the Library. A dark, shining orb, like hematite, hung before us with no visible means of support, accessed by a quartet of ladders. Each ladder was carved from a single gloss-black stone. Zia motioned at the orb eagerly.

We took the nearest ladder, awkwardly tilted, making for a dicey two story climb. Our ascent terminated at a porthole. The inside of the orb was dark, thirty feet in diameter. Shelving displayed mechanical objects and books of a sinister appearance. On a lone pedestal at the center of the room, a huge tome lay already open.

This was the Chamber of the Coethyphys.

The light within was adequate but had an unholy feel, like a black electric light's distortion of color. The tome was lit by a white spotlight that lacked a discernible source.

Bierce closed the book to survey its cover.

Of the Transformation of Fedosei and the Rituals of the Coethyphys.

Bierce reopened the book and read. As the afternoon wore away, he scanned its water-damaged pages and read aloud the salient parts. Soon we had learned more about the dreamflesh eaters than any mortal man or woman.

The *Fedosei* of the book's title had been an Aedolae, doubtless a being represented by one of the five mysterious statues. He was slain in cold blood, his spirit doomed to wander the chaos of unshaped dreams. He strayed long in unknown places, refusing to be extinguished, hatred rankling. After long years, he found a vessel, a body to inhabit.

He took possession of a Coethyphys body, reshaping it in his own image, but the Coethyphys body in turn shaped Fedosei's spirit, twisting it until only will and cunning and a long hunger remained. He drew to himself the other murdered Aedolae, and they too took Coethyphys form. By virtue of their power and intelligence, they mastered the other Coethyphys and became their lords, a *de facto* dominion unsanctioned by their Aedolae creators.

"Have you ever heard of this?" I interrupted.

"No, I have not," he replied, clearly fascinated.

"Timothy hadn't either," I added, thinking of the journal even now tucked in my pocket. Bierce continued.

Fedosei built a grand castle for the Coethyphys, who were exiled and plagued with starvation. He and his fellows were its lords, and he gathered the Coethyphys to live in its bowels. And he developed the Feast of Millennia, to satisfy the hunger of his charges.

"What is that?" I wondered aloud. Bierce flipped pages hungrily, questing for an explanation. I drummed my fingers on the pedestal, and Bierce scowled me into silence. I didn't have to wait long.

"Essentially," Bierce explained, "Fedosei found Deana's secret, or rather she found his: the secret of anchoring. Listen:

The priest then removes the outer fingers and toes from the aliment, and encases them in the hermetus. With these trapped within the hermetus, the aliment is bound to the temple of the Coethyphys and its psyche must return to regrow the alimentary body, again and again. Thus the aliment becomes a source of eternal—not transitory—nourishment. To safeguard the equitable distribution of the precious sustenance, the priests of the Coethyphys codified its consumption in a ritual of thanksgiving in which the aliment is vivisected and rationed amongst all of the eaters. This is the Feast of Millennia, in which the Coethyphys en masse celebrate the timeless resolution of their hunger and are elevated from carnivorous assassins of the Aedolae to a race of purpose and beauty."

"I've seen Coethyphys," I commented, "so fuck that. What kind of propaganda is this?" But my bravado didn't exorcise sinking feeling in my gut. I knew what *aliment* was. It was Bierce, it was Daevon, it was me. "So they eat the dreamer, the dreamer wakes up, the dreamer dreams again, and the hermeti pull the dreamer right back to the site of the Feast."

"Precisely," said Bierce.

Not only was the *aliment* me. It was Timothy.

As if reading my mind, Ambrose said, "We can only hope the Coethyphys do not in fact have your brother."

Despite my dread—or perhaps because of it—my mind was busy puzzling things out.

"Does this have to do with Timothy's disappearance from the waking world?"

Bierce pondered. "I've read of dreamers who had run-ins with Coethyphys and refused to dream again, using drugs to block their dreaming. A dreamer subject to this Feast would have even more reason to do so."

My mind raced. "So that could have been the goal, to circumvent my brother's escape route. To take him out of the world, to trap him in a dream of endless death and rebirth."

"Yes," Bierce agreed, "to achieve endless regeneration at the site of the Feast, with no waking up or drug-induced dreamlessness to interfere."

"Would that work?"

"Who knows? It was likely a gamble, a conjecture of Ghislain's."

"Why would Ghislain help the Coethyphys this way? Wouldn't a singular brutal dying be deterrent enough?"

"I do not know, but I'm sure his cooperation is not a good sign."

We fell silent. The air was still and oppressive. Inside the orb time was impossible to gauge so Bierce consulted his pocket watch. It read two o'clock.

"Keep your mind on strategy. You will have time later to think about your brother. We know now what Deana did, and we know what you need to do."

"Which is?"

Bierce studied me as if disappointed in the results of his tutelage.

"If this is Ghislain's experiment you will be next. You must anchor your dreamself somewhere. This might block their machinations, should you come under their power. I cannot say what would happen if your dreambody were anchored in two different places, but it is your best hope. And it has another advantage: this anchoring will keep you Within the Detheros, where you belong."

"You're telling me to cut my pinkies off!" I made a face at him.

"Credit that idea to our friend Fedosei here," Bierce shot back. "In any case, that's the easy part—"

"Easy for you," I interrupted, knowing Bierce hated interruptions.

"We need to find a hermetus. And I doubt there's any special magic in your pinkies. Anything will do."

"Hair?"

"No, I'd say not essential enough."

"Which one of your body parts would you do without?" I argued, poking him in the shoulder with my staff.

"I'm old, I could spare a few," Bierce returned, unfazed, still reading. "I have already lost a finger to a skull someone tossed in my lap."

"I'd like you to lose your mouth: so good at giving masochistic advice."

"We better get to work." Bierce pointed out a detailed illustration of the hermeti.

We ransacked the interior of the orb for an hour but had no luck finding a hermetus amid the shelves' sundry gadgets and items. Zia flitted in and out occasionally, and scowled at us if we left a shelf messy. She merely shrugged her baby shoulders at the illustration, as if to say, *I have never seen such a thing.*

"Just take us to the most likely place," Bierce instructed, "wherever that might be."

Zia nodded.

We left the orb and retraced our steps to the main part of the Library. Zia's agitation at the subdued light in the Hall of the Ancients was palpable. According to Bierce's pocket watch the day was already growing late. A question nagged at my mind.

"How is it the orb of the Coethyphys has information about things that happened after the Library was brought here?"

"There are still Librarians here, despite the Spaerodont," Bierce answered, "and the Library, though crippled, continues in its purpose, drawing all information to itself. The *how* of it I do not understand."

"How can we find a hermetus outside the orb? Why would the Library have one?"

"It may be a long shot, but the Library follows its own logic. It has many things it should not have. We can hope one is here, because if you get close enough to Fedosei to steal one, at that point it's probably too late."

Guided by Zia's guesswork, we spent several more hours rummaging through a wide variety of rooms.

"Will they let us take it?" I asked at one point.

"That's a good question," Bierce confessed, "but let's find it first."

"What time do we need to be out of here?"

"In about an hour," Bierce answered. His watch read five o'clock.

I wish I'd had more time in that wondrous place, and that the end of the day had been more than a mad rush against time. I was forced to tear my eyes away from a thousand curiosities in those last hours, some gorgeous, some fascinating, many both. Later in my travels I tried to recreate some in the margins of Timothy's journal, but I found both my memory and my skill unequal to the task of resurrecting such hastily apprehended beauties.

In one room lay specimens of a bewildering array of dreamworld races, preserved in somnolent stasis. In another chamber, low ceilinged, a score of spectral women sat at weathered wood tables inscribing exquisite books. I couldn't tell if they were living or ghosts or whatnot; they took no notice of me as I moved among them. Their faces were impossibly ancient.

Zia led us in a circle about this chamber, through a series of rooms containing religious and ceremonial artifacts. The (lack of) light had grown difficult.

"Um, what happens," I asked Bierce, "if we are still here at night?"

"The Spaerodont becomes wakeful," he answered, "and that is not good."

He said no more, but kept to our task.

I glanced back into the chamber of the ghostly clerics. They were closing their books with great ceremony, laying them at precise angles on the surfaces of the tables, peering into the adjoining rooms with a guarded attention they had entirely lacked before. Then they stood and gathered up their robes. Zia, flitting in and out of the inscribing room, took this as a sign. She tugged at Bierce's pant leg. He paid her no heed, up on a ladder and engrossed in a shelf. I was having difficulty concentrating, instead watching the women file out into unseen hallways. Soon the inscribing room was empty and still, and as if on cue, a deep shadow fell on it.

"I'm on to something here," Bierce said. With some stiffness he climbed bodily onto the cyclopean shelf. I figured he knew what he was doing and would ask for my help if needed. So I paced the floor below.

Three things happened at once.

1) I chanced to glance upward and found myself looking through an oculus at a completely dark sky. A single baleful star gazed down the tube. My sudden perception of darkness and the cold brilliance of that single night star combined to produce in me a horrible prickling fear.

2) Bierce shouted out, "Found the buggers!" and hoisted aloft several small objects, glinting faintly bronze.

3) The entire Library rumbled with thunder.

"It's night!" I shouted in panic. Bierce, crouching on shelf's edge and shoving three hermeti in his knapsack, pulled out his pocket watch. He grimaced. I climbed partway up the ladder. The face of the watch still read five o'clock.

"Damn thing," he sputtered, "it hasn't failed since the day I bought it in 1879."

"I don't think it's the watch's fault."

Rushing down the ladder, I found Zia was gone. Well, at least we wouldn't have to explain our thievery.

The floor grumbled and shook, knocking me off balance. A dim phosphorescence clung to the floors and walls, but I sensed it faded, slowly but undeniably.

"Come"—Bierce grasped my arm—"I think I know the way."

Thus began our wild race out of the Library of the Ancients at night. As we ran, the phosphorescence continue to fade and I had the stifling sense of a great weight pressing down from above. Whenever Bierce paused at a junction, I found myself watching the ceiling, reassuring myself it wasn't dropping closer. Nonetheless my spine felt compressed by freak gravity.

Next stalactites and rock chips began falling, striking the slick stone floors inches from our bodies. We ran as fast as we dared. A sudden, *sentient* malevolence eclipsed the Library's grandeur; the shadows in the niches and adjacent rooms *watched* us, commanded us to freeze or stumble. The Librarian and Zia were nowhere to be seen, and I had the weird apprehension they no longer existed, not in that moment of evil.

It was nearly pitch black by the time we reached the last rooms. A sickly green light traced the razor edges where walls and floor met, and clung to the frames of doors, but did nothing to illuminate our path: an architect's blueprint in phantasmagoric *3D*.

I wondered if the overshadowing of the Spaerodont was slowly poisoning the Library's soul.

The stone floor of the gallery where we had first met Zia split like plates of ice. We hopped as best we could from plate to plate, straining to keep our balance as we made for the stairs.

As we mounted the stair, it splintered behind us. We rushed through the square hall and into the grotto. A gelid breeze from the bowl of the extinct volcano refreshed our lungs. The air of the Library had grown stiflingly close.

Then an arm from one of the deposed statues flew past my head.

"The key!" I shouted. Bierce fumbled in his pack.

With an eldritch creak another statue broke from its base, and was hurled at us by an unseen force. It missed us but left a broad oval indentation in the metal bars of the portcullis. Bierce was now unlocking the small door. We rushed through, panting, and crushed our aching bodies against the firm stone of the mountainside below the Gate.

Below us we saw, by cold starlight, the rustling, clicking bodies of a hundred Achthroi filling the bowl.

"Damn," Bierce commented.

"I'd fly over," I said. My brain was numb from our mad flight. "But you can't and I'm not confident I can carry you."

"Then through them we go," Bierce said with steel in his eyes.

"Wait. Let's try this first." With one hand I touched the Torc, and with the other reached for the Star in my pocket.

I became an Achthron.

Bierce recoiled. I suppressed a smile. My gash of a mouth wouldn't have accommodated a smile anyway. I pulled Bierce's hands behind him and pressed them together as if bound. I marched him down the hilly path.

At the bottom several Achthroi congregated in shadow. Each different—as was the way with their race—each hideous. Most had some form of antennae and were eagerly touching them to mine. A grotesque electricity ran through my transformed body. The Star struggled but managed to convert the impulses into some form of crude language.

"Are there others of us up in the Library?" they said. *"There aren't supposed to be."* Their primitive electrical thoughts conveyed confusion. I focused my desire to speak commandingly in the Achthroin tongue on the Star. Electrical impulses flowed from my antennae. My beak clacked.

"I am taking this prisoner to Him, on his orders," was what I attempted to say.

"Let us escort you," they said obsequiously, eager to please Him. To my discomfort, they crowded in, forming a circle, and I heard not only the incessant clacking of beak-like maws but the same sniffing I'd heard when I had eluded the Achthron at Jico's as a tree. The sniffing worried me.

Two thirds of the way across my ruse began to slip.

The Achthroi crowded closer. The Star translated expressions of distrust and alarm. Their clicking grew louder, and they halted our forward progress. Most turned to face us, antennae touching furiously. Jungle was just ahead. Bierce released his hands from my fake bonds.

"This resolves a mystery," he whispered. "I should have figured it out sooner: Achthroi scent dreamflesh."

Bierce reached in his knapsack. I transformed and drew Daevon's sword. The Achthroi howled and clicked. My sword found purchase in flesh. The report of Bierce's six shooter reverberated off the Peak of the Spaerodont. A wall of fangs and claws lunged at me. Soldiers take for granted opponents having fixed proportions, two legs and two arms. Achthroi are harder. There is no fixed form in their biology. Six arms or one. Eight feet tall or four.

More Achthroi rushed, some coasting down on grasshopper wings that folded into insectoid carapaces at their backs. I guarded Bierce as he reloaded.

"We must attain the hill. We can't beat them all," Bierce huffed. I brainstormed what might scare them off, buy us time. I had no idea.

The coming of the Spaerodont spared me the effort. Shadow pooled in the sky above the Library. It extinguished the light of the stars as it spread. The dread I felt inside the Library returned. The night sky vanished behind a deeper darkness. The Achthroi quivered and cowered.

"This is our chance," Bierce whispered. We ascended the remaining distance, as I boxed away unmoving Achthroi with my staff. What I can only describe as silent thunder shook the world behind us. As we reached the escarpment, the air tasted bitter. Lightning ripped into a tree ten feet away, reducing it to flying shards.

"Shit!" I cursed.

We raced down the trail, hearing trees explode behind us. The jungle cover must have foiled Him, or perhaps He did not stray from His home. After ten minutes of dark, downhill stumbling, all was silent. In our haste we had made it half of the distance of the morning's climb.

Daevon found us pausing to rest at a junction between two trails. The disc at his wrist glowed faintly.

"We can't return to the house," he said. "There have been Coethyphys in the village and the jungle teems with Achthroi. The Coethyphys were on the move uphill last I saw them."

"What do we do?" Bierce asked.

"We get her out of here," Daevon answered, placing his arm behind me. "Master, a Glowship has arrived. It's docked at Jico's."

Bierce's eyes went wide, clear even in the inferior light.

"What is a—" I began but Bierce interrupted.

"Perfect," he said. "We put her aboard. That solves the problem of her taking passage again with the Orsians." They must been discussing this out of my hearing.

"Master," said Daevon, "we should go. Think of the opportunity!"

"No," Bierce dismissed.

"Master," Daevon implored, "you have heard Siana's arguments, her challenge that you get involved. Traveling aboard this Glowship would be a safe way to abet her mission, and to see long denied wonders. When were the Gau last seen here?"

I could hear Bierce's scowl in the dark.

Daevon continued, knowing Bierce's objections before he had a chance to voice them.

"Ambrose, where does knowledge reside? Only in your charts, your maps, your books? They'll be safe while we are gone. Is knowledge also in your mind and what you apprehend with your own two eyes?"

"My old two eyes."

"Not too old for the Summer Isles. Not too old to dare the Library for her."

"But the Tablets—"

"Curse the Tablets. They'll still be here when you return. The Achthroi won't pilfer such things. Regardless, I go with her."

I had never heard Daevon speak with such force.

"I forbid it," Bierce barked.

"Then release me from your service. Master, we are running out of time. I *will* see her safely away."

"Cursed woman," Bierce directed at me. "All women are the same in the end, addling a man's wits." Nonetheless he sounded defeated. He loved Daevon, and I forgave him his words. I was shocked at the depth of Daevon's commitment to me.

"Master, release me or don't," Daevon said. "I don't care. You know I will return to you. But will you go with us now?"

Bierce was quiet a long while.

"I will not," he said. "I am not ready to leave my things behind." He pulled two of the hermeti from his sack and handed them to me. "If Coethyphys are here, then the Aedolae know she is here. I don't know what evil that portends. I wish you no ill will whatever you decide. But neither do I release you. Rather I charge you with the care of this young lady, on your life. And I charge you to return by the time the Orsians complete their tour again. Now go! I can take care of myself."

Thus my first association with Bierce ended with this unexpected magnanimity.

Daevon and I plummeted downwards in the dark, speaking little, listening for Achthroi. Where the trail allowed, Daevon held my hand. We arrived at Jico's outpost without incident and I thought of the day I eluded the Achthron as a tree. A lantern burned in Jico's shack. But the light from the pier below caught my eye instead.

A beautiful craft, every surface illuminated, was moored at pier's end. As we dropped from the ropes to hard-packed earth and descended rudely constructed stairs, I realized the ship was tethered to—and hovering above—the aging pier. Lanterns shone from within round glass bubbles along its hull. The craft was metal, but its workmanship was exquisite rather than utilitarian, light splashing off curved and filigreed surfaces—gold, silver, and bronze.

Jico stood beside it, talking to a tall creature with a gecko's paws, marmalade skin, and a face both humanoid and equine. Its clothing resembled phosphorescent moss, with trappings of metalwork similar to the ship's. It folded its hands (paws?) together and bowed to us.

"You have brought her." Its tone was airy, its Orsian perfect.

"Yes," Daevon replied, "may we both take passage?"

"Of course," it replied. I decided it was female. "All seekers of truth are welcome." Apparently we met that criterion. She beckoned toward a woven ladder depending from an open porthole. Our invitation was that simple and soon we were closeted within.

The interior of the Glowship was even more amazing. At the center of the craft, visible from every common area, was a complex globe of machinery, a 19th century inventor's dream, all gleaming gears and oscillating pendulums, woven into a single mechanical sphere and encased in thick but entirely transparent glass.

"This is our mechanism of transport," the creature explained. "We read the magnetic patterns of the ground, water and air and magnetize the body of our ship to either repulse or attract." I hadn't paid much attention in science class, but my waking world brain protested this explanation. Oh well, I was in the dreamworlds now.

Fantastically detailed maps adorned the interior walls of the Glowship, rendered in raised strips of colored metal. Soon other Gau—the equine beings—filled the room, crowding about me, some of both genders.

There was a commotion outside. A whizz of arrows. Through a porthole, I watched Jico's longbow pick off Achthroi who tried to gain the pier. Daevon spoke quietly with a different Gau. The ship began to move, utterly fluid and smooth.

We flew over the pier and toward Jico's, flying low to scare the Achthroi away. Daevon struck several with crossbow bolts fired through a window. They scattered as we banked and headed out over open sea. The dark silhouette of Ebon Port gradually disappeared into night at our back.

We were away. Daevon sat on the floor and I nestled in his arms, sighing relief.

THE MIRROR ROOM

E llie had drowsed through the final pages. She shook herself awake. She forced herself to reread the end carefully. By the time she was done, the Time Room was shadowy and the night was late. She fell asleep on the bench nearest to the statue of Siana.

And dreamt.

· · · · ● · ● · ● · ·

S iana was in the Glowship, moving through a belt of floating island rocks like Mihali, numerous but not nearly as big. At sunset they tethered the Glowship to a smaller rock.

In Ellie's dream, the ensuing night was a feeling, a moment of darkness, and then a flaming white sun rose from the nebulous gases below. All was silent and still.

Until a small Orsian craft, propelled by balloons, stole around the edge of the rock and bore down on the Glowship.

A trio of grappling hooks whistled through the air, bright metal flashing, tearing at the filigreed workmanship of the Glowship's hull. Fierce men, some Orsian, some light-skinned pirates, hauled on the lines and pulled their craft abreast.

Ellie's dream consciousness moved inside the Glowship, where echoing thuds from the hooks' impact roused the Gau. The butt ends of spears smashed through portholes, pried open doors. In the main room where the magnetic mechanism of the

Glowship was housed, Daevon and Siana sprang awake, looking as Ellie imagined them from the books. The Gau, an unmilitant race, were thrust aside or slain as the pirates crashed in.

Ellie knew Siana was their target.

Daevon and Siana were the nucleus of a ring of flashing blades, their own swords whirring and clashing against the steel of their adversaries. Ellie watched with horror as Daevon's blade clattered across the floor. Daevon crumpled, clutching his chest.

Siana fell upon him, turning over his bloodied body. The pirates stayed their attack as Siana held him, slowly closing their ring tighter.

Siana screamed in anguish as she released his body, and in the same movement, flung a trio of daggers secreted from his person into her adversaries. One howled in pain. Siana was on her feet, sword slashing wildly. She boxed away a man to her left while running through a man to her right. She spun with elegant precision, engaging men on all sides, anger and anguish making her deadly.

But they were too many, and Siana knew it. She reached for the Kalimba.

A shimmering halo rent the air, and Siana dove through. As it closed an Orsian pirate lunged after her. Then the portal closed and Ellie's consciousness was outside the Glowship again. Sunlight glinted off its ruined surface as it listed to one side and bumped against the stone walls of the island. There was that weird calm that has reigned after battle since time immemorial. Siana's absence from the scene was a palpable feeling, a great emptiness. Ellie imagined Daevon lying crumpled on the ship's floor.

· · · · ● · ● · · ·

E llie awoke to morning sunlight, tears coursing down her face.

How could he die? she protested. *Siana's beautiful lover can't be dead!*

Siana mentioned the pirates' attack briefly in the second book Ellie read. Neikolan had followed Siana through the portal to the forest above Forgotten Town. That same book chronicled her finding the Eterokon of Time.

Why hadn't Siana mentioned losing Daevon?

Maybe she didn't lose him. Maybe I merely dreamt his death. Siana didn't mention him in either of the first two books. But he still could be alive. But why would I dream his death?

She had no answers to any of her questions.

She moped about the Time Room long into the morning, dwelling on the vividness of her dream. It might not be true, but nonetheless she ached for Siana and burst into tears again and again. The tragedy of Siana losing Daevon was too much. She tried to reason herself out of her emotions without success.

Around noon, she heard a footfall outside of the Time Room, just as the sunlight struck the sundial on the statue. Her red-rimmed eyes met Graham's kind face.

"Are you alright little miss?" he asked. "Have you been hurt?"

She shook her head, feeling young and foolish.

"I was grateful I could come today," Graham explained. "To my surprise, the morning clouds cleared." A radiant halo of light surrounded his face, even though that part of the room lay in shadow. "I packed for two today. I brought you food from my garden."

Graham smiled, and she smiled back through her tears.

Pocketed in Graham's cloak were red apples, crisp and juicy. A dim memory of an apple tree beside an old house surfaced as she ate. But the memory refused to yield more, and soon faded, evanescent. Juice ran down her chin, and her eyes cleared. The Parson was staring at her. She wiped her face with the back of her hand.

"Do you want to tell me why you were crying?" he asked.

"A dream I had, about someone very lovely and good, and they died. Can we not talk about it?" Tears threatened again.

"Certainly. Why don't you describe the room we are in? That will take your mind off the dream."

Graham listened intently for someone who didn't share her vision and could have dismissed the results of the exercise as unimportant. Graham processed everything with a thoughtful, measured intensity.

"Do you still have the key?" he asked, as she abandoned the endeavor for another round of apple consumption.

"It's on my sleeping bench," she said, and went to fetch it.

"How does one pick a bench to sleep on?" Graham laughed. "Something special?"

"It's the one closest to the statue, that's all. Nothing special about it. Here it is." She held up the key.

"I'm curious about this key," Graham said. "Unraveling a mystery is a series of small discoveries, so let's put all that good apple to work"—he patted his own belly—"and find out what this key is for."

Once they set themselves to that task, the castle presented an endless series of doorknobs. None of which sported a lock. She had never noticed that before.

The Parson's thoroughness both calmed and annoyed her. He wouldn't let her rush to a new room without checking everything. Since he couldn't see the castle, this kept them in constant dialogue and she had to describe everything. But he insisted the only way to resolve a mystery was through his exhaustive methodology.

"Otherwise," he said more than once (and this repetition was one of things that vexed her), "you'll have to do the same room again, wasting more time than doing it right once."

In the end, she had to thank him for his methodology. He sharpened her focus, and God only knew how long it might have taken her on her own. Indeed, they had both begun to despair, and he had started talking of his need to return home. And then they found it.

They had stuck to the general perimeter of Ellie's prior explorations between the Time Room and the library. The right door could be between the Time Room and the Gallery where she once slept. It could be somewhere she hadn't yet explored. But they had agreed to leave those areas until another day. Besides, Ellie had no desire to retrace her steps to the Gallery, where she had spent so many days in forlorn confusion.

Very late in the afternoon they came to the antechamber below the library. She was tired, despite the food and the Parson's company. The glow about his face had softened with failing daylight. They agreed to search the antechamber before giving up.

It was not a door, merely a keyhole in the rich russet paneling on the left wall, just shy of the stairs to the library. She called to Graham excitedly. She slipped in the key and turned. With a click, seams appeared in the wood, outlining a door she never would have seen. She pushed and the door separated from the paneling and slid forward over rough gray stone. She peered inside.

She knew at once they had discovered something immensely important.

Below her was a goliath sunken amphitheater, by far the largest chamber she had found. A hundred rows of stone seats dropped from where she stood. A bowl-shaped ceiling curved up from just above her head. After the warm candlelight and rich woods of the antechamber, it was strange and primitive. At its center, far below, was an empty square stage, also gray stone.

On the opposite side of the amphitheater was another paneled door, partially ajar. Painted on the convex of the ceiling in faded colors were three huge figures. She was sure one was Daevon. Another must be Paris, veiled and voluptuous. The third, with piercing blue eyes, must be Timothy, not bearded and wild like the xemenos of the ice, but clean-shaven and handsome. The importance of this place was this trio: the first images she had found not of Siana or her enemies, but of her friends, her loves.

"What do *you* see?" she asked Parson Graham.

"A huge bowl in the earth, like a long extinct volcano."

She described for him the amphitheater she saw.

When she was done, he said, "Ellie, I'm sorry, but I must go. I am so glad the key revealed this place. Keep exploring, go on without me"—he gave her a nudge forward—"and tell me tomorrow what you find. I believe your mystery continues to unravel."

After Graham left, she was too excited to feel dejected. She made a circuit of the whole room, keeping to the highest step. Her gaze kept returning to the massive images of Daevon, Paris and Timothy. The workmanship was indescribably beautiful, and tears threatened her eyes again.

When she reached the door opposite, and pulled it all the way open, she was surprised to find the ballroom.

"That is interesting," she said aloud. "I've come full circle then." She stepped inside, and that first image of Siana greeted her, its stained glass subdued and colorless in the lateness of the day. Trembling, she climbed the staircase to her first memories: the small dusty gallery. Perhaps something would be different. But inside was the same peeling green paint, the same small window, the same dirty pallet on the floor. Like countless times before, she used her palm to smudge aside the window's dirt. Rolling hills stretched to the horizon, olives fading to browns.

Her heart leapt.

In that dead and barren landscape she spotted a billowing cloak and red-gold hair. The Parson strolling a beaten trail she had never noticed before. She found herself smiling.

And then a house dropped from the sky and exploded against the hill to Graham's right. Timbers shattered and flew over his head. He took no notice, and ploughed on unawares.

So strange. The castle and the houses, part of her same weird reality.

She watched until dusk and distance hid him.

She was not afraid at the coming of night. She resolved to spend it in her gallery. It might look the same but it *felt* totally different. She was no longer the lost and lonely Ellie who first awoke here.

The proximity of her chosen sleeping place gave her time to further explore the amphitheater. It had seemed empty, but the Parson's thoroughness had rubbed off on her. Was the key's purpose merely to bring her back here to her gallery? The return felt momentous, but she sensed there was more than that.

It didn't take long to find out. For the stage at the bottom of the amphitheater was no longer empty. At its center, a door floated a few feet above the stone. She rushed down the nearest aisle and up onto the stage. She studied the door, now seeing that it hung from the ceiling on a very fine chain. Only one side had a doorknob, the other was featureless and flat. She studied the doorknob and found it had a lock. She tried her key. The lock turned and the door opened, revealing a small room completely invisible from the outside.

Her toe stubbed against an invisible stair. She went within.

The room inside was fifteen feet wide and thirty feet deep; she had entered through a door in the middle of the near wall. On the wall opposite was an identical door, closed. It, like the room, must be invisible from the outside, for she had only seen one door. The dark wood floor was old and scuffed and the same wood paneled the walls and ceiling. Candles on sconces lit the room, regularly spaced along the left and right walls.

In front of her was the back of an empty chair. Ten feet further away, along the same axis, was an identical chair facing her. She walked to the left of the first chair and made for the other door, intrigued as to where it might lead.

She ran smack into some invisible barrier. The painful collision toppled her backwards into the chair, the chair scuttled sideways, and she fell on her bottom. She rubbed her bruised nose.

The other chair had also moved, now turned perpendicular to the doors. Ellie looked behind. The chair she had collided with stood at an identical angle, a perfect mirror image. She reached out and found the barrier again. She held the key up to it. An identical key appeared in the air an inch away.

A mirror.

A mirror in which she didn't show.

What am I? Ellie thought, *a ghost?* Yet the Parson saw her. *I suppose since I'm in a dream, all's fair.*

She returned the chair to its original position. The chair in the mirror followed. She sat down, frowning, but no Ellie appeared in the glass. She was about to get up, when a most curious thing happened. The knob on the door in the reflection turned and it opened. Heart pounding, she jumped up and glanced behind. The real door was firmly shut, as she left it. Only the *reflected* door was opening. How strange! She could do things that didn't reflect in the mirror, and the reflection could do things that didn't show in her half of the room! But then a greater surprise. In through the door strode a woman, as vividly real as Parson Graham.

She was fairly tall, slender and muscular, dressed in black. Candlelight flashed on metal: a ringmail vest, the steel vambraces on her arms. Hilts of daggers protruded from sheaths at both thighs, and her unusual belt sported a myriad pockets and clasps. Flowing blonde hair, many strands woven into tight braids.

Siana!

The woman strode to the chair, eyes downcast, and sat down, placing her hands in her lap. Ellie was frozen. The castle's icons paled beneath the overwhelming nearness of this human Siana.

She raised her chin and looked Ellie full in the face, just like the Cathedral Room when the icon on the altar had raised its ice-blue eyes to meet her gaze. The same penetrating stare. Siana did not appear as Ellie expected. In her imagination she had attributed to Siana a plenitude of virtues, picturing her beautiful, fiery, and strong. This Siana was not exactly beautiful. Her eyes were striking, as were her full and sensuous lips. But her face was drawn and pained, and darkness that ringed the crystal blue of her eyes. Was this the real Siana or yet another image?

"Hello," Siana said. "Who are you?" Her voice was low. She sounded displeased.

"I'm Ellie," she stammered back, her voice cracking. "I am pleased to meet you, my mistress."

"Your mistress?"

"Well, I've been living in your castle here..." How could she explain? To Siana, she must be a pathetic non-entity.

Siana said nothing. Ellie gazed at her hands, folded in her lap, at the key in her open palm. Siana's stare pummeled her.

"Is Daevon really dead?" she whispered.

"Yes," Siana answered. Hot tears rose to Ellie's face again. She didn't want to cry in front of Siana, to appear more pathetic than she already must. She dared to raise her eyes. Siana's expression was cold.

"I'm sorry for you," Ellie said, immediately regretting it. She had wanted to express sympathy. But she cringed at the condescension of her words.

"He was a good man," Siana said simply, "but it is of no consequence now."

Ellie's heart lurched. An uncomfortable silence settled between them. Siana's stare was defiant. But Ellie's hunger for information drove her on.

"Can you help me?" she pleaded. "I'm in this castle, somewhere in the dreamworlds, and I'm surrounded by images of you. Your face is on every wall, and I figure you must know this place, must know where I am."

In response, Siana slowly studied her portion of the paneled room as if she had never been here before.

"I know of no castle," Siana responded at last. Ellie was about to explain this room wasn't the castle when Siana continued absently.

"I sought for years for the lair of the Coethyphys, their refuge, but I could never find it..." Her rich voice subsided into private memories.

"You have not found Timothy," Ellie said flatly.

"No," Siana replied, shifting in her chair, "I never could."

"That is terrible," Ellie said, afraid to sympathize too much.

"At least I've had my revenge," Siana said, steel infiltrating her voice. "I made the Aedolae pay for what they did, to him, to me, to all of us." Her brows creased and her eyes glinted fire.

They were both silent again. To Ellie's relief, Siana showed no inclination to leave the room. So far, this Siana had offered Ellie no assistance with her predicament. But she could ask more questions the books raised.

"I have dreamt of you, here in the castle," Ellie said, "several times. You dreamt your way across the Detheros and the Edoi Sea. And I dreamt of the attack in the Glowship, just last night. This place is weird, it gives me dreams of you. And I guess these dreams are true stories. Why did the pirates attack you?"

"Ghislain bade them," Siana answered.

A contradiction struck Ellie.

"Neikolan's men killed your lover," she said. "How could you take them as comrades? Why not seek revenge against them?"

"They were mercenaries for hire, lawless men doing what lawless men do. Like me, they had no love for the Aedolae. Ghislain was merely a player in their game of predation and reward. But I gave them power and focus, a chance to change their world. They were an opportunity I couldn't pass up. They were skilled, daring, with nothing to lose."

Ellie found herself nodding assent. Siana's words made *logical* sense, and she wanted to think the best of her mistress. But somehow they didn't really answer her question. As if sensing Ellie's uneasiness, Siana continued.

"I left them as often as I could, to continue to recover the Eterokoni, to explore the passages, to seek for the Coethyphys. But I had to keep them busy, keep them striking against the Aedolae, putting our plans into action. I couldn't let them get aimless."

"But Timothy! What about him all that time?"

"I kept up my quest," Siana answered, apparently nonplussed by an unknown waif's interrogation. "But I didn't want to drag the issue of Timothy into it. I wanted my saboteurs' motives—my motives as their leader—to be impersonal. I didn't want them to become suspicious of me. I had plenty of reason to destroy the Aedolae without Timothy."

Ellie was increasingly confused. The *issue* of Timothy?

"What reasons?" she asked.

"The Detheros. Their segregation of the places of deep dreams from humankind. The lands they have appropriated from the Estringites. The depravity of Kadesh. The cruelty of Ghislain. I could go on." Siana shrugged, sounding petulant.

"So where are you now?" Ellie asked, thinking of the first book she read. "What happened after your attack on Kadesh?"

Siana appeared confused.

"I'm *here*," she said finally, as if stating the ridiculously obvious.

"OK," Ellie acknowledged, not sure *who* or *what* she was talking to, "but what is the last thing that you remember?"

Siana cocked her head. "I remember fighting Kadesh in the Traverse of Stones, I remember an army of Achthroi upon the plains of Mihali..."

"That is the first book I read!" Ellie interrupted. "You see, here in the castle there is a whole library of books written about you. I think you wrote them!"

Mirror-Siana laughed for the first time. "When would I have time to write a bunch of books?"

Ellie ploughed on. "I read about that fight. The book ended with Paris falling, grabbing a rope, hanging above the abyss. Is she dead too?" The question tasted sour in her mouth, what with Siana's dismissal of Daevon and her brother's fate.

"I don't recall." Siana rolled her eyes upwards. "There is so much shadow..." The harshness left her expression, and she looked tired.

Another question, the natural conclusion, came out of Ellie's mouth. "Then are you dead now?"

Siana's eyes flashed. "Do I *look* dead?"

"Then why is your Sundial here in the castle?"

"You have my Eterokon?" Siana gripped the arms of the chair. "You must return it to me!"

"I will," Ellie flinched, "if you tell me how to! But I don't even know where you are. You're here everywhere, on the walls, in my dreams, in this room, but I still don't know where you *really* are!"

Silence again. Ellie's mind raced.

"What happens when you leave this room?" Ellie asked.

"I haven't left it before," Siana answered. "I only just came in."

"OK," Ellie said irritably. "Where were you right before you came in?"

Siana seemed truly perplexed. "I can't say."

Ellie thought of the Parson and how he might proceed toward solving this riddle. But she came up with nothing.

So instead she asked, "Tell me about Paris."

"What is there to say?" Siana said flatly.

"She was very special to you," Ellie bumbled.

"Paris is beautiful and sweet, but she is a dreamworld creature, a phantom of the night. And frankly an impediment to my mission, more times than not."

Ellie's ire rose for the first time. "How can you say that? She wasn't a soldier and she risked her life to be there with you. You're not making sense!" Ellie realized her impertinence, and lowered her voice. "My mistress, I don't understand how you can care so much about the Aedolae, and not about Paris? Aren't the Aedolae phantoms as well?"

"They may be phantoms but they are ageless phantoms of great power who have taken something from me."

"Just as Paris gave much for you," Ellie argued, not sure her scant knowledge of Paris justified this impertinence but compelled to argue all the same.

"Who are *you* to tell me about Paris and me?"

Ellie lowered her eyes. "I am only trying to understand. I know nothing about myself, I am trapped here in this unknown place, and your story, your life is the only light I have."

"I am sorry for you," Siana said, not without warmth. "I would help you if I could."

Ellie felt defeated. She was arguing with her patron, senselessly, instead of getting answers. Was Siana dead? What happened after the first book? She had reasoned Siana must have survived Mihali, in order to later earn her title *Princess of Time*. Then Ellie learned the title came from Siana's childhood fantasies. In light of this conversation, Siana might indeed be dead, along with Paris and all her troops. Was this creature a phantom, an artifact like the frescoes and the books? Ellie felt cold and alone, trapped in a world where the Aedolae had triumphed unequivocally. But where was she really? In that world or some other? Where was the castle? She must ask the Parson. Thinking of the Parson made her think again of his patient methodology. He had divined the nature of the castle's reality with such clarity. Could she not do the same with this mirror-Siana, and gain the certainty that eluded her?

"Siana," Ellie suggested, "why don't you go out the door and then come back and tell me what you saw there?"

Siana's immediate acquiescence surprised her. She rose stiffly and without another glance turned her back and left. Ellie heard the door behind her open and shut. She shivered. When Siana had entered, the door behind her hadn't moved. Another curiosity.

Then she waited.

And waited.

Siana didn't return.

She smacked herself on the forehead for her stupidity. She had tried to imitate the Parson and ended up foolish. *Maybe if I leave and come back in.* She tried that, but after another equally long wait for Siana to reappear she gave up and left the room for good.

She climbed out of the amphitheater toward the library.

It was getting late. Dare she stay out? She was only two rooms away from her pallet. The ghosts of the ballroom had never harmed her, and she had survived the Achthroi shadows in the Time Room. She needed to know more.

• • • ● • ● • • •

T hus began a week of fevered reading. Freed of the necessity to travel daily to the library from the Time Room, Ellie could spend most of her time in the library itself. All that week, the fire of curiosity quelled the new hunger of her belly and drove her through a pile of books. She picked up the thread of Siana's story after Daevon's death, and found mirror-Siana was truthful about her subsequent attempts to locate the Coethyphys' lair and any glimpse of the shining ribbon that helped her trail Timothy through the Fringe years earlier. Siana had returned to Neikolan's pirates, established her new saboteurs in Forgotten Town, and explored throughout the demesnes, testing the Kalimba's powers. Ellie figured out how the second book she'd read fit the narrative, placing it after Siana began to lead successful raids against the demesnes, but before her fateful reunion with Bierce (this was painful to read, dominated by Bierce's rancor at Daevon's death). All that week the Parson never came, but she hardly noticed. Her goal was to arrive at a certain point in the narrative, and though she stuck to her plan to read the books in order, all the way through, she really was waiting for that one book.

She hardly dared to think it, but she was trying to prove Siana wrong. The dissonance of Siana's dismissal of her loves, those grand figures on the amphitheater ceiling, clanged like a bell in Ellie's head. She would not admit to herself that she was disappointed in her demigoddess, but the dissonance drove her, harder than her prior admiration and wonder. She felt she owed Paris, as if *she* could somehow pay the debt of Siana's denial. *She* would read Paris' story and pay homage to it. She was sure that book would deny Siana's callousness. Hadn't even the first book demonstrated Siana's deep concern for her friend? Who was this mirror image of Siana to deny it?

She reached that book late in the week, plucked from the second floor shelves: the story of Siana's third trip to Kadesh, some months after her second visit with Bierce, two years after Daevon's death. Into the heart of that jungled demesne: to test her cunning against an Aedolae for the first time since Cylindrax. To recover two more of the Eterokoni.

And, unwittingly, to rescue a maharani.

THE DANCES OF PARIS

One year before the Attack on Kadesh

K adesh.
I had been to his realm many times, but only once to the heart of his kingdom, years before as Jaena. Now I possessed the Star, the Bracelet, the Torc, the Kalimba, and the Sundial, though of the latter I could make neither heads nor tails. My army had swelled and exhibited its power in skirmishes and raids throughout the dreamworlds. My knowledge of secret ways through, around and between the worlds of the Via had grown. But our sabotage was often little more than a casual nuisance to the Aedolae. I needed more power, and for that I needed more Eterokoni. I lacked five my brother had possessed. The best hope of recovering these lay with the remaining xemeni.

The xemenos on the ice floe mentioned seeing himself fall three times, once below the moon, once into torch-lit jungle and once into desert. The first reference might be to the moon-haunted passage where I recovered the Sundial. The second sounded like Kadesh; so by deduction the third would be the desert between Kadesh and Cylindrax. My spies spotted the desert xemenos on a rarely used route paralleling the Via, and heard tales in Kadesh of another man matching Timothy's description.

In returning to Kadesh I intended to find both.

I reveled at the opportunity to test my strength and cunning against an Aedolae in his place of power. Alone.

I was prideful.

I entered Kadesh in the Dark Quarter, where the Kalimba has always taken me. But rather than sneak through jungle, I decided on an obvious approach. The last thing Kadesh would expect would be Siana passing his front gate in broad daylight. I followed ill-used trails to the Aedol Via, which here was a great road of orange paving stones, linking Kadesh's bamboo compound with the far desert.

As I took to the road at daybreak, I shifted my face and form into the slim but well-muscled man I first discovered in the mirror at Bierce's house. My hair was close-cropped, dark blonde. I had brought a walking stick and a trader's pack which was suspended on a wood frame and rolled behind me on tiny wheels. By the time I reached the gates I was amid a throng of merchants and travelers, representing every conceivable race under the dreamworld's suns. All were in an uproar of celebration for it was the third day of a weeklong festival, and rumor was at the end of seven days Kadesh would distribute great rewards to his loyalists.

The crowd was wild with expectation of that night's feasting and bizarreries.

So much the better.

I surveyed the massiveness of Kadesh's palace. Towering tubes of giant bamboo formed the outer frame. Each of these tubes I could only get my arms half around. In between, smaller tubes of myriad sizes were bound together to form walls, balconies and turrets. Windows were merely openings with thick cloth drawn back to welcome in morning light. The bamboo was chiefly blonde, but russet red and jet black outlined different floors and sections. On two semicircular platforms suspended by vines from the roof, guardsmen and their massive green eagle mounts paced, surveying the courtyard.

Between these platforms an instrument with features of both pan pipes and a pipe organ was built into the palace face. I knew from experience its stentorious tones would summon us to the evening's revelry at the waning of the day. And below the pipes hung swaying skeletons, visceral reminders of Kadesh's displeasure, held together by bits of decaying flesh and muscle and the sun-bleached remnants of clothes.

I climbed the ramp to the gate.

In the Merchants' Book in the inner courtyard I signed with the name I had chosen. In the unusual frenzy of the festival the scrutiny to which the Orsian traders had been subjected seemed nonexistent. I was grateful there were no further requests for details about my origins.

Just as it was when I was Orsian Jaena, on that first trip along the Via, visiting merchants were escorted next through the fabulous Fire Gardens, where the Seraphi were stationed in military position along the paths, their countenances black shadows ringed with fire. Our guide, a majordomo of the Palace, explained the Gardens were sustained by the powers of the Prism. As part of the festival, the Prism itself would be on display later that week, and this incited a fury of whispers.

During the ensuing three days I asked as many questions as I dared.

A quarter mile west of the palace I discovered a decaying ziggurat, and climbed its stairs past the tree line to survey the surrounding landscape. At its apex a plinth, akin to the one in Zoorn, sported the rune for Kadesh's kingdom: circle atop a cross, the fifth key of the Kalimba.

And nearby I found the xemenos, in a subterranean jungle prison for those both criminal and insane, bound with chains.

A little strategic shapeshifting and an unconscious guard allowed me to speak with him, not as long as I desired. The xemenos was only marginally coherent, failing to recognize me but revealing in a torturous fashion that he had once possessed both Glass Sword and Beetle. They had been taken from him. He mentioned the royal armory.

This too painful reminder of my brother irritated me. I wanted the Eterokoni, but I no longer wanted to think about Timothy. I wouldn't have wanted to admit it, but I had given up the quest to find him. My second trip to Bierce had been a plea for more information, but Bierce, grief stricken at the loss of Daevon, was deaf to my entreaties. I had bared my desperate soul to him and I had been spurned. So I had resolved to put those thoughts aside. I had become a dreamer to escape from suffering, to become a person of power. I was no longer willing to have Ghislain define me otherwise. I was now only Siana, Princess of Time, His Enemy.

The sixth night of the festival arrived. In two days the city would empty out and it would be harder to achieve my goals. That afternoon, I pinpointed the armory among the guards' chambers in Kadesh's personal lair at the heart of the palace. The question was when to raid it: during the nightly fete, when the vast majority of the palace's occupants were assembled, or later, when drunken sleep claimed them?

I was outside the palace, and still undecided when the fete began.

The throaty wailing of the gate pipes hushed the crowds, sellers commenced to store their wares, and from within the open gates of Kadesh's palace drums began to sound. With remarkable restraint, the occupants of the outer courtyard proceeded within, moving in time to the quarter notes of the drums and the even splash of tambourines. I fell in step, feeling the massive pipes shake my ribcage as we passed under. In the inner courtyard, we passed the Merchant's Book on its pedestal, where faded names went back six hundred years. Kadesh and his ilk had lived a long time.

Once past the inner courtyard, the excitement of the crowd grew as the harmonies of unseen musicians enveloped us. Some of my fellows took sharp-edged metal pipettes and rammed them into the largest bamboo columns, blowing their own melodies into the framework of the building. I had never witnessed this before, but perforations down the length of the hall showed the tradition was not new.

As we approached the banquet hall, the song changed as the insistent drumming of a percussionist further within set a faster beat. Radiant light in a rainbow palette—rich red, sparkling emerald green, succulent orange—flooded from open doorways ahead. The crowd hushed. A chorus, embellished with the chromatic ululations of tribal singers, chanted to the fast pulse of the drum.

We entered the feasting hall of Kadesh.

At the center of the fan-shaped floor was the Prism. Not a triangular scientist's prism, but circular and irregular, a natural prodigy of the dreamworlds. It was an amalgam of melted and translucent porcelains, rippled together in a seven-colored whorl, each color emitting broad and roving beams of light. As the crowd spilled out and surrounded it, I could see the people on the far side through the body of the Prism, their faces distorted and stained surreal hues.

I wondered if I alone noticed the jagged wound at the Prism's base, where a man-sized shard had been cut away. I had seen that shard in the Fringe, and a Singer perched atop it.

On my left, steps climbed to Kadesh' dais. His corpulent belly shuddered with rich laughter. And to my right the banquet space was open to the Prismatic Pool and the setting sun, ending in a terrace over the boardwalk trail and glistening waters beyond, framed in a fence of torches.

At Kadesh's gesture, a torchbearer approached the Prism, and the crowd parted for him. He threw his flame into the Prism's sparkling depths. Lightning rippled across its surface. Then it exhaled warm air in all directions, blowing back our hair and clothing. The Prism had magnified the torch's energy a thousandfold.

Pity we don't have such things in our world.

The Prism rested on a metal circle, and now a hundred of Kadesh's slaves strained to hoist and carry it up the stairs. They placed it behind his throne, silhouetting him a blaze of color. I now noticed a line of molten silver liquid ran from the wound, down the length of the hall before dropping off the edge of the terrace. This was source of the Prismatic Pool.

The silver blood of the Singer.

The music stopped.

A tall being disengaged herself from Kadesh's crowd of guards and slaves and descended to address the crowd. This was the first Gnish I had seen. She wore a robe of sparkling silver. Her mouth, dominating her face, was a vertical maw of curving fangs.

"We celebrate the beneficence of our great Lord and Master, whose Will established this great realm amid the jungle's chaos, and whose fashioning of the beauteous Prism gave us beauty, light and power."

The crowd roared approval. *Oh, you all don't know your dreamworld history*, I thought bitterly. Such is always the way of conquerors and usurpers, co-opting the past. I so wanted to point out the Prism's wound.

"We have yet two nights of celebration," the fanged thing continued. "Tonight the Lady Paris will dance. And she will dance again tomorrow." This too met with a roar. It was the first time I heard her name but I was too busy being disgusted with Kadesh's revisionist history and the name washed over me. Little did I know that Paris would soon outshine for me the vulgarity of her surroundings.

And little did I know that in twenty-four hours I would be fleeing the realm with her beside me.

The feasting began with colorful drinks in tall tubes of transparent bamboo. Next small ovens on wheels were pulled throughout the crowd to offer delicacies, many repulsive to several of my senses, some delicious. Fortunately as a dreamer I didn't rely on dreamworld food for sustenance; I could eat or not as I fancied. Bierce told me this changed somewhat when one fully entered the dreamworlds, as he and Daevon had. Then there was a true need for food, though still much, much less than in the waking world.

During all the feast the musicians played and chanted, gorgeous melodies interwoven with frenzied drumming—strange beats that at times made my skin crawl. As ever, Kadesh's realm was a place for all tastes and predilections, the beautiful and the bizarre mixed in equal and careless measures, a vivid wash of indulgence.

For a time I forgot my mission to the armory. The power of the Star made me an enthusiastic eavesdropper. I had gleaned much information over the years from members of dreamworld races who falsely assumed I did not understand their speech.

A significant portion of the night's conversation was about Paris.

I easily overheard the following: she belonged to Kadesh's harem, his harem was on the fourth floor of the palace, and the only stairs to that floor were inside the guard chambers. And that Paris was his favorite, but she had never been bedded, by him or any other man. So went the rumor.

Intriguing.

A series of spectacles followed the meal. Acrobatics, impressive enough but then eclipsed by the detachable people from Onissia. I had never seen Onissians before, and judging by the raucous response of the crowd neither had they. Someone whispered that all Onissians were female.

They resembled ordinary women, but took their bodies apart, limb by limb, and tossed around their appendages and heads like living Starmen. I stared awestruck. Their theatrics, though executed with grace and skill, were nonetheless stomach-churning.

Next handlers paraded in exotic species, including gigantic many-tailed serpents, and man-eating flowers to which Kadesh fed several dissidents. Lurid and provocative dances followed. Certain women of his harem led these, not without some art, but the scene eventually disintegrated into invitations to public coitus, to which several members of the audience eagerly assented.

My mind wandered. I surveyed the scene, noting the placement of the guards, noting where pools of shadow separated ovals of torchlight, noting which archways framed the darkest halls. I chose one and moved a little at a time to hide my intent. Few went in and out of the banquet hall now, most eyes riveted to the amorous scenery. This was both good and bad. The masses would pay me no heed, but a stray eye might easily notice my idiosyncratic movements.

I took my time. Thirty minutes of it in fact. I was about to slip away when the music stopped and everyone fell silent.

I was a minute too late. Or was I? Everyone's gaze was intent on the center of the room. Most of the torches had been extinguished, tendrils of black smoke spooling out from their stumps. With cunning artifice, a servant on the dais used a silver tray to direct the light of the Prism, creating a blue spotlight in which a single figure stood.

I chose to stay. A different decision would have cost me the Beetle. It would have cost me so much more.

I climbed onto the pedestal of a statue to see better. A man nearby smiled at me knowingly. For the first part of Paris' dance, I thought she was of a new and exotic dreamworld race. For her face was a rich velvet blue, a procession of tiny dots radiated from the bridge of her nose upwards, and her cheeks were striped. Her black lips pursed in a strange animal shape. The overall effect a black-and-blue striped lion's face, a feline muzzle. Her dark hair was piled in a bun atop her head.

But it was not her appearance that seized me, for I had seen more unusual things that night. It was her motion. With slow fluidity, she traced a slow arc across the open space at the center of the crowd, oblivious to their stares. The spotlight from the Prism followed her. There was silence in her slowness, opposite the frenetic intensity that preceded her. Singers at the foot of the dais intoned low syllables, and to my surprise the Star did not translate. Sacred syllables, not words? Their voices matched the mood of her dance, but Paris led the scene.

She wore a loose fitting shirt and trousers dyed in black and blue stripes to match her face. This eventually convinced me her leonine face was an effect of makeup. A lion's mane of fringes hung from the backside of her sleeves and pants, and such was her art that she controlled how they rippled and fanned out behind her, making it a part of her dance.

THE DANCES OF PARIS

A male voice spoke and the chanting voices dropped to hushed tones. He began a story of the creation of the demesnes, with many details I had never heard. I should have listened carefully, for likely no dreamer had heard this mythical narrative unfold. But I couldn't concentrate. My eyes were drawn again and again to the lone figure in blue. What little of the story I caught were those details Paris enacted in her dance.

As the story unfolded, musicians joined, and Paris matched their drums with quicker dance steps. The speaker described wars between the Aedolae and the Coethyphys, and the crowd now recited *en masse*, prompted by the speaker, a common lay to which they knew ritual responses. One which they anticipated, accompanied by the sublime dance of this woman of Kadesh's keeping.

But I heard their recitation as if from afar. I could not sway my attention from Paris. When she finished I couldn't remember the music or the words. I couldn't remember the chronology of her dance. All I remembered was a disordered but vivid collage of images— the movement of her body divorced and freed from the distractions of context.

The way she balanced and spun on her toes. The wide shock of her eyes at the evils of the story. The sorrow she conveyed, a wilted flower crumpling to the ground. The elation, expressed in curving, arcing hands, as her arms wove and intertwined. The bounce of her breasts beneath her linen blouse. The spiraling colors, sapphire and ebony, as she twirled. Her twisting contortions were somehow as graceful as her lightest steps. Paris had consummate skill, as acrobatic and athletic as the best performers of the fete. But her dance was far above skill; she was art and not spectacle. She shamed and diminished all who had gone before her. I had never seen anything so beautiful in any world.

I had never seen anything so beautiful in my life.

And it was the last thing I had expected at Kadesh.

Her dance ended. I had no idea how long it had gone on and shook my head as if awaking from a trance. The crowd murmured disapproval, for the epic lay had ended prematurely. Paris stood frozen in the last curve of her dance, eyes downcast. Having gathered the crowd's attention, she unfolded herself and nodded toward the dais. The spotlight disappeared and torches were relit.

Kadesh had orchestrated an unexpected ending.

All eyes turned as the Lord of the Night descended the stairs. He was taller than human height, seven feet perhaps, both muscled and corpulent, clad in a bright red sampot and trappings of black leather. His face was ugly and leering, with strangely arched eyebrows and pocked skin. A naked scimitar hung at his side. At the foot of the stair, he leaned on one of his great javelins.

"It is time," he boomed with power and barely veiled condescension, "to announce a great joy, timed to coincide with this celebration of my demesne. You, my guests and vassals, have the privilege and pleasure of witnessing and paying homage to this prodigy. For in two days hence, I shall be married, and take to myself, after a thousand years of dominion, a bride."

The assembly did not expect this, and yet murmurs of confusion soon gave way to shouts of approval. If nothing else, a wedding meant more spectacle and more feasting—at Kadesh's expense.

"My feasters and friends, I present my bride," Kadesh continued, as a sick knowing dawned on my mind. "At last she has attained the marriageable age of her people. Come forth, my maharani."

Confirming my sickness, he stretched out his powerful hand to Paris.

In response she walked down the open aisle toward him, with stately poise. At his feet she sank to her knees in abjection and in a single fluid movement unbound her hair. It fell in lush brunette waves about her shoulders and cascaded down her back. She leaned forward and let it cover her as she folded herself upon her legs.

Kadesh stooped and touched the crown of her head. She raised her head and he helped her to her feet. She turned to face the crowd. Her expression was unreadable in her leonine face.

"My bride-to-be, the Apotheosis of the Aedol Via, Paris Christianne de Na-vaylah." The crowd screamed its approval, fully in tune. "We shall be wed on the morning of the Eighth Day, and there shall be another night of Festival." The crowd screamed even louder. "And tomorrow Paris will dance again for you, her final night as a maiden."

I clutched the statue for support. The man who had smiled at me before glanced my way.

"It is a shame that no mortal man shall taste her loveliness now," he said in a tone of confidence.

"It is beyond shame," I said out loud without meaning to.

My mind went back to the Gardens, where Ghislain had lulled me into mindless dreaming. There a phantasm of his design had courted and used my body, again and again. I thought of this rape as Kadesh grinned lasciviously at the beautiful young woman by his side. It was everything I abhorred, the Aedolae's defilement of all things lovely and free and fair. My senses reeled.

Paris had donned a black veil and danced again, slow and sensuous before Kadesh. She controlled the flow of her hair with the same grace as the fringes of her costume. If she shared my horror at her fate, harbored any dread within her soul, it did not show; the elegant perfection of her movements was unmarred by Kadesh's revelation.

Somehow this sickened me all the more. I felt betrayed in the tribute my rapt soul had paid her gracility. Now she was a lamb acceding to slaughter. Did she not hate him? How could something that fair fail to be abhorred by Kadesh? I imagined him possessing her, that blasphemous leering Buddha, and my mind recoiled.

To one pledged to fight the Aedolae at all cost, her acquiescence was revolting.

But I had done the same in the Gardens. And this too fueled my revulsion, though I was not fain to admit it.

I could watch no more, and oblivious to any risk of detection, fled from the room.

The corridor was empty. I turned my focus to attaining the guards' chambers. They weren't far, and only a pair of blonde amazons stood watch. A shake of my wrist and the Eterokon of Petrifaction took care of them. They hadn't seen me, so they would have no sense of lost minutes when their flesh quickened again. Neikolan and I had tested the Bracelet at length. He always awoke from the spell of my surprise attacks incognizant of what had happened in the meantime.

It didn't take long to find the Glass Sword in a display case sporting many other elegant weapons, deceptively fragile, gleaming even in the dim light. I tried to draw it but it wouldn't leave the sheath for me either. I stole a number of other exquisite and well-tempered weapons, whatever I could easily carry and conceal. One is always losing daggers.

Energized by recovering the Sword, I was eager to complete my quest and exit the demesne. Eager to flee my own emotions about what had happened in the banquet hall. I searched long—long past when the guards resumed low conversation outside, and longer than I should have—but the Beetle Eterokon was nowhere to be found.

And thus I got caught in the armory. The fete was over, and women of the harem ascended the nearby stair, giggling and talking. The adjoining chambers flooded with guards, drinking, laughing, many paired with women of the household. I froze in place, crouching uncomfortably behind a display case. I wondered if Kadesh ever came here, to gloat over his treasures. I reassured myself there was little chance he would tonight. An hour passed before conversation and carousing retreated behind closed curtains, and talk mixed with murmured ecstasies of lovemaking.

To my own surprise I climbed the spiral staircase (this too was cleverly fashioned of bamboo) to the harem floor. I told myself I only wanted to ensure the Beetle lay nowhere within. Perhaps a harem girl had fancied it a brooch, or received it as a token from Kadesh.

But it was more than that. An hour earlier I had wanted to find the Eterokoni and be gone. But sixty minutes of my dark, cramped hiding space in the armory had made me face what I could not bury in activity: I could not dismiss Paris from my mind, nor dismiss my disquieting horror at her betrothal. My heart would not yield up the beauty I had witnessed, and could not forsake what had awakened in a forgotten corner of my soul. I wouldn't see that beauty sullied by callous revulsion. It had felt, in those moments before my disillusionment, a rare and precious thing. Paris still danced, brilliant blue, in the spotlight of my soul. And she wouldn't leave.

I slipped past the guards at the top of the stair by shapechanging my skin and hair to jet and then crept along the fourth floor. The Star translated the talk of women hidden beyond gauzy curtains.

Only one door in the harem had a private guard. Hers.

With the guards easily petrified on either side, I tried the door to Paris' chambers and found it unlocked. Taking a deep breath, not knowing what I expected to do, I went inside.

Her rooms were open and airy, a series of adjoining chambers with high archways and windows to the outside. Candles burned low on small tables and on the arms of a divan. A magnificent silk-strewn bed occupied one wall. I saw no one in the room or its shadowy corners. I had seen Paris enter, minutes before. I stepped lightly and explored each chamber but they seemed unoccupied. A breeze blew in from an open doorway.

"I can hear you," a female voice spoke from outside. I detected a suppressed quaver in its tone. A lone figure stood in torchlight on a small balcony; the doorway and all of the windows opened on this semicircular space. She leaned on the bamboo railing, back to me, her waist-length tresses of brown hair dark against the brilliant red of a knee-length robe.

"I mean you no harm," I said as kindly as I could. My masculine voice sounded queer.

"I hope that is true, for I have no defenses," the woman said. "Whatever you intend, come join me. The night is beautiful. If you are clever enough to gain admittance to my chambers, I suppose you have earned my audience." I stepped onto the balcony. The woman turned toward me and I suppose we both stared.

It was Paris, her face still painted blue and black, and around her neck on a gleaming golden chain was the Beetle Eterokon.

She stared as if I was not what she expected. I don't know how it feels to a man when a woman sizes him up, or stares as if she finds him handsome, but there was something in her gaze analogous to the way Daevon once looked at me. Similar but different. In my masculine guise I had not received such an appraisal before. What Paris saw must have been pleasantly surprising to her. But she quickly recovered her composure.

"How do I know you pose no threat?" she said guardedly.

"Because I seek not you," I answered, "but something you have." She wrinkled her brow in doubt. I didn't believe my words any more than she did, but they were truthful enough to build on. "It is around your neck."

"This?" She touched it with one graceful hand, her perfectly manicured nails flashing in the torchlight, long and painted in blue and black stripes to match her face. "This is a gift of a dear friend but it has no value. It is just an ornament of common brass." I hadn't known the Beetle's exact appearance, but I sensed the pull of an Eterokon. Had that same magnetism pulled me up the stairs? I was eager to justify my churning emotion as a dreamer's instincts.

"Nonetheless, my lady," I said, "I have sought for it long. But I am not a thief and I am not going to steal it from you."

I wasn't sure I believed those words either, but for the moment they were true.

"Well, that is good," Paris said, "but if I will not surrender it, you have come in vain." Her rising inflection made it more question than statement. She cast me a sidelong glance before returning to the railing. Surveying the glorious colors of the Prismatic Pool, she sighed deeply.

"Your dances were incredibly beautiful," I said, attempting to avoid an impasse over the Beetle. And I needed to understand, to make sense of her betrothal and her acquiescence. She sighed, her shoulders rising and falling heavily.

"You don't want to marry him," I said. She turned toward me. Her eyes flashed, exquisitely shaped and lustrous beneath heavy painted lids. They knocked the breath out of me.

"Of course I do not want to marry him," she said with force, but without anger. "I am grateful he protected me, fostered me, but he terrifies me." The uncanny animalistic effect of her face paint made her expressions unreadable, but her eyes spoke volumes.

"I have been dreading this week all my life," she continued. "Long have I known he desired me, and that his protection of my honor would have a terrible price." She cast her eyes downward. Her left hand trembled where it gripped the rail. We were far above the Pool here, with only one higher level of the massive palace between us and dark sky. A gust of wind blew her hair across her face. She brushed it away, her fingers moving with the same elegance of her dance, as if she were still on stage. As she adjusted her hair, her robe parted to reveal the pale flesh of a full bosom and a purple silken breechclout, sparkling with immense dreamworld diamonds and weighted down with beads and dangling gems.

My disgust and dread mutated into a raw but focused sympathy. She was a target for the lust and greed of my enemies. About to become their victim, like I had been in the Gardens, drugged by the poppy-laden air, every day for months of senseless dreaming.

"I will make you a bargain," I said.

Paris met my eyes again. Mine had never left her face. Her eyes had filled with tears.

"What?" she breathed.

"In exchange for your beetle, I will take you from Kadesh's kingdom." She wiped at her tears with the back of her hand, an elegant angle to her wrist.

"You do not jest," she said.

"No, I do not jest," I answered. "No one should be forced to wed against their will, especially not a beautiful girl to a wicked Aedolae." Her tears had dried. She was staring me up, taking my measure.

"Come inside," she said. "The paint is starting to burn."

I followed. She lit more candles. Opposite the bed was a porcelain basin, fashioned in the form of swan-like bird.

"Tell me how you will do this," she said, leaning to wash her face. Candlelight sparkled on the rippling water and cast a soft glowing lightning onto her skin.

"I am a spy for the Brigandrie," I explained, "and I know secret ways in and out of every demesne. If I anyone can get you out, it is me. But I cannot promise it will be without risk."

The Brigandrie was what the Mihalians called us.

Paris' face vanished between her lathering hands. After she had raised up and dried it her face with a towel, I found myself staring again. For the animal appearance I had thought a cunning artifice of her makeup was still there. She walked toward me, the beads on her silken breechclout tinkling. In the candlelight I saw her upper lip was cleft, an inverted Y between her nose and her full and sensuous lower lip. This, and not makeup, had been the cause of her leonine appearance.

She smiled. After her initial skepticism, I wasn't expecting her hopeful expression. I had only really seen her figure and her eyes before, but her heart-shaped face was finely crafted and very beautiful.

"You have heard of us?"

"Yes, I have," she breathed.

"I will be taking the desert passage toward Cylindrax, where I have another mission, and if you choose, I will take you with me. Should we encounter pursuit, I have an artifact that can transport us immediately to a safer place. Your beetle is another such artifact. But you must not mention this to anyone, for Kadesh knows what they are, and this would betray me."

"I won't say a word. And I am not afraid," Paris said. "I agree to your bargain. For safe passage from Kadesh, I will surrender my beetle." I made to shake her hand. She looked confused by the gesture, but touched my palm gently.

"Agreed," we said at the same time and laughed.

"My lady, are you alone?" a guard called through the door. The petrifaction had worn off. Paris gathered her robe about her, a strange modesty after her unselfconsciousness around me, a stranger in her rooms, and went to the door. She opened it a crack.

"It is of no worry," she chirped happily. "It is my costumier."

"We haven't let anyone pass since you returned tonight..." The guard sounded confused.

"Well, he is here," Paris returned, "so you must have forgotten. You *must* be more mindful." She didn't sound condemning. She shivered visibly. To me the night was not cold, not after the cool mists and rains of Forgotten Town.

"Excuse me while I change," she said, "then we can talk more."

She drew a curtain across the near corner of the room. I hadn't seen any kind of wardrobe there, only a bare wall of bamboo tubing. Nonetheless behind the curtain she rustled through garments. A single candle behind the barrier cast a plenty revealing shadow of Paris onto the creamy fabric. As her shadow tried on multiple sets of clothing, I argued with myself that despite my appearance I was female too and I shouldn't feel like a voyeur. Through every outfit change, Paris kept up a charming and partially indecipherable babble. She didn't, apparently, need any response from me. I wasn't sure if she was talking to her clothes or what.

At one point she said, a bit louder, "I don't even know your name."

"Peredur," I lied. I had been using the name since entering Kadesh. Another name that along with Siana featured in my childhood fantasies. I had gleaned this one from some forgotten book of my brother's.

She drew back the curtain. The area behind was still empty of anything resembling a wardrobe.

She drew close and spoke in low tones. "I can hardly believe you are true. I have dreamt and hoped for the last few years of an opportunity to escape, but I couldn't think of a way. I am not good at such things. It was too huge of an endeavor."

Paris had settled on a loose-fitting dress of resplendent cerulean satin. An unusual style of fingerless glove that reached the elbow. Cloth-of-gold sandals. What I had seen so far of Paris' clothing must be insanely expensive.

I matched her quiet tone. "I have a couple questions. Do you have clothing suitable for rough travel? How will Kadesh react if you disappear? I want to know what we're up against."

"As to your first question: I have *every* kind of clothing," Paris giggled. Where she was *keeping* said clothing? It seemed well-nigh invisible. "As to Kadesh, he is truly fond of me. He would be angry, but I think he would chalk it up to my nervousness and forgive me. But he would kill you if he had the chance."

"I'm sure of that," I laughed, "but are you sure he would be so kind to you?"

"Yes, I think so," Paris concluded.

"Well, that's good." I was trying to strategize, but the intensity of the last two hours overwhelmed coherent thought. "After Kadesh announced your betrothal, you were every bit the ecstatic bride. Your dance, your composure, was so assured, and beautiful, and even sensuous toward him. How could you do that, if it is so abhorrent to you?"

"Do you not understand?" She put her hands on her hips. "Dance is all I have, all I am. If I must marry Kadesh, all the more so! I would sooner kill myself than dance without grace. To lower myself to the lewdness of a courtesan, or dance artlessly just to protest—"

"*Beauty is the last protest of the honorable,*" I interrupted.

"What?"

"I read that somewhere. Anyway, it describes what you're saying."

She placed her index finger in the crook of her cleft lip, looking pensive. She scratched the tip of her nose with her long nail.

"Yes, you are right. Absolutely right." She smiled again, seeming pleased I understood. She gave me that look again, the female version of the Daevon look. "I'm tired. Can I lay down while we discuss what we must do?" She moved toward her luxurious bed and sat down on the covers.

The bed let out a howl.

Paris jumped and in her fluid leap put far more space between herself and the bed than I could have. My thigh daggers were in my hands instantly as I rushed between Paris and the bed. A dark face peered out of the silken blankets.

"On your feet unarmed or I slit your throat," I commanded. A jet-skinned youth, maybe fifteen, crawled from the covers. He was slender, with tousled curls. A inappropriate grin, considering the circumstances, split his homely face.

"Explain why I shouldn't throw you to the guards," I said.

"Number one," the youth said, scratching the back of his head, rearranging his clothes, and acting completely unfazed, "I've heard your whole conversation. Number two, I can't see the difference between my sneaking in here and your doing the same." I scowled, but he kept going. "You can *say* you're after her beetle, but really you're trying to catch the most celebrated beauty in all the Demesnes with her clothes off, just like me." He finished with an even bigger grin.

My response was a dagger at his throat. But Paris broke the tension.

"I am quite used to this kind of thing," she laughed, pushing my blade hand away from his throat, "and it's quite alright. He's just a boy. And a very clever one."

"And how old are *you*?" I asked of her, feeling miffed.

"Nineteen," she replied. "But what's your point?"

She turned to the lad and curtsied. "Paris Christianne de Na-vaylah. And you are?"

"Assav"—he bowed back—"at your service."

"And what service might that be?" I inquired. Despite myself, the Orsian's infectious grin was beginning to spread to my face.

"I heard you talking of escape," Assav answered, "and I have what you need."

"And what is that?"

"A patchwork ox with ultra-dimensional saddlebags."

I had no idea what he was talking about.

A SINGER'S STORY

I awoke early the next morning, sun streaming into my rented quarters. I dressed quickly, hoisted my pack, and headed up to Paris' rooms. On Paris' orders I was given admittance to the harem stairs, and soon stood outside her suite. My heart pounded. I would have preferred to be away before now. How long until they discovered my theft of the Glass Sword? How long until the rumor mill of the palace brought to Kadesh word of Peredur, so-called costumier who resembled a mercenary?

At least we would be away this morning. Assav, Paris and I had whispered until late in the night, forging a plan. It began with Assav meeting us—with his ox—south of the Fire Gardens, after Paris and I gave her guards the slip. I still wasn't sure how we'd do that.

I had brought my pack to hide the Sword, which was still under her bed as last night I hadn't been able to slip it past the guards on my way out. I had brought an old scabbard into Kadesh's realm to conceal it, but the Glass Sword would not be parted from its own translucent sheath. So my pack would have to do.

The morning guards eyed me suspiciously. My black breeches, shirt and ringmail tunic didn't match the role of costumier, but we would be leaving the demesne within the hour and I didn't much care. I wouldn't leave my things behind. They had their orders and let me pass.

What I found inside was not the mental image I had expected.

Paris sat in the white sunlight, surrounded by a gaggle of giggling female attendants.

This was the first red flag.

"Come in, Peredur." Paris smiled broadly. "It is so nice to see you again." The women lowered their eyes and hid behind their hands, but they were measuring me up and down all the same. For her part, Paris was not shy at all, sitting on a stool in her black lace undergarments. Her eye makeup was a rainbow of pinks, her rich brunette tresses were neatly divided into a score of tiny pigtails (each adorned with miniature tinkling bells) and her lips were painted in two colors: her lower lip brilliant coral and her upper, cleft, lip cerise. This darker color above had the effect of deemphasizing the cleft and balancing the fullness of her lower lip.

The women returned to painting her nails and threading bells in her hair.

"Oh my God," I blurted out loud, "it's Barbie of the Dreamworlds."

Of course, no one in the room had a clue what I meant. Paris didn't react, but the tone of my voice brought scowls from a pair of eunuchs who stood by the open door to her balcony.

"Peredur is going to take me shopping today," Paris explained to her attendants.

Second red flag.

Paris was supposed to be alone, ready to flee, clad in the travel gear she swore she had.

She noticed my open mouth.

"I think Peredur is surprised I am not happy with the wonderful things he has designed already," she said, all sweetness and light, "but I have a whole new idea for my last dance, and I'm sure he will welcome another chance to demonstrate his brilliance."

Last dance?

I met her eyes, and found a keen intelligence there. She knew exactly what she was doing. Or better put, she was doing exactly what she wanted.

I had no choice but to play along.

And I had no idea at what we were playing.

Paris stood up, the ministrations of her helpers complete. One of her ladies fetched a strange garment from the bed. I thought of my sword, stuck under that same bed.

The lady helped Paris into the close-fitting tunic, which buttoned up the front, snow-white and brocaded in sable. She donned matching pantaloons. The outfit left her belly bare, where her navel sported a magnificent black stone. But I barely noticed these things. I was focused on the cloud of diminutive hematite orbs hovering, by no apparent means, two inches above the surface of the fabric. Spaced evenly across the outfit's length and breadth, they formed in the air a gleaming black and silver aura of Paris' exact figure.

She crossed the room, and the aura dissolved, as the orbs chased her through the air like a slow motion shadow and settled around her body again. Her spicy perfume encircled me as she stretched up and balanced perfectly on her toes to kiss my cheek.

"Trust me, it will be better," she whispered in my ear.

And so—with my mind racing and my body surrounded by a cloud of attendants, eunuchs and guards—Siana, Princess of Time, Nemesis of the Aedolae, went shopping.

• • • ● ●• ● • • •

At the bazaar by the Gates, I caught Assav's eye. He was atop his ox, more mountain than animal, its heavy, drooping fur suited for arctic conditions and colored a magnificent patchwork of deep greens and blues. I discretely raised one hand, palm upwards, in a gesture of helplessness. He shrugged and grinned back, as unfazed as when I'd held a blade to his throat the night before.

At least my co-conspirator wasn't going to do something hasty and stupid.

Paris waltzed me through the bewildering variety of booths in search of items to costume her as a bird. She kept up an amiable chatter the whole time. At first this concerned me, for the bulk of it seemed free and careless. But after the first hour I concluded she was anything but. She did a masterful job of concealing from her entourage my total ignorance about anything related to costuming, orchestrating our exchanges so I appeared to be the source of her ideas.

Sample:

"You think this one is the material for the shoes? Oh, that's perfect. And of course, I should have known, it is perfectly supple too, the way I like it to flex. You know me so well."

And so on and so on. Perhaps had I been more of a Barbie doll myself, in my waking world youth, she wouldn't have had to work so hard.

I noticed Assav was shadowing us nonchalantly on foot, doubtless making himself available for any moment I could communicate. He was skillful. Good, he needed to be. Paris was keeping me so busy it would fall to Assav to fetch the Glass Sword from her rooms sometime today.

Paris meant to stay in the realm until nightfall and dance. I didn't yet know why, nor how to salvage our plan. But I couldn't be mad at her; she was so charming, and so completely and good-naturedly oblivious to my frustration. She seemed utterly confident she could do no wrong by me.

Well, I sighed to myself, *she's got that sized up right.*

After another hour, we entered a merchant's booth that was plainly decorated (unlike the rest) and sold only prodigious feathers that ranged from six inches to six feet in length. I couldn't imagine the size of the bird.

"They are *perfect*," Paris exclaimed, repeating one of her favorite words, "a good color match". But my attention was drawn to the merchant: Egyptian in appearance, painted eyes, rich brown skin, and barely a stitch of clothing. His unabashed stare indicated recognition, but I couldn't place him. I hadn't run into anyone with his features or dress in my travels.

He smiled knowingly.

Paris was busy collecting a pile of feathers, pink tinged with purple. The Egyptian sidled up to me.

"Remember, friend," he whispered in a low baritone, "when you are in need, the same key will get you *out* through the *in* door." After speaking, he immediately withdrew and turned his attention to Paris.

I was stunned. Immediately I thought of the Kalimba. Could he know? I had hidden the Kalimba and the Torc away during my transformation into Peredur, merchant. Who was this man?

I never got a chance to learn more. Paris bought the feathers and distributed them amongst her entourage and then we headed back in the direction of the palace. We did stop briefly at a few more shops. In one I found Assav beside me. I whispered to him a meeting time and place. Not knowing Paris' further plans, I hoped I could keep the rendezvous.

Back in her rooms, Paris got busy giving explicit directions to her tailors regarding her new outfit, all the while making me the mastermind behind her design. Apparently I was a conceptual costumier, a *costumier of costumiers*, and actual needlecraft was as beneath me as carrying her own things was beneath Paris.

Our next stop was the banquet hall, abandoned at this hour and swept clean of the nocturnal festivities. To my relief, Paris dismissed her eunuchs and attending women (these were not in fact handmaidens or servants, but fellow women of the harem, whose subservience to Paris was a function of their kinship and adoration). Only a single guard was left behind, and the rest escorted her entourage back to the fourth floor. Paris left this man at the main entrance and swept me to the center of the room.

"I need to practice, for I have designed a whole new dance," she explained in a quiet voice. "Later the musicians will be here, and doubtless my lord will come at some point to see what I am doing, but for a bit we can talk freely. I am sorry to leave you in the dark, and I am sorry if I disturbed you." Her apology was unexpected, after her cheerful disregard. "But I must dance tonight."

"I know you take your art very seriously—" I began, but she held her hand up.

"That's true," she said, "but it isn't what you think, not this time. I'm not going to dance the dance they expect. This is something that weighs on my heart, Peredur. You will see." The seriousness of her tone arrested me.

She assayed the room, measuring its dimensions against the boundaries of her dance, moving across the smooth wood floor with a ballerina's step. I noticed for the first time that the dance floor was not bamboo but true wood, the only wood in the whole compound.

For a while I was occupied watching the hematite orbs shadow her movements across the room and form a trailing black arc behind her. And listening to the ring of the bells in her hair.

Then she invited me to join her at the edge of the dance space, near the Pool.

"There is a trapdoor here." She ran her toes along a barely perceptible seam in the wood. "It hasn't been used for years and it's probably locked underneath. But it leads down to a narrow catwalk above the Pool that meets the boardwalk. Have Assav to free the lock and make sure the passage is clear." I nodded and then she said loudly, for the benefit of the guard, "You are so right, Peredur, if I arch my arms so, then moonlight will shine on the feathers of my wings."

She flowed through a few more steps, then returned to me and explained the remainder of her plan. I had my misgivings, but the drama of it appealed to my young mind. And the gall of it struck me as *very* satisfying. For Paris, even her escape needed to be artful, part of her dance. So be it. Go out with a bang, I thought.

I hope none of us gets killed.

A rippling metallic sound interrupted us, as the curtain of the dais was drawn back. The Prism was gone. Through the part in the curtain strode Kadesh, so confident in his place of power that he was unguarded and alone.

"My maharani," he said, in booming tones dripping with possession, "you grace my afternoon with your loveliness." Paris bowed. "Who accompanies you? Present him to me."

A moment to dread. Without betraying any nervousness, Paris took my hand and led me to the throne. I could learn a thing or two from Paris about hiding intent. We mounted the bamboo stair. Kadesh had sat down in his chair, its rim adorned with humanoid skulls.

"This is Peredur, who, despite his rough garb, is a skilled costumier. He took a fast and perilous way to reach me in time for this special night, and his road was dangerous. From his tales, I can tell you he is as brave as he is as skilled." She ended her introduction with her customary curtsey. I had no idea what protocol Kadesh expected and kept my eyes downcast.

"You look familiar," Kadesh said. I hoped he didn't notice my shudder.

"You honor me, Lord Kadesh," I returned, "with the thought you should notice and remember such as me."

Perhaps Paris' poise had rubbed off a little, not bad.

"Have you visited us before?" Kadesh asked. My mind raced.

"Only as a child, my parents brought me. They were merchants from the desert," I answered. I didn't want anyone searching the Merchant's Book for my name. A child's first name would not be listed. I hoped this would satisfy Kadesh's sense of recognition.

He had never seen me as Siana, only as Jaena. Could it be he discerned the same cast of features in both an Orsian girl and a white-skinned man?

Paris, wisely, turned Kadesh's attention before more details were sought.

"Lord, if it please you, I have designed something special for this night. Unprecedented." She stressed this last word, and then, I observed, dared to meet his eye.

"I have full confidence in your abilities," Kadesh said, without much apparent interest.

"My lord," Paris said, "this is something for which I, your betrothed, must ask your permission." Kadesh nodded his heavy head. As with Daphne, there was something disturbingly wrong about his features. So close to human, yet not.

"I wish to display my loveliness in a way none have seen, to show the world what wonders your greatness is about to possess," Paris said and cast down her eyes. After a moment's silence, Kadesh laughed, a rich, booming laughter that evidenced his thorough approval.

The sly way she explained it. The unexpected brazenness, hinting that Kadesh had already corrupted her nubile innocence. I admired Paris' strategy. She knew how to play Kadesh. Perfectly.

She sashayed down the stairs and ran to the spot above the trapdoor.

"When I collapse here," she shouted, "I will slip from my costume, so that none will see. And when they think the dance is over, when they have waited long, I will emerge, my flesh naked to all eyes. Then they will know the glories of your bride. Does this please you, my lord?"

Kadesh's only answer was more laughter. Paris nodded and smiled. She returned to the foot of the stairs.

"Feel free, my lord," she advised, with honey in her voice, "to spread the rumor of this impending wonder. It will insure and safeguard the drama of the moment."

I'd been watching the shadows cast by the torch poles along the Pool, and knew it was time to meet Assav. I excused myself graciously, on the pretense of some costumier's mission, and with relief left Kadesh behind.

Out in the bazaar, I was grateful to find Assav hooded and disguised. I explained to him about the trapdoor and the retrieval of the sword. He asked a few questions and then was gone.

With all our plans laid, we could do little but wait.

· · · ●·●· ● · ·

D uring the night's first entertainments a low mist effused from the jungle and wafted across the Pool like the tattered garments of ghosts. The afternoon had passed to evening, with no uproar indicating that my theft had been discovered. During her garment-fitting and into the banquet, Paris had resumed her upbeat prattle. It was too genuine and sweet-spirited to be an act, yet she was either blessedly lucky or quite smart—to say so much and speak so freely without disclosing a single fatal detail. Throughout dinner she had dropped various hints about her dance, but never any part of that secret she was keeping even from me.

I wondered if she had been at the feast last night and I had missed her, or if her presence at the meal tonight was a result of her new status.

Though I sat nearby, her prattle kept all attention focused away from me. I soon realized no one would notice if I changed seats and positioned myself closer to the Pool. So I took a position along the far wall, with the Prismatic Pool to my left. Ignored by Paris and everyone else, I had time to worry about Assav failing to show up at our second and final covert meeting before the fete. I wanted to assume his jobs had taken long than expected and all was still well. But if not, my military mettle would be sorely tested before the night was up. Or we weren't going to get Paris out at all. I didn't welcome the idea of stealing the Beetle and leaving her behind.

My worries kept my focus off the festivities until Paris took the stage. Two of Kadesh's moons had begun to cast their light into the hall, blending with the roseate light of torches. Paris would take advantage of this later on. As would I.

Of course I watched Paris. Watching for the cue, because I didn't know the length of her dance and had to be ready. But soon rapture consumed my anxiety. Anxious Peredur was stripped away, and a younger Siana remained. The Siana who dreamt seeking beautiful and wondrous things to assuage her pain. Who dreamt to submerge the banality of her waking world existence in something grandiose and free. Before she became Princess of Time and her vendetta against the Aedolae transformed her.

A Siana I had been seeing less and less of.

Even in my rapture I fought against the rawness of my feelings. I tried to dismiss them as dangerous distractions. But I couldn't. Paris spoke too strongly to a dreaming girl's longings. Piercing through the veneer of the Siana I had become.

Paris stood in the Prism's spotlight, now tuned rosy pink to accent her costume's color. Paris' back and arms sported feathers, with the biggest forming her arms into wings. Her legs were clad in form-fitting white and her knees were crested with tufts of down. Her hair was pulled back and dyed white, and her face was again cleverly painted, this time in whites and golds. Her amber lips contrasted with the deep purple rings around her eyes. There was something familiar to that, but I couldn't place it and soon forgot.

At the start of her story her avian character was seeking a landmark in unfamiliar worlds and I admired her artfulness in the telling. The way I could *see* the flowers she stooped to smell, and could *see* the water trickling from her hands when she bathed at dawn, the way I could hear her thoughts as she wrinkled her brow and cast about for sign of home. I could taste her anguish and confusion, as Paris shaped it with fingers and enlaced arms. She had exquisite control over the pace of her movements, accelerating their rhythm to express anxiety, slowing to express her contentment at finding home again.

And then shock. Paris pantomimed ascending a long incline, hunching her feathered shoulders, and then collapsed to the floor. I snapped to attention. No, she was nowhere near the trapdoor. The bird-woman was on her feet again, running about with great agitation, and in all this frenzy Paris never lost her grace.

She was surveying her homeland, rediscovered at last, and it lay in ruin.

Slowly I came to realize the story Paris was telling. To understand her immense courage in telling it. The depth of her defiance. I wondered how she knew the tale.

She found something large and ovoid in the ruined forest. My heart pulsed with the sway of her hips, the undulations of her body as she circumscribed it. Gingerly she climbed it, and Paris' skill made us see the ascent, despite the absence of any prop. She sliced her foot on some sharp edge and knelt to press her fingers to the wound. Now hobbling, she continued up and perched on its apex.

Despite great variation in her moves, Paris was remarkably adept so far in concealing the front of her outfit from the eye, her pink wings shrouding her body in shadow. Now, at the summit, her foot still crooked in pain, she spread her wings and pirouetted, making a full circuit of the crowd, ending with her face toward the throne. Her blouse was thin and gauzy, and her brown nipples and the comely shape of her breasts were clearly visible beneath. A wise provocation, a confirmation of the rumored spectacle to come.

But yet that was not all Paris intended. With all eyes drawn to her she began to sing. On cue, the spotlight was cut off, and all the torches extinguished. After my eyes adjusted I saw she was still bathed in light, the light of the moons, one white, one yellow, casting shadows along the folds of her costume. Mist from the Pool snaked along the floor, surrounding Paris in mystery.

I now had no doubt of the story. I could tell it from the wound in her foot, the purple and gold cast of her features, from the shard of the Prism she had circled. I knew it from my passage through the Fringe years before, for in the Prismatic Jungle I had spoken to a Singer, the same day the shining ribbon of my brother's soul had shattered and frayed.

Paris told, in risky defiance of her betrothed lord and master, the story of the Solmikaedes. Their realm had been shattered by Kadesh's greed. My promise of escape allowed her this defiance.

Music had accompanied her dance so far, but with the extinction of light all drumming and piping ceased, leaving only Paris' high, sweet singing. I judged from the collective intake of breath no one had heard it before. She sang only syllables, no words in any known tongue, but they were plenty sufficient to punctuate her anguish and to evoke roiling tears from many. It didn't matter if they understood the tale.

Her song encapsulated all my losses. The loss of my mother. The loss of my brother. The loss of my naiveté, the wistful dreams before Timothy was taken. My cheeks were wet and my chest heaved.

One who understood her tale all too well was Kadesh. Was it my imagination or could I see even at this distance his eyes narrow and his fists clench on the arm of his chair? At an almost imperceptible motion of one hand, his guards began to fan out through the crowd. This was getting dangerous.

I had no idea how long she had sung. Paris' voice dropped in slow undulations and faded away. The hall was dead silent. And then she spun, once, at the center of the hall. With a flash in the moonlight, her costume took flight in multiple directions.

She had released a flock of Vinna birds, hidden somehow among her feathers. They scattered in all directions, startling onlookers.

Power shuddered in me, fleeing my body and spiraling toward the bamboo rafters. The Bracelet Eterokon acted without my conscious control. It had never happened before.

The Vinna birds fell mid-flight and struck the floor with a percussive rain of thuds. Even in the dim light, their glossy black plumage was clearly stone grey.

Shit, I thought frantically, *how did that happen? Did the anguish of her story engulf my mind and spark the Bracelet's power?*

Paris stayed in character. She climbed down and ran to the nearest bird, picking it up with infinite tenderness and stroking its stone back. As she ran to each bird in turn, her composure disintegrated into a keening wail. Her dance had gone way beyond theater, as she poured all her fear of Kadesh, all the anguish of the Singer's story, into a frenzied survey of her dead friends. Her voice rose and fell in waves of torment, piercing our souls. The audience gasped. She had taken them where their festal mood had no intention of going, but now they were fully there. She took a feather from her costume for each of the birds and laid it upon their breasts.

And then she retreated, one slow step at a time toward the Pool, her shoulders bowing under a tremendous weight, her body crumpled and defeated. I dared not look at Kadesh now. He knew Paris' story, even if no one else did. And he would know what petrified the birds.

Paris reached the trapdoor and collapsed beneath her feathers. She disappeared from view beneath them but the heaving of her body shook the feathers, as she pantomimed breaths of sorrow, subsiding as the Singer died. On this cue, the musicians resumed, softly but growing in intensity.

Music to cover our exit, though they were unaware.

Mist had filled the chamber. Paris' costume had been contrived so that the feathers would retain its form even after she slipped out of it. I found myself staring too long, watching to see if I could detect any movement as she escaped, but roused myself to action. I should have been away immediately. Watching for guards, I vanished into the garden of shrubs and jungle flowers behind me, walking twenty paces before dropping off the lip of the terrace and onto the boardwalk below, my shapechanged feet landing without a sound.

The mist was thicker here, making visibility only fifteen feet or so. A diffuse white light surrounded me. Before me was deep shadow where the boardwalk tunneled under the overhang of the banquet hall.

Out of that shadow stepped an angel.

Paris. Naked save for the Beetle about her neck and a red ring that flashed on one finger. Her body was beaded with perspiration, her face glowed white and gold. She was as exquisitely beautiful as the rumors of myriad worlds proclaimed, from the voluptuous curves of her figure to the rich luster of her smooth and unblemished skin. This was the opulent sight denied hundreds of onlookers above and revealed only to Peredur, brigand and would-be hero.

A part of me I didn't even know I had stiffened inside my clothing. I blushed.

The drums grew louder, pounding through the fog. A cue for action. I hustled Paris to me, whispering, "You can't go like that."

"Don't worry." Her chest still heaved from the exertion of her dance and the difficulty of slipping from her clothes without betraying her disappearance. She touched her glowing red ring. "It'll be fine."

I had no idea what she meant, but what could I do anyway?

Where was Assav?

In answer to my thought, something huge parted the mists to our left. The ox. Assav slipped deftly from his high perch upon its towering back, and handed the Glass Sword to me with a smile, the ivory of his teeth the only color in his face. He pointed to the sizeable leather pack on the ox's left flank. I climbed the rope ladder first. I pushed aside the heavy leather flap and hissed back, "It's full of fruit!"

"Open it again," Assav whispered. I did, and found it empty. Ultra-dimensional saddlebags indeed. Another intriguing wonder of the world of dreams. Holding the flap aside I motioned to Assav to help Paris up. When she reached me, I took her hand and helped her inside the bag. Soon she was stowed inside.

I joined her, enclosed in complete darkness. There was a bitter scent, but the bag was empty. Paris had already figured out that with the flex in the bottom of the bag sitting up was impossible. I jostled my way in behind her, cursing the scabbard where it poked me in the back and feeling generally awkward. What an ignominious way for the Princess of Time to depart her enemy's realm.

"It's OK," Paris giggled, "you can touch me."

"I'll have to," I replied, realizing touching her was exactly what I'd been avoiding. The ox shuffled forwards, throwing me against her. I found my arm encircling her naked belly. Her perfume wafted over me and her body shuddered at my touch. Great. I quickly shapeshifted the tumescent part of my anatomy out of existence.

I'm a woman, I argued with myself, *I can hold her*. But my Peredur-self protested. I wondered at the perils of staying too long in shapeshifted form.

Outside sounds were muffled by the thickness of the bag. Our plan was clever but I hadn't counted on my own impatience. Feeling the ox's slow stride and not seeing what transpired outside was maddening. Not knowing if our ruse had been discovered. These past two years I had become a creature of action. I abhorred being carried like so much dead weight. The ox's pace was horribly slow. There would be no hope if Assav couldn't step it up.

A shift in direction. Perhaps that was Assav turning toward the board-walked trails of the Dark Quarter. I hoped so. It would not be good to be discovered along the Pool's perimeter. How long before the music stopped and the crowd awoke from the spell of anticipating Paris' nakedness? I heard nothing, no faint rumor of music. The fog made the jungle uncharacteristically silent. What would they do first? The unconscious action of the Bracelet was unfortunate, despite the brilliant way Paris had played to it. We had assumed they would waste time searching the palace for her. Now Kadesh would suspect Siana's involvement. He would be searching the whole demesne before long.

Warm and cradled in my arms, Paris suddenly sneezed.

"I'm allergic to it," she whispered.

"To what?"

"Pinnia."

"What's that?" I whispered back, wishing we weren't talking.

"The smell in here," she explained. "It's obviously what Assav has been smuggling. It's the drug half the palace and the harem are addicted to."

Great, the smiling kid is a drug dealer. And he's all that stands between us and disaster.

Paris sneezed again. It was amazing her tremendously pungent perfume didn't make *me* sneeze.

"You've got to try not to do that," I whispered back. A payload of fruit wouldn't sneeze.

Paris' allergy must be another reason for her beauty and purity, her dedication to her art. She'd been protected from another danger of harem life.

A half hour passed. The ox's hooves struck stone, a change in sound. We'd left the Dark Quarter and struck the Aedol Via, far enough from the palace to appear uninvolved in any crime.

Good.

Another quarter hour passed with only the thud of heavy hooves against surface of the road. And then a whoosh of wings, a bellow of surprise from the ox. We stopped moving. Paris' body stiffened in my arms.

"Calm," I whispered in her ear. I held her closer, sensing she needed this even as part of me resisted. She placed my hand between her breasts. Her breathing slowed.

Guards' boots clicked on stone, no doubt as they dropped from the backs of Kadesh's green eagles. I tried to count their numbers from the sound. Fragments of conversation penetrated the leather of the bag. Accusations.

"Why are you traveling by night, trader?"

Assav answering. *"I enjoy the solitude, the road is so crowded by day."*

"It is dangerous.

"We would inspect your goods....routine procedure."

Someone climbed the rope ladder, jostling us. I cupped Paris' mouth with the hand she had laid on her chest. The flap was thrust aside and fog-veiled moonlight, dazzling after our dark ride, flooded the interior of the bag. I didn't know if smell could escape a parallel dimension but I was glad all the same for the bitter scent of pinnia to hide Paris' perfume.

The guard looked right through us.

"Nothing but fruit," he called over his shoulder. Amazing. The flap closed. The guard's metal-trimmed boots clicked again on pavement. He checked the other side of the ox.

Then more conversation.

"Since you are out here, trader, in the middle of the night, trader, you can help us—"

"—escaped from the palace, Kadesh's favorite—"

"—substantial reward—"

"—help us look—"

Paris' body shuddered, her chest convulsed. Oh no.

I had cupped her mouth to help her stay quiet. But my hands had brushed against the lining of the bag. Bringing the traces of the pinnia drug closer to her nose.

Such a small mistake to unhinge a plan.

Paris sneezed. Only once, but once was too much. The conversation stopped. More clicks on stone.

"Lower your bag, trader."

There was venom in the voice. Assav sputtered a protest, but was cut off by a jolt and a thud. I hoped they hadn't hurt him. We struck the ground.

The flap was raised again, and this time javelins were aimed at our throats. They saw us now. They recognized me, the strangely dressed costumier, and their eyes went wide at Paris' nakedness.

"Get out," one commanded. I helped Paris to her feet and we stepped out, awkwardly, for the lip of the bag was high and stiff. The four backed away slowly, ringing us in. They were all men, the fiercest of his guard. Four eagles surrounded the patchwork ox, wings folded, talons flexing in impatience, snapping and pecking in the direction of its shaggy hide.

"You foolish girl," another said. "How high in his Lordship's honors will you sit now?" He prodded her toward an eagle, about to separate us. I was still sizing up the situation, not sure what to do.

Assav's ox made my decision for me.

Patchwork oxen have an ankylosaur's spiked club-tail. This ox, tiring of the eagles' gall, smashed the nearest offender full in its feathered breast, sending it flying across the Via and into the jungle. The bones of its wings snapped audibly on impact.

The other eagles shrieked and lunged. A guard moved on me.

"Throw down your scabbard, deceiver," he demanded.

I reached back, directing the energy of my will at the Eterokon at my back. It slid from its scabbard, for the first time since ancient days. Timothy had never succeeding in wresting it free. To him the sword was a curiosity; my brother had never wanted to fight.

The Glass Sword sliced the guard's javelin in two like cleaving paper.

Chaos followed. Paris shrank against the ox, hiding in its fur, while it thrashed its tail and I laid about me with my new weapon. For all my hatred of the Aedolae, I did not relish the actual bloodshed, especially not human blood. In our conspiracy we had tried to avoid it, but now I had no choice. Assav jumped into the fray, sporting a rusty short sword and a purpling bruise on his forehead from the butt end of a spear.

The guards were no match for the Glass Sword. The melee ended with their bodies splayed across the Via and my weapon lodged in the breast of the remaining eagle not yet ricocheted by the ox into the woods. Assav was okay. I exhaled relief and freed my Sword. It showed no gore. Paris came to my side, wide-eyed at the carnage.

A fresh problem: something glowed on the road back to Kadesh. Flames in the center of the road, seen through fog. The moons had set behind the jungle.

They came, too quickly, ripples of muted orange light growing more intense. Sharp contours of fire burst forth from the mist and coalesced into human shape. A Serap of Kadesh, astride a night-black six-legged wolf.

Assav left my side, backing away.

From the utter black of her face, trailing gouts of fire, came words, thunderously spoken.

"Come, Sojourner, and meet thy doom."

She stepped from her mount, the fiery tendrils of her two-ended whip cutting the air with a vicious crackle. I parried with the Glass Sword and watched with satisfaction as it cut a smoking fragment off one end. She surrounded me, boxing me in with her whip and making coherent thought difficult. I tried to lead her away from Paris and Assav, toward the jungle. My blade sparkled in her firelight, and I was thankful for Daevon's tutelage. Not for the first or last time.

Fragments of the whip flew in all directions. Stray strands of my hair smoked and curled from the heat of her body.

I ducked and came up at her very feet, slicing outwards and cleaving her weapon in two at its haft. She staggered backwards. Pushing my advantage, I hewed at her torso. The Sword passed through her body without purchase.

The Serap's immateriality was only a one-way disadvantage. She regained her footing and struck my face with the back of her arm, burning my cheek and sprawling me face down in gravel at the edge of the Via. I rolled away in time to avoid the stomp of her feet.

The power of the Bracelet shuddered out of me, hurled at her with an intensity of rage. Her flaming body coagulated into the stone figure of a woman and dropped. I jumped to my feet and sliced the statue into a myriad pieces. I had no idea if that would kill her when the petrifaction wore off.

I looked back. Assav had his arm about Paris protectively, shadowed by the ox. A blur of movement my eye: the Serap's wolf fleeing down the road to Kadesh. I couldn't let it escape. My body transformed into a mimicry of its form, leaping after it on six legs. The fog enveloped us as I gave chase and soon I was gaining on it. Then, in a sudden feint, it turned and reared on its hindmost legs and I crashed headlong into it. Its middle legs boxed me in the chest with prodigious force. A black tongue snaked from its crimson red mouth as I flew backwards, and unexpectedly it spoke. Curses from a canine throat.

"Siana, you will not escape Kadesh's wrath for long."

As I fell, I left wolf form and became Peredur again. It bounded off into the mist. I struggled to my feet as Assav clattered up.

"Let it go," he wheezed. "Our hope is in flight. You can't kill everything Kadesh sends after us." I exhaled in frustration, staring at the place the mist had closed around the wolf's retreating form. "It's not over. You are a tremendous fighter. I've never seen anything like it. Hurry!"

He tugged at me and I acquiesced. As we jogged back to Paris, I brought up a concern.

"With your ox in tow, we won't be able to elude them now. It would be easier to hide a purple mountain."

"Don't worry," Assav said. That sounded too familiar. We hadn't resolved the issue of the ox before something new presented itself. A glistening cube had appeared in the middle of the road, edges alight with ruby fire. Were my eyes failing me in the dim light and the fog? I remembered my last glimpse of the Library of the Ancients as Bierce and I raced up the crumbling stair, the way the edges of the rooms had glowed in the dark.

Inside the cube, as we drew our weapons, we heard Paris humming.

KOIDENANG CREVASSE

I lowered the point of the Glass Sword and laughed. On that cue, a ruby-edged seam appeared and split the cube's shimmering surface. Through this doorway stepped Paris, fully dressed. She touched her ring and the entirety of the cube disappeared into the brilliant red depths of the ring's gemstone.

In response to our apparent bafflement, she said cheerfully, "It's a room ring. Haven't you ever seen one? A girl with my kind of wardrobe *has* to have one. I told you not to worry, Peredur."

She smiled sweetly with mischief in her eyes. She had sponged off her face paint and stripped the dye from her hair.

"That couldn't have fit inside your rooms at the palace," I protested.

"Oh," she said, "a lot of times it's bigger on the inside than the outside."

(Silly me!)

"Anyway," she continued, fanning her hand down the front of her outfit, "what do you think?"

Paris' version of travel gear was an elegantly tailored leather jacket studded with gems, a broad yellow sunhat tied below her chin, and dark thick pants. The linen blouse beneath her jacket was cut low and showed off her ample cleavage. But I noted that the pants were of rough material and her hand-sewn leather boots looked both sturdy and supple, fitting her dancer's feet perfectly.

"That's good enough," I nodded. Paris pursed her lips as if my reply wasn't adequate praise. I turned to Assav. "What about the ox? We need to be off this road in minutes."

"Can I put him in the room ring?" Assav suggested meekly. Paris' eyes blazed.

"Paris," I intervened, "we're safe so far, but what's left of the Serap will cease being stone and we can't count on it staying dead. Besides which, she had plenty of friends, and I'd bet they're coming this way. I can't hide the ox. Is there room in there?"

"Maybe in the back with my *older* clothes," Paris growled.

I hadn't heard *that* tone of voice before.

"OK, so how do we get him in?" I asked.

Paris touched the ring and the giant cube reappeared. A much wider door split its side. She turned to Assav.

"If he goes—" Paris began.

"He won't," Assav interrupted, "I promise. He never soils his stable."

"*Stable!*"

Paris swatted him with her sunhat. Assav defended himself with upraised hands.

"Kids!" I stepped between them. "We are going to die out here. Assav, lead your ox in there, and do it now." I retrieved my pack from the ox. A beautiful creature and steady, it showed no resistance being led into such an unusual place. Paris went in with Assav to insure the safety of her wardrobe, while I watched from outside. From my vantage point it seemed like a department store's worth of clothing.

When they reemerged Paris was scowling and Assav was wearing his trademark grin.

The cube dematerialized leaving only the three of us in the fog. I distributed to Assav weapons purloined from the armory. Paris handed me back the dagger I gave her.

"I'm not a fighter," she said with a shrug. "I couldn't do it."

"So we run as far and as long as we can," I explained. "There is a network of old trails that shortcuts a huge loop in the Via. It's maybe a fifteen minute run from here. It will deposit us back onto the Via just shy of the desert wall. We'll figure things out from there. I'm sorry, Assav, that your lot is thrown in with us now. I appreciate your help and your bravery."

"Thank you," he said. "It's OK. Maybe I'll join the Brigandrie someday. Does Kadesh know these trails?"

"I don't know," I confessed.

"When will we hit the Via again?"

"If we travel fast and don't sleep, sometime late tomorrow," I answered.

"Then let's hope they don't know about this shortcut," Assav said.

I had hinted about the power of the Kalimba the night before. But they didn't ask now, and I was loathe to abandon my desert mission. The Kalimba gave no direct access to the desert, and traveling through Kadesh's realm again would be perilous. I reasoned that I must recover the last of my brother's Eterokoni, but I felt a pang of guilt all the same. *I won't risk their lives; I still have time to use the Kalimba if it comes to that.*

We took off down the Aedol Via at a run. I was grateful for Paris' athleticism and Assav's youth. We found the landmark ten minutes later, a stump so prodigious the ancient builders of the road had opted to leave it undisturbed in the gravel shoulder. The trail I sought would be invisible from the Via. We crashed about the undergrowth for a few minutes but found it: a narrow line, the barest of trails, winding into deep jungle. The fog-laden road had been spectral, but this was worse. A tangle of low-hanging limbs roofed the long-neglected passageway, making us crouch and stoop. Dripping tendrils of moss stroked our backs like ghostly fingers. We were sucked along a thin tunnel of the palest white light.

There was a crackling sound behind us and we turned to see the black latticework of the jungle silhouetted against an orange glow. An entire squadron of Seraphi was passing on the road. We crouched, already drenched, Paris' linen blouse plastered to her breasts, and sat motionless as they glided past. Their blazing glow lit different sections of jungle as they passed us by.

I breathed a sigh of relief and beckoned my companions on.

The ground grew rockier, and the jungle opened up into sparser stands of trees. It had been a half hour since the Via, and Assav dared to asked a question.

"Where is this trail taking us?"

We were now among stone outcroppings that may have been statues of men, features worn by weather and menacing in the mist. We stubbed our toes on rocks in the path and I was starting to have trouble finding the path, no longer framed by trees and undergrowth.

"Over Koidenang Crevasse" I answered, trying to sound matter-of-fact.

"That passage is a legend," he shot back, sounding like he misdoubted his own skepticism.

"No," I said, "it's not."

Assav turned to Paris. "We're going to die."

As it turned out, we didn't die, nor were we pursued. A few minutes later we arrived at the lip of a dreamworld wonder, a crevasse like a raw wound that clove the jungle, deeper than any explorer had penetrated. From its floor, unseen even by daylight, the famed black willows of Koidenang grew thousands of feet toward the light, their feathery tops so spindly that they were swayed by the lightest breeze.

Our trail became a suspension bridge anchored to these frail and slender trees, framed by the gentle sweep of their branches. Surrounded by acres of open air.

"No," Assav said simply.

I chuckled. "We could leave you and the ox here at the edge."

"Come on, Assav," Paris said and sprang nimbly onto the bridge, leather boots flexing with her step. There was a rope railing to either side, and the floor of the bridge was formed of wide bamboo slats. Even in the dark it was obvious quite a few slats were missing.

"How far does this trail go on like this?" Assav asked. Paris had turned back to wait for us, hands on either rail and looking unconcerned.

"Seven or eight thousand feet lateral feet," I replied, enjoying his anxiety. I was young and brash enough at that time to take a self-satisfied pleasure in my greater experience. "It is rarely used now so watch your step."

Paris was balancing the weight of her body on the ropes and doing ballet poses with her legs in the air.

"Show off," Assav grumbled and stepped forwards.

"Let me lead," I said.

"No, Peredur, let me lead," Paris said mildly. "I have better balance than either of you and I'll be able to tell quickest if something is amiss." Despite my authoritarian attitude with Assav, I took to Paris' leadership without complaint.

It was different with Paris, already.

So began my second crossing of the Koidenang Divide.

With three of us the bridge swayed alarmingly. The willow trunks flexed more than seemed safe.

"Are you *sure* about this?" Assav glanced over his shoulder.

"No," I smiled, "but I have crossed before and I know where to go at the junctions. The trees sway a lot but I've never seen one fail."

Unlike any suspension bridge in the waking world the whole pathway dipped and our weight bent the trees' hoary heads—less bridge crossing and more amusement park ride. Watching Paris' deft movements now was a pleasure. Her body was one with the dips and bends, no matter how random.

We reached the center of the labyrinthine system of bridges around midnight. If an Orsian face can be ashen, Assav's was, and his palms were raw. The center was a bamboo platform, forty feet square and buttressed by four massive trees, from which bridges led off in many directions. These four trees stood alone, separated from their fellows by a hundred feet of open air. The mist had begun to clear and a few stars winked overhead. Assav was panting, while Paris looked nonplussed, though fatigue showed in her eyes. A different one of Kadesh's moons glowed behind a distant line of trees, throwing a white halo above the horizon.

"Ten minutes rest," I said. Assav collapsed on his back in the middle of the platform. Paris walked to the far side and peered over, as if she hadn't yet seen enough of boundless open air. I joined her at the bamboo railing.

"Your dance was marvelous," I said. The words were hopelessly inadequate. "It wasn't just beautiful. You dared to tell the truth about the Aedolae. About the kind of injustice the Brigandrie fights."

"Thank you." She turned toward me. She must have repainted her lips in the room ring, for, like that morning, her upper lip was darker. Its unusual shape made her lipstick striking. There was a leonine cast to her features.

"No one had heard you sing before?"

"No, at least not in performance."

"Why did you never sing?"

"Well," Paris said, leaning over the rail again, "it never occurred to me, if you can believe that, not until today. I love singing, but it was always for my own amusement. It never occurred to me to combine it with my dance."

"Your voice is heavenly," I said. "I wish I had an iota of your ability."

"So you know who the Singers are?" Paris asked.

"Yes, I know."

Paris looked puzzled. "How? That story is a secret Kadesh believes guarded well."

"I could ask you the same question."

"I asked you first," Paris teased. She had taken my arm and was leaning against me. Her long brunette hair was soft and silky across my hand. And again her perfume! A different scent now, honey and cinnamon.

I answered. "The Brigandrie is led by a Sojourner, who journeyed through the lands of the Solmikaedes to reach the

Aedolae's realms. She encountered one and spoke with her at length."

Close enough to the truth. I was beginning to feel uncomfortable with my disguise. It had been meant to fool Kadesh and his guards, but the deception had begun to feel inappropriate. I was lying to this fine and gentle girl, whom I had come to deeply respect.

"So the Sojourners are real..." Paris mused. "I heard that one led the rebellion."

"Yes, they are real," I said, wanting to say more, but not knowing how. I was interrupted by an undeniable lightening in the surrounding darkness. Now I could see the grey sparkle of Paris' eyes. Color swirled in the dark abyss below.

"Look," Paris pointed. A translucent purple balloon floated past the railing, lit from within, and trailing feathery tendrils. A pair of fleshy goggly eyes winked at us. Wriggling its tendrils, it *swam* through the air toward us. My free hand strayed to the hilt of the Glass Sword.

"No," Paris said with alarm. "See, it is just curious."

The balloon creature had approached Paris, bathing her face in violet light. It blinked its eyes and made a slow circuit of her head. The tendril-like fins swirled in an arc about her. There seemed no menace to it.

My attention had been riveted to the one, but now a swarm of balloon fish, each lit a different jewel-like hue, came over the railing and swam around us. The bamboo planking was now a kaleidoscope of rich color, brilliant in the dark and fog. They were clumsy as they crowded about us, bumping together and sometimes propelling each other into slow spins through the air.

"Oh, Peredur," Paris giggled, "they are so funny, and so beautiful." One nuzzled in her hair, and she pantomimed flight into my arms. My arms closed about her back as she buried her head in the hollow of my neck. My spirit lifted, eased by the unexpected appearance of the comical fish, eased by Paris' delight.

"Thank you," she whispered, "for saving me."

Assav was encouraging the fish to chase him about the terrace. Paris turned to watch the antics, but she stayed nestled in my embrace. One by one, lazily, the fish dispersed, floating back into the depths, until they were but shining jewels against black velvet, the glowing silhouette of their bodies softened by the fog that still clung to the great trunks of the willow trees below. And then one by one they winked out of sight and were lost. Paris laughed in my arms, and I found myself laughing with her.

"You never know what's going to happen in the dreamworlds," I said quietly. Paris raised her face. I was only a few inches taller than her; I hadn't increased my height in my male guise.

"Why do you say that? What do you mean?" she asked.

I cursed myself for the indiscretion. My thoughts were pulled back to my disguise. Paris thought I was someone I was not. I needed to come clean.

"Where will you go, when we get out of Kadesh?" I asked.

Paris wrinkled her brow and pursed her lips like I was stupid.

"You can come with me," Assav grinned hopefully, now standing a few feet away.

"And where are *you* going, my dear Orsian drug smuggler?" I asked. Assav looked sheepish. "You said you'd like to join the Brigandrie. Your ox will mark you now, for which I am sorry—"

"I said *maybe*," Assav said. "Actually, I don't know what I'll do."

Paris had stepped from my arms and now faced both of us.

"As for me, Peredur, I'm going with you," she said. "I am so happy to be away from Kadesh, from the threat that I tried to dismiss from my mind all these years. I never thought about where I would go if I could escape. I didn't believe that I could. I've left all my friends, my entire life behind, and I have no idea where to go. You are kind, Peredur, and you risked your life for me. I trust you to lead me to a place of safety."

"I go into the desert on a dangerous mission. And then I return to the hiding places of the Brigandrie. I can't take non-combatants there, nor can I take anyone who has not pledged to our cause—"

"Why not?" Paris frowned.

"You won't even hold a dagger. I don't want to take you out of the frying pan and throw you in the fire."

"I can fight, you've seen—" Assav interjected.

I held up my hand. "There is something you two must know. But first, you must promise never to act against the Brigandrie in any way."

Assav's face grew serious. "I promise. I have no love for the Aedolae."

"Then I will tell you the truth: I disguised myself to penetrate Kadesh's demesne. My name is not Peredur, and this face is not mine. I didn't mean to deceive you. I didn't expect to find friends amid Kadesh's people. I am so sorry. I meant only to evade my enemies."

There, it was done.

"Then who are you?" Paris breathed.

"I am not one of the Brigandrie," I answered. "I *am* the Brigandrie. And I am their Sojourner."

Assav and Paris both stared intently, as if this might explain a thing or two.

I took it to its conclusion. "My name is Siana, Princess of Time." Dark consternation settled on Paris' face.

"*What?*" she exclaimed.

I let the Torc release my Peredur disguise, grown too familiar over these past days. *Siana* returned with a subtle shift in the proportions and weight distribution of my body. Straight blonde hair brushed my shoulders. I can only imagine what it looked like to Paris, seeing the handsome face of her rescuer soften into a woman's face, a face with the same eyes, the same basic character, yet somehow so different. To see my hips fill out and my shoulders narrow within my black martial attire.

Confusion and surprise washed across her beautiful face, then passed like storm clouds fading into clear blue sky.

I never saw a single flash of anger.

Paris folded her hands in front of her chest and spoke with a poise that was, given the circumstances, every bit as graceful as her most sublime dancing.

"Then I thank you again, Siana," she spoke my name gently, "for rescuing me, for risking your life and your mission to save me, for treating me with kindness. It means even more now, because you weren't one of the many men who have sought my favor. I will go with you, into the desert, and I will go with you as long as you will have me."

With that, she laid her sunhat aside and knelt before me, letting the waves of her hair shroud her body as she folded herself upon her legs. As she had for Kadesh the night before.

I loved her for it. How could I not?

"I'll go with you too," Assav chimed with a grin. "I might as well."

I touched the crown of Paris' head, as Kadesh had done, and helped her to her feet. We stood an arm's length apart, holding hands. An electricity passed between us. I had found a sister, a friend, something both dear and beautiful. Timothy and I had both sought beautiful things in the world of dreams. But Paris was a deeper wonder, a human creature that somehow embodied all the beauty for which I had longed.

She was beautiful as I had yearned to be.

Paris nodded, a slightest of motions.

"We'd better go," I said, and led my troupe into the dark.

MORE QUESTIONS

E llie finished the book late and felt exhausted. She left the library and used her new key to the amphitheater. She wanted to head down, to the suspended door marking the entrance to the Mirror Room, and confront Siana with the truth.

But it's too late in the day, she reasoned, *and I'm yawning where I stand*. So she crossed to the ballroom, keeping the amphitheater wall tight on her left, and climbed the stair to the gallery and small pallet where her odyssey in the castle had begun.

She was asleep in seconds, but images from the book accompanied her, for in the middle of the night she dreamt about Siana and Paris.

• • • ● • ● • • • •

I n the dream, Ellie looked down on a small town bathed in muted sunlight. The scene was peaceful, restive, and the streets, wet from night-time rain, shone in the white light. Ellie heard birds chirping in the bushes, but every yard and avenue were empty.

Then a woman stepped from one of the houses. The screen door clapped shut behind her, as Ellie's dreaming consciousness hovered closer. Siana, not clad in black like the icons, but wearing soft pants and a clingy white shirt. Ellie followed Siana down the streets of what must be Forgotten Town, watching Siana pause at the bay window of a small house, cupping her eyes to fend off sunlight and see within. She shook her head and returned to the sidewalk, walking several more blocks and climbing a tall flight of stairs into an ugly concrete building.

A "gymnasium", Ellie thought, not knowing how she knew the word.

Instead of following Siana inside, Ellie's dreaming mind was drawn to a high window and she peered down, past rows of bleachers, to a lone figure dancing at the center of a broad and open space. Paris. Her spiraling movements were every bit as beautiful as Siana described. As Paris finished her dance, Siana appeared from underneath the bleachers. Paris and Siana spoke, but even though Ellie had heard the birds outside, this part of the dream was silent.

Then the two danced, Siana mimicking Paris' moves. Siana was not a bad dancer but appeared inelegant beside Paris' grace. She collapsed on the floor midstride, scowling. Paris soon laid down on the floor next to her, and Ellie saw that they spoke. She strained to hear, but nothing clear reached her, only a muted ripple like the echo of voices cast down a bending corridor. Then something strange happened. They had stood and Paris struggled to pick up Siana from behind. Then Siana tried to lift Paris. They were laughing. Siana tackled Paris from the front, then staggered and fell. Paris' smile was beautiful.

They lay there entwined as laughter subsided into conversation. And then, inexplicably, Ellie's consciousness drew close. She fancied she was Siana, feeling the weight of Paris' body on top of her. Paris traced the line of her lips with one finger and then in the dream Paris was kissing her, Siana, and she, Siana, was kissing back with relish, wrapping Paris in her arms.

Then the scene darkened and faded, dispersed like mists before the wind.

· • • ● ●• ● •• ·

E llie awoke to morning light, dimmed by the grime on her little window, as it ever was. She could tell, though, from the quality of the light that the Siana window in the ballroom would be blazing with color. Before she even remembered the dream, there was a queer sensation in the pit of her stomach, a palpable sense of loss. She shook her head and ran her fingers through her hair, which felt longer and smoother beneath her touch. Then memories of the Paris book and the dream returned and she rushed out of the room.

She froze on the balcony. Someone stood on the ballroom floor below, but in the fierce light from the stained glass she couldn't see who. Slow movements of the person's arms cut through and deflected slanting beams of sunlight.

As her eyes too slowly adjusted and she held her breath, she recognized Parson Graham, sorting through a new collection of plants and herbs. For the first time, his appearance matched conditions inside the castle, for his hair shone gold.

"Hello, Ellie," he said, once again sensing her presence without turning his head. She went down the stairs.

"Why didn't you come?" she asked, then cursed herself for her rudeness. "I'm sorry. I missed you, Parson Graham."

"I was waiting for the rains to abate," he said matter-of-factly. He stood up, brushing dirt from his cloak. "I'm sorry I wasn't here for you. But today is beautiful, both inside and out. For once I see you in the sunlight."

She pointed at stained-glass Siana, which of course he couldn't see.

"There's a window in this room. I've only found three total in the castle," she explained. "Did you watch me come down the stairs? What did it look like to you?"

"I only saw you from the corner of my eye, I was still sorting my plants. But there is a low hillock behind you now. I suppose that hillock is your stairs."

He smiled, but with the hint of a frown.

"How did you know where I slept?" Ellie asked, assuming it was a purposeful rendezvous.

"I didn't, but I assumed near your amphitheater was a good place to run into you. And I was right." The hint of a frown was gone. "Tell me about your week, my young mystery-solver."

She felt like she was smiling inside, Graham was so reassuring and so sweet. She described what she had been reading, and then she told him about meeting Siana in the mirror. Stammering all the while, for she feared she must sound crazy.

"Intriguing," Graham replied. "This is a magnificent opportunity to unravel some of the threads of our tangled skein. Have you been back to see her again?"

"Not yet," Ellie answered, "but I want to go today."

"Make a list of questions for Siana before you go," the Parson said, tucking away his floral finds. "It will focus your mind and insure a more productive session." Ellie tracked his advice with little nods of her head.

"Tell me, Parson—"

"You can call me Graham."

"—okay, Graham, where are we? I mean, I know I'm in the castle, but where is it that you live?"

"It's a small village beyond the heath, near the river Calmbrook. This country is mostly wild, with villages and pockets of farms breaking up the wilderness. The whole region is called Vaelonn-Marr, though I can't tell you why. No kingdom of that name has existed in human memory. We are simple folk, tending our land and animals. In all my life, I have traveled no further than this heath."

Ellie thought this over. It didn't place them anywhere in the worlds of Siana's exploits.

"Did you bring me any food?" she asked, biting her lip. He nodded and took bread and cheese from his pocket.

"I only ask, in barter for breakfast," he said, "that you take me into this library of yours. Let's eat and walk." She immediately began stuffing her face. She wondered if the condition of her hair at daybreak was related to the food. How long had she wandered without eating? And her legs were less scrawny below the threadbare shift.

Ellie led him through the amphitheater. The Parson's posture was odd as he followed her into the foyer below the library, which she noticed despite her fevered involvement with a block of cheese, for he crouched and ducked like her. She eyeballed him as she munched.

"Graham," she began with her mouth full.

"What?"

She held up her index finger and finished chewing.

"You're not in the sunlight anymore," she said, finally.

His face erupted in a huge grin.

"Very good!" He patted her shoulder. "My sleuth!" Then said nothing more, smiling.

"Well, why?" she said, a bit exasperated.

"You tell me." She thought back to his posture entering the room.

"You can see the castle now!" she burst out, wildly excited.

"Not quite," the Parson explained, "but this morning, I saw something strange on the horizon. A building stripped of its roofs and doors, a decayed skeleton of a castle. Ruins that *grew* overnight. What I see now is a rectangular room with stone walls, ancient and broken. The door you led me through is just a frame and it's a few steps above the floor of this room, which is about half gone. I am standing in the shadow of the broken wall separating us from the volcanic bowl. Remains of stone stairs rise to a missing balcony on my left; there's another doorframe up there and skeletal vestiges of a second and third floor—"

"That's the library!" Ellie interjected. "This is amazing! I wonder if you will see more tomorrow. What does it mean?"

The Parson rubbed his chin. "I would argue the world you inhabit is shifting into line with my world. This is a deeper puzzle than anything I've ever read about. I wouldn't have believed any of it if we hadn't made a careful test the day we met. Experience is a wonderful teacher, for she keeps our Reasoning pure and unsullied by the prejudices of our assumptions."

She laughed.

"You are a funny man. *You* sound like a teacher."

"Take me up." He pointed to the landing. She led him up the stairs, and he had to pick his way around gaps in the staircase that existed for him. Strange he saw the stairs as stone and she saw them as paneled with wood.

"I'll have to jump to get to the door," he explained.

"Do you *know* the floor I'm standing on won't support you?" she wondered. "It might be different now."

"Good reasoning. Let's see." He stepped forward and his foot appeared to sink into the wood. "Guess not."

So the Parson jumped instead, more lithe in his long cloak than she expected.

"Find me a book," Graham said once they were inside. "I want to see at what point it becomes visible to me."

"Can I look for the one about my dream?" she asked. "It might take a while."

"I'm in no hurry. I had a whole week to tend my garden and visit my flock. In the rain, no less. What dream are you talking about?"

"I dreamt about Siana and Paris in Siana's hideout."

"Had you read about that too?"

"No, but Paris pledged herself to stay with Siana, in the last book I read. After her desert mission, Siana probably took Paris to Forgotten Town."

Graham's brow wrinkled. "It was a dream, yet you speak as if it had the same authority as a book."

"You're right," Ellie said, frowning in turn. "Well, it was very vivid, and it felt true. That's why I thought I'd look for it in the books, to see if it was the same there."

"That sounds like a good idea." The Parson waved her onwards.

"I'll have to go up to the second floor," she explained and climbed the stair. "What do I look like now?"

"You're levitating," Graham said excitedly. "Every other day I've been here, you have walked on solid ground, no matter what architecture you've been describing. But if I had any doubts as to the reality of your castle, I don't have them anymore."

She began poking through a familiar shelf. She found a reference to Paris' first days in Forgotten Town. She hunted through several adjacent books, but found no mention of her dream.

Nothing referring to a kiss.

The Parson was infinitely patient as she skimmed. He didn't act bored. Nonetheless she felt pressured to produce something.

"I can't find it," she said. "But it could be anywhere, because it sounds like Paris stayed there awhile."

"Just select one, then," he said, "and bring it down."

Ellie grabbed a book and scurried down the stairs. Graham received it from her with confident movements and turned it over in his hands.

"Did you see it before you touched it?" she asked.

"I saw all the books, but only once you touched them. It's as if you pull them out of the air." He opened the worn front board.

"After I read that first book in the ballroom, I found it later here in the library, on the table," Ellie recollected, "and I assumed you moved it. But you can't see the table, and since you couldn't see the castle back then, how could you have left it here?"

"I cannot say, but it makes me think the phenomenon of your castle is rather intricate and unpredictable."

"Did you find that book where you met me today?"

Parson Graham squinted his left eye. "Yes, I think it was, and I passed by the amphitheater place that day."

Ellie nodded. At least that made sense.

"Should I read this book to you?"

"Sure," Ellie said, and sat on the floor, leaning against the shelf. Graham remained standing and read in a measured way, his voice clear and pure. As it turned out, the randomly selected book confirmed the truthfulness of her dream.

UNRAVELING

O ne always enters Forgotten Town at evening.
    I had been gone thirteen days.

When we pass through the portal to the forest above town it is always midmorning on a late autumn day, and no matter how long we spend in the forest, it is always dusk when we descend into town.

Today in town must have been beautiful. Slanting beams of sunlight filtered through buildings and cast a deep orange glow onto Main Street. Electric lampposts were flickering to life. I was weary and glad to return. A large contingent of Estringites, refugees from a counter-attack on their homes, strode at our rear. Many of my saboteurs were gleeful, gloating over weapons and valuables gleaned from the slain. But I was just tired.

Neikolan took charge of the troops, and I let Talmei take charge of the Estringites, new and old. I was grateful to be free of responsibility. My mind was wearier, perhaps, than my body, for it took focus and energy to direct the power of the Eterokoni. Nonetheless I found my feet leading me to Paris' door, not mine. She had established herself in a small house two blocks from mine, in a part of the town that was a grid of small homes, each with its quaint yard and fence. When we first came here, it had had the same aspect, carefully tended but uninhabited. An unlikely headquarters for a rebellion.

I knocked on her door. She smiled broadly as she let me in.

The sun had set outside, and her rooms were brightly lit. Paris sat down on the edge of her bed (nothing compared to her bed in Kadesh's palace) and I busied myself unstrapping the Glass Sword and removing my belt, mailed vest and boots. Her eyes lingered on the bloodstains on my gear. She was fixing me with the "Daevon look". The first time I had been Peredur and it felt like the kind of look a woman gave a man. But she had never stopped looking at me that way.

"I saw you come into town," she said, "but I didn't want to interrupt. I'm really glad you came by. I can't believe how much I've missed you these two weeks."

She stood up and melted into my arms. Her hair was bound in a single ponytail, and my hands met on the backside of her satin blouse. Despite the athleticism of her body, she was all softness to me.

"Ow!" she scolded, disengaging herself. "How many belts do you wear?" The thick brass buckle of my regular belt had bit into the bare flesh of her waist. Both her shirt and pantaloons were loose-fitting cherry-red satin. Paris was radiant in any color. The shirt ended below her bust, weighted there with diamond pendants, and a braided black belt circled the smooth expanse of her bared belly.

"How was the campaign?" Paris inquired.

"We saved the Estringite population but we lost the outpost."

"Are you OK, unhurt?" she asked, solicitous.

"Basically," I said, passing my fingers over a deep cut on my right arm. She came over to kiss it. I tried not to flinch.

"Please kiss something that doesn't hurt," I teased, remembering the kiss we had shared in the gym. I'd thought about her constantly while I was gone, even when my focus should have been elsewhere. Paris cupped my belt buckle with one hand, and raised her lips. Her sweet scent filled my nose. Her perfumes had annoyed me in the beginning, but they were something quintessentially Paris that I had come to expect and enjoy. I felt, while kissing her, that I shared in her beauty, that something of her rubbed off on me. I hadn't admitted it yet but Paris' beauty spoke to something in me that Siana's war did not. To that part of me that had first sparked my dreaming. I ran my hand down the length of her back as we kissed, straying on her bottom. She kissed me more deeply and pressed tighter into me.

"Siah, will you walk with me? I've been cooped up all day, practicing, thinking of you, and I'm tired."

"So you want to go for a walk?" I laughed, thinking of my aching muscles, but knowing this was Paris' wont.

"It's restful," she explained, as she had before. "The Town is beautiful at twilight, and it is nice to move in only one direction, as slowly as I want, with no guards. I love dancing, but…"

"I'll join you," I consented, "but let's focus on *slowly*."

And so we walked, after Paris wasted fifteen minutes of her precious twilight getting dressed. She still seemed acclimated to the jungle and horribly overdressed for the cool but not cold nights here. In this case donning fur-lined boots and a long fur coat. She put her hair in twin pigtails that stuck out perpendicular to her cheekbones and this made me laugh. She was equal parts beautiful and random.

By Paris' standards, we were quiet for the first fifteen minutes, walking slow. Clouds had hidden the remains of the sunset and a misty drizzle was wetting our faces and our hair. For all her warming fur, Paris appeared to relish the mist. We held hands and she spent a few humorous moments trying to lick the mist off her face. But then she surprised me with an earnest question.

"Who was that man, the man who gave you the Glove and the Eye?" she asked. "You never told us. Why would he have Eterokoni?"

I hadn't seen her express much interest in the affairs of the war before. I hadn't explained the xemenos because I hadn't wanted to talk about it, but now that she asked, I wasn't going to dissemble. I was never good at lying. At least not to people I cared about.

"He was a xemenos," I answered, "a fragment of a person."

"What person?"

I should have seen that coming.

"To be honest," I said, feeling all the fatigue of the last two weeks descend on me anew, "my brother, Timothy."

"Your brother?" she exclaimed. "Of course I would want to know about that. You can talk about anything, anything about your life and I would want to know. I love you."

I winced.

That was the first time she had said *that*. Daevon hadn't said that, per se. The only person from whom I had ever accepted, or believed, those words was my brother. Paris' unexpected confession left me in a confused mix of emotion. But I wouldn't shrug off her confession. For I had to confess to myself I loved her too, my dear sister and friend.

We had come to a wide creek, where the street went over a small bridge. Paris stopped on the bridge, leaning over to watch the dark water pass below. It never reached full dark in Forgotten Town. As I was thinking of Timothy and love, the wheels of Paris' mind had been turning.

"So this world is the world of your dreaming each night," she said, biting her lower lip and scrunching it around. "So when you wake up why doesn't that interrupt the flow of things here?"

"I don't know," I replied, hoping we'd left off the topic of my brother. "But my mind always picks up where it left off. I think the flow of time here is different, faster somehow, because I sleep here, too, all while I am dreaming there."

"Tell me about your brother," she said absently, studying the water. She turned her face to me in the ensuing silence. I could feel my own frown. "I'm sorry, Siah. I'm being awfully stupid. I am stepping all over something I clearly don't understand." She paused but then couldn't contain the momentum of her curiosity. "But is he—"

"Dead?" I spat, "no, but he might as well be. He was captured by Ghislain years ago, and all I can find of him are these God damned xemeni." Unwanted tears brimmed in my eyes. I turned away from her. I didn't want to feel this anymore.

Paris reached for me, but I shrugged her off. I wanted her embrace, to blubber like a child in her arms, but I couldn't. I couldn't allow myself that luxury.

Her hand stopped in the air between us, a bird frozen in flight.

"Is that why you're here, to find him?" Paris said softly, her voice tremulous with understanding.

"Is that more acceptable to you than Siana, Princess of Time, Avenger of the Gods? Do you prefer Miss Grey, hapless dreamer who—though armed with the Eterokoni—cannot find a single man?" I was lashing out, stating for the first time the unspoken tension between us. I was being unfair. Why do we take advantage of the meek? Abuse those whose mildness we should cherish?

Paris' eyes flashed in the twilight as she met my stare. But then she lowered her face, as if deserving my reproof, and settled her hands about her waist, nestled in fur. Without raising her face she spoke, so softly.

"You can't give up. Don't give up on finding him."

"Do you even know what I've gone through?" My words rose to a shout, as if to swallow up the softness of her voice. "Does anyone know all the haunted and forsaken places I have sought for him, the terror of them, the terror of being alone?"

I could feel the sadness breaking through my voice, the tears starting to pour forth. She was making me a child again and I hated it.

"Siah," Paris said, stepping close, not retreating from my ugliness as she should. She reached for my hand, but my clenched fist was piercing my palms with my nails. "You're aren't alone, I will go with you. I hate military things but if you go looking for him, I will go with you."

"But I am alone," I bawled. "When I wake up in my world in the morning, I *am* alone. You're not there. Timothy was my family, and he isn't there. He is gone. And my dreams, *my* beautiful dreams, my escape from all the ugliness of my world, are now full of *this*, war, fear and frustration. God damn them, God damn the Aedolae, God *fucking* damn Ghislain!"

I had stepped away from the bridge and my legs collapsed under me, leaving me a pathetic ball on the side of the road, chest heaving under the weight of long repressed grief.

Paris seemed both cruel and compassionate. She had forced me to give her my raw and bloody heart, which I had hidden from both of us. Now I needed someone to hold me, to forgive me, to exonerate me, to tell me it wasn't my fault and everything would be OK. And this too she did.

She opened her fur coat, slipping out one arm and placing the coat over both our shoulders. She let me rest on her shoulder, kissing the top of my head and then tenderly kissing away my tears. After I had sobbed awhile, she raised my chin and kissed me full on the mouth.

As our lips parted, and my eyes locked on the inverted V of her lip, her tone changed. "If it were me, would you give up?"

"What?" I breathed, utterly drained.

"If it were me who was taken, would you give up searching for me?"

I felt like she'd struck me. My brain was a paralyzed muddle of guilt, anger, love and despair.

"Because you can't give up," she continued, merciless.

I began to sputter an echo of my prior protests but she interrupted.

"Because if you do, girlfriend," she said, "the Aedolae have already won, because they've destroyed your heart."

· · · ● · ● · · ·

The Parson handed the book back to Ellie. She held it to her chest. A nimbus of sunlight clung to the Parson's face.

"That is quite fascinating," he said, squinting again as was his wont.

Ellie found tears on her cheeks, and wiped them away unceremoniously.

"I am such a crybaby," she said.

"Don't call yourself such. You just have a kind heart. That is nothing to rue."

"I wish I could go home with you. I don't feel like solving any more mysteries."

"I wish you could come with me. My wife would relish the opportunity to fatten you up. She finds even me frustratingly thin." He smiled kindly. "Maybe—extrapolating logically from current circumstances—this gradual blending of our two realities will someday soon make that possible. But for now, we have to be thankful for the additional clues."

"What clue did that book give us?" she said peevishly.

"That your dreams about Siana are accurate," the Parson said. He never got irritated at her, even when he should. "So you gather good information both waking and asleep. Many a researcher would envy that!"

He laughed freely. A breeze stirred his hair. It was very odd in the stillness of the library.

"I must admit," he remarked, "I'm not keen on heights. Can we go back down?"

"Sure!"

Ellie stood up, encouraged by his amiable and even personality. They returned to the foyer.

"I'm want to go back to the mirror," Ellie admitted. "Now that I've bartered for my breakfast." She smiled.

"You are quite a young lady," Graham praised, "to maintain your good humor in these circumstances. Let's make your list of questions for her."

They spoke for several hours, lunching on more bread and cheese. The sunlight shifted behind his head, casting his face in shadow and a long shadow stretched from his body as the day outside moved on. Her own shadow was different, cast lightly in many directions by the multitude of candles in the candelabra above.

The Parson had now read two accounts of Siana's life. Ellie had read many more, and had had two dreams that turned out to be true. All this presented a lot of information, and as they wrangled over it, the Parson firmly but gently corrected her if her conclusions were illogical. He was only satisfied if they moved carefully from point to point; like before, his approach energized and annoyed her in equal turns. But at the end the spider webs crowding the chambers of her mind were systematically cleaned away. The food and the conversation left her more excited than ever before.

"I must go, Ellie, for my wife will begin to worry. But I think we have discovered a lot today. Go and see if your friend in the mirror is there."

"I will," she said, and her own voice sounded deep and robust. A sudden impulse moved her. She spread her arms to hug him, but then drew back uncertainly. But Graham drew her into a firm embrace.

"Thank you, thank you. How can I ever repay you?"

"Don't worry about that, little miss. Kindness is its own reward. It has been an unexpected pleasure for me." He stroked the back of her head. "You feel a lot more substantial already. A wind could have blown you away the day we met."

He stepped from the embrace and gave her a little bow, hands folded at his chest as if he were praying. Then he pulled his cowl about his face and took his leave.

She stood there in a daze, until she heard his already far away voice call from another part of the castle.

"Ellie, good luck!"

BACK TO THE MIRROR ROOM

Ellie walked down to the dais at the floor of the amphitheater. The hanging door was still there. She reached for the knob but it was locked. *Silly me*, Ellie thought, and ran back to the gallery. She had hidden the key under her pallet. Five minutes later she was back.

Inside the room was the same as before, candles casting dim pools of light on the dark wood floor. She sat down in the chair, folding her hands in her lap. The door in the reflection stayed closed. While she waited, she mentally rehearsed her list of questions. She began to fear disappointment.

Then the door opened.

Siana stepped in, wearing the same outfit. This time she scanned the room warily, her icy eyes upcast and roving. She approached the chair in the reflection and placed her hands on its rungs, appearing ill at ease.

"You're here again," she said, her voice low and rich but the inflection almost monotone. "Your name was?" It was either disdain or sarcasm in her voice.

"Ellie," she replied. She was just as daunted by Siana's presence today. Her list of questions seemed impertinent.

"Ellie," Siana said slowly, as if pondering the name.

"You remember talking to me then, before," Ellie asked, adding "my mistress."

"I do," Siana answered, sitting down stiffly as if compelled against her will.

"Can you tell me," Ellie asked, "where you've been since then? Since you left this room?"

"It feels as if I've been dreaming, dreams of blood and fire."

"Like your dreams of leading the Brigandrie?"

"No, not like that," Siana answered, "like the dreams I have when falling asleep inside the dreamworlds, sketchy dreams."

"You haven't been back with the Brigandrie, or with Paris, since talking to me?"

"No, I don't think so," Siana said, "only dreaming." She sounded hazy, as hazy as the castle had often made Ellie. But Ellie didn't feel that way now.

Her replies confirmed Ellie's sense that Siana was indeed dead and she was speaking with a ghost, a vestige of Siana's soul entombed in the castle. But the Parson would have lectured her for being hasty. She put aside her sense of dread.

"Where are your Eterokoni? Do you have them?" Another question she and Graham had thought up.

Siana looked down at her belt, the broad belt mentioned in the book Graham had read. She rummaged through its pockets, confusion and anger deepening on her features. Her hands went to her throat, searching for Torc and Kalimba.

"Where are they?" Siana bellowed from the mirror. "Did you take them? Are you mocking me?" She stood up.

Ellie cowered in her chair.

"No, no, mistress," she said, the smallness of her voice genuine. "The Sundial is here, in the castle. I told you. But I don't know why, and I've never seen the others."

Siana's rage cooled, suggesting it was not about Ellie but the absence of her precious artifacts. She sat down forcefully.

"They are my birthright," Siana said flatly. "They should be here with me. I do not understand. Will you look for them?"

"I can try, mistress," Ellie replied. Siana's appeal for her help was unexpected—and gratifying. In the books Siana never expressed any concern about the Eterokoni being taken from her, though that would have been a logical stratagem for her enemies. The Parson had pointed this out, arguing the

Eterokoni must be inseparable from their mistress. Therefore, Ellie reasoned, the fact this Siana does not have them confirms the direness of her fate. Or, maybe this Siana is not the real one. Her head ached. How could Graham expect her to tease this apart?

"Do you remember what happened after the Traverse of Stones?" Ellie asked. The first book had ended with an intimation of disaster. Graham reasoned the showdown at Mihali was a reasonable time and place for her to have died. So she should probe for details beyond that point in Siana's memory, to find out if they were any.

"I remember the army of the Achthroi, I remember Ghislain there, and Daphne, and the Twins. I remember my men and women dying," Siana answered, "but that is all." That was past the events in the book and more than Siana had said the last time. Would this specter of Siana remember more and more?

"But you remember Daevon, and Mercedes, and Paris, and going to Mercair's World ... before that?"

"Yes, I remember all of that," Siana said.

"But no battles beyond that day at Mihali," Ellie pressed.

"No," Siana conceded. This confirmed Graham's argument. Ellie couldn't think of more to ask along that line. But what did it all mean? Siana was a dream warrior, and Ellie knew death inside the Detheros meant only a dreamworld death, not the extinction of Siana's soul. Ellie recalled Siana's conversations with Bierce. If Siana had been killed, her dreamself should be back outside the Detheros now, dreaming again in the shallows of the Fringe. Not trapped in this castle, conversing with her. A strange and clever thought struck her. Was this Siana a xemenos, splintered off from Siana's dreamself? She thought Graham would congratulate her for her reasoning. Or was Siana's presence in the dreamworlds so vivid that in the wake of her destruction this castle of memories was left behind? They were stimulating possibilities. But they didn't tell Ellie where the castle was.

Where *she* was.

She calmed her mind. There would be time to sort it out. One step at a time, Graham had cautioned. But she didn't know what else to say. She wished she could freeze time, leave the room and talk to him somehow. Then come back with something useful.

But she was here and didn't want to lose her patron's attention.

"I read about you meeting Paris, here in a book in the library. You were struck with her beauty, her skill, and you found in her the kind of thing you were seeking in dreams in the first place." Ellie remembered her week of fevered reading, searching for the truth about Paris.

"Is that what the book said?" Siana's voice was edged with a vexed boredom.

"Yes, it is," Ellie affirmed, emboldened, "and whether you wrote them or not, the books are written from your perspective. They speak your thoughts."

"Let me tell the writer of *said* book a thing or two," Siana sounded angry again, this time with a quiet venom. "I was a man, Peredur, when I met Paris, and she was a beautiful woman needing succor. That is why I was taken with her. Nothing more."

"But, but," Ellie sputtered at this patent lie, "I dreamt of you and Paris in the gym, her teaching you to dance. She kissed you, and you kissed her back. You weren't Peredur then!"

Siana seemed taken aback. But she recovered a taciturn cool.

"Just a dream, a dream fashioned by your own fancy for Paris. Which is obvious, since you are always coming back to that subject."

Ellie's own anger astounded her.

"Why would I care about Paris?" she shot back hotly. "I am telling you your own story as I've read it. Listen, it's not only my dream, it's in this book too. Listen." She had brought the book with her, and hastily opened it, reading aloud to the image in the mirror.

"I felt, kissing her, that I shared in her beauty, that something of her rubbed off on me. I hadn't admitted it yet but Paris' beauty spoke to something in me that Siana's war did not."

Ellie couldn't look up. She was angry but afraid of Siana's eyes. "Do you deny this is true?"

Siana's chair scraped against the floor.

"What right do *you* have to tell me about my life?" Siana said, her pacing footsteps audible. "Have *you* explored worlds of nightmare, or fought Seraphi and Achthroi and other minions of the Aedolae? What other things do you dare accuse me of?"

Ellie was glad Siana was trapped in her side of the mirror. She wouldn't have wanted to face her in battle. Nonetheless, she pressed on, with courage born of both indignation and desperation.

"Why in the attack on Kadesh could you shapechange at will with no problems, but when you turned into the flying thing at Orse the Torc destroyed your clothes?" This was the first point on a list of inconsistencies Graham and Ellie had drawn up.

"Is that your big complaint?" Siana mocked. "As I mastered the Torc I learned how to shift my clothing back and forth at will. Do you think the design of the Torc would have been so ineffectual? What are you accusing me of? I told you, I didn't write these books so don't accuse me of lying through them."

Ellie couldn't answer that. Siana must have taken her silence as acquiescence for she stopped pacing and the chair feet scraped again as she sat down. Whatever this version of Siana thought, Ellie didn't believe the books were fabrications. They *felt* truthful. They revealed things this Siana wanted to deny and keep hidden. Ellie thought of the tone of the first book she had read. In that book Siana was most similar to the Siana before her, dismissive of all but her campaign against the Aedolae. As if at that point in Siana's history, that particular Siana had finally won out. That book hadn't mentioned even Timothy at all!

Siana had wept at the side of the road in Forgotten Town. There was no trace of that woman in the Princess of Time sitting before her. Was the vulnerable woman in the book a fabrication?

Was it some writer daring to speak in Siana's voice and trying to humanize her? No, that didn't feel truthful. Ellie believed Siana had retreated from her feelings and cast Paris and Timothy aside.

But you must know for sure, the Parson spoke in her mind.

In the books, Siana had confessed she was a poor liar.

Ellie dared to raise her eyes. The Princess met her gaze with simmering defiance.

"I want to ask you one more time," Ellie willed her voice to be even and firm. "Do you deny that you kissed Paris, that you loved her dearly? Please tell me the truth, Siana, I need to know."

Siana stared at her harshly, drawing breaths. A minute of silence. Then she huffed and exhaled forcefully. Her shoulders slumped.

"I do not deny it."

"Thank you. Thank you for telling me. Please know, Siana, I was never trying to accuse you, and I have no bad feelings against you. I just want to know the truth, about you and about the books in the library, and about this place where I am trapped. Can we work together? Will you trust me?"

Siana had taken a dagger from its sheath along her leg and idly tested its edge with her left index finger. "How do I know you're trustworthy, that you're not here just to interrogate me?"

Ellie bit her lip.

"My mistress, when I dreamt of Daevon's death, I woke up crying and couldn't stop. When I dreamt about you and Paris, I woke up with a hollow feeling in my tummy, like I'd been torn away from someone dear. When I read today"—she didn't mention Graham was the actual reader—"about the time you went walking with Paris, and she first told you she loved you, and you got frustrated"—she chose her words carefully—"when she pressed you about Timothy, my eyes filled with tears. It makes me angry that I cry so easily over words and dreams, but it at least proves that I care. Would you trust that? You wouldn't trust someone who reacted to your story with callousness."

Siana laid the knife across her lap, and asked, "It makes you mad that you cry?"

That was not the detail Ellie expected Siana to light upon.

"Yes it does," Ellie said with a small laugh, "but I have trouble stopping all the same."

"I hate tears too," Siana said. She smiled slightly.

"Why?" Ellie asked, shifting forward in her seat, excited.

"Because..." Siana paused. She rolled her eyes as if searching for words. But Ellie noticed that her posture was relaxed for the first time. "Because I'm afraid of them."

"Afraid?" Ellie repeated.

"Afraid that they will make me weak, that I will crumple under the weight of them and cease to exist." Siana pulled up one leg and tucked it under her. The gesture made her more human. "I put all that girlish emotion behind me. I had to change the order of things. I couldn't be a victim."

"Why not?" Ellie was surprised at the question, but it popped out of her.

"What do you mean why not?" Siana sounded indignant but her expression didn't match. She was now treating Ellie like an equal, like they were two girlfriends having a tiff. "What warrior goes around blubbering about what she has lost?"

"I don't know. But perhaps you should expand your definition of a warrior. I agree with Paris, you can't let the Aedolae destroy your heart."

Siana pursed her lips. "You and Paris again!"

Ellie forged on. "Your grief at losing Timothy drove you in the first place. You were their victim, but that didn't stop you from taking action. You were never *that* kind of victim. I don't think you should fear your feelings will make you passive. They never did, and from what I've read of you, they never will." She couldn't, while dialoguing with this living, breathing image of Siana, talk as if Siana were dead. She could only think of Siana in the present tense. "I think your grief and your sadness are good; they keep your anger from destroying you, from making you inhuman."

Ellie was quite shocked by her own elucidation. The Parson had definitely rubbed off on her.

"And this from a girl who said her tears made her angry." Siana was smiling. Her drawn face had lightened, and more of its beauty shone out. "Your words are wise, Ellie. They challenge me and I will think on them."

"I'll try to find more of your Eterokoni. I don't know if I can, but I will try."

"Can you bring me the Sundial, let me see it?"

Ellie nodded. She was ecstatic at turn in the conversation, and she wanted to end it on a good note, before its tone could change. She stood up and curtsied to the image in the mirror.

Siana stood and nodded in reply.

"Goodbye," Ellie said, "for now." And she went out the door.

She spent the remainder of the day fetching the Sundial from its hiding place in the Time Room. By the time she returned to the gallery night had fallen. She lay down and dreamt a deep sleep without dreams.

· · · ● · ● · ● · · ·

A strange sound awoke Ellie the next day. The patter of rain. Of course, it had rained before outside, streaking the grime on her little window. But it had never woken her. She sat up in bed. The room was darker than usual. She was conscious for the first time of the bareness of her legs, poking from her threadbare dress. The air had a nip of cold. The unexpected sensation yanked her from her bed.

A drumming noise sounded from behind the door. She shrieked as something wet touched her toe. A trickle of water threaded across the floor, carving a maze-like path through the omnipresent dust. Her eye traced it back to the doorframe. She burst open the door and ran out.

Into a blinding sheet of rain.

Inside the ballroom.

She was so shocked she gaped open-mouthed, while the rain soaked her hair and the wet weight of it fell over her eyes. The room was full of rain, rivulets trailing down the stairs, pools of water collecting on the floor. The ceiling was intact but the rainstorm paid no heed to that.

She rushed down the stairs, twirling and laughing. The rain was cold but exquisite. She hadn't felt rain, the outdoors, in so long! Her shift plastered itself to her thin form. Ellie ran crazily from room to room, exploring places between the ballroom and Time Room that she hadn't been in for weeks, all fear of those places forgotten in the delight of the rain. She ran, splashed in puddles and rolled on the floor. Some rooms were impervious to the rain, bone dry like her gallery, but most weren't.

Hours later she was back in the ballroom, spread out on the marble floor, basking in the sunlight now streaming through stained-glass Siana, wringing out her sopping dress. She even napped, a thing she had never done during her days in the castle.

When she woke the water was gone, evaporated by the sun or simply gone. She analyzed the situation logically. As her castle became part of the Parson's world, his world must be intruding inside. Would their realities meet, and a partially ruined castle allow her to escape? The hazy dread of her first days in the castle felt so long ago. Things had changed so fast.

Ellie sat up and stretched her arms above her head. She twisted her spine. The marble floor hadn't been comfortable. Something caught her eye. A book, lying below the balcony. She walked over to it. She had never seen this slight, faded pink volume before, and most of the pages were blank. She had only found two books outside the library. The first had come of its own volition, but the second had appeared as if in answer to her ruminations about Siana's title *Princess of Time*. Perhaps the castle listened to her and revealed things with purpose. Perhaps this book would do the same.

With fluttering anticipation she sat down cross-legged to read.

TEARS

F all swept through Forgotten Town. Main Street was ablaze with sun. It was October of the year Paris and I met, and Assav had caught up with me in the middle of town.

"I know you only returned last night and there is so much to do, but you need to go see Paris," he implored.

"Why? Where is she?" I asked.

"In the gym. I think she's quite upset, but she won't admit it. I would have comforted her," Assav explained with an impish grin both mischievous and innocent, "but as you know she only has eyes for you."

"Thank you." I nodded and headed off.

I found Paris doing her stretches. She studied me up and down, but her expression was veiled. I sat on the floor a polite distance off. At last Paris spoke, looking away, while she lay her left ear against her leg.

"Assav told me where you've been going," she said, in what was for her a virtual monotone.

"Which is...?" I narrowed my eyes.

"Seeking the Coethyphys." Same tone.

"Isn't that what you recommended?" I said unpleasantly, angry at her anger. I didn't feel like dealing with anyone else's feelings.

"Siana"—Paris straightened up and then flattened her torso flush to the ground between her outspread legs—"you didn't tell me what you've been doing, and you didn't take me with you." The first hint of emotion crept into her voice.

"I didn't want you to worry, and I didn't want you to get hurt."

"I have the right to worry about a person I love," Paris countered. She sat up and toweled off her brow, pulling her brunette tresses tighter in her ponytail. She studied my face, her eyes defiant. I hadn't seen her like this before.

I realized recently I hadn't been *seeing* her at all.

"You've been exhausting yourself for months, Siah. At first I was mad at you for ignoring my advice, and now you follow my advice without telling me?"

"But aren't you happy I'm trying again?" I whined. "I'm not giving up on him."

"Yes, I'm happy"—Paris exhaled forcefully—"I guess. But I wanted you to share it with me. I didn't want you to go off and shut me out."

"I haven't been shutting you out..." I said irritably.

"When you don't reveal your heart," she said, as if lecturing a child, "you build a wall between us. Besides which, you have been gone half the time and when you are here you're taciturn and stressed out."

I rested my head on my knees. "This is what I do. I am their leader. I hold the Eterokoni. You can't change that."

"No, but *you* can," Paris blurted, then cast her eyes aside, knowing she had overstepped her bounds. I said nothing.

"All I'm saying," she said, wearily, "is you'll destroy yourself trying to be Timothy's savior and Brigand both. What supreme good is the Brigandrie doing that you must sacrifice yourself for it?"

She seemed determined to infuriate me.

"We're standing up to the tyrants, which no one has done for a millennium," I argued. "Someday, we will cast down Ghislain. And when they are all gone the Detheros will fall."

"Someday," Paris repeated the word, and it sounded hollow in her mouth. "Meanwhile Neikolan builds a pile of dreamworld treasures in Forgotten Town. And his pirates bring home battlefield widows to be their brides."

I opened my mouth to interject but Paris held up her hand. She was breathing fast and doubtless saying a lot of things that she'd wanted to say for a long time.

"I'm not stupid. I pay attention and I listen and I hear. I'm not saying they are all bad men, or that any of them are all bad. But I don't really see the difference between kinds of suffering. Or kinds of theft. They steal from the Aedolae's guardsmen and vassals, they wreak suffering. Yet it is always suffering and theft that you hold up as your complaint against the Aedolae. What is the difference? When is your someday going to happen? Or is it just the convenient excuse for all this?"

I stood up. She couldn't have struck me more forcefully with her fist.

"Are—you—quite—done?" I said, jaw set, each word coldly articulated.

"Yes, Siah," she said, "I am". Tears welled in her beautiful grey eyes but I refused to care. I left the gym.

• • • ● • ● • • •

E llie felt like the wind had been knocked out of her. *Poor Siana*. She knew how much Paris had come to mean to Siana. Could it have changed so fast?

Love is like tears, Ellie thought. Something Siana had pushed away, but there under the surface, unchanged.

Ellie tried to reason like the Parson. Everything in the two books she'd read since her dream jived with it; she had no doubt her dreams of Siana's life were truthful. But they were more than truthful. They described Siana's most personal or painful moments: her first kiss with Paris, or the tragedy that befell Daevon. Yet, even though the books in the library had edited out those two events, other similarly painful things had been left in, like the rancor of their conversation in the book she'd just read. There was no strong logic to it.

"The illogical or the partially logical are also logical possibilities.

She remembered Graham saying that, and laughed to herself. So.

She got up and stretched, the stray ends of her thoughts beginning to unravel. But before they were gone she seized upon a thread.

"Hmm," she said aloud. The book she'd found in the Time Room had seemed like a deliberate answer to her curiosity. And this pink book fit so well with her recent conversation with Siana.

Why of all the books housed in the castle, did that first book fall into her possession? Was it chance? Or was it because it best expressed the kind of Siana portrayed in the iconography of the castle, the Siana she'd now met in the Mirror Room? Siana, Princess of Time, Warlord Siana. We are all many things, and out of all her selves, Siana had chosen that persona, the one she thought served her best.

The persona in which her dreamself had died, Ellie thought.

The persona *by* which she had died.

In their last conversation, Ellie had told mirror Siana her sadness and grief were good, in ways that Siana did not see. In denying them Siana stripped herself of her loves. Siana's vengeful persona was beyond cold; it was arrogant. Even the narrator of the first book had realized that in the end.

Perhaps the library—the castle itself—responded to Ellie. If she had shown no interest in Siana's first tale, perhaps the castle would have restated forever its images of Siana as triumphant and powerful. But she *had* expressed interest, and in time found the library, which revealed to her, in order, the true story of Siana's life, and then that story was augmented with dreams.

Giving her what mirror Siana wanted to deny.

Explaining, in the pink book, what lay behind Siana's attitude. Responding to Ellie's empathy and her desire to understand.

She was tired despite her nap. Her body was sore, not with the customary pathological fatigue of day's end, but healthy aches from her wild romp in the rain. Her body was unaccustomed to such things, and she did little else that day, productive thought slipping away. She retired early to her little bed. She put off to tomorrow her promise of retrieving the Sundial.

· · · ● ●· ● ●· · ·

S he awoke from barely remembered dreams in the middle of the night, finding her hand pressed between her thighs and her body hot and flushed. The room was darker than she'd ever seen it. The only other time she'd been awake in the castle at full night was when shadows of Achthroi had menaced the walls of the Time Room. Her heart pounded with fear.

A red glow filtered through the crack under the door. Though she was wide awake, her body was compelled to rise from the pallet and cross the room, like a sleepwalker. She turned the knob slowly and quietly as if afraid to wake a sleeping child. As if afraid of disturbing whatever lay beyond but despite that fear unable to turn back.

A floor lamp with an embroidered scarlet lampshade threw a wide circle of ruddy light onto the ballroom floor. The waltzing ghosts were gone, but in that circle sat a figure at a vanity. Her back was turned, but Ellie saw her reflection in the vanity's mirror. The muted light cast shadows between the cherry-red highlights of the woman's unclothed figure. She was brushing her hair, her posture both relaxed and erect.

Ellie sidled silently down the stairs, her feet feeling the familiar way in the darkness. She was no longer afraid, but her heart pounded all the same at this new revelation of the castle.

The figure took no notice as she crept up behind the woman's right side. She sat on a simple wooden stool and combed tangles from the ends of her very long brunette hair. The lamp was to Ellie's right, and as her right arm raised the brush her right breast was exposed to the light. The finer details of her face in the mirror were lost in the dimness, but Ellie could see the shape of her lips.

Paris.

Ellie's skin tingled.

First mirror Siana, and now this: a living breathing image of Siana's friend. Paris stood up, placing the brush on the crowded vanity, and deftly tied back the voluminous tresses of her hair with a dark ribbon. Ellie watched the muscles ripple beneath the smooth glow of her shoulders. Now her hair no longer hid the perfect hourglass of her figure.

"Siana," Paris said into the darkness before her. Her voice was just as Ellie imagined it, smooth and melodious, but the tremor inside it grew as she talked. "What did I drive you to? I knew there was truth to your war, you didn't have to prove it. But I guess you did, after all I said. I was so selfish, Siah. I believed I was criticizing you for your sake, but it was more for me than I admitted. I didn't want you to die."

She turned toward Ellie. Ellie froze, but Paris' face was hidden behind her hands. Her long nails were the color of a Luna moth. Her shoulders heaved. She sat down, her hands dropping to her sides, revealing every detail of her body to the light. Ellie found herself, like Siana, stricken by Paris' beauty. Paris' cheeks were wet, her eyes shining.

"But it wasn't just for me," she sobbed. "You loved your brother and losing him, never finding him, broke your heart. I wanted that pain to be over for you. I didn't think your war could heal that wound, no matter its success. But, but .... oh, why do I argue with you still, when you're not here, when I know I've been wrong? I want you back, safe, here with me..." Her voice vanished in her tears.

This, Ellie thought, can't be a scene from Siana's memory. She was already gone. Am I dreaming, a dream inside this world of dreams, and I just think I'm awake? Is the castle showing me this, or is it my imagination? But Paris' appearance—just as the books describe her—well, that must come from the same source as the books and other dreams.

The image faded, plunging Ellie into a terrible darkness, the likes of which she had never experienced. She turned about but could see nothing, no glimmer from the veins of the stained-glass window, no trace of the stairs back to her balcony. She began to panic when a new image coalesced before her.

A girl sat in the dappled shade of a gnarled apple tree. Unlike the vividness of Paris at her vanity, this image was hazy and ethereal, floating above the floor of the room. A car pulled up the graveled driveway below the tree. Though Ellie had no conscious memory of such things, the car's appearance was natural, unsurprising. A lanky youth stepped from the car and walked toward the girl. The girl hid the notebook in which she'd been doodling.

The young man sat beside the girl shoulder to shoulder, intentionally crowding her in a good-natured way.

"C'mon, show me what you're working on."

The girl had long, unkempt blonde hair. Her overalls were patched at the knees. She mumbled something, then opened the notebook for her companion. Suddenly Ellie recognized the young man. From the ceiling of the amphitheater. Timothy!

"That's really good," Timothy said. "'*Siana, Princess of Time.*' You're such a good artist. I can tell that's supposed to be you."

"Is it *that* obvious?" The girl blushed.

"Yes, but that's good, it means you draw realistically," Timothy persisted.

"You're not making fun of me?" She closed the book with a snap. She turned her head away and starting picking under her thumbnail.

"I'd never make fun of you."

"Good," the girl replied finally, looking away but smiling all the time, "because maybe someday *Siana, Princess of Time* is going to save your ass." She rammed him with her shoulder.

"Don't swear," Timothy chided, pushing her back. "Mom won't like it."

"Dad says *ass*," the girl argued.

"All the same." Timothy stood up. "Let's go, you can come with me into town." The girl jumped up excitedly, tall and gangly for her age, clutching the notebook to her chest.

"Will you buy me a Slurpee?"

"Sure, sis." Timothy laughed, and tousled her hair.

As they walked to the car, the scene faded. Not wanting to be left in the dark Ellie quickly went up the stairs, her back to the wall. By the time the scene went dark, she was on the balcony, but she kept her eyes on the ballroom floor, just in case. But no further vision pierced the inky dark, so she groped her way back to her pallet on the floor and fell quickly asleep.

A THIRD VISIT TO THE MIRROR

E llie had the sense she'd slept late. What finally woke her was the cold. She had never needed blankets before. But something was changing. Her body was stiff from both the prior day's exertion and the cold. The floor was cold beneath her toes as she left her room and crossed the ballroom, not the comfortable cool of a basement floor in the summer but truly cold. She noticed a draft from the amphitheater, where the door was ajar. Brightness flooded along its edge. She peeked in.

The amphitheater ceiling was gone, the triple mural of Daevon, Timothy and Paris replaced by cloud-streaked sky, brilliant with midday sun. She rushed in. She had not expected this, not even after experiencing the rain. Though the air was more chill here, the sun was glorious against her skin and she lifted her dress to let it warm her legs. The amphitheater today was like being outside, and she walked along the stone bleachers, arms raised like an ancient worshipper of the sun.

After her exaltation passed, she studied whether she could reach the wide opening in the convex roof of the chamber. The answer was a resounding no, unless she could build a stair up to the rim of the opening, twenty feet above the top row of bleachers. She touched the walls. Smooth and sloping gradually outward. No way to climb those. She had seen little in the castle that wasn't built into the architecture, nothing with which to build a ladder or a stair. She would have to search harder.

So she contented herself with sunbathing. With the autumn sun blazing down and her back to the stone she wasn't cold. The peaceful warmth lulled her back to sleep, despite a long night's rest. She estimated she napped an hour or so, for when she came to, the sun had moved noticeably in the sky.

What woke her was a low humming. A smooth voice singing a little nonsense song, sweet and feminine. A delicious scent wafted across her. And then something entirely unexpected, the light touch of a palm on her belly and long nails gently trailing along her arm. A warm exhalation of breath on her neck and forehead. Soft lips pressed to her cheek. Despite the gentleness, a thrill of alarm went through her drowsy mind.

She opened her eyes, narrowing them against the glorious light. The filtered sunlight formed a hazy corona around a face, framed in brunette hair and cast in shadow. A plush red bottom lip.

"Paris," Ellie breathed, hearing the tremor in her own voice, as the sense of another person's presence, so often pantomimed in dreams, faded into solitude. Paris' face withdrew into the distance, absorbed into the bright, hazy air. Her mind fully woke. She was alone, and her dress fell down across her belly as she sat up. Had it been her own touch against her belly? Her gut feeling was someone else had been there. She canvassed her surroundings. There was no one in sight.

Below her, on the raised dais, floated the sorcerous door to the Mirror Room.

"I have a promise to keep," Ellie said aloud and rushed back to her gallery for the Sundial. She hurried down to the floating door. As she did, scents of honey and cinnamon struck her nose.

Strange, she thought.

But she was beginning to be unsurprised at the strange place in which she was imprisoned.

Holding the Sundial like an offering in her left palm, she carefully opened the door and stepped in. She sat and didn't wait long for Siana to join her. Siana was dressed the same.

"I brought it for you, mistress," Ellie pronounced with excitement.

Siana's eyes locked on the Sundial.

"That is it," she said, in a tone that suggested she had doubted Ellie before. She crossed the room. "Bring it to me."

Ellie approached the imposing figure of her patron with tingling nervousness in her stomach. Siana's lips were set in a cold line. Mascara smudged beneath each icy blue eye. As yet there was no trace of the warmer terms on which they had parted. Ellie held out the Sundial, the tips of her fingers touching cold glass. Siana's outstretched fingers met the other side of the glass as frustration settled in creases along her brow.

"I cannot touch it," Siana growled, pushing the finger pads of both hands against the transparent barrier. She pushed herself back from the mirror with a huff and sat down in the chair. Ellie found herself thinking of this Siana as a xemenos. She didn't know what was going on, but having a working hypothesis stilled her mind. She felt responsible for Siana's incapacity to the touch the object of her desire.

"Siana," she said, "perhaps you can help me. In your travels did you hear of Vaelonn-Marr?"

Siana cocked her head.

"Maybe, it sounds vaguely familiar. But I couldn't say anything definite."

"That is where this castle is," Ellie explained. "But you don't know where that is?"

"No, I'm sorry."

"There might be more Eterokoni here," Ellie said, "if I could only find them. Perhaps I could use one to escape." She had been thinking aloud, and regretted the comment. She glanced up at Siana, whose face had darkened even more.

"What makes you think you could use them?" Siana said icily

"I'm sorry, mistress," Ellie bumbled. "I want to get out of here, I've been here forever, I am trapped."

"Only dreamers can use an Eterokon," Siana replied factually, a little less glacial.

"I think I am a dreamer," Ellie said, "like you. Well, not *like* you..." She gave what she hoped was a convincingly self-effacing laugh. She had no pretensions to Siana's power, but if the Torc *were* here, and she *could* wield it, she would be free. That was all she wanted.

"Why do you *think* you're a dreamer? Wouldn't you know?" Siana asked with interest. Siana had shown little interest in Ellie before.

"The problem is I remember nothing about myself other than my name."

Siana's eyes narrowed. "Then why would you fancy yourself a dreamer?"

Ellie tried to explain to Siana the reasoning she had done, and then told her she had tried, to no avail, to wake up. When she finished, Siana was silent. Ellie watched her, her still face clouded with thoughts.

"So," Ellie breathed finally, "what do you think?"

"What you have said makes sense," Siana said simply, "as far as it goes."

"You are the dreamworld warrior. What do you think is going on with me? Why can't I wake up?"

"I am not sure you are drawing the right conclusions," Siana said. "When I was trapped in the Gardens, my waking mind had no idea what I dreamt, only that my dreams were frustrated, locked, that I wasn't making any more progress toward the Detheros. I can only imagine that while I dreamt I had no sense of who I was, that my identity had been entirely stripped from me—that I had no idea I was anything more than a sensate girl-child lolling about my bower. And I probably didn't have any memory of waking between dreams."

"But I *do* know I'm trapped here. You never did?"

"No, not until Mercair came and broke the spell. But I think the mechanism might be the same."

"So," Ellie said, pushing the idea around her mind and finding its edges barbed, "I might have been waking up, the day I bashed myself around the Time Room, but *this* me, the one that's trapped here, had no memory of it."

"Perhaps," Siana said. She sounded impatient with the topic. Ellie decided to change the subject.

"Would you tell me about your childhood?" She was thinking of the vision.

"Look," Siana said, and in a seamless move whisked a dagger from its thigh pocket and twirled it into a upright position before her face. "I am the nemesis of the Aedolae. My childhood is long gone." She spun the dagger deftly and returned it to its sheath.

"*Timothy*," Ellie breathed.

"Why do you say his name?"

"Because *he* was your childhood," Ellie said, the words feeling just right.

"Why do you say that?" Siana shot back.

"It's what I see, from all the books," Ellie pitched her voice soft and sympathetic. "Last night, I had a vision of you drawing under a big apple tree. You were just a girl, and Timothy drove up and wanted to see what you'd drawn, and you didn't want to show him. And you told him 'Someday Siana, Princess of Time is going to save your ass'."

"Actually I said 'maybe'." Siana cupped her chin in both hands. Chagrin had blended with impatience in her expression.

"So my vision was real."

"It was a day from my life," Siana said, "so long ago." A wistful sadness rode on her voice.

"Siana, Princess of Time," Ellie said, "not nemesis of the Aedolae, but rescuer of Timothy. That's how you described yourself that day. But you never rescued him."

"Oh fuck you," Siana exploded, baring her teeth. She looked feral. Ellie's heart skipped a beat.

"Oh, mistress," Ellie blurted, "I didn't mean it that way. I just feel bad for you, the way you suffered and struggled, the way Paris criticized you, the way you tried to find him, to no avail."

"Like I said, go fuck yourself, starveling," Siana shouted back, standing. "I will bring the dreamworld to its knees, and the Aedolae will beg me to spare them. But I will exact from them the vengeance of thirty generations of dreamers. They will pay for what they have done, Ghislain most brutally of all. And *my* suffering—that will be the blade to pierce his Aedolae throat."

This time Siana ended the conversation, striding from the room and slamming the door behind her. The tiny candlelit room shook with the reverberations, and Ellie trembled. Her hand shook so hard she could barely work the doorknob. She fled through gathering shadows, up the amphitheater stairs, and threw herself sobbing onto the pallet in her room.

WINTER

E llie rode a river of tears, a furious swollen river. All the angst of her unmeasured time in the castle returned as if Graham's clarity had been nothing but a fragile veneer.

She huddled on the dusty bed, and sobbed for hours, until she forgot her name and had to search to find it again. She watched light come and go through the grimy window and tears ushered her each night into the darkness of sleep. Uncounted days passed this way, until one morning the increasing cold forced her out of the gallery.

Sunlight shone through the crack below the door, the bright sun of a cold winter day, the coldest yet, and her body ached with it. Her limbs barely functioned when she uncurled herself from the floor.

"Come on, Ellie," she said aloud, "you're not going to lie here in the cold, crying yourself to death." But despite her chipper words, inside she was as numb as her chilled body. She stumbled and had to grab the doorknob to keep from falling.

The doorknob broke off in her hand.

The weight of her body tore a path through the wood panels of the door. The wood had become pulp. She checked her forward motion, barely, and stared at the doorknob in her hand. The door twisted on its hinges and fell with a muffled slap. The strangeness of the occurrence woke her cobwebbed mind and reminded her of the mystery to be solved.

She stepped around the door and walked onto the balcony. The Siana window blazed, her eyes daggers. Ellie turned her head away, unable to tolerate even the inanimate glare of her patron. Something dazzled in the sunlight at her feet, light on a sheen of water. The thought came unbidden.

My tears, flooding across the floor.

The doorknob, her tears, all connected in a mental flash, in time to propel her down the staircase as the balcony came apart behind her. Sodden woodwork crumpled and splayed out on the marble floor of the ballroom. The stairs remained, but the rivulets of her tears had scored them like acid. The open doorway to her gallery was a long jumping distance from the orphaned staircase, and an impossible distance above the marble floor.

"There you go, Ellie," she said aloud, "you've gone and ruined your bedroom."

The ballroom air was even colder. She shivered. She had to find something warm to wear or she would freeze. She remembered what the Parson had said, the day they'd met: winter was coming. The castle, obviously, was changing, and no longer insulated her from the cold. She could die, for real.

Her search was long and fruitless.

She started by taking what had been her accustomed route every morning, through the hall to the Vicious Room. Ellie shielded her eyes. She didn't want to see the paintings, not now. She groped her way down the spiral staircase beyond and went through the archway to Cathedral Room. The oval icon of Siana drew her, for within it the stare of her mistress was veiled by closed lids. She knelt before the icon, like the day she'd found the first book.

"I'm sorry, I'm so sorry," she blurted. She didn't know what to say, but wanted to unload the weight that lay on her heart. The icon didn't change. Something darkened inside her.

"So ignore me then," Ellie shouted, surprised as anger replaced her sadness. "I didn't have to care about your story. I didn't have to give you advice. I was only trying to help. I'll just worry about me now." She knew she blustered. She couldn't be free of Siana's story, not while she remained captive in a prison strewn with Siana, and where Siana's story was as yet the only clue.

She pushed on.

Coherent thought returned. She remembered the open ceiling of the amphitheater. To her mental list of target items, she added the Torc, or, more practically, a ladder.

She passed the Copper Landing with its concentric circle motif, gem-encrusted. She remembered the Time Room dream of Siana's soul wending its way back to Ebon Port. Those same circles had floated above the Edoi Sea, in the same order: haunted green, brilliant orange, sapphire, emerald, sun-yellow, amethyst.

She descended the staircase whose railing sported tiny tiles of the Eterokoni. She studied them awhile then tried to pick them loose, managing only to shred her nails, and then searched the room for any sign of the real thing, for seams, cracks, secret places. But to no avail, and the cold settled on her hard now that she wasn't walking. She sighed and moved on.

She came to the sitting room with the gilt chairs. Wind howled down the chimney, exhaling frigid air and old ash. She tried to move one of the chairs, and it squeaked and groaned in protest. The noise echoed through the adjacent rooms with a lonely ring. She had once fled in terror from that noise, dashing along the armory corridor and pitching herself headlong into the Time Room. She was struck again by the vast emptiness of the castle. She had forgotten that feeling in the euphoria of mystery-solving and the reassurance of Graham's presence.

"I need you Graham," she said. "Where are you today?"

The thought of him was only a small balm against all that empty silent space. She returned to her task, shivering in the cold draught. She tried to stack two of the chairs but they were too heavy to get more than a couple inches off the ground. No luck there.

She moved on to the circular room that connected via the armory to the Time Room. Here she found a great jagged gap in the ceiling letting in both wind and light. The air was fresh and she would have welcomed it had she not been so cold.

The ladder!

She ran to the far wall, where a ladder provided access through a trap door to the otherwise inaccessible balcony. She measured it with her eye and sized up the distance from the balcony to the hole in the ceiling. It might work.

The ladder wasn't attached to the floor, but only to the wall at eye level by a pair of wooden supports screwed into the wall. It angled slightly and rested against the edge of the trap door opening. She climbed up to verify it wasn't attached there.

Oh, for the want of the screwdriver, she mused angrily several bruised minutes later. She rattled the wooden supports as hard as she could, and feared she would break the ladder in the process. Where they were affixed to the ladder, the joints loosened, but wouldn't come free.

She rushed up the ladder and went into the armory. One suit of armor yielded a glove easily. She shoved her hand inside and went back down. Two karate chops from her gauntleted hand and the ladder clattered free, falling to the floor.

"Oh great," Ellie said. "Now how do I get back up?" She reset the ladder gingerly against the trapdoor rim and found its end would catch in a warped seam in the floor. She climbed it with the gentle steps of a ballet dancer. It held her. Exhaling relief, she reached through the hole and hauled it up.

It barely reached the hole in the ceiling. She lodged its butt end in a crack in one tier of the slanted floor. She was afraid to get her hopes up, but she climbed.

Cold wind tore at her dress and distressed her raw, bruised hands. She stood on the roof of the castle in the brilliant sun and surveyed her surroundings.

The castle spread to three horizons, a sprawling architectural beast, impossibly huge, hugging the contours of the landscape, a monstrous turtle shell cast in stone. In the haze of the distance she fancied she could see a line of trees, but the line turned out to be more rooflines, parapets, towers, domes, squares of obsidian.

This isn't possible, she thought.

She realized how paltry a portion she had explored of this gargantuan building stretching as far as the eye could see. A single percent, maybe? Hopeless despair flooded her heart.

And yet throughout the building the roof had holes. And on one horizon the castle ended, the direction of the ballroom. She could see the great convex dome of the amphitheater, now mostly open to the sky. And beyond that the castle fell away. She could see the barren heath, and the sloping hills visible from her window.

And as she watched a house fell from an unseen height and crashed upon the heath, splintering open with violence. A tremor shook the length of the castle. The ladder, precariously perched on the rim of the jagged hole, slipped free and fell onto the balcony. She peered over the edge with alarm, and watched gravity pull the ladder down the slanted tiers of the balcony, under the railing, and onto the floor below, where its sides split off from the impact and all its rungs scattered and rolled.

Ellie studied the section of roof on which she sat. Beyond its circle was a thirty foot drop to other nearby roofs.

This isn't possible either, Ellie thought. *The roof of the armory, the Time Room, the sitting room with the chairs should all be a few feet below where I'm sitting. I didn't climb a three story tower to get up here.*

Equally impossible: the blazing morning sunshine through the stained-glass window of the ballroom. The path of the sun's rays along the floor of the Time Room. Neither matched the orientation of the sprawling castle relative to the arc of the autumn sun.

"Well, castle, you're making it hard to escape when you don't follow the rules of physics," she said out loud. She thought of Paris' room ring being larger on the inside. No doubt she inhabited that same world.

"Maybe I'll have to wait until you completely disintegrate," she concluded. But obviously the castle wasn't going to give up that easy.

She stayed on the roof, soaking up the sun's grudging warmth. She didn't want the afternoon to end. There was no way down to the other parts of the roof, so she would have to go down inside, but she didn't want to relinquish her dearly won perch. *I'll stay up here all night, and the next day, until the castle melts out from underneath me,* she thought perversely. Why was she so sure the castle's disintegration would eventually happen? Did she bank too much on the Parson's analysis of things?

A more concrete logic won out. Dreamworld or not, her limbs became stiff and painful as the sun fell. The wind had picked up with renewed fury. She couldn't stay longer. With the ladder shattered there might not be another chance to get back up, but she had no choice.

Lying on her stomach on the cold, gritty surface of the roof she peered into dark shadow. As her eyes adjusted, she estimated the distance to the balcony as too far for a straight jump. She spun around, and lowered her legs into the hole. The rough edges of the hole tore at her thin dress. Soon she was dangling by the undersides of her arms. Deciding to let go and fall into the darkness was exceedingly hard. The sky glowed with the flat, radiant white that is the last light of day. Her heart yearned to soar into it, to fly after the light, and chase the sun over the horizon. How could she return to the prison below?

She let go. Her feet jolted against the floor, and one shin bashed a tier in the slanted floor. As she rubbed her leg, her eyes locked on the jagged white circle of sky. It wasn't over. She would escape.

She stood up and brushed and flattened her dress. Little crumbles of masonry ticked against the floor. She would have to sleep in the Time Room, for her tears had destroyed her gallery. Oh well. The castle's night was beginning to settle in. But she didn't feel tired and spent a few hours searching rooms adjacent to the Time Room for any clue to the other Eterokoni.

At last she retired, her searches in vain.

· · · · ● · ● · · ·

F or five days Ellie made the Time Room her base of operations and searched for the Torc or any other useful thing. She knew at some point she must expand her perimeter and explore unfamiliar passages and chambers—for she knew now the immense breadth of her prison—but cold was increasingly her enemy. It became harder to fall asleep at night, harder to get going in the morning. And harder to concentrate, for wistful images of blankets and coats danced in her mind. She took to napping in the amphitheater in the sun during the warmest part of the day, despite the ever present reminder of Siana's door. This necessity tied her to that part of the castle and made it harder to explore during daytime hours. And as the cold compromised her sleep her old exhaustion returned, further crippling her searching.

"I'm going to die for lack of something I don't have the energy to find," she chastised herself, laying on the cold pew and trying not to look at the statue of Siana and its Eterokon of Time. She had more trouble than ever falling to sleep that night, and slept only a little before finding herself awake again. She had the sense there had just been a noise in the room.

She strained her ears to catch a repetition of the sound. She remembered the dancing Achthroi shadows with fear. But nothing seemed amiss in the soft grey twilight.

Then she caught a glow of light from an adjacent room. She sat bolt upright and padded to the open archway. Male voices sounded from two or three rooms away and a flickering yellow light bobbed and swayed. Something in her gut told her this was not a vision, a phantasm of the castle like Paris or the Achthroi, but something real, from the world without. She couldn't say why, but the sense was strong.

The light was a lantern, held by a hooded figure. A group huddled in heavy winter clothes. Young male faces peeked out from stiff cowls, each caught briefly in the xanthous glare of the lantern. Some looked scared, but most of the faces seemed to harbor darker thoughts. Ellie's heart pounded. They must be adolescents from Graham's village. They came her way.

She caught smatterings of whispered conversation.

"—She is out here somewhere, Jonathan saw her at sunset last week—"

"—Floating in the air—"

"—So **he** *says, but* **I** *say we get out of here—"*

"—Maybe she was a young crazy, perched on the ruins—"

"—Maybe she will sleep with us, Jon said she was beautiful—"

"—And maybe she'll turn you into a toad, you idiot—"

"—I'm freezing—"

"—Shut up, Carlin—"

"—All of you, be quiet, how do you expect to sneak up on a sorceress—"

"—Magic is a bunch of bunk—"

"—Then where did the ruins come from, there was nothing here—"

That was all Ellie caught before she decided to hide. She didn't know what part of the "ruins" they could see, what to hide behind. A stray comment informed her.

"—Look at that statue—"

She ducked behind the image of Siana. The boys' footfalls made incongruous crunching noises like hard-soled shoes on frozen ground. She could hear them clearly now.

"That's probably what Jon saw," one voice said, "a statue of a woman, and he was too chicken to find out more."

"Don't you think he'd notice she has no head?" another argued.

"Nah," a third voice scoffed, gruffer, "that's the type of girl he fancies anyway, just tits and no brain—"

"Oh, shut *up*," the first voice said. "Let's keep looking."

To their eye, with the castle in ruins, the sculpture must be headless. The boys fanned out through the room. Some had long cloaks, swishing about their legs. A lust for warmth filled Ellie. She coveted their clothing. But what could she do? She didn't think she should accost this kind of group for help.

"Hey! An old birdbath or something."

"That's too big for a birdbath, birdbrain." (This must be the basin in which she'd bathed.)

"Here's a gauntlet."

"Wow, that looks like a piece of armor."

One set of footfalls came closer, too close, on her left. A second boy was to her right. Imminently they would circumscribe the statue and discover her hiding place. If she was going to be discovered, she might as well seize the upper hand.

She stood up and put her head right behind the statue's head.

It had the impact she'd hoped for. The closest of the youths let out a wail. To them the decapitated image had grown a living head, lurid in the lantern light. She grimaced for effect.

The adolescent search party dissolved in panic. A brave willfulness seized Ellie and she launched her thin body at the nearest boy, shrieking. She tackled him from behind. She aimed for the sleeves of his cloak and her ragged nails tore flesh. The boy screamed. She yanked on his cloak as hard as possible with both hands, and found that he was more than willing to leave it behind. She drew it about her and raced on all fours back behind the statue. The yellow lantern light faded away.

When it was completely silent, Ellie rolled on her back and permitted herself a long, loud laugh. She laughed first thinking of the boys' terror, then laughed at her own boldness and the indescribable pleasure of the warm fabric clothing her aching bones. Warmth, a forgotten heavenly dream, settled on her limbs. She fell asleep on the pew and slept more soundly than she had for many nights.

• • • • • • • • • •

She awoke with the sun, exhaling frosty breath. Her face was cold but her body was joyously warm inside the well-made cloak. A sheen of ice covered the water in the basin. She had stolen the cloak just in time. It dragged on the floor behind her; the boy had been considerably taller.

With the most pressing concern crossed off her list, she tackled in earnest finding a means of escape. Despite her recent exhaustion, over the past five days she had thoroughly scrutinized all the places she had been before. Time to search further afield.

She was about to leave the Time Room when she heard the same crunching noise that had accompanied the boys' approach. She wheeled about, knowing she had no time for evasion. But it was just Graham. He was laughing.

"You, my young friend, need a better tailor."

"Hello," she said, her voice as chipper as she felt. "I've really missed you." She could have been irritated at his absence, but she was too blissfully comfortable to be mad. His absence seemed suddenly reasonable.

He was still studying her attire.

"I stole it from a village boy—" she explained.

"The story is all over the village, and your pilfered cloak will mark you as everyone's new bugbear." Graham crunched his way over the frozen ground and held out a grey, fur-lined garment. "So I brought you a replacement. I'll take yours back to town, and do my best to discredit the boys' outlandish tale."

She stripped off the cloak and slipped her arms into Graham's gift. It was every bit as warm, and fit her perfectly.

"Thank you," she said and kissed him on the cheek. "Where did you get it?"

"It was my cousin's. She passed away last winter. You remind me of how she was as a girl, willowy."

"I'm sorry."

"Thank you," he said simply. "Regardless of how the boys' tale is regarded, things have become dangerous. The ruins of your castle grow in size, and are visible from our hunters' trails. There will be no end to the curiosity and the folk of Vaelonn-Marr are not, as a rule, very sensible about things they don't understand. Unlike them, I have read much that makes me discriminating about extraordinary things. I had hoped to keep you a secret. But you won't be my secret much longer. I'm not sure what to do, other than urge you to be careful and help you quickly unravel the last of your mystery. I don't want to have to mediate your presence to my people, because I'm not sure how successful I would be."

"Graham," she teased, "you use so many words. What you're saying is that they will think I'm a witch, burn me at the stake, that kind of thing—"

"That's the gist of it," he sighed, smiling wryly.

"Well, if you bring me a ladder and some rope, I think I can escape." Ellie told him about the hole in the roof.

Graham scrunched up his face, squinting. She knew him well enough to know he was thinking and would speak when he was ready. So she examined the charcoal-flecked grey fur lining her sleeves.

"I will aim to do that, next time I come. But your escaping now gives me pause."

"Why? That's what I want, more than anything—"

"It's what you want, but what comes next? You can't stay in my village. So you flee to another village in Vaelonn-Marr. Do you want to live out the rest of your days with country folk who eye you with suspicion because they don't know where you came from?"

"Couldn't you arrange something?"

Graham had complicated the simplicity of her desire for freedom but she knew he was right.

"I don't fully understand Siana's tale, the idea of another world, and Vaelonn-Marr being part of a world of dreams. My world feels quite concrete, annoyingly so," Graham laughed. "But I believe knowing the end of Siana's tale is at least as valuable as your escape."

"I've been reading in the library for a month," Ellie argued half-heartedly, "and it's gotten me nothing but trouble."

"Give it more time," Graham said, his voice level and cool. "I'll do my best to discourage curiosity and keep my parishioners busy with other things. I can buy you a couple of days."

"I was in that library for a week reading up to where Paris and Siana meet," Ellie protested.

"Well, then, we have to get you to whatever book is most critical. I need to return this cloak, but let's walk to the library before I go, and discuss what you should read."

As they walked, Graham had to duck and circumvent an increasing number of castle features. Ellie pondered her natural acceptance of his authority. His kindness and reasonableness were an insuperable combination. They made it impossible for her to do otherwise.

She both trusted and loved him for it.

Ellie recounted her past two weeks, the bitter end of her talk with Siana, and the vision of Paris.

"Paris spoke of something she drove Siana to, that Siana did to prove herself. I wonder what it was," Ellie mused as they arrived at the candlelit antechamber below the library.

"It makes me think of the issue of Siana's death. Why is mirror Siana here, stripped of her Eterokoni? But in the first book, Siana says she died previously. You have never read about *that* death, and I reason that account would provide additional clues. It would help with the puzzle of a dreamer's death and rebirth. Do you agree?"

"Yes, I do," Ellie said.

The staircase and landing were more solid to Graham now and he was able to walk up beside her to the library.

"It is tempting," Ellie said, "to jump ahead in the story but I will go in order and find the book about her dying before."

"Good. After that you should read what happened after the Traverse of Stones. I may be away a couple days and that should give you time. I get the feeling those two books may be enough."

An hour later, after Graham took his leave, she found the first.

DREAMSLAYER

3 months before the Attack on Kadesh

Paris was right. I had pissed around long enough. Each night in the waking world I arranged daggers about my bed, aimed Within. But I had failed to strike often enough, hard enough, close enough, at my Enemy.

I had become nothing but a dagger. My soul shone with a cold light, stripped of Paris' love, stripped of everything but an icy resolve. On a moonless autumn night, in the frosty air of the limitless aether surrounding Mihali, I aimed the weapon of my soul at a pulsing vein of Aedolae power, and in an hour I penetrated to the doors of Iakovos and Ilanit's chamber as my forces took the Palace of the Twins. I spared none, and left a wake of corpses on the marble hallways of their abode. Death came stealthy and brutal that night.

The twin doors of the throne room stood tall as my Estringites, fashioned from single pieces of onyx, products of some cyclopean dreamworld quarry. At our feet, dead hands held sputtering torches, and in that flickering light Neikolan's black face returned my steely gaze. He betrayed no fear. Talmei placed his woody hand on my shoulder. Behind us, arrayed in the shadows of the oval gallery were my forces: Rungeains, Chaotics, Orsians, Estringites, white-skinned pirates, tan desert nomads from the wastes between Kadesh and Cylindrax. A contingent of Gnish, fang-faced humanoids like Kadesh's speaker, some flower species, some leonine. Further behind, beyond the outer gates of the diamond-shaped Palace, in the broad and octagonal courtyard below, Assav and a group of Tzi, with their translucent honey-filled limbs, held the Omphalos for our return. And not far underground, down the hidden and forgotten shaft of the Omphalos in impenetrable dark, a final contingent held an abandoned storeroom for our translation back to Forgotten Town, a chamber with a barred door and enough room for all of us, two hundred or so, to fit inside.

The gallery, with its high-buttressed ceiling, dark skylights and mammoth black and white pillars was dead silent. The guards had made little noise, taken as they were by an invisible warrioress with a vorpal sword. I hesitated in the silence, heart pounding. What Rubicon was I about to cross? Beyond this door, for the first time I would kill an Aedolae.

When I came here with Mercedes, I was surprised to find the Twins holding audience in the dead of night. Now I knew better. The Twins were rarely seen elsewhere, and seemed to have no need of sleep.

"It is time, do not stall," Neikolan whispered. Only the three of us, I had decided, would go in. I did not want to cower behind the safety of numbers.

I was still naïve.

I motioned to Talmei, and replaced the Glass Sword in its scabbard at my back. The Estringite leveraged his weight against the heavy doors and forced them open.

The chamber was as I remembered it. I remembered Ghislain's vision in Cylindrax, my body held aloft in a cage, naked and transfixed with spikes, borne into this very room. I pushed that from my mind.

At the far end sat the Twins, the King clad in sable like his skin, the Queen in a porcelain white gown. Something about their placidity rang a bell, resonated with my uneasiness. Why no alarm at our intrusion? Iakovos had leapt from his throne with a fulminant energy when Mercedes took his guards.

We crossed the length of the chamber to stand below them. The Vinna birds sat quietly on their candelabra perch. Iakovos' face was impassive, Ilanit's petulant. Their faces betrayed nothing.

The echoes of our steps died out. In the brightness of the throne room the silence was more disturbing than the silence of the umbrageous gallery behind. As I dared to meet her gaze, Ilanit arched one eyebrow.

Neikolan growled and hefted his two-handed sword.

"Put that thing away, Orsian," Ilanit said, her voice harsher, more grating than I recalled. She didn't move.

"Who comes before us with such intransigence?" Iakovos boomed.

"I am Siana, and I have come to exact punishment for your injustices, Aedolae."

Iakovos laughed, a rich laughter that was utterly condescending.

"*Siana,*" he scoffed, "the interloper, the dreaming brat, with her collection of trinkets." He turned to Talmei. "You, Estringite, are a cursed rebel who has broken your treaty with Mihali. And Neikolan: maledict ruffian and not long ago Ghislain's lackey. On what authority does this trio enter my realm and mouth such outrage?"

"The Aedolae are murderers and thieves," I answered, "slaying Solmikaedes, taking from the Fringe, erecting the Detheros to hide your sins. Your sister Isabiel stole the childhood of a thousand Mihalians. Your brother Kadesh feeds his people to the Trophina for his amusement. Ghislain imprisoned me and stripped my mind, when I came to the gates of your realms to rescue the brother he stole from me. As a victim of your injustice I claim authority. And I claim vengeance!"

I rushed the throne, mounting the stairs in a bound, swinging the Glass Sword in a wide arc. Neither of the Twins stirred. The sword passed through Ilanit's flesh. I didn't wait to see her head topple from her shoulders before striking the other direction, through the space between Iakovos' head and massive barrel chest.

Nothing resisted the Sword's arc. The tip of the Sword came to a rest and clicked on the stone at my feet.

No spray of blood, no tumble of headless forms. Rather, Iakovos and Ilanit sat tranquil and expressionless. Neikolan cursed behind me, and his boots clattered on the stairs. He plunged his broadsword into Iakovos' chest. Nothing. He slashed at Ilanit's arms. The shining metal disappeared into her sleeves and emerged out the other side.

The King and Queen said nothing.

Dread settled on my heart. I gently touched Ilanit's albino cheek. My hand passed through her face and disappeared from view. I closed my eyes and waved my hands in all directions. The Twins simply weren't there.

I cut their thrones from the dais, elegantly wrought chairs a thousand years old. I kicked them down the stairs, gems scattering across the tiles, delicate workmanship shattering on marble. The images of Iakovos and Ilanit floated in the air where their chairs had been. Ghosts. Projections.

"You fucking cowards!" I yelled toward the open door of the chamber. "Where are you? Come fight me!" I left the dais, brandishing my sword, Neikolan beside me.

"Destroy the Palace," I hissed to Talmei.

Neikolan and I ran to the gallery and instructed our troops to destroy everything in sight. Stone creaked behind us as Talmei's woody arms latched onto a great column and began to heave it from its base. Estringites ranged through the gallery and its antechambers, tearing through masonry, flinging blocks of stone against the skylights and walls. It quickly grew too dangerous for the rest of us to stay inside.

A fan-shaped stair five hundred feet in width links the front of the Twins' palace with the recessed piazza below. Atop this stair is a V-shaped roof formed of two membranes of a prodigious dreamworld insect. We rushed onto the terrace below, threading between a triple line of spire-like pillars resembling the grey boles of trees in the starlit darkness. I lit into the nearest pillar with the Glass Sword, twice, taking out a four foot chunk. The weight of the spire closed the gap with a smack and the spire toppled into its neighbor. I clipped several other spires the same way. Soon the entire terrace was a chaos of falling pillars, the membranes ripping and tearing free a hundred feet above.

We could have escaped then. We had already effected a punishing insult to the Aedolae. But Paris' criticisms of my Brigandrie rang in my ears. I had come here for blood, to dethrone the Aedolae. I would not flee.

With ear-splitting groans the Palace was coming apart behind us as we fled to the top of the stair. Glass shattered and tremors tossed us to our knees. Estringites, spider-like, rushed past, fleeing their own demolition.

Two roads, gentle whorls of Onyx and Porcelain, cut through the dizzying black and white checkerboard of the sunken octagonal piazza. In the center was the raised square of Iakovos and Ilanit's garden and statuary, which hid the neglected well of the Omphalos. This well had been our access to this protected compound within the City. Atop the enclosing wall, at regular intervals, brooded high towers. The wall was only pierced in two places, where the Onyx and Porcelain Roads left to thread their way through the City. The gates were metal portcullises, barred and closed.

A lone figure left the cover of the garden and dropped to the courtyard, running toward us, unguarded. It must be Assav, for it did not have the gait of a Tzi. Why would he defy orders to make this mad dash across?

He had gained the lowest stair when a loud *thwunk* clove the air to my right.

The projectile struck Assav's running form and threw him backward onto the stones. He clutched a twenty-foot harpoon projecting from his gut.

I tore down the stairs.

"It's a trap!" he yelled hoarsely and collapsed. There was another thwunk and I wheeled, raising the Glass Sword in defense. The sword shattered in a rain of tiny particles. The harpoon clattered away, deflected.

I stared at the jagged hilt of the fragmented sword in disbelief.

The courtyard flooded with light. Great bonfires were suddenly lit atop the towers, which bristled with Mihalian soldiers and the mechanical contrivances that fired the harpoons.

The Tzi, with their superior senses, had penetrated the darkness and spotted the ambush, and Assav had taken it upon himself to warn us.

Now he was dead.

I grew wings and took to the air.

"Take out the towers," I screamed to the Estringites. They seized chunks of stones from the ruined spires and catapulted them toward the harpoon guns. Sparks flew as the burning wood of the fires was scattered. Mihalians fell to their deaths. Harpoons whistled in all directions, transfixing many who failed to take refuge behind the wreckage. A torn section of membrane flapped and glistened in the firelight.

The wreck of the Palace was visible now, largely roofless. Walls tottered and crashed into the jumbled heap of masonry within. From my winged vantage, I watched the disintegration of the balcony where Mercedes and I had stood. The Estringites had done well.

I shapechanged my lungs and bellowed, beating my wings and turning about to face each of the towers.

"Iakovos, Ilanit, come forth to face me. Unlike you, I am not cowering behind my men."

My answer was the whistle of harpoons. The guns were ill-suited for firing upwards and all fell short of me. They returned to firing on my people. With 270 degrees of antagonists, my brigands couldn't dodge every projectile, despite options for cover. Peals of anguish accompanied the thwunks and thuds.

I altered my form to something more eagle-like and flew at the nearest tower. Power from the Bracelet of Petrifaction preceded me in a wave and I crashed down amid petrified men. With my talons I heaved them over the battlements. Even over the roar of the bonfire, I caught the satisfying sound of their dismemberment on stone below. I added a club-tail, thinking of Assav's patchwork ox, and smashed the harpoon gun into metal matchsticks.

I launched myself toward the next tower. Before I could reach it, a massive block of onyx projectile swept clean its top, throwing flailing forms of Mihalian warriors high into the air. *Good work, Talmei.* No need to visit that one.

A stratagem occurred to me. I swooped toward the gardens, catching from the corner of my eye the portcullis of the Porcelain Gate admitting a swarm of black forms. More trouble. Landing by the Omphalos I explained my plan to the Tzi and several of the diminutive orb-eyed creatures crawled onto my back. I took off and flew toward a different tower. A harpoon whizzed past my ear. I directed the energy of the Bracelet at the line of men in front of us. As I crashed down, their immobilized forms clattered backwards, alarm still etched on gray faces. My Tzi riders set to figuring out the harpoon gun, clicking and popping excitedly. Even before I lifted off, they had turned the weapon on the other towers.

With their superior eyesight every shot was deadly.

The piazza now swarmed with black forms, burly soldiers who surrounded the raised statuary. I dove toward the Omphalos. The soldiers' heads turned to track me, swarthy animal faces with beady eyes and projecting muzzles. They held stout halberds and what I'd thought was armor was a bristling mass of quills which rustled and clicked against the pavement. I had never heard of this creature.

I landed beside the Tzi, finding them unharried.

"Can you pick them off with your bows?" I asked. "I don't think that kind will climb well." The Tzi are effective archers, and their diminutive arrows are carved of a fiery red tree poisonous to most other beings.

The Tzi wrinkled their brows and blinked their goldfish eyes. It was obvious enough they hadn't understood a word I'd said. I'd thought I was speaking their tongue, my long use of the Star Eterokon so second nature I didn't often think about it.

The Tzi popped and clicked. No translation entered my mind. First the Sword and now this. Why would the Eterokoni fail? They had understood me minutes before. I remembered how the Torc had failed near Ghislain, but I had no time to puzzle it out. I pointed at their bows and waved them toward the Palace side of the gardens. They nodded and took up their weapons.

I ran ahead, wings retreating into my back. A quick survey of the scene around me revealed that the tops of several towers were gone, and most of the harpoons now came from the Tzi. Few Mihalian men survived. The swarm of porcupine men mounted the stairs now, seeking out my forces. Freed of the harpoon scourge, Neikolan had brought the Brigandrie to the top of the stair, where we rained down arrows on the advancing enemy. Estringites tossed fragments of Palace, landing them with crunching sounds amid the porcupine army and upending the slabs that formed the stairs. The porcupine warriors persisted, grimly continuing their ascent regardless of casualties. They outnumbered us four to one. Their rearguard was rapidly diminished by the precise bow-craft of the Tzi. But my forces would still be hard pressed by the number I estimated would gain the top stair.

I didn't need to tolerate this.

I wanted to end this as quickly as possible, rout the Mihalian forces and defang their trap, so Iakovos and Ilanit would have to confront me themselves or lose their city.

I regrew wings and flapped out over the porcupine army, releasing waves of petrifaction. I landed beside Neikolan as the first wave of porcupine men—those who dodged my assault—gained the terrace. They grabbed their noses, feral mouths snapped shut, spun about, and blew hard.

Quills exploded off their backs into our front line. Men and women stumbled backwards, shouting with pain. It would have been comical in a movie. It wasn't comical here. Here were people with whom I'd laughed and dined at Forgotten Town, pierced like human pincushions.

Neikolan was unhurt and beat down the porcupine men on our right with his two-handed sword. I drew Daevon's blade from its scabbard beside the Glass Sword and threw myself leftwards, weaving a circle of death. I was tossed off my feet by the impact of a boulder nearby, thrown by an Estringite to break apart the ossified. A porcupine warrior closed in on my prostrate form. A young Chaotic with mirrored mail and streaming silver hair deflected the axe blade aimed at my head and in the same motion plunged her scimitar into his neck. She hauled me to my feet.

"Thanks," I said as I unclasped her arm.

"My pleasure, lady Siana." She nodded her head. So young, I thought, looking into the colorless irises of her eyes.

The tide had turned. Many the Bracelet had struck would not rise again. No more harpoons. It grew dark as the bonfires exhausted their fuel. Where were the Twins?

Judging my soldiers to have the upper hand, I flew into the air, beating my wings to flap in place. I sent my voice throughout the City.

"Where are you, Iaakovos, Ilanit? What else will you send against me? Come, cravens, or your City will be mine!"

Something that flashed silver emerged from the eye of the Omphalos. A metal chariot rising by no apparent means, tinctured with argent. It bore two forms, side by side, who faced off with me in the air.

Iakovos and Ilanit.

Why would they come from the Omphalos? I thought of my men and women guarding the underground storeroom for our escape and shuddered. I had felt uneasy throughout the day, traveling a network of ancient tunnels from the rope bridges at the edge of Mihali to the Omphalos. I couldn't pinpoint what was wrong. The Twins were ascending from the same shaft I thought was a secure retreat.

They hovered closer. Something was strange about them, different from the familiar phantasms I had tried to cleave in the throne room. Streaks the color of blood laced Ilanit's corn-silk hair. A wild fire burned in the dark of Iaakovos' face. A giant steel crossbow rested against Iaakovos' massive thighs.

They were not alone on the chariot. Something stood behind, dark and misshapen.

"You have brought us together at last, Sojourner," Iaakovos boomed. "All of the sundered cousins, Ghislain, Kadesh, even our lost sister."

Isabiel.

Isabiel, the presence at their back, came forward. The fanged statue in the Library of the Ancients, brought to malevolent life. Downturned violet eyes set in a once beautiful face ruined by hatred. Pendulous breasts, crooked back, skin mottled and reptilian. Toes splayed out into talons. A lashing devil's tail.

"Welcome to our feast," she purred, her voice incongruently smooth. With a wave of her hand wind rushed from the Omphalos, alive with half-glimpsed forms, throbbing with greed and hunger. The Tzi clicked and squealed. And then were silenced by the death in that wind.

Isabiel. Mistress of the Incubi and Succubae.

I had sensed them, the presence of Isabiel's creatures, close up under the City, in tunnels and caves where I had never felt them before. But I had been unable to name my misgivings.

The remaining porcupine soldiers parted to let that satanic wind flow up the stairs and into my forces.

Ilanit smiled sweetly, her teeth now white fangs in her petulant mouth. Making peace with Isabiel had changed the Twins.

I rushed to my troops' succor. I dared not use the Bracelet amid such chaos. The porcupine men redoubled their attack, shooting quills haphazardly. Some struck succubae and incubi, blue-veined flesh materializing from the wind to lie cold on the ground. I struck with staff and sword, at shadowy forms I could barely see. Things instantly turned against us.

A woman's voice, familiar, sounded at my ear.

"Siana, to your right, to the edge of the terrace," she urged. There was no one there. Something moved away from me in that direction, fast, tracing a faint silvery arc of light and came to rest four feet off the ground, right where the voice indicated I go.

I sharpened my eyes with the Torc. An effigy of Zoorn, naked girl transfixed with spikes, hung mid-air on a silver chain.

I slipped on the Glove Eterokon and strode invisible toward it. As I took it off, my rematerialization was matched by a young girl's. The effigy of Zoorn now lay on her naked bosom. Strawberry-blonde curls framed a familiar face.

"Mercedes!"

She smiled in response, but only briefly.

"They hate me," she said. "Once they sense me, they will forego your people and attack me. Isabiel's commands will matter less than destroying me."

I wrinkled my brow.

"It's your only chance," Mercedes explained. "When they crowd about me, you can petrify them all."

"But what about you?"

She smiled wanly.

"Can you control what it petrifies?" Her glance fell on the bracelet of tiny stones on my wrist.

"Not very well," I grimaced.

"But it won't kill me?"

"No. If it strikes you, I'll carry you someplace safe until it wears off." I touched her pale arm. "Are you sure? You haven't lived this long to die here."

"I won't die," Mercedes concluded. "Now I go, before it's too late." She didn't dematerialize. Rather she *flowed*, quicker than human motion, down the stairs in a diagonal line toward the center of the courtyard. She didn't have to do anything more to announce her presence. Her presence was a beacon.

The wind of her accursed fellows hissed down the stairs and surrounded her en masse. She was the center of a sputtering maelstrom, slashing with her talons in all directions. I flew to the edge of that circle, focused my mind and let loose the Eterokon's power.

A thicket of lapidified succubae and incubi appeared, whorled about the lone living form of Mercedes. I grew a club-tail and smashed my way through them to rejoin her. Her heaving chest was ribboned with slashing cuts. But the Eterokon's power hadn't taken her. It had obeyed my mind. Interesting.

"I'll heal," she huffed when I put my arm around her.

"It's not that," I said, and scooped her up in my arms. I took us straight up in the air, to the levitating chariot that bore three of the seven Aedolae.

I fixed my eyes on Isabiel. "I charge you to release this woman from your power. And lift your curses from the innocent children of this place."

Isabiel snarled, her clawed hands groping toward Mercedes as if they could reach across thirty feet of open air. Iaakovos bent down, reaching for something.

Holding Mercedes was awkward, but I freed a hand long enough to pull forth a thigh dagger and fling it at Isabiel's heart. Light, blinding in the darkness, burst from Ilanit's fingertips and incinerated my weapon as it flew. In its wake, I saw only white flashes before my eyes.

Iakovos spoke.

"We have for you a gift from the Spaerodont, recovered from the Library of the Ancients, forged in the age when your kind last pestered us." His voice was dark with hatred, no longer the regal voice of Mihali's King. "It is called Dreamslayer."

My vision cleared to see a barbed bolt leave the massive silver crossbow in Iakovos' hands. I was too close, and too encumbered with Mercedes, to evade its flight. The bolt whammed into my body and lodged in my ribs directly below my left breast.

In the overwhelming shock and pain, all I could do was keep Mercedes from tumbling to the courtyard below. The bolt had just missed her. I managed to land feet first but then crumpled from the pain. Mercedes leapt free of me. A glistening filament scrolled out between my chest and the chariot above, joining the wicked barbed end of the bolt to Iakovos' weapon. My waving fingers could not disrupt it.

Lounging backward on the stones pummeled me with fresh agony. The bolt protruded from my back and pressed against the pavement, jarring its position within my lung. I forced myself back up, dizzy.

"There will be no escape for you now," Iakovos leered over the edge of the chariot. "You will see."

The chariot glided toward my forces. Translucent globes of albescent energy left Ilanit's hands, each settling around one of my warriors. The spheres rose, holding the warriors aloft, then incinerated them to ash within.

Mercedes hovered over me, spellbound.

"Go," I waved her off. "You did what you could. I won't have Isabiel retake you. Go to Faisanne." She hesitated, doubt shadowing her beautiful face.

The way the bolt pierced caused, as yet, little blood. I groped at my back. The point of the bolt had become a clever hook that lodged like a crab's pincers in my ringmail. I tried to focus on the other end projecting below my breast. I couldn't push the bolt through; its tail was a mess of barbed protrusions, forged of the same piece of metal as the shaft. I staggered to my feet and tried instead to push it through my body from the backside. I almost passed out from the pain as the shaft torqued inside my chest. And the hooks were unyielding.

I was unprepared for this. So far my Eterokoni had protected me from grave injury. Nothing had prepared me for the claustrophobic horror of Dreamslayer stuck fast in my body, refusing to be pulled free.

I seized upon a new hope, even amid that lancinating haze. I let the Torc shift my body through a flickering parade of forms. No luck. I had shapeshifted holes in my body to avoid injury before, but the bolt held fast to every shape I took.

The effort left me dizzier, and my horror deepened as I realized I couldn't rid myself of it.

The portcullis creaked and a fresh wave of porcupine warriors, much greater than the first, flooded the piazza.

I was about to lose my army. My attack on the Twins had failed.

"Mercedes," I croaked. "Neikolan knows your story, he will recognize you. Go and tell him to sound the retreat."

"I won't leave you" was her reply.

Before I could make it far the reinforcements would surround us. A commander had to decide quickly. There would be no escape through the Omphalos, for we would have to push through an onrushing tide of enemies to gain it. And the Tzi guarding it—and the forces I had left underground—had doubtless been slain by Isabiel's minions.

"We need to get up the stairs." I pointed weakly toward the ruined Palace. Mercedes helped me gain my feet and we began an agonizing climb back to the remains of my army.

The piazza filled with dark, armored forms. Neikolan met us halfway up the stairs and scooped me up in his burly arms. Mercedes still stayed close. For some reason, Ilanit had laid off her attack, and the chariot of the Aedolae had retreated to hover above the statuary. The silver line still spooled out between my chest and Iaakovos' weapon, unaffected by widening distance.

At the top of the stair, the terrace was littered with bodies, porcupine creatures but also far too many of my own. Half of the force I had brought from Forgotten Town had perished. We were far too few to resist the crowd of enemies starting up the stair. And I could no longer trust in my own strength to defend them.

I was both the Demigoddess and the Achilles Heel of my army.

At least I could get them out.

"Put me down," I croaked at Neikolan. "I can walk. We must retreat. We can translate from inside the Palace. I'll hold the portal and come through last. You lead them through, and Talmei and Mercedes can guard me until the last moment. Let's go."

Neikolan barked commands. We threaded through the wreck of the terrace toward the thrown-down gates of the Twins' abode.

A screech clove my hearing and snapped my head back toward the Aedolae. The sky behind them was filling with a bevy of aphotic winged forms flowing from the Omphalos, black ink pooling against the stars. They flapped about Isabiel's head with the mindlessness of greedy gulls, jostling one another for the favor of her attention. Spindly insectoid legs hung from their torsos, and their prehensile tails curled and uncurled nervously, sporting a scorpion's sting. They dwarfed Isabiel in size, twenty feet from wingtip to wingtip.

"I command you, *Tsidhaevai*," Isabiel purred, audible somehow despite the distance, "to pursue this woman until you destroy her, no matter you all perish in the doing."

She waved her hand to dismiss them, pointing one crooked finger along the line of silver cord flashing in the darkness. They shot toward me with rapid pumps of their tattered reptilian wings. Grey forms with the heart-shaped faces and long noses of barn owls rushed in, their white pupil-less eyes shining. Lurching with eccentric speed and framed in darkness, they were faces of nightmare coming out of the void.

"*Nightwings*!" a Rungeain prince shouted, copper braids snapping as he dove for cover. But the circle of Estringites about me did not balk. They pummeled the Tsidhaevai with powerful fists and sent them spinning and slamming into the skeletal walls of the destroyed Palace. One Estringite, Nao, took up a harpoon from the battle litter and speared one by the wing, swinging this makeshift weapon in an oval about his head. The hooked Nightwing crashed into one after the other of its fellows, but nothing deterred them. They kept trying to maneuver around, above and through that whirling circle, heedless of their own safety. A crazed but relentless stupidity, expressed in both their fevered attack and the jagged elastic grins that split the space below their long noses.

We were all inside the gallery now. Mercedes and Neikolan hustled me toward the back, where one onyx door to the throne room still hung askew on its frame. The first line of porcupine warriors was streaming in, but their attack was hindered by the surging mass of insane Tsidhaevai that kept dive-bombing in my direction. Heedless of anything but me, the Tsidhaevai inflicted many unintentional wounds on both my army and the porcupine men, grazing combatants with their dangling legs or crushing them when they fell.

Strangely, something prevented them from reaching me. Not the Estringites, for they couldn't keep all at bay. It was as if I was protected by a force field.

Mercedes.

Something in her presence or energy. The icon of Zoorn, the protection of Daphne.

"Thank you sister," I breathed. "You're keeping them from me. Thank you for saving me, again." She smiled back, staying close. I took the Kalimba from its chain and activated the portal to Forgotten Town. A window between worlds, brilliant with early morning sun, opened beside the onyx door. Neikolan began the retreat, while our rearguard held off the porcupines with a cloud of arrows.

With so few of us it did not take long. The Estringites stooped to pass through, still brandishing harpoons at the crazed Nightwings. Soon only Mercedes and I remained. I released the Kalimba button and the portal began to close.

"I still owe you a debt, greater now, and I will pay it," I said. The space behind her was a collage of ravening Tsidhaevai faces, now only stayed by icon of Daphne between her breasts. Her face was softened by white sunlight from the rain-washed forest as the portal closed. She smiled once more then dematerialized, leaving only a wall of slavering faces pressing in vain against a tightening portal through which they could not fit.

AMPIZAND

Neikolan's voice sounded on the trail ahead, congratulating the saboteurs. Wounded were laid on litters recovered from our nearby storehouse. Nao brought one for me.

"No," I waved it away. "I will walk. I won't return from this campaign lying down." Something akin to a frown settled on his hoary face, as he stooped over me. My breath came in ragged gasps and I think my left lung had collapsed. Every inspiration was painful.

We walked, trailing behind. Individuals from the group disengaged in turns to check on me, their faces worried, solicitous. No one tried to remove the bolt, not here. I managed to smile, whispering affirmations I have since forgotten, but my consciousness was overshadowed by jarring agony.

Fifteen minutes down the trail a sound I never expected to hear split the rain-washed tranquility of the forest.

The screech of a Nightwing.

"No," I said, blood cold in my veins. "I must be dreaming. Nao, tell me you didn't hear that."

"I'm afraid I heard it too, my lady."

Another screech rent the air. Neikolan's voice barked, far ahead, but I couldn't discern the words. Wheeling about, I saw it. Hard to see against the sunlight, which dappled through maple branches overhead. But unmistakable all the same: the silver cord.

It scrolled along the path behind me, making wavy curlicues in the air. Still attached to the bolt lodged in my ribs, still connecting me, somehow, to the Twins' demesne.

No sign yet of the Tsidhaevai but there soon would be. I imagined a cloud of those things descending on Forgotten Town, on children playing in the streets, slaying wives and lovers. I thought of Paris, in her little green house.

No, it shouldn't be. They were after *me*. If the Tsidhaevai were able to pursue how long before this damned filament brought the Aedolae down on my dreamworld refuge, the only place safe from their power. I knew what I must do.

"I'm sorry, Nao. Tell them I'm sorry, tell them I will return."

I was going to die, and lose the dreamself I had built for years within the Detheros. I slipped on the Glove.

"Lady Siana!" Nao said in alarm.

"Go!" I yelled. "Get them back safe, don't let them come after me."

I didn't stay to see if he obeyed. I forced my body to run. Dreamslayer jounced inside me, tearing tissue. The fabric of my shirt was wet with blood.

Branches cracked and rained down on me as the Nightwings shrieked and dove. I reached for Daevon's sword and was surprised to brush against the hilt of the Glass Sword, renewed within its scabbard. I had thrown it aside at Mihali. I drew it and found it unshattered. Strange, but I wasn't arguing.

I sliced the legs from an attacking Nightwing. I shook the Bracelet and a cone of power blasted into the others nearby. A rain of solidified bodies crashed through the undergrowth. I had returned to the grotto. A tiny black circle floated in the air before me, silver cord running through its center. It had prevented the portal from closing. I recalled Iaakovos' threat.

A Tsidhaeva's claws dug at the portal from the other side, forcing it open. I had never opened a second portal while the first remained but now was time to try.

Circle atop a cross. The key for Zoorn. Between Forgotten Town and some demesnes there was no intermediary world, such as with Kadesh or Mihali. But Ampizand lay between here and Zoorn, a place of limitless sea. If I still had the strength I could transform into something amphibious and I could evade the winged Tsidhaevai. In the deeps of that sea were sentient beings who might help me, though my contact with them had been fleeting so far.

A portal opened, superimposed upon the other. Nightwings screeched behind me, doubtless frustrated by my invisibility and the inhibiting trees and brush. The second portal must have imposed a secondary reality because I passed through the grasping limbs of the incoming Nightwing as if it wasn't there.

I stood on a dark hill above a vast urban center at night.

No sea.

Wheeling about in consternation I found the hillside behind me crowned with soot-damaged trees. The silver cord disappeared through the small hole of the mostly closed portal. I had no idea if the first portal from Mihali would stay open, or only this new one. I wasn't to find out for some time, but I hoped dearly for the latter.

Why had the key to Zoorn led to this unfamiliar place? But I couldn't risk going back. This would have to do.

With considerable difficulty I sidled down the loose scree of the hillside. At the bottom was a metal guardrail and an empty freeway. Beyond a lofty urban skyline twinkled with a million electric lights. I had never seen anything so modern, so like my world, within the Detheros. Despite all the light, the city exhaled desolation. No living thing was abroad and not a single vehicle, moving or stationary, in sight.

A Nightwing screeched behind me. I jumped the guardrail. I had to cross the road and get to somewhere enclosed. My flight back to the grotto had cost me more strength. It was harder and harder to breathe.

I stepped onto the gray concrete ribbon of road stretching the length of the city in either direction, empty and forlorn.

A flying vehicle zoomed out of nowhere at inconceivable speed and passed within inches of my head. I dropped to my side on the hard pavement. On the cue of my presence, the road was awash with roaring airborne vehicles, filling all the lanes in both directions. I lay stunned and in excruciating pain. There was no end to the flow of traffic. I had to crawl, shuffling on all fours, to stay below the rush.

The second I passed over the faded white stripe of the final lane, it was silent behind me. I stood on the shoulder and glanced back. The road was empty.

But the air wasn't. A flock of Tsidhaevai filled the far side of the road, blocking the hill from sight. They wheeled about, waiting for more of their number to arrive. I had started to climb the steel ladder set into the concrete barrier on my side of the road when they made for me.

Instantaneously the space between us was awash again with phantasmagoric traffic, materializing from literally nowhere. Vehicles ranging in size from small cars to small buildings plowed into the flapping Nightwings and flung out streamers of blood and shredded wings.

I like this place, I thought.

I would soon find it less to my liking.

The Tsidhaevai were not deterred. Only those few happening to fly above the lethal vehicles survived. Not smart, these pets of Isabiel. But the survivors were more than enough trouble. I reached the top of the ladder, and passed through a gap in the railing of the sidewalk. Across a smaller avenue was a line of storefronts, plate glass windows, dark inside. Streetlamps cast a rosy glow onto cracked pavement. I espied a narrow alley between two buildings, and with some trepidation placed an experimental foot into the roadway. No traffic answered, and I crossed quickly without incident. I slipped into the enclosing blackness of the alley as the first screech sounded atop the wall behind.

I rushed down the alley, unable to see my hand in front of my face. Wings flapped behind me and a scorpion tail was thrust into the narrow slit and pounded the empty pavement at my back. The alley seemed to extend forever. The sound of my pursuit faded as I stumbled my way along clammy stone walls. I came to a junction with another alley. A pool of water to my right caught the yellow sheen of light from beneath a door. I crept up a short stair and wedged my fingers in the crack. It opened.

Inside was the last thing I expected. Gleaming rows of washers flanking a narrow aisle. The perfumed smell of laundered clothes. I remembered the Laundromat in my hometown, air heavy with moisture, the heat of dryers. Another row of machines to my left was partially hidden from view. My blood speckled across grimy tiles.

A pair of plate glass windows, opaque with darkness, faced another street in the empty city. The front door was closed, and like the door of the laundromat we frequented as children when our appliances at home invariably broke down, it was adorned with bells on a chain, to signal customers entering. But what customers here? A dryer in the neighboring aisle hummed with tumbling clothes.

My legs trembled, and I felt feverish.

I realized I was not alone.

A small table in the corner by the left window was flanked by white plastic chairs that were cracked and chipped. In one chair a figure in a fur-lined greatcoat sat at ease, smoking a long pipe of red wood. He didn't startle at my approach. The hood of his dark brown tunic hid his face.

"I've seen lots of piercings, but that is the most dramatic," the figure said, setting down his pipe. His hands were gloved. The voice was low and richly sardonic.

I leaned on a washer for support. I was speechless.

The figure pulled back his hood with both hands. His head was a tiger's, or as close to a tiger's as possible while mounted on a human body and evincing a keen, wry intelligence. The tiger-man replaced the pipe in his white muzzle and blew a series of lazy smoke rings. I realized the fur trim of his greatcoat was actually the fur of his neck.

He regarded me coldly with black-rimmed green eyes. The tumbling dryer dinged, a loud chime that made me jump, and the dryer drum decelerated into silence.

"Don't just stand there," the tiger-man said. I had been gazing into his eyes as if hypnotized and shook my head. My consciousness was hazing over with pain. "Your clothes are done."

"*My* clothes?" I gawked. He reminded me of something, some illustration I'd seen in the waking world.

"Go see." He motioned me on with a dismissive and lethargic grace.

I stumbled into the other aisle, trying not to fall and keep him in my peripheral vision. One dryer had a lit purple button. I yanked open the chrome door, and pulled the garments into the basket positioned below it. The slightly damp clothes slapped against the plastic.

"They're a little wet. Shake them out," the tiger-man purred in bass tones. I obeyed, even as the motion made me grit my teeth in pain.

The first garment was a bodysuit, its extremities coal-black and the torso a collage of browns. I shook it out and felt a weird tug as the garment rippled out of my hands. The garment was *standing* in the aisle beside me, and was filling out as if being inflated. Though only a few inches thick, I recognized it: Benjamine, the Orsian sailor lad infatuated with me. The coal-black extremities were his Orsian hands and face. His expression was the last I had seen, as his crushed and lifeless body slid into the icy water of Cylindrax, eyes wide in shock and pain. But now his eyes came to life, narrowing and fixing on my face.

"You killed me, and I will never see my parents again." His quiet voice throbbed with hatred.

"No, you were my friend," I protested.

"You could have saved me," he countered, his inflating form taking a jittery step toward me. "You didn't use the Torc in time."

"Benjamine," I argued but my voice became a sob. A liquid agony of loss and regret was fusing with the pain in my chest.

I turned instead to the shrouded figure in the corner. "What madness is this?"

The tiger-man took the pipe from his muzzle and blew out a ring.

"It is not *I* that accuses you." He ran his gloved fingertips along one stiff whisker. I turned back to Benjamine, but he had collapsed, a jumbled heap.

"Go on," the tiger-man instructed.

I pulled out another garment, even as I tried to avert my eyes. Compelled, my arms shook out the garment, and it took the form of Assav.

"No," I grimaced, but the face of this other Orsian lad filled out despite my protest. The laughing eyes and irrepressible grin that had lightened my mood so many times. The pain of losing him at Mihali descended on me, grief I had been too hard-pressed to feel before.

Awareness descended on his face, erased the wrinkles of laughter, and transformed his expression into a mask of fury.

"No, no, no," I wailed, knowing what was coming. His wrinkled two-dimensional arm thumped wetly against my bloody chest in accusation.

"I died for your foolish ideas," he said. "I trusted you, and you cared more about the Aedolae than your friends. Was slaying them more important than our lives? And we didn't even succeed! What did I die for?"

"Assav wouldn't say these things," I sputtered at the tiger-man seated at ease in the corner.

"How do you know, Miss Grey?" the tiger-man said. "Who knows what rancor overshadows the once kind souls of the dead? Have *you* been dead, Miss Grey? Though from the looks of it, you will be soon." Blood pooled beneath me on the tiled floor.

"Shut up!" I barked. "That's not Assav."

I turned back to the image of Assav and slashed at it with my remaining dagger. Where its garments tore, blood spurted.

"Shit!" I cried. It crumpled to the floor beside the other.

"How appropriate," the tiger-man purred. "You killed him again."

"*Shut up!*" I turned on him, stumbling in fury and pain but still strong enough to throw aside the white plastic chair separating us. I dropped my dagger and seized the flimsy table, clattering it against the wreck of the chair.

"What are you going to do?" the tiger-man said quietly. He hadn't budged an inch. "Kill *another* innocent?"

Recognition dawned.

"You're a rakshasa," I said.

"You always were well read," he purred, blinking his inhuman green eyes. "Go see what is left in the basket."

"No," I said, but I obeyed all the same. I was a warrior. I wasn't good at fighting seated foes that invaded my mind.

Two garments remained in the basket. I pulled out the topmost, shaking it out. Daevon materialized in the air.

I fell to my knees.

"Don't make me hear this," I pleaded.

My peripheral vision was blurring. The only defined space was in front of me, occupied by the expanding phantom of my dead lover. His beautiful face, the finely formed cheekbones, the dark eyes. How I had longed for him after his death, how many private tears I wept. I had longed to be back in his arms, safe and protected, the young girl who first voyaged Within.

I backed away, expecting accusation. But instead he spoke in a faraway voice, looking over my head. He described in a strange detached way his emotions when the pirates slashed into him. He had felt only love for me, focusing on my fading face as he collapsed and consciousness fled. And now his spirit wandered in a shadow realm of lost dreams and yearned without hope to see me again.

My guilt now was accusation enough. Who was I to merit this devotion, from a man who lost his hard-won immortality to protect me?

I had killed everyone who loved me.

"Daevon, I'm sorry, I'm so sorry," I sobbed. "You were so good to me."

The Daevon-garment deflated, a dying balloon sinking to the floor.

The remaining item in the basket was satin cloth that changed colors with the light, rich turquoise and dark plum at the same time.

"You might as well get it over with," the rakshasa mocked.

I reached down and shook it out.

This one was Paris, as I knew it would be. Standing in her iridescent nightdress, her rich tresses unbound and rippling about her shoulders, at nightfall in her little green house. I longed to run my fingers through her hair, to enfold her in my arms, but Dreamslayer protruded from my chest, welling blood, a visible reminder of the war that stood between us.

Her eyes were full with unshed tears, her mouth set in a hard line. This was Paris striving to be strong and resolute when her heart was breaking. She'd worn this look when I left her in the gym before setting out for Mihali.

"How long, Siah," she said, "how long before you kill me too?"

Her voice was empty of passion, and the coldness of her tone—coming from my sweet Paris—hurt much as the words. Indeed, how long? Perhaps she was dead already, slain by the Tsidhaevai that trailed me to Forgotten Town.

"Do not despair, Miss Grey," the tiger-man said. "She speaks the truth: she isn't dead yet. But isn't it all up to you? *Can* you desist from your futile schemes? Or are you as incapable of that as everything else you attempt to do?"

The utterness of my failure sank in my gut like a stone. I had lost everything to the Aedolae. What business did I have, foolish girl, taking on the gods? I had lost friend after friend, sacrificing them to my vanity. Perhaps I should forsake the deeper worlds of dreams, allow my dreaming spirit to be cast out. Then Paris would be safe and at least one life would be spared.

I would die alone in this hell-hole of a dreamscape. But whether I'd be coming back again was up to me. I would have to choose.

"It's not right," I argued, turning to the rakshasa. "It's not right that the Aedolae prevail. It's not about me. I'm only one woman, and a fool to play the hero, but I can't let them get away with their sins. It's not just."

"*Just?*" the tiger-man laughed. "Justice! Who ever heard of such a thing!"

I turned back to Paris, but the last of the garments had crumpled to the floor.

"It is easy," the tiger-man continued, "for you to speak of justice, when the worst you suffer is death in a dream. What of these, who died for real because of your *justice*?"

He gestured languidly at the rumpled heap of deflated garments.

"Those are lies," I spat.

"Are they?" he retorted. "Do you think I made them? They are *your* clothes."

I opened my mouth to protest, but then the wall behind him exploded into a thousand shards.

Several things happened at once. Two Nightwings burst through the plate glass windows and ploughed into the dryers in front of me, sending several flying into the air. The walls and ceiling disappeared. And the entire scene flooded with light.

I sliced the leering face off the first Tsidhaeva with the Glass Sword and spun to face the second as its scorpion tail slammed into my leg. Its barb pierced my pants and sank into muscle. I sliced it off and pulled out what was left, but it was too late. My thigh already throbbed with the poison.

The cityscape was gone. The true nature of the passage between Mihali and Zoorn had reasserted itself, a bare islet of sea-green rock a thousand feet across, surrounded by churning ocean. The overcast sky was bright after the darkness of the city and the dim light of the laundromat. I stood in a halo of glass fragments and tumbled chrome machinery, the two injured Nightwings thrashing amid the litter. I dispatched them. The rest flew low over the ocean, coming for me.

"This should be interesting," a voice said behind me. I wheeled about. I'd hoped I'd left him behind. No such luck.

The rakshasa sat in a plushy brown chair. He pulled a different pipe from a deep pocket and began to smoke again. "Get on with whatever you're going to do. You're running out of time." He pointed at the advancing cloud of Tsidhaevai.

"To hell with you," I said, and rushed him. I swung my sword at his head and watched it sink a couple inches into his furred cheek and stick fast as if enveloped in a clinging, sucking mud.

"A rakshasa is not so easily gotten rid of," he growled throatily, and pushed the sword out of his face like a trifle. "Don't worry about me, miss. I'll just sit here and give you more of my capital advice."

I took to heart the first piece of his advice. I ignored him.

I knew where I was. The knobby center of this island was smoothed off and crowned with the weather-beaten idol of some amphibious deity. The idol was the other translation point of the passage because I'd been through Ampizand both ways, from Zoorn to Forgotten Town, and from Forgotten Town to Zoorn. At the idol the Kalimba's power would engage. I could get there before the Nightwings struck, barely. But then they would follow me to Zoorn, and Zoorn would be less hospitable to a mortally injured enemy of the Aedolae than the cityscape of the rakshasa. I needed to escape them for good.

I knelt down, legs unsteady, and awkwardly twisted my wrist to poise the Glass Sword against the protruding crossbow bolt. I didn't want to end up cutting off some part of me. I fiddled with the angle, breathing heavily, and pushed. The Sword went through the bolt like butter and its wickedly barbed shaft clattered on the rock before my knees.

"Ah, I wondered when you'd get to that," the rakshasa commented drily. "Of course now you'll bleed to death." I ignored him, and used the hilt of the Sword to push the bolt out my back. My vision went black for a moment as pain greater than any I had ever imagined pummeled my consciousness. In futility I pressed my hand against the wound, as my lifeblood pumped out.

Then the Nightwings, shrieking, descended on me.

There was no use fighting. I took the severed barbed end and threw it out over the sea, changing and strengthening the muscles of my arm. The filament attached to the fragment shimmered in the light as it spun. The Nightwings gave it chase. I would have laughed at their stupidity if I'd had any resources left with which to laugh. My vision was greying but for some reason I could clearly see the rakshasa, calmly stroking his whiskers.

A thought struck my swooning brain. I was as stupid as the Nightwings. With Dreamslayer gone, I could shapechange the hole in my chest! I tried and willed a firm veneer of new flesh to staunch the flow of blood. But something was wrong inside. My lung remained collapsed and the pain just as great. I didn't know enough—or couldn't use the Torc well enough—to mend my internal wounds. But at least I wouldn't bleed to death. I wouldn't die here.

I refused to die.

I stood up, eyes fixed on the primitive stone altar.

Or rather I *tried* to stand up. My legs wouldn't obey me. The rakshasa laughed.

"Have you forgotten?" he asked.

The poison from the Tsidhaeva's barb. My legs had frozen, folded in a kneeling position.

"I'll drag myself there," I hissed, and pulled myself along the rock, trailing the dead weight of my lower body.

"There isn't time," the rakshasa said with more animation, "and even if there was, you'd arrive in Zoorn a blue and lifeless corpse. You must accept, sojourner, that you are now dead and your mission is over."

"You're wrong," I gasped.

Now I must choose. Should I die and leave Paris free of me? Was I committed to my war or would I retreat behind the Detheros, to wander the Fringe defeated and forlorn? I had carried the hermetus in its pouch about my belt for two and a half years. Why had I never used it? Did some part of me balk at the terror and insecurity of my vendetta against the Aedolae? Secretly wish for an end, a way out?

No, I lacked the guts to lop off one of my digits. It was that simple.

What a sissy.

I placed the hermetus on the rock beside me. I still held the Glass Sword. I imagined my toes inside my boots. Fedosei's book in the Library of the Ancients described how the priests of the Coethyphys removed the outside fingers and toes. Bierce said hair wouldn't work, but any essential part of the body would. I didn't want to lose fingers and spend the rest of my dreams looking like a fucking Coethyphys' *aliment*.

I didn't want to lose toes either. I may have called Paris a Barbie, but I too was a girl, as well as a warrior, in the end.

I lay on my back and held the Glass Sword aloft. My arm trembled. Deadness moved up my abdomen. The Nightwings' cries sounded somewhere to my right but I could no longer see them. Were they coming back?

"Ah, this is grand," the rakshasa commented. "The sojourner cannot bear to see her fate." I had placed the tip of the Sword below my breasts.

"You've had great fun mocking me," I replied. "Now you are the fool." And I laid open my ribcage, moving as carefully as I could with my hand shaking from the awkwardness of the angle and my body weakening from the poison. Woozy from the fresh pain, I pulled the flap of skin and flesh aside and, to be safe, cut out two pieces of rib.

"What are you doing?" the rakshasa hissed. The chair legs scraped against stone.

"Defying you and everyone else who thinks they control my fate," I said, my last words before I died.

I groped for the hermetus, dragging it onto my blood-soaked belly. My fingers trembled horribly and fumbled with the latch, but I managed to drop two gory fragments of my body into the vessel's brazen interior. I closed the latch.

The rakshasa stood over me. I was well-read indeed and knew it could not directly jeopardize my well-being. Its hope had been that I would slaughter myself so it could feast on me. In any case, the poison in my flesh would make me a poor snack now. Would the rakshasa trouble the hermetus, could it undo my work? I didn't know but somehow figured not. I would return, growing a new dreambody at this very spot.

Within the Detheros.

As many times as they could kill me.

The rakshasa glared down at me, green eyes blazing, angered by his own impotence and failure, gloved hands clenching and unclenching at his sides. Behind his head the whirring, thrashing cloud of Tsidhaevai dove toward us. I tried to raise the Glass Sword but my hand barely left the ground. The poison was attacking my ravaged chest and suffocating me like a hand clamping over my mouth.

The last thing I felt was a wave of power from the Bracelet coning upwards, born aloft by anger and anguish, the death throes of a Dreamer. As my vision went black, the petrified forms of Nightwings smacked down on the rock and shattered all around me, and then I knew no more.

OUT THROUGH THE IN DOOR

My next awareness was dreaming, dreaming in some dim corner of myself.

I dreamt of an island, little more than a circle of bare green rock, the only thing visible in a twilit, storm-tossed sea. A skeleton lay upon it, grey bones buffeted by a cold wind. But in the dream a gauziness clove to them and in flashes of lightning I fancied I saw, superimposed upon the skeleton, the translucent body of a young woman.

Time passed. My dreaming mind shifted through night and twilit day, and night and day again. On the rock lay a pallid female form, laying on her side, chill as death. The wind cast her long hair about her face. Then rain fell, beading on her body and plastering her hair dark to her scalp. Rivulets ran from her skin and pooled in the cragginess of the stone. Night fell.

The next day dawned colorless: no sun, only a lightening of the cloud masses overhead. A freezing rain woke me. My chest lurched and coughed and sucked air into my legs, raw and painful to my throat. My face lay smashed against the stone, and I watched rain splash up from the rocks. My body was frozen and sore. I struggled to sit up.

A flat sea spread to the horizon. I remembered that nearby an ancient altar marked the portal to Zoorn.

I was naked. My head ached. I couldn't remember how I had gotten there or what I'd been doing. Something stirred in my memory. I lifted my left breast. The white flesh below was crisscrossed with scars, a puckered tautness where Dreamslayer had pierced me and ragged lines where I had cut open my chest. I remembered the gleaming bolt, the pain. But I couldn't remember who shot me or why.

But I remembered dying. The blood. Pain fierce enough to unseat my reason. The destruction of my body, poisoned and broken.

As I shifted, uncomfortable on the rock, something clanked between my legs. I picked up and studied the small bronze vessel. It brought back my last act before dying: slicing open my own chest.

The hermetus had worked. Inside lay the small part of me I'd sliced away, in defiance and desperation. I glanced about, suddenly afraid, but the rakshasa and his plush brown chair were gone. He had disappeared and left my corpse and the hermetus alone.

I was alive, my dreamself regenerated here where my flesh was anchored inside the hermetus. I had not been cast over the Detheros, fated to penetrate its horrors again.

Instead I was here in Ampizand.

Where I'd slowly freeze to death.

I touched my throat and found the Kalimba despite my nakedness. I had to remember what it did. Mostly from instinct, for my thoughts were hazy, I clambered up to the hideous idol where it squatted on its circlet of stone and regarded the cold sea with empty eyes. Those few steps took only a moment, but for inability to take them I had died. How much time had passed? Days, weeks? I hoped not months or years.

I pressed the key for Forgotten Town. I didn't remember what it stood for. I had no image of the forest in my mind, only a need to get away and the sense that key meant safety and reprieve. Nothing happened. My fingers, stiff and painful, traced the Kalimba's other keys. Another symbol jumped out at me. Zoorn. I had to go there first to get to Forgotten Town. Some portion of my mind still functioned logically. I stumbled back down the slick rock and grabbed the hermetus. Returning to the idol, I pressed the key for Zoorn.

Beyond the portal was a dense fog. My bare toes sunk inches into oozing mud, cold and loathsome. Broken spires jutted from the fog, vast fingers clutching at a dead sky. Masts of seagoing vessels, shattered and old. I stood in the Graveyard of Ships, so the Temple of the Zoorn Cult, Daphne's Temple, was nearby, hidden today by mist. It was even colder than Ampizand and I didn't want to be here either. My finger returned to the key for Forgotten Town.

Next was a dark place that lacked depth, like stepping into a painting. The usual scents and sounds of the dripping forest above Forgotten Town were absent, but it was a forest of sorts, skeletal trees against a flat, dim sky. The two small evergreens marking the location of the portal were still there. So I was in the right place, but it had never resembled this.

I tried to follow the gravel road toward town, but immediately stumbled. Walking was perilous, because in the bizarre flatness of this world there was no way to gauge the proximity of anything around me or the slope of the road ahead. I sat down to nurse a stubbed toe and pick gravel from the flesh of my knees. My new dreamself was strange, arms too thin, the skin of my belly and thighs too smooth and soft. The forest was warmer but my muscles were still cold and stiff. I turned back. Normally the portal would have vanished but a shimmering oval still hovered there, framing a black void that was the only three dimensional depth in the scene.

Words came to my mind unbidden, the words of the Egyptian-countenanced man at the bazaar in Kadesh. I don't why I remembered them, when I could barely remember my name.

"Remember, friend," he had said, *"when you are in need, the same key will get you out through the in door."*

That key—cross, circle and half-moon—had always been the key to Forgotten Town. For the first time, it had transported me to a perverse and suffocating facsimile of that destination. What would happen if I pressed the key again, here inside that world? It might get me out, but out to where?

I pressed it. The blackness framed by the ovate portal became blazing light. I shielded my eyes. A warm breeze flooded through, instantly washing away my soreness, coldness and wounds.

When my eyes adjusted, I saw a cloudless blue sky, so beautiful my eyes filled with tears. I heard the mournful cries of sea gulls, far off. And for the first time I stepped into Mercair's World, his hidden oasis in the world of the Aedolae.

I laughed out loud later, thinking about it. I had always wondered at the uniqueness of Forgotten Town, why it wasn't like the other demesnes, why it functioned like a passage as well as a destination world. Why had I never tried the obvious experiment? Treating its fixed translation point like that of a passage and pressing again the original key on the Kalimba that took me into it? It was the old adage of missing what is right before your face. All my systematic exploration with the other keys, portals and passages, finding their fixed translation points, had been done subsequent to my original naïve discovery of Forgotten Town. Did this fact blind me? My naiveté had returned me to the grotto in the wood and compelled me to press a *different* key. My instinct had been to return to Ebon Port and Daevon. Because this had worked it fixed in my mind that Forgotten Town was a demesne, albeit unique, and it worked this way and no other way.

But if it was instead a passage, it was still unique, for pressing a *different* key within any other passage was useless—one had to continue on to the original destination. But I had never thought to make this exact test. Not until some magic of Mercair's compelled me to try. Some magic of memory.

The portal closed behind me. I stood on a beach, a vast crescent spanning perhaps six miles between rocky headlands. Low undulating mountains, carpeted in green, sloped down to meet the sand. Dots of color—pink, red and orange—moved against them. Later I would see them up close, the guardian birds of Mercair's realm, striding among the trees on their impossibly tall and spindly legs.

My mind was still full of cobwebs, but my soul felt instantly lighter, and my body felt healed and at peace.

At the foot of the mountains a mile off was a cluster of buildings, flanked by a long boardwalk. A warm but not hot sun beat down upon my back, and a cool breeze, rising and falling mercurially, balanced the heat of the sun. My naked body felt strong and I walked toward the buildings, drawn by instinct. The sand was cool and firm beneath my toes, wetted by the receding tide.

I discerned small figures huddled on the beach ahead. As I passed among the first group, the figures were suddenly all around me, children on their knees in the sand, scooping and digging, building sandcastles at the tide line. Both girls and boys, clad in outfits from different centuries of waking world fashion, never speaking, and never turning my way, engaged in the seriousness of their play. To them I did not exist.

The chance arrangement of the groups of children left a purposeful avenue of open space. Down this avenue strode a man. Something was immediately familiar about him, and the unexpectedness of that familiarity, in this strange world, froze me in my tracks. He had sighted me but did not hurry. His hat was stiff, a perfect circle, and he held a hooked cane in his left hand. His apparel—black slacks and neat vest over a long-sleeved striped shirt—seemed less anachronistic than last time I saw him, surrounded as we were now by children from the waking world.

My heart lightened.

"Mercair," I cried. My mind cleared. I rushed to him like a daughter greeting her father.

"Well met again, young Siana." He stopped and leaned on his cane. "You have foiled your enemies again. Well done, dreamer."

His compliment felt undeserved, waking in me an echo of my sense of failure at Mihali.

"I am always meeting you when I am ill-disposed," I said, blushing at my naked bosom and loins.

"Do not fuss," he shrugged, paying my nudity absolutely no heed. He offered me his arm. "This is a place of beauty, a place for healing dreams, and such things do not matter. Walk with me."

I forgot my self-consciousness in the blissful comfort of his presence.

I remembered Ghislain, how he reminded me of Mercair. *But truly*, spoke my heart, *there is no similarity*. I took Mercair's arm. He smiled, jet-black eyes sparkling in the sun. He appeared no older than that day five years ago. The same, sparse, flecks of white in his black goatee.

"But where are we?" I asked.

"Haven't you guessed, little Siana?" he laughed. "This is my world, my home, and it appears you have traveled through the Detheros and all those horrors to take another stroll with me."

He spoke like my passage through the Detheros were yesterday, and nothing else had happened since. Perhaps he perceived time this way?

"This is my realm, long hidden from the Aedolae. It is my long protest against their rule."

"And who are the children?"

"They are dream orphans," he said, "finding their salvation the way such things are best found."

A bright feather from one of his great flamingo-like birds had drifted down to the beach, and he hooked it with his cane, balancing it precariously in the crook and offering it to me.

I smiled and held it to my chest, folding my arms about my scarred chest. The feather radiated purple light against my skin, making it beautiful.

"Thank you," I grinned. Memories of how he rescued me in the Gardens, and treated me with such patient kindness, played like a movie in my head.

"You are welcome," Mercair said.

We said little more that night. He walked me to his abode, a sprawling complex like an elegant seaside hotel. We strolled the long boardwalk at nightfall, watching the setting sun cast an orange avenue across the waves. Then we retired to his solar, a many-windowed room that drank in the rainbow-hued light of the gloaming. There on a shelf I left my hermetus, judging this the safest place within the Detheros for that piece of myself to reside.

All queries, and agonies, and memories were subdued and blanketed under a deep sense of peace as night fell. Not the forgetfulness of the Gardens. Rather a peace that left all things clear in my mind, but separated out my soul. Drawing a veil around my concerns. I went to bed in my own little room on the highest floor of his hotel, finding my black war garb and the rest of the Eterokoni laid out on the vanity. Before I retired I trailed my fingers over them, inviting memories to return. There were nine. Something nagged at me. Shouldn't there be ten? No, I'd never found one that was mentioned in my brother's journal. He had called it the Eterokon of Destruction, but described it as both a cluster of pearls and grapes. I felt too peaceful to puzzle over it further.

On the bed was a simple cotton shift, sheer and finely made, and I put that on instead of my war garb, pleased at my reflection in the mirror. Then I crawled into the neatly made bed and had a divine and restful sleep within the world of dreams.

· • • ● ●• ● ●• • ·

T he morning cries of seagulls woke me slowly. If not for the deep feeling of rest, I would have thought I had just fallen asleep. I found Mercair breakfasting on a terrace flanking the boardwalk below. Our waiter, it turned out, was the Egyptian from the bazaar, looking strange here in his desert garb. The Egyptian winked at me as he retreated from our table.

"Why did you save me from the Gardens?" I sipped a glorious glass of orange juice. I had been far too dazed to ask the question back then.

Mercair left off buttering his toast.

"Because a Dreamer is a noble thing, and not to be chained. Dreamers should be the ones to shape the *prima materia* of this world, projecting onto it the stuff of their longings and imaginations. Leaving it free and uncorrupted when they are done, to be shaped and enjoyed anew by Dreamers of a myriad races. The Aedolae have hoarded these worlds for their selfish ends. They are Shapers too, and I once respected that. But in their hubris they made these worlds like yours, cold and rigid. And they go too far when they bind Dreamers as they have bound their worlds."

Mercair paused. Sunlight glinted off his butter knife.

"But couldn't a powerful Dreamer do the same?"

"That is true," Mercair studied my face. "In the past such has been against the unspoken code of Dreamers. The famed dreamers of old did not bind the *prima materia* in permanent shape, but left it free for all. They became heroes, explorers, demigoddesses, but not conquerors or tyrants like the Aedolae. You are of their ilk, a great Dreamer."

That was a lot to digest.

"I don't know that I am a 'great Dreamer'," I stammered. "Lately I am just an angry girl." Or so Paris accused.

Mercair meticulously scraped at a small burnt patch on his second piece of toast. It struck me as a humorous behavior for such an ancient being.

"I don't pretend to understand the emotions of your kind," he admitted. "I can only judge your actions, which have shown determination, pluck and skill, time and time again. This world is not like it used to be. That you are still alive within their great Wall, persecuted as you have been, is tribute to my judgment of you."

"You say the Dreamers of the past were explorers, heroes," I said, helping myself to more orange juice from the carafe. "But if the Aedolae are tyrants, what does that make me, the anti-tyrant? Is a guerilla dreamer a respectable thing?"

Mercair stroked his trimmed beard. "Are you asking if I find your War an acceptable vocation for a dreamer?"

"Basically," I laughed. To tell the truth, I was having a hard time remembering that war. I remembered the rakshasa, the Nightwings, my death, but not what led to it. It seemed significant elements of my memory had been lost with my body.

"It is not mine to judge the pursuits of dreamers," Mercair shrugged and sunk his teeth into his toast.

I cocked my head and pointed a finger at him playfully. "Yet you are happy to judge the Aedolae."

Even though this man—who was, perhaps, not a man—confessed his ignorance of human emotions, I nonetheless was unguarded around him. I didn't feel like Siana the warrior, or a great Dreamer. I felt wrapped in the affectionate comfort of a friend, or a father.

"I have judged them, yes, in your hearing," Mercair said, looking a shade uncomfortable, "but I have left them alone to pursue their aims. So far."

I fancied Mercair was surprised at his own words. The expression on his face made me smile.

"Why leave them alone?" I asked.

"I do not know that it is my role, my destiny, to confront them. I am a friend to Dreamers. That is all."

"But do you have the power to confront them?"

Mercair finished his toast and went back to stroking his beard.

"Rightfully, my dear, I do not know," he answered. "I have never really considered that."

"Perhaps you should!" I said, with a level of vehemence I immediately judged impertinent. I hid behind my hands. Peeking in between my laced fingers I saw Mercair didn't look angry.

"Why haven't I seen you in all these years?" I asked, dropping my hand.

The Egyptian was bringing out plates laden with thin pancakes.

Crepes, is that the word? I thought. My upbringing hadn't exactly been high-class. I was struck by the humor of being served something with a French name by a mostly naked

Egyptian in a 19th century seaside resort. Mercair, not being of my world, must be blithely unaware of this humorous anachronism.

"You didn't need me," Mercair answered simply and began to slice his crepes with elegant precision.

"Why did you think I needed you now?"

"Dying on a rock in a middle of an ocean doesn't strike you as need enough?" Mercair shot back with a slight smile, but then his face grew serious. "It is not my business to interfere with your dreams, only to keep them free of unfair interferences from the Aedolae."

"You seem plenty ready to oppose them," I said. Typical me: picking at old topics like a scab. "Perhaps you should step it up a bit. Oh, and get rid of the Coethyphys while you're at it."

I found myself hiding behind my hand again.

"My lady!" Mercair chuckled. "It seems I will learn about human emotion if I keep talking with you. I expected your resurrection to leave you befuddled and lost. My world has been more restorative than I expected. How *do* you feel?"

"Even better if I stopped talking and ate this lovely food," I laughed. "You make me garrulous and that is not what I am known for. That is Paris' job."

"Your Paris is a lovely thing," Mercair commented absently.

"Do you know about *everything*?" I said, wrinkling my brow, wondering if he knew what went on in her bedroom at Forgotten Town too.

"Not everything," he replied. "But I have many ways of traveling about and learning what I seek to know. Let me speak while you enjoy Alt's cooking."

"Alt? That is a funny name."

"He has some longer name, but I can't pronounce it. Now stop talking." Mercair motioned at my plate.

"I named you a great Dreamer," he continued, once he was satisfied I was keeping my mouth full of Alt's cuisine, "because of your spunk and because of the Eterokoni. And those are one and the same thing, for your spunk, your will, brought them into your possession, the sign of a master dreamer. And in your possession lies the greatest concentration of Eterokoni in the history of these worlds—"

"My brother had eight," I interrupted, doubtless unladylike with my mouth full of food.

"I didn't know that. That is interesting. Your family has quite a pedigree—"

"Ghislain said that too," I said, swallowing heartily.

"Did he? In any case, your brother did not have them long."

I detected something in Mercair's gaze sharpen at mention of Ghislain. "What are the Eterokoni, really?"

"Their creation goes back to the time when the Aedolae first came to these worlds," Mercair replied, motioning again at my plate. "Really, you can ask me questions later. The Eterokoni's purpose was to focus and enhance dreamers' power, as a check against the growing power of the Aedolae. To help them Shape dreams with a grandiosity never before seen. You have done well harnessing that power.

"When you are well and rested, you can return to Forgotten Town, to Paris, to your Brigands, to your War if that is what you like. But rest here awhile; it is why I fashioned this World and hid it behind the veneer of what you call Forgotten Town.

"Now you know where it is, it will always be here for you, my dreamer," he said, and I did not miss the possessive in his reference. "But guard the secret well. For now, eat and walk my beach in peace, and remember your dreams."

And so I did, walking the beach alone. He had affirmed, needlessly for my heart knew no dread here, that his realm was guarded and safe. I walked for hours, splashing about at water's edge, watching his amazing birds as they came on their stilt-like legs to drink from the waves. I wondered if here even the sea was sweet? I did a whole lot of blissful nothing for a long time. But as the morning wore on, thoughts swirled about my mind and took form. Memories reforming, emotions churning inside. My mind replayed the whole sequence of my dreamlife within the Detheros: meeting Daevon at Ebon Port, my trip as Jaena

along the Aedol Via, my confrontation with Ghislain, finding
Forgotten Town. Raiding the Library of the Ancients, losing
my first lover to the men who became the core of my Brigandrie.
A myriad explorations in dark and forgotten places between
demesnes. Meeting Paris, huddled up and laughing with her in
an underground bunker beneath sand storms in the desert, the
feel of her hair beneath my fingers. Attacking the Twins at their
palace and the ambush of Isabiel's various minions.

As these thoughts took shape, my simple joy was punctured
and I hoofed it back to Mercair.

"I remember everything now. And I am a failure." I scowled
at him while we stood at one end of the boardwalk, doubtless
looking a windswept and ridiculously grubby Hero.

"No dreamer is a failure, as long as they dream," he said.
He had been gazing off toward the horizon. I felt like I was
interrupting him but I was too peeved not to persist.

"I about lost my force, and myself, in my last move against
the Aedolae. If it hadn't been for Bierce's foresight and
the hermetus, I would be outside the Detheros banging on
Ghislain's front door again right now. I want you to help me.
I want to finish the dream I have begun and I want to succeed
this time. I have the power, I have the will, but I misdoubt I have
the wisdom I need. Help me, make me wise."

This got Mercair's attention.

"If only wisdom were so easy," he smiled gently and laid his
hand on my shoulder. "I wonder, ofttimes, if I am wise. But I
will try, Siana, I will try."

• • • ● ● ● ● • •

A nd he tried, through those weeks I stayed at his seaside
estate. Under his tutelage I harnessed the power of the
Eye for the first time. Mercair indulged my many questions,
answering them deftly, though I found his attitude toward the
Aedolae frustrating. With Alt as sparring partner and goad, I

recovered the strength and dexterity of the dreambody that died in Ampizand, transforming the softness of my new self into the lean hardihood of the Siana I remembered.

As Alt and I fought with staves and wooden swords, my hatred and my anger returned.

I thought to become both wise and strong, wiser and stronger than before. Mercair tried and his help was above reproach. I fancied myself so much smarter than the young girl who penetrated the Detheros and arrived at the docks of Ebon as a mermaid. But things turned out more complex than the wisdom of my adulthood could manage. How often this is true, even in dreams.

I told Mercair, on the boardwalk that second day, that I remembered everything. I remembered many things, but not nearly enough. The things most painful—the rakshasa's phantoms in the laundromat—I didn't yet remember. The accusations of those phantoms might have tempered both my anger and my zeal to confront the Aedolae again so soon. But I didn't remember, and my quest to dethrone the Aedolae and pay them back for my death burned a fire in my mind, brighter and brighter, leaving no room for shadows of doubt or hesitation.

Thereby my wisdom—and thus Mercair's—was compromised. I still failed to respond to the events at Mihali with anything other than blind determination to atone for what happened—through vengeance and victory. I still framed doubt as an untenable accession to the sovereignty of my opponents.

Was I any wiser by the time I left the refuge of Mercair's World and returned to my saboteurs? Mercair's tutelage was crippled by his uncritical adoration of dreamers, and honestly by his love for me.

But I would remember the things I had lost, at last, when I found Paris beside me on the battlefield, unsought and unexpected, exposed to the terrors of the Aedolae.

By then it would be too late.

WHAT WAS HIDDEN IN THE FRAME

E llie startled awake when the book fell from her drowsing fingers and slammed on the library floor. She had no idea how long she had napped, only that she was warm and sluggish in the thick cloak the Parson had brought her, nestled into the tiny alcove in the back of the lower floor of the library. The light between the stacks was the same as ever but she had the sense that she had slept for a while. She stood up and cursed at the pins and needles sensation in the leg that had been crooked beneath her.

She walked out from under the upper story, into the recessed entryway where, as ever, the castle's sole electric lamp shed a pool of friendly light onto the plush chair nearby. Something struck her odd about the chair. She ran her palm over the indentation in the cushion. It was warm.

A chill ran the length of her spine. She glanced at the statues, Mercair on one side and the Achthron-like thing on the other. Nothing different there. She shook her head and left the library. By the time she entered the amphitheater to gauge the time of day, she had half convinced herself it was her imagination. The air was bracing and fresh, clearing out the cobwebs of sleep. It looked to be late afternoon. But she wanted no part of the Mirror Room.

So she wandered into the gallery below her ruined bedroom. Siana's implacable face was dim in the failing light. Ellie thought of the events in the book she'd read. She no longer believed the expression on that face. The power, the invincibility, the righteousness. She couldn't decide if she sympathized with, or was disgusted by, the Siana in the books. A little of both, a mixture of many emotions. Concern for the heroine she had come to know. Frustration with her choices, her insensitivity to those she loved. Identification with how she had been wronged. She now knew the heart of the woman within that icon. Siana was flesh and blood to her, human fallacies and desires, the lost girl within the warrior. Ellie had read too much—and felt too much as she'd read—to think differently.

She turned from the window, and was momentarily blinded to the rest of the room, despite the lateness of the day. She was eager to know more, to return to the library, but she had the sense that she must think things through first. The Parson had said he'd be away for several days. She wished he were here. *I'll have to find a place to have a good think, and do my best.*

Ellie froze.

There was something new in her field of vision, a dark painting on the wall near the door. That wall had always been empty. The painting hung at eye level in a tarnished silver frame. The dark canvas showed a solitary figure. She approached it as if approaching a viper.

The figure was a rakshasa.

The painting was vividly realistic. In it a tiger-man sat at a circular table of dark wood scarred and pocked with age and abuse, smoking an elegantly inscribed pipe. On the table lay a slim black book, very similar to the ones in the library. Though he sat at an angle to the frame and his furred head was shown in partial profile, his black-rimmed green eyes stared right at her. His gaze was so intense that Ellie found herself crossing her arms across her chest as if in defense.

She knew it: the creature in the painting saw her.

She backed away a few steps, then fled in terror through the amphitheater and into the antechamber below the library. She leaned, panting, against the wall. Her mind raced with self-loathing. *Silly Ellie, this isn't the first time you have seen Siana's enemies portrayed—remember the Achthroi shadows!*

But the confidence of the past few days was slipping through her fingers, threatening to plunge her back into her old terror of the castle at night.

"No!" she shouted and punched herself in the arm. She stomped across the room, forcing herself to walk slowly, up toward the library.

And then she saw the second painting.

Or was it the same one?

To the left along the staircase was the same silver frame, and even at this angle she could see the same rakshasa staring down at her. The illustration was the same but she swore the eyes looked a different direction.

Fright almost knocked her down the steps. She recovered herself at the bottom, legs shaking. She turned her head, still feeling the rakshasa's eyes on her back. *But I want to go up the stair!*

A fury rose in her, as it had that night in the Time Room. She marched up the stairs.

"I have no business with you. I am not Siana and I don't need to be afraid of you because your business is with her," Ellie yelled. As is the case with fury, she was not easily satisfied. To her own surprise she hefted the painting off the wall, carried it into the library and smashed it on the upraised arm of the statue of Mercair. The canvas tore and shredded and soon she was smashing apart the frame. The silver had been cast in segments and came apart easily. Soon the rakshasa was black and orange strips on the floor. She ground them beneath her bare feet.

She sat in the plush chair, which was now cold, and laughed.

When her laughter subsided she found the remnants of the painting a visual distraction and returned to the alcove. She wanted to think fast, and find the last book, the one that must contain the secret of Siana's final fate. Her defiance had quelled her terror, but nonetheless she was on edge. The encounter with the rakshasa had unsettled her in a way the Parson's admonitions of running out of time had not.

Lists always helped. So she constructed a new one in her head.

What I've learned from the last book:

1. Siana used the hermetus when she died, and so her dreamself is anchored within the Detheros. Therefore if she died again at Mihali, she should have just regenerated again within the Detheros.

2. I know her whole story, basically. I've read right up to the events of the first book I found. I know why Siana went back to attack Kadesh: to get vengeance for her death.

3. I've never found a book that tells of events after the first book I read. (That's not something I learned from this book. Maybe I should retitle my list *Things I Know.* Whatever.) So even though I don't know for sure it sure seems like the events of that book must have led to the existence of this place, with Siana's ghost now trapped in the mirror.

4. Maybe something happened to Siana like what happened to Timothy. Maybe this is only a fragment of her, this whole place, and there is a bigger fragment of her somewhere else, out there in the dreamworld. But if so, she isn't OK anymore, just as Timothy doesn't seem to be.

5. Oh fuck, this isn't getting me anywhere. I read that damn book and the Parson's logic failed. I only know something went dreadfully wrong with Siana, something that shouldn't have happened given the hermetus, she never found her brother, and time is running out for me. I have to figure everything out before I'm stuck in the dreamworlds being chased by people with pitchforks.

6. This isn't a list anymore.

7. I need to find the end of the story.

8. *Duh, Ellie!*

Frustrated and restless, Ellie stood up. The floor was suddenly rippling water. Her stomach lurched. The library became a latticework skeleton of shredded concrete, filtering rays of white winter sun.

The way the Parson saw it.

She looked down. Below her feet was a hole in the broken floor. She started to fall.

A flash of light. The close air of the library and the smell of old books returned. She sank to her ankles in the floor. Instinctively she raised a foot and it trailed the floor behind it in long streamers like viscous glue. She struggled to free both feet while her stomach churned. A moment later her feet were free and clean and the floor hardened beneath her.

Her gut was sick, threatening to heave. She cast about for some clue to what had happened. To the right of the spiraling staircase, on the upper floor, several books poked over the edge, strewn carelessly. She hadn't done that. Wrinkling her brow, she crossed to the foot of the stair.

Another flash. So bright she could see nothing at first. Her hands groped and seized the railing of the stair. A second later, that iron rail was the only firm thing in a maelstrom. A screaming wind tore across a barren land. A figure stood on the ground a few feet from Ellie, blonde hair whipped about a hidden face. To Ellie's horror a vortex of air alit on the woman and lifted her bodily, spinning her and shredding her body into ribbons. But there was no blood, only streamers of flesh, and an anguished, disembodied face in 2D that spun at the outside of the vortex like a piece of paper.

The walls of the library returned, phantom-like, then hardened. At the same time, the vortex released its captive and slammed the spinning blur of pink flesh onto the coagulating material of the walls. This version of the library had no second floor, only walls and ceiling, with Siana splintered and crushed against them.

These were the bas reliefs of Siana on the upper floor, face distorted in distress. Perhaps Ellie had just witnessed their making.

The noise and wind disappeared. The dim light of the library returned, along with books and shelves, the cold wilderness gone. Had this been Siana's last moment? It still didn't make much sense.

Ellie leaned over and tried to vomit but nothing came. She felt a sudden hunger, combined with the nausea. Her hand still gripped the railing and she remembered why she was there. With trepidation, she climbed to the second floor.

The shelf to the right of the staircase had been ravaged, books torn from it and scattered in a jumble on the floor. Only the edge of this mess had been visible below. She knew this wasn't the Parson's work, nor hers. She wasn't alone in the castle anymore and she shared it with more than a phantasm. Was it boys from the village? Was all this now visible to them? The explanation didn't feel right.

She knew the truth. The warm spot in the chair below, the mess here on the second floor, the painting that moved from wall to wall. The rakshasa had been here—real and in the flesh—and he had done this.

What had he sought?

Had she killed him when she destroyed the painting? On the lower floor, fragments of gilt frame gleamed like metal bones in the light of the reading lamp, but she saw nothing else. She rushed down the stairs. In her haste and nausea she tripped on the third stair from the bottom and pitched headlong.

She fell on her shoulder, striking not floor but ground. Coarse soil abraded her skin. She rolled onto her back, feeling cold muddy moss beneath her bottom. The sky was a dim winter twilight. She sat up. The library was gone as was everything else but low barren hills and a sun whose lower rim was striking the horizon.

"I'm free," she thought. *"The castle is gone!"*

Something passed in front of the sun, casting shadow, and the ground shook with the impact. A falling house. Timbers exploded in all directions, at this distance looking like matchsticks scattered from a box.

A single black book lay on the barren ground. The same book had been in the painting of the rakshasa.

Ellie got up and walked toward it.

Something unseen scratched a line of blood on her right arm. She shrieked with surprise more than pain, and clutched her arm. A veil descended over her vision and the heath and hills disappeared.

She stood beside the bookshelf whose edge had scraped her arm. She was near the semicircular sitting area. She rounded the railing separating it from the main floor and descended the ramp to the statue of Mercair. Her stomach felt better, perhaps the pain had pushed away the nausea.

What was going on? Her mind was overwhelmed.

The shattered frame was there, forming a loose diamond on the floor. In its center lay the black book, the one she'd been walking towards. But the scraps of canvas, black background, orange fur and brown greatcoat were gone.

"So the rakshasa isn't dead, I just blew his hiding place," Ellie said out loud. The scraps she trod into the floor were him, transformed, and when she wasn't watching he had fled. The thought of Siana's ominous tormentor in the castle somewhere, perhaps very close, was not comforting. But if he meant her ill, why did he play the craven?

"If he could stand up to Siana, he could stand up to me!" Ellie thought. But his goal seemed to be hiding things from her, a book for which he had ransacked the upper story. When he'd heard her wake he had run off.

"See, Ellie. He doesn't want to confront you." But she wasn't sure she believed herself.

She removed the slim book from its halo of broken argent splinters.

"Well, let's see what he was hiding," she said. Like the rest, its cover was blank. She opened the book and scanned a paragraph in the middle. It described Siana and Paris in the gym at Forgotten Town and Siana goading Paris to pick her up.

Ellie had dreamt that scene, and here it was. Why would this matter to the rakshasa? She already knew about this. She closed the volume and glanced about nervously. If the rakshasa was still alive and fled the scene he had very politely closed the library doors behind him. Nonetheless she felt funny standing there, so close to the door. So she took the book back to the alcove, feeling safer with stone walls behind her. She arranged the voluminous fabric of the cloak comfortably about her and set the book on her lap.

"We'll just have to read the whole thing and find out what's the big deal," she said. She would look again for the end of Siana's story after this.

The book confirmed the truthfulness of her dream, down to the last detail. In her dream she had watched this scene from above, but now she saw it from Siana's perspective, and was privy to all the dialogue she'd been unable to catch. This is how the book read.

• • • • ● • ● • • •

T hat morning, Paris was at the gym before me. Over Forgotten Town, a rare sunshine broke through banks of shifting clouds. There was birdsong in the bushes, but aside from the twittering all was quiet. The peacefulness made my step light as I trod the rain-washed concrete.

I couldn't fathom why Forgotten Town was there, why this gym and its adjoining empty school? I had walked the school's empty halls and thought of my own youth in a faraway world.

Mornings at the gym were a ritual grown familiar in this month of peace, away from the violence of war. I could hear Paris humming, as happy and unselfconscious as the birds outside. I paused to listen before breaking in, smiling. I opened the door quietly, but while she didn't stop dancing she stopped humming, so I knew she'd heard me.

Paris never broke off in the middle of a dance. She explained that such would insult the integrity of the dance. So I watched her and waited. Cloud-filtered sunlight glowed in the high windows. Paris' dancing here at the gym was more beautiful than her dancing at Kadesh. Perhaps because the firelit trappings of Kadesh's palace competed with the singular elegance of her dancing. Perhaps because the gym was a place from my world. Whatever the reason, watching her each morning in the pure white light was an anticipated joy. I always enjoyed her company, but in this part of the morning nothing was expected of me, and that made it sweeter.

She came over when she was done. I teased her that she pranced (not walked) for a few hours after dancing, and she did so now, stepping lightly as if music were playing. She pushed her sweaty hair from her forehead and the inverted V of her upper lip disappeared in a smile.

"What do you want to work on?" she asked, taking my hand.

"How about that twirly thing?" I suggested.

Paris wrinkled her brow. She had a specific vocabulary, mostly of her own design, to refer to dance moves, but found *my* vocabulary impossibly obtuse. I admit I had tangled motives in spending time with her at the gym.

In our first days at Forgotten Town she had sought for a place to keep her art intact and we had found the gym. I watched for a few days, and then she offered to teach me. She explained a majority of the women in Kadesh's harem danced, whether they were skilled or not, for dancing constituted entertainment and sociability. I agreed to learn, but whether from a desire to watch her without spying on her, to exorcise my own awkwardness, or to augment the skills I learned from Daevon I'm not sure. Probably all three.

Today I felt twice as awkward as the day before. I have a classic dancer's figure, slender and tall. But that didn't help me at all this day. Paris was several inches shorter, with much fuller breasts and broad hips, but she had invested her entire life in her art. She was more muscular than she looked, and ridiculously supple. I often teased her about Pretzel Hour, the stretches she did in the afternoons.

We danced—or she danced and I tried—for a half hour then my mood bottomed out. I collapsed, breaking her rule about finishing moves, and stared up at the ceiling. Paris made a legalistic attempt at wrapping up her dance fluidly, and lay next to me.

"What's up, Siah?"

"I suck at this."

"What does that mean?" she asked.

"Sorry, waking world term," I said, a common comment. "It means that I'm a graceless toad and you are the most beautiful thing in the universe." I was staring at the big silver gym lights we never turned on. I fancied I could hear her frown.

I had gleaned from Paris' past lectures, delivered with self-effacing kindness but full of strong opinions, that she didn't approve this kind of self-evaluation. Dance was self-expression, equally valid for the less skilled. I thought that was easy for her to say, and had told her so.

"I used to think I was better at something," I laughed, "but you are stronger than me too. I tire out way faster."

"I have seen you fight," Paris said quietly. Even her speaking voice was beautiful, damn it. "You are amazingly strong."

"Well, you're strong enough to pick me up and throw me around," I said, hoping banter would lift me from my mood. "I know that now."

"I don't know about the throwing part," Paris said slyly. We had turned our heads toward each other. She was about to burst out laughing.

"OK, girlfriend," I sat up. "You try to pick me up."

"Let me try"—she got to her feet with a jump—"then we can settle this silly argument."

She pushed up her open sleeves, that resembled something from the Renaissance, and set her feet in a lifting stance. She motioned a circle so I'd spin about, then grabbed me around the waist and lifted me a couple inches off the floor.

After she'd set me down, I walked a pace away and clapped.

"OK, my turn," I said and lunged at her. Unlike her systematic attempt, I grabbed her from the front and crushed her in my arms as I hefted her, pinning her arms to her sides. She squirmed and threw me off balance. I fell backwards, with Paris on top of me.

"See, you're stronger," I said, lying on my back laughing, arms spread-eagled.

"Sabotage!" she argued.

She lay half on top of me, purple skirt spread out, one hand on the floor at my side. She didn't move away, and as my laughter died out I found her staring at me.

"Why do you say I'm so beautiful?" she asked with sudden seriousness. I knew, against all odds, Paris was not the least bit vain.

"You want me to tell you?"

"Yes," she nodded.

"OK," I said tentatively. Flip comments about her beauty were a lot easier than the murky mix of feelings behind them. "You are sweet, and even-tempered, and kind. You dance, and walk for that matter, like you communicate with every muscle in your body. You have that wonderful flowing dark wavy hair, a heart-shaped face, ruby-colored lips, and, topping it off, a luscious figure with really big boobs."

"Boobs?" she asked, but I gleaned from her tone that she understood.

"Breasts. You are every man's dream girl. I would have hated you back in school. I ought to hate you now, but I don't. I love everything about you."

"Why, if you ought to hate me?"

"Because you are so kind, and so humble. I can't hate you. I wish I *were* you half the time. I wish I was more like you, in all sorts of ways."

"But you *are* beautiful, Siah," Paris said. To my surprise she lay her head on my chest.

"Name one thing that's beautiful about me," I said, with more than a gracious amount of challenge in my voice.

Paris raised her head from my chest.

"Your lips," she said, "they are incredible. I wish *I* had them." Paris had never given any indication she was anything but fine with the cleft in her upper lip, but I couldn't help thinking that now.

I couldn't manufacture a response, and my mental protests died unspoken. Paris surprised me further by shimmying up my body, dragging the softness of her breasts along my belly. She took both my hands in hers.

"I think I would like to feel what your lips are like," she said softly. "May I?"

I was too stunned by what was happening and the tingling excitement in my body to think straight. I nodded like a dazed fool. She touched my lips with one finger, tracing them slowly. All the grace of a thousand dances was compacted in that simple motion.

And then she kissed me, with slow and infinite sweetness.

She stood up and pulled me to my feet.

"Kiss me back, Siah," she said, wrapping herself about me. In the wake of her kiss, I'm sure I was staring stupidly. She was in my arms, glowing like a jewel. I lifted her chin and met her lips.

Her bottom lip was full and exquisite and I could feel the shape of her cleft as I kissed her. Our kisses had the careful first steps of a dance, but grew passionate. When our lips parted she sighed and laid her head against my neck.

"Paris Christianne," I said.

"Princess Siana," she murmured, "I do indeed think you are beautiful."

I didn't know what to say. I hadn't expected this at all, but I suppose the seeds were sown the first night I watched her at Kadesh, utterly entranced, when I was a man. My waking world life had been singularly devoid of romance. But within the Detheros, first Daevon, and now this.

Two magnificences I felt unworthy of.

In my silence, Paris detached herself from my embrace. She held my hand.

"There is something I want to know," she sounded concerned.

"What?"

"I know Siana isn't your real name, that you have a real name in your 'waking world'. Now that I have kissed you, I want to know what it is."

I hadn't expected this either, but it struck me as somehow appropriate.

"I haven't told anyone else in this world," I answered, "and you shouldn't either, because it might give power to certain of my enemies. But of course I will tell you." I answered honestly. "My real name is Elizabeth Grey."

"So Elizabeth is what people call you in your world?"

"Well, that's what teachers called me at school. But more often I go by my nickname."

"What is it?"

"It's funny I use it, because the nickname was my dad's idea, who I don't really like. He's the one who coined it."

"What is it, *Elizabeth*?" Paris insisted, scrunching her bottom lip like she was tasting my new name. "Stop beating around the bush."

"My nickname is Ellie."

· · · ● ●● ● ● · ·

E llie jumped to her feet, heart pounding. The black book fell unceremoniously to the floor, splaying out its pages.

My name is Ellie.

Siana's nickname was Ellie.

No, it cannot be.

I—I, Ellie—

I am Siana.

She fainted dead away and collapsed beside the book on the library floor.

WHAT ELLIE DREAMT

I n a sprawling monolith of interconnecting buildings that
dominates a wilderness of heath and low hills—more a
complex than a castle—a young woman lies on the cold floor of
a library as if dead. An old book lies next to her, spine broken,
pages crumpled against the floor. Her palm is stretched out as
if reaching for it. But her eyes are closed and fluttering beneath
the lids as she dreams a rapid succession of images in this deep
dream within a dream.

This is what Ellie dreamt as she swooned.

She is in a small circular house whose windows open on sunlit
gardens framed by woods. The windows are open and a light
breeze stirs the draperies and wafts into the room. She sits on
a bamboo chair and wears a thin cotton dress, a better kept
version of her shift in the castle. Her feet are sandaled. She feels
rested and peaceful, but something nags at her mind.

She stands up, to the sound of birds chirping in the gardens.
Within the house is a small square room, enclosed on three sides
and open on the side closest to her, a square inside the circular
gallery that is the rest of the house. Drawn by that nagging
something, she walks in. Its walls are rich cinnamon. Inside all
is still and silent, without birdsong or breeze. On a plinth lies a
sizable dagger and a motley collection of objects: a cheap gold
chain with heart-shaped ruby pendant; a green hardcover book
whose cover depicts a tentacled monster dangling a tiny man
over a field of boulders; a large plastic pen with a number of

buttons on its side; a skeleton key on a length of florescent nylon cord; a wooden duck on wheels attached to a long stick.

These are mine, but I don't recognize them is the exact thought that goes through Ellie's mind. Each object glistens with a dreamworld radiance. She is afraid to touch them but knows she must. She thinks of the sun-dappled gardens without, and thinks of taking a long leisurely walk in the woods. She has the sense she has done that before, but no concrete memory of it.

But then she remembers being lost in another sun-drenched wood, and misplacing her name for months.

"My name is Ellie, Elizabeth," she says out loud, and her own voice is deafeningly loud. "I must remember who I am."

She picks up the wooden duck.

She feels compressed and nauseous as her vision goes black. When the light returns, she is small and the world huge around her. She is pushing the toy duck, twice the size it was on the plinth, over a hill of dirt and gravel. The sun is hot on her back and she wears only a pair of cotton underpants.

"Ellie," a familiar voice barks from behind. She spins unsteadily on her feet and falls back on her bottom. She is three years old. Her dad sits in a rusty lounge chair in the shade of the gnarled pine by the driveway, drinking beer. Traffic whizzes by at fifty miles per hour on the country road. "Are you going to push that thing all over the yard?"

She giggles and stands, pushing the duck through ruts of partially dried mud. She likes the feel of the mud squishing between her naked toes.

The screen door bangs and her mother—an overweight blonde with greasy hair and a hard face—yells.

"Look at her, Evan, she is filthy. Can't you watch her for ten minutes without—"

"Dahlia, it's just good old country dirt," her dad says, pleasant but dismissive, waving Dahlia away with his hand. He smiles at Ellie. He is missing a tooth.

She is tall again, standing at the plinth.

This time she touches the pen.

She rests against her favorite tree, the ancient apple tree at the high end of the blackberry-crowded property. She is drawing on construction paper clipped to a clipboard. The pen's buttons light up different colors when she writes. She won the pen at a school fair, fishing for plastic fish in a plastic pond. A car pulls off the country road and narrowly misses the row of mailboxes: Timothy learning to drive. Her mom jumps out the passenger side, but Ellie can't hear her words, only her admonitory tone.

Her mother and brother walk up the broken concrete steps, passing the moss-covered satellite dish with its dressing of clean and not so clean laundry. She didn't think Timothy saw her, but at the front door he looks straight at her and motions her inside. She puts down the clipboard and runs. He is pouring her Kool Aid in the kitchen. Mom is still mad but Timothy is good at ignoring Dahlia. He asks her to accompany him to the stream.

"What for?" nine-year-old Ellie asks.

"We've got to fix the pump."

"Why can't Dad do it?"

"The better question," he whispers, "is why *won't* he? That is why we gotta. Personally I like to take a shower once in a while. Besides I'm smarter than Dad."

"Don't say that," Ellie hisses. Her regard of her father hasn't yet deteriorated; her father and the ideal of father in her head haven't yet parted ways. But that rift is beginning.

Timothy just grins.

At the creek, a water pump slurps out of a cracked bathtub sitting in a depression midstream. The electrical portion of the pump occupies a makeshift pump-house whose walls are a stump of Western red cedar, whose roof is a piece of corrugated aluminum metal, and whose doors are a pair of old kitchen cabinet doors hinged to the stump.

They say little, as Ellie hands him things from the toolbox on request and Timothy sets to work splicing and wiring with quiet confidence.

"You almost hit the mailbox," Ellie says for no particular reason.

"I always knew you were my biggest fan," Timothy says back with a smile. As she grows older, Ellie will envy his calm, the way nothing about their family life seems to bother him.

Because that same life will begin to wear her down, its barbs shredding the unconscious happiness of her earlier childhood.

Ellie is back at the plinth.

She is afraid to touch another object but she must. She picks up the chain with the fake ruby heart. It sparkles in her upturned palm.

There is a moment of vertigo and then she is sitting in the farmhouse kitchen. It is raining outside, endless Washington rain. Timothy is camping with a friend, and her mom is in the hospital. Sixth-grade Ellie came home from school to a strange woman. This woman now sits across from her as Ellie makes a half-hearted attempt at her homework, resisting the urge to doodle. The woman's young but not pretty face is framed by long black hair with outrageous curls and sports way too much makeup. The ruby pendant from the plinth hangs above her huge breasts, which threaten to escape a low cut, extremely clingy shirt. Frankly, Ellie is fascinated by her tits. The woman, Veronica, assumes Ellie's eyes are on the necklace and unclasps it with long brightly painted nails, her movement jiggling both breasts and curls.

"Do you like it? You can keep it."

Why was this woman sent to care for her? Veronica says she is Evan's friend. In a few more years she will figure out what this means: the kind of "friendship" her imagination can't yet ascribe to her father. It is about that time that Ellie stops wearing the necklace and hurls it across the gorge into the woods.

Ellie is back at the plinth. A growing unease has replaced her sense of peace at the beginning of the dream, the feeling one gets when reading a story and knows the ending will be tragic. But she can't turn aside. She picks up the book, the one with the squid-headed monster.

She is suddenly in her bedroom, crying and mad that she is crying. Timothy is saying goodbye. She is thirteen and trying to be cool. But he is going to college and she is despairing.

"Elizabeth," he says in a quieter voice than usual, "I'll be back all the time, it's only in the city. I could have gone to WSU, but I stayed for you."

"You stayed because WSU didn't give you any money," she argues through her tears.

"Well, I'm glad I didn't have to choose between my sister and money," he says. "Here, you can have my anthology." He hands her the Cthulhu-adorned volume. "Now you can read it and think of me, and Mom can't give you a hard time for stealing it from my room, since it's yours."

"But it's your favorite, don't you—" Ellie tries to hand it back.

"I've about got it memorized. Anyway, all the more reason for me to come back and visit a lot."

Ellie stares at the volume in her hand. Lovecraft. The author that started it all, for Timothy and then for her. Lovecraft hadn't gotten the specifics right, but he knew the dreamworlds were there.

As time passes, she will steal other things from Timothy's room, more rare and more esoteric. This behavior leads her to his journal, and from there to the edge of the Detheros.

Back at the plinth a few objects remain. She examines the dagger, a wicked military knife with none of the artistic touches of prior civilizations. She is starting to remember her life now, without first reaching for an object. She stole the knife from the Army Navy Surplus store, needing to have it, but knowing she has no money and there is no reason for a fifteen-year-old girl to purchase such a thing. She remembers getting caught for a different theft and her mother slapping her across the face.

Ellie doesn't touch the dagger. Instead she picks up the skeleton key.

The school bus travels south on a country road. It is early spring but uncommonly warm and she is seventeen now. Timothy has been gone for over a year, reckoned dead by everyone in the waking world, but against all reason she knows it's not true. Her long and still awkward legs poke out from her short black skirt. Her shirt is tight, her bellybutton showing, after the fashion of the other girls at school. The skeleton key to her front door hangs around her neck. She has made a nominal effort to fit in, acquiring through petty theft and bartering some of the things she'd never have money to buy. But she feels wrong in her skin. Her eyes are too big and her breasts are too small and she's still riding the bus in eleventh grade.

Her first boyfriend sits next to her touching her knee. He must have been attracted by her recent attempts at normalcy. He's still fifteen, too young to drive and he lives up the country lane from her farmhouse. But she can tell he's starting to lose interest because she can't bring herself to fuck him.

The school bus lets them off. She clutches the house key in one hand and hefts her backpack over one shoulder. Her eyes rove past the old trailer in the driveway, where Evan's lowlife friend John lived until Ellie falsely accused him of propositioning her. Something unexpected is parked behind it. She runs past the trailer, her boyfriend in tow, heart pumping. It is a police car, lights off, under the old pine. Beyond is an ambulance she didn't see before.

For years she has known this day was coming, deep in her bones, but she has refused to think about it, to let the possibility enter her mind. But the day has come, all the same. Now all those repressed thoughts flood her mind. A sick feeling pervades her being. She rushes up the walk to the door. A group of uniformed men and women block her way.

"Whoa, miss." An older policeman, very tall, holds his hand against her chest. "Slow down. Who are you?"

Ellie tries to talk but only strangled syllables come out. She holds out her house key on its nylon thong.

"Her name's Elizabeth Grey and this is her house," her boyfriend chimes from behind her.

"Is Dahlia Grey your mother?" a uniformed woman asks.

"Yes," Ellie croaks, "what's going on?"

But she knows already.

"I don't know how to tell you this, Elizabeth—" the tall policeman begins but she pushes past. She wants to run inside and be a thousand miles away at the same time. Downstairs in the unfinished basement where her mother has been sleeping is another group of people. She can see past them to the leg poking from under the sheets and the crimson pool of blood on the hard concrete floor.

Ellie is back at the plinth. The last memory has shattered her. She collapses at the base of the plinth and cries for a long time. When she dries her eyes an object has appeared on the floor. It is a hypodermic needle with a broken tip, lying in a slanting patch of sunlight. Her brain flashes black, a half remembered struggle in the dark. She has the strange sense that this fractured memory is her last.

She doesn't want to pick the needle up but she must remember more.

She is twenty two and standing in her tiny apartment high above Puget Sound. The view is gray sky above gray water. She is wearing black cargo pants and a gray T, and her long blonde hair is pulled back with a single red ribbon. She wore the same to work, because it is Saturday and no one else was in. She has been working as a graphic artist for a couple years; someone saw her drawings and gave her a break. But her firm does uninspiring ad work and she doesn't much care. Ellie's focus is lost within the Detheros now, firmly ensconced in her alternate reality. Her roommate left a year ago because she found Ellie "too freaky." Now it's just her place, but she doesn't care about the apartment either and it shows in the hodgepodge of books, art journals, computer hardware and antique weapons.

She leaves the flat white light of the main room and goes to the bathroom mirror. She stares at her gaunt face. She contemplates changing into something else for the occasion but thinks *screw it*. She paints her full lips dark red and tries to do something with her eyes. She clips up her hair and curls some of the loose bits.

She frowns at the curling iron. She never would have bought one but her roommate left it behind.

It will take her the rest of the afternoon on multiple buses to get to the farmhouse in the foothills. She contemplates not going for the hundredth time in three days. Ellie doesn't care for the world anymore, and she tells herself she doesn't care a whit for her father either. But she has a lingering sense of family obligation. She wants to do the right thing. She can't bring herself to totally abandon her past.

She arrives at six PM, walking the last mile from the bus stop. It is dark and cold but she didn't bring a coat, telling herself she is the Princess of Time and has braved far worse than a Washington winter. She hasn't been back to the house for several years. The yard is the same or worse, unkempt, with broken down cars, scattered tools and trash. What must be Veronica's car is parked by the walk, a BMW. Even though she has never liked Veronica, she wonders how her dad scored such a flashy woman. Perhaps a bitch like Veronica required someone as mellow as Evan to even her out.

The house is lit up and cleaner than usual. Her dad meets her at the entryway and appears genuinely happy to see her. He gives her a hug, which she returns stiffly. He looks good, shaved. He is marrying Veronica at last, which is the occasion for dinner.

An attempt to patch things up with your daughter, Ellie thinks sourly. *Well, I came all this way, and I've got to stay here until the next bus tomorrow so I might as well make the best of it.*

She drops her backpack on the floor. She has never had a purse.

Veronica appears at the kitchen doorway, smiling. Her hair is blonde now which is dreadful. But otherwise she appears the same, no older, tons of makeup. Ellie tries not to think of her as the woman over which her mother killed herself and manages to smile back.

Hating her won't bring back my mom.

A third voice, low and grating, startles her: "Is that little Ellie, come home to the roost?"

Fury seizes her and she gracelessly hauls her dad to the porch.

"I can't believe you invite me to dinner, *Evan*," she says through gritted teeth, "and have that beast in the house." She has never trusted John since the day Timothy disappeared. She didn't like the way he talked in the wake of that day, the way he looked at her. It wasn't sexual, like she'd claimed to her parents, but predatory all the same, violent. "I told you—"

"I'm sorry," Evan says, cringing before her adult wrath in a way wholly unfamiliar to her. "He needed a place to go and I've been at Veronica's most of the time. You're all grown up now, he can't hurt you, and I thought—"

"I *told* you to send him away for this weekend," Veronica harps from behind her father.

Ellie glares silently. She ponders turning around, walking seven miles back to town and getting a motel room. Her last shred of moral obligation wins out, barely. She stuffs her fury and goes inside.

In the last part of her vision, she is in her bedroom, which has changed little since she left home. She got through dinner with silence and cold answers and the shreds of adult social skills she has managed to acquire, which aren't much. She goes to bed exhausted. But in the middle of the night someone is in the room with her, pressing something cold and sharp against her arm. When it penetrates her skin she jumps full awake and tries to clock the dark form in the head. The needle hangs from her vein as she struggles with a sweaty, stinking hulk that must be John. She feels a strange tingling in her head and flails at the needle, breaking it off in her skin near her elbow. John pins her thrashing limbs to her sides and she is suddenly weak.

Then Ellie remembers and dreams no more.

A LAST TIME AT THE MIRROR

The cawing of crows awoke Ellie from her trance. She stirred, groaning, every limb stiff from sleeping on concrete. She had slept through the night and a new day had dawned; she could tell from the flat winter sky above.

She sat up with a start. *Sky!* The library walls were still around her, the rakshasa's book still lay on the floor. But part of the ceiling had crumbled away and was letting in the colorless light of a late winter morning. She watched as a flock of crows passed across the opening. She stood and gathered the long furred cloak about her to ward off the extreme cold. She placed the fallen book in the nook. Some instinct drew her up the spiral stair. The evidence of the rakshasa's hunt still lay on the floor near the railing, scattered books.

The bas reliefs of Siana in torment were gone. The plaster walls were bare.

Her mind cleared. She remembered her dreams, and with them a rush of childhood memories.

I am Ellie.

Of course she had known her name, for weeks and weeks. But she hadn't known who Ellie *was*. Now she did, remembering all the details of her life: childhood at the old farmhouse, the death of her mother, her grim friendless life in Seattle.

And then she recalled the last line of the book.

"My nickname is Ellie."

No.

Siana was still something alien to her, outside of the boundaries of her memory. *I don't remember the details of being Siana, so it cannot be. How can I be her, if I have no memories of her life beyond what I have read?*

Ellie stormed down the staircase, past the sitting place and the twin statues. The chamber beyond the library was infused with white light, the candles of the candelabras extinguished. This light filled every crevice and corner, not a single shadow to be found. Something was different about the room, the whole castle. Empty, completely empty of menace for the first time.

She ran to the amphitheater. The door to the Mirror Room still hung in impossible suspension from a ceiling that was no longer there. She propelled herself down the wide step-like tiers, her frantic motion a plea against the thoughts threatening to coalesce in her head.

She threw open the door and plunged into the Mirror Room. The door slammed open in the mirror.

Siana entered the room with her, matching her every move.

Siana was clothed in a fur-trimmed cloak. Her expression was open and confused, unlike any she had seen on the face of her patron goddess.

Ellie approached the mirror and so did Siana. Ellie reached out her right hand and Siana matched it with her left, fingertips meeting at cold glass. Ellie's breath fogged the mirror. She stepped back. Siana stepped back too.

Slowly Ellie parted the grey folds of cloth, drawing the cloak from her shoulders. Mirror-Siana did the same.

Beneath was a thin body in a tattered linen dress, a pathetic garment riddled with tiny holes. Not the body of a warrior or a princess, but the body of a young woman lost and starving, weakened by hunger and exhaustion.

She stared at the face in the mirror. The big crystal blue eyes, the dark blonde hair, the full lips. A dusting of freckles across the bridge of the nose. This was Siana's face, there could be no doubt, the face that haunted her wandering days.

My face.

No!

She began to hyperventilate. The chest of her twin heaved in the mirror. She closed her eyes and steeled herself to calm.

When she opened her eyes, Ellie pulled the hem of her dress and up and over her head. She had never undressed in the castle.

Her eyes took in the length of the naked body before her. Matted hair that barely struck the shoulders. Collarbone too pronounced beneath pale flesh. Slight bosom. Ellie bent and gripped her right ankle, and looked at the reflection. A scar along her calf.

The dagger of an Orsian sailor.

Ellie drew closer, taking care to breathe away from the glass. She examined her too-prominent ribs, placing a hand beneath her left breast and pushing it up and away. A grid work of white scars lay beneath.

The scars of Dreamslayer, scars from the Glass Sword cutting deep.

The body in the mirror was Siana's and she was Siana, after all.

This final admission stilled her panic.

The face in the mirror frowned.

She recalled standing at the mirror in her little studio above the Sound, and frowning at that same face, painting her lips. It didn't matter that Siana's face stared back at her. This was *her* face, the same face that frowned at her from her mirror at home.

In the waking world.

Ellie examined her body again. Thin. Battle scarred. She noticed many more scars now, though no others were as dramatic as those from her death in Ampizand.

Another memory burst to mind. Toweling herself off in front of a different mirror, while an orange cat mewled at her feet. *What was that cat's name? Oh yes, Olivia...*

She had appraised this same body in that mirror. She had watched the crack in the mirror descend as she grew (when she was little the crack had been at her throat) until it settled at her navel, where it stayed. All that time there had been no money to replace the mirror. That day Olivia meowed while Ellie took the measure of her teenage body, wondering if the dress for the dance would look good, but unhappy with what she saw.

Having memories was strange. She had sought after Siana and had given little thought to her own identity.

She had found herself instead.

She shivered violently. Her nipples were stiff with cold. She put on her dress. It looked utterly pathetic, as did her hair.

"Why did you never ask Graham for a comb?" she said out loud.

She wrapped herself in Graham's fur-lined cloak and sat in the Mirror Room's only chair. She was still there a half hour later, flooded with memories familiar and unfamiliar at the same time.

I should be happy to know who I am.

But she wasn't. Much of her life had not been happy, and now her mind was polluted with so much information.

"They do say ignorance is bliss," she said out loud, looking up from her reverie to see a wry smile on her face. It took a moment to register again the face in the mirror as her own. For so long in her amnesia that face had been Siana's. The face in all the icons.

Siana, Princess of Time.

She remembered her sketchbook where she invented the name and drew pictures of a fighting maiden, ninja princess, under the apple tree to while away summer hours. They'd been pictures, innocent daydreams for so long.

But all that changed, when Timothy's bright light, the light sustaining her universe, was extinguished from the world.

It had grown serious then, became a mania. *A kind of mental illness*, Ellie thought, knowing she'd never have framed it that way before. This was her first inkling she was not the Ellie she'd been before, and that the empty reservoir of her mind—fast refilling with the memories of a life—had been changed by its emptying. How many people have the chance to step outside of themselves? How many people have the opportunity to *truly* argue with themselves, to tell themselves to fuck off. Siana had told her that.

I told *myself* that, she thought with bitter mirth.

Siana. The name cut through her memories like the keen edge of the Glass Sword. Sitting in the Mirror Room, Ellie sifted her memories with that keen edge, remembering the first time she arrayed herself like the warrior princess of her drawings, behind the locked door of her bedroom. She had clumsily braided her hair and surrounded her eyes with grey eye shadow and put on her worn combat boots. A tight black shirt to make her breasts look bigger. She had held her stolen knife flat against the fabric in between them.

That night sixteen-year-old Ellie had crossed the graveyard of Nathnang. A tall being in a dark cloak waited at the far side, holding a lantern with a floating kaleidoscopic light.

"How is it that a young dreamer comes this way?" he had asked in a voice as ancient as the surrounding graves.

"I am Siana, Princess of Time," she had answered. The being nodded its hoary head. "I am seeking my brother."

"What is your brother's name?" the guardian of Nathnang asked.

"He calls himself Llywd Emyr," answered Siana, Princess of Time. Her beauty and cold puissance were a glowing white gem in the dim wasteland.

"Then I have something for you," the being had answered and withdrew a packet from its voluminous garment. Inside was a weathered map tooled on old leather, and a key. These things would lead her to the first of the Eterokoni, the Kalimba.

Ellie retraced her memories of dreaming, following the path of Siana's crystal radiance through the Fringe worlds of sleep. She remembered her first glimpse of the Detheros from high mountains fifty miles off, a grey ash-choked blight on the landscape under sullen turquoise and black clouds.

She had adjusted her vambraces and saluted it with her middle finger.

And then the Gardens. Her descent from those cold mountains brought her against all reason to a closeted vale of surpassing loveliness, warm and drowsy with sheltered summer. She had tarried there, too long, always promising herself just another minute more, until days passed and she forgot all else. One by one the military trappings of her daydream persona were lost, and soon she shed her clothing as well, becoming an amnesic nymph in a sun-dappled bower. She remembered her lover, but not his face. His warm skin had been haloed in light and he stroked her flesh and crowned it with tender kisses.

But he was a scion of the Aedolae. While her folly distracted her, the vale was raised by Ghislain's power to become a circular prison above the Detheros, surrounded by acres of open air. She had wasted nearly a year of dreams, Siana neutralized. She remembered her frustration in the waking world, riding the school bus each morning, knowing something had gone terribly awry.

Until Mercair saved her.

He strode into her bower and asked her for the pleasure of her company as if he had walked there every afternoon for years. He had woken her to sense, reminded her of the Kalimba which alone had stayed with her, hanging about her neck. He had shown her where to recover the Torc, in the grave of a Starman lich who had fallen prey to the charms of the Gardens uncounted years before. And the Torc had given her the power to cross the Detheros unseen, to tunnel under its far wall and to emerge at the edge of the Edoi Sea.

There her memories of her Siana self stopped. There was nothing more, nothing that matched the vividness of her passage through the Graveyard of Nathnang or the nightmarish tunnels under the Detheros. Only her memories of the books she had read. Her feverish reading had made her feel she knew the woman behind the militant persona. But now, knowing she had created Siana—that she *was* Siana—she felt the very opposite. Her knowledge of Siana's history was secondhand, divorced from the firsthand emotion of her other memories of waking world life.

She had made herself a stranger, let some other alien being borrow the body and face that confronted her in the mirror, leaving it battered and scattered.

What have I done?

Why did I try to live a dream, a foolishness that normal people grow out of?

What have I done, in making an enemy of ancient powers beyond the ken of humankind?

Ellie felt none of Siana's bravado now. She supposed she should be wishing for the Eterokoni, feeling their lack, as mirror-Siana had expressed in their conversations before. But there was no emotional connection, no longing for the lost trappings of her childhood alter ego. Only fear.

In the Gardens, Ghislain made me forget myself. I wandered about there for a year, amnesic. Is that what happened here? Is this another cat-and-mouse game for his enjoyment? Watching me pad about this prison, clueless, shivering and afraid?

If so, things were dangerous, for now she knew who she was. Would the Aedolae come for her now, now the trap was neutralized? She was suddenly afraid of what lay outside the Mirror Room. She imagined faceless enemies creeping down the tiers of the amphitheater. She wrapped the cloak closer about her.

She didn't feel like Siana at all. Nonetheless she would have to reap the fruits of Siana's history. Everything had changed, and yet nothing had. She still didn't know what happened after Paris' fall at Mihali. She needed to know where Vaelonn-Marr was. She knew so little, despite her reading and remembering. And what of the last waking world memories—John binding her arms, the needle hanging from her veins? She was sure those were part of the mystery.

Standing up she was suddenly weak. She longed to feel strong like Siana, to be hale and well. She was hungry and thought of Graham's bread and cheese and apples. Her yearning for

Graham was abrupt and palpable in its intensity. When would he return?

She crossed to the doorway. She hadn't closed the door. The amphitheater beyond was washed in sunshine, for the clouds had separated into white continents in an azure sky. There were no enemies in sight, only empty concrete tiers. *But if there were, what would I do?*

Well, I wouldn't have surrendered, or groveled and pleaded for my life. I won't ever do that, whatever my name is.

If that name must be Siana again, so be it, I will be Siana. For it isn't Ellie who they trapped here but Siana. The Princess of Time. Nemesis of the Lords of the Night. Mistress of the Eterokoni. Saying "I am Ellie and Siana was a girl's fancy, pardon me my hubris" won't help me any when they come for me. For better or worse, I made Siana something real. Something dangerous.

And if I'm going to be Siana, I must do three things:

1) Get my butt out of here before it's too late.

2) Find Paris.

3) Find my brother

If they're both not dead.

ACCUSATION

A nd how do I do *that*? Ellie thought as she climbed the amphitheater stairs and returned to the antechamber below the library.

She knew she should delve back into the books—for reading about her life as Siana held more promise than squinching up her face trying to remember. But sitting down to *read* was at odds with her resolve to *do* something. So she found herself walking instead, and her mind fixed upon the Time Room as her destination. She would go get the Sundial, the one Eterokon whose location she knew. She had put it back in the floor, after the disastrous talk with her mirror self. She remembered how afraid she had been of Siana's wrath. *I was afraid of my own alter ego. Well, no more. She is going to obey me this time.*

She had walked half way there, forcing her body to keep a fast pace (*the first step in getting my muscle tone back*) when she realized all the iconography was gone. No Siana images anywhere. Gone like the bas reliefs in the library. She wondered if the statue in the Time Room would be gone.

She reached Time Room quickly for the walk seemed shorter. Throughout the castle there had been further evolution in its shattering, familiar walls fragmented or missing, more rifts in the ceiling. The Time Room was no different, its near wall about gone and open to adjacent rooms. The church pews were scattered and broken. And the statue of Siana was indeed gone, the point of the oversize Sundial at its feet broken off. But in place of Siana there an all too familiar figure. Ellie froze in her tracks. But the figure had already seen her; he faced her and stared in her direction. She had had no warning of his presence, no sense of impinging danger.

"Come, come. I mean you no harm," he purred, his sonorous voice both soothing and menacing. "If I did, I would have taken more advantage of you in Ampizand."

She thought of fleeing. The castle was a big place. But she rejected that notion as soundly as she had rejected the passivity of reading. Fleeing the rakshasa would not be *doing* something toward her goals. He was an impediment, and she needed to *do* something about him.

If these are my instincts, no wonder I got into so much trouble.

"What do you want from me now?" Ellie asked.

She tried to keep her voice even. She strode into the room. She noticed that the glass of the skylight was shattered and a halo of glassy debris lay behind the rakshasa. He was perched on the shattered stump of the Siana sculpture, languidly smoking from one of his pipes. She avoided his gaze. The green black-flecked depth of his eyes made her feel lost.

"A better question might be 'What do *you* want from *me*?'" he replied.

His eyes never left her face but he dug in the pocket of his greatcoat and held forth the Sundial in one gloved hand. Such a small thing glinting in the light. The boxlike piece of marble lay on its side on the floor, removed. How had the rakshasa known?

"That is mine, it belongs to dreamers, not the likes of you. Give it to me and get out of my castle," she said.

"Aren't we impertinent?" the rakshasa said, sounding amused.

"Did the Aedolae send you after me? Into Ampizand?" Ellie hissed.

"No. I merely wait for miserable riffraff like you to chance along. I am an opportunist and a scavenger by trade"—the rakshasa nodded—"and you proved most enterprising sport. But then you made me angry, with your little tricks. Thus I am still here, and not at all happy that you are at your tricks again. I suggest that you treat me with more regard, given I possess your precious Eterokon."

"Is remembering my name a trick?" Ellie said. She had always hated being patronized.

"To what great use will you put this momentous discovery? Elizabeth has been a byword for depression and frustration so far. Or perhaps you were speaking of Siana? She has fared little better, being nothing but a disorganized little terrorist whose actions have made her a nuisance to her enemies and poisonous to her friends."

Ellie's mouth went agape. The rakshasa purred louder, replacing the Sundial in his pocket. If a tiger could look smug, he looked it.

"Nothing to say? Then perhaps I shall leave, and take the Eterokon with me as a souvenir of our pleasant association." He stood up.

Her hands itched for a weapon, for the feel of the Glass Sword.

"You see," the rakshasa said, pacing about the dais on which the statue had stood, "you are more terrorist than you think, Elizabeth. Confronted with an enemy, with something that *angers* you, frustrates your hot little will, you'll become Siana all over again. You may not remember her, your conscious mind may not identify with her, but you—*you*, Ellie—made her out of the stuff of your being. Think that you are any different now? Hah!"

The rakshasa turned with a sashay of his greatcoat and began to walk away.

"You are a liar," Ellie said. "You are no more done with me now than I am done with you."

The rakshasa stiffened. He turned, enough to fix her with one baleful eye.

"And on what authority do you call me liar?" the rakshasa argued.

She knew from her brother's books that rakshasas delighted in tormenting their victims with words, using rumor, insinuation and accusation. Perhaps the rakshasa couldn't bear being the accused.

"Number one, you have no intention of striding off with my Sundial and giving up the sport of bothering me," Ellie answered. "Number two, you have always meant me harm and you know it. When I was Siana on that island, you wanted to drive me to ruin and despair."

"*When you were Siana*," the rakshasa countered with emphasis, striding closer. "As if you aren't still the Princess of Time. If you are no longer Siana, let me take your Eterokon." He watched Ellie's face in the ensuing silence. "Be Siana then. Be Ellie. I don't care. Either way, you are every bit the deceiver that I am."

"Don't compare me to you, you beast—"

"And why not?" the rakshasa replied, purring once again, as if back in his element. "What to think of a dreamer who has to fabricate a name for herself, and then, as if that were not enough, hides as an Orsian girl, or disguises herself as a *man*?"

"I couldn't very well stride down the Aedol Via saying 'Hi, I'm Elizabeth Grey, first dreamer to be here in a while, can you give my brother back?'"

"And I couldn't very well say 'Hello, Elizabeth Grey, would you care to lie down peacefully while I sink my fangs into your tender flesh?'" The rakshasa gave a feline snort. Something like a smile spread across his striped muzzle. "We all deceive, we deceive each other, we deceive our enemies. We say our lies are justified by our noble purposes. We lie to ourselves until we think our hungers are not passions but noble aims. So what?"

"My aims were noble," Ellie said. "I came here to rescue my brother, that alone and nothing more."

"Then I agree with your sweet Paris," the rakshasa said, "that you have a funny way of going about it."

"She didn't say that," Ellie argued.

"How do you know? You hardly remember her."

The rakshasa's words cut like daggers. They were only too true. She had felt sick in her gut when mirror-Siana denounced

Paris. She had felt Paris' anguish when she had seen the ghostly image of Paris at her vanity. But she couldn't *remember*. She had only feelings, and the words she had read. Ellie couldn't remember Paris' face. Couldn't remember the kisses they had shared.

"Nothing you say can change what I do know," Ellie said, trying to keep her bearings. "I remember why it began. I remember why I crossed the Detheros and came Within. I may have done things as Siana that didn't fit the intent of finding my brother. I may have done things as Siana that I would regret, if I could even remember what they were. I know precious little about Siana beyond what I have read here in the library."

"Does that absolve you of those deeds?" the rakshasa questioned. "Please. You may not remember them now, but you were fully yourself and fully cognizant when you did them. And therefore I judge you would happily do them again. Your noble aim to rescue your brother, when frustrated, became a passion like all other hungers. A passion—a hunger—for vengeance. Do you think for one minute that I, or anyone else, would believe you had some lofty goal to liberate the dreamworlds from the Aedolae? You just wanted to pay them back."

"Are the Aedolae so virtuous that you must defend them?"

"You beg my point. I don't care if they are virtuous, any more than I care about your virtue. I hate hypocrisy. Call your war what it is: a struggle for power, not principle."

"What it *was*," Ellie countered, but the argument was weak in her mouth.

"Are you so sure? What if they are outside this castle waiting to get at you?"

"Are you telling me something I don't know?"

"No," the rakshasa replied but Ellie didn't trust his expression.

"All I know," Ellie said, "is from here on I am going to worry about those that I love, as I should have been doing all along, and to hell with the Aedolae and what they are doing."

"If that were so easy to do, Siana," the rakshasa said, insisting on her dreamworld name, "you would have done it the first time. To worry about your loved ones, you are going to have to fight the Aedolae again and you know it. It wouldn't be so easy to be on the defensive, to be on the run. You'll be sucked back into the same campaign that consumed you before, and it will consume you again. Or did you enjoy being stuck here nine months? Perhaps you would like to lose your mind and your liberty yet another time, perhaps for good?"

Nine months!

What could have happened outside during that time?

"Has it really been nine months?" Ellie asked.

"You can't know for sure, because you don't trust me," the rakshasa said, stroking a whisker.

"Did Ghislain put me here?"

"I'm not about to answer that," the rakshasa said, "but I will do you the favor of being completely straightforward with you about something else. Completely honest and not in the least hypocritical."

He came even closer.

"What?" Ellie said, resisting the urge to back away. The rakshasa's posture had changed. He slowly and meticulously removed one glove. Beneath his hand was furred and taloned.

"I grow tired, even for a rakshasa, of all this talk." His whiskers quivered. "I have hungered for a taste of you and I am ready to have it."

Ellie shrieked in a most un-Siana-like way as the tiger-man lunged.

She stumbled against the stump of the statue and ducked behind it as he sprang over her, the open folds of his greatcoat undermining his accuracy. She scurried, trying to keep the dais between them. He had alit on all fours but drew himself up to man height again. As he did so, his furred flesh sloughed off and faded, leaving a grinning skeleton with a tiger-shaped skull. At the end of its finger bones talons still gleamed, dripping crimson and green ichor.

Her eyes cast wildly about. A wooden cudgel of sorts lay amid the dust and debris. Had the village boys left this behind? She seized it.

"Ah, brave Siana." The voice of the rakshasa, unchanged, came from the skeleton's vacuous grin. "You're an unkempt cave girl with a weap—"

Ellie hurled the cudgel at the skeleton's head. Her aim had decayed during the time of her imprisonment for it struck the skeleton's ribcage. There was a dark fog in the empty space behind the ribs, then a huge bird stood where the skeleton had been. It stood on powerfully muscled legs, with an ostrich's body and a yellow beak curved and sharp as a scythe. Greasy, ill-plumaged feathers stuck out like uncombed hair and beady eyes stared her down. Ellie was now weaponless. The bird, a thing of Cenozoic nightmare, advanced, pecking around the edge of the shattered sculpture.

"Begone!" a man's voice shouted.

The bird withdrew its head with a snap and bristled its dirty feathers. Ellie whipped around. Graham stood in the doorway of the armory beyond the basin. He brandished a rusted sword from one of the suits of armor and frankly looked foolish.

She was at once both grateful and worried for his safety.

The rakshasa-bird charged down the remains of the aisle between the pews, shrieking and flapping its vestigial wings. As it ran it morphed into a black dog and leapt.

It stopped mid-flight, as if striking a force field. Its black form crumpled and fell, yelping. Parson Graham held something aloft in his other hand, a kind of staff. Ellie ran toward him, stopping when she saw the rakshasa stand up beside the basin, a tiger-headed humanoid once again.

"Begone," Graham repeated. "She is innocent of the crimes you lay at her feet. You only mean to torment her and there is no truth in you. Leave off your cruelty and go."

The rakshasa circled about Graham, talons extended and upraised, but he was held at bay by some power. Embedded in the wood of Graham's staff were interlocking circles of vivid color. She had seen them before, on the floor of the Copper Landing. The sequence was the same: green, a brilliant orange, sapphire, emerald, sun-yellow, amethyst.

The colors of Siana's vision over the Edoi Sea.

The rakshasa snarled in defeat and backed away. His upright form melted into the black shadow of his dog form and sprang away. He bounded out of view through the adjacent rooms of the castle. She could hear the patter of his feet on stone and then silence.

The silence was broken by her sobs as she fell into Graham's arms.

Graham leaned the staff against an overturned pew and held her.

"I had the sense I was needed here," Graham said softly, and she could feel his breath in her hair atop her head. "I am glad I came back earlier than I had planned."

"But how did you drive it away? What power—" She detached herself from his arms.

"Perhaps it was the staff," Graham replied. "I've had it a long time, but the other day I saw the same colored circles in a fragment of floor here. I brought it with me today to ask you about it. But more than the staff, I think it was my love for you, Ellie. Rakshasas have a particular aversion to love and absolution."

"But I am *not* innocent. I know who I am now, I'm Siana!" Ellie spat in a rush.

"All the same, you're innocent of that thing's accusations," Graham said with quiet assurance.

"You heard what he said?"

"The last part of the conversation," Graham answered, "yes."

Ellie studied his face.

"You don't sound the least bit surprised," she said, narrowing her eyes in suspicion. His dark eyes sparkled.

"You knew!" she accused. "You knew all along I was her!" She made a mock show of boxing him in the chest.

"Not all along," Graham replied. "I would not deceive you so. I've known since yesterday. The statue was visible to me for the first time"—he swept his hand toward the stump—"and it was you."

"Why didn't you tell me?" she accused, but she wasn't really mad. He had saved her, and she trusted him implicitly. She figured he had his didactic reasons.

"I would have told you today," Graham explained, "or whenever I next saw you."

"But how can you say I'm innocent? You've heard her stories."

"The rakshasa would hold each of your actions against you, but examine your heart. Your heart has never grown cold. If you are Siana, then the same Siana who attacked the Aedolae is the girl who was imprisoned here. And I've watched that girl cry at her own story. This same girl was morally indignant at the lies and half-truths her mirror-self told her. That girl cried at Daevon's death and championed Paris' cause without even knowing the full truth of things. That girl faced the rakshasa's charges and rejected the path of vengeance and anger for the first time. So I say you are innocent of the failings of your past. And free to do what's right, with a freedom very few get the opportunity to possess."

Ellie couldn't say anything to that. She dearly hoped Graham, and not the rakshasa, was right.

The rakshasa—he still had her Sundial!

"Graham, he's taken it!" she said with alarm.

Graham smiled. "No he hasn't. See behind you." It sat there on the floor next to the hole in the marble, flashing in the sun. "It seems hard to rob a dreamer of the Eterokoni."

Just like the Glass Sword returned to Siana after she lost it at Mihali.

"Then the rest of them must be here somewhere," Ellie reasoned.

"Even so," Graham assured.

"Then I must find them!" Ellie asserted, without the lust she'd heard in her mirror twin's voice. Instead she had only a tired expediency.

"Yes, you should," Graham agreed, "but there is something else I must tell you first. Another reason I had to come today."

"What?" Ellie sat in one of the remaining pews.

"Some of our hunters range far in the winter to find game, even as far as the Va'e River, up by the mountains. One returned yesterday and told of an army, massed on the far side of the river and building a bridge over it. Very strange tidings, for no army has been seen here in living memory. We have nothing of value, nothing to steal, nothing to protect, no role in the machinations of the Aedolae."

"This army is of the Aedolae?" Ellie asked, her heart beating faster.

"The huntsman didn't know. To us the Aedolae are little more than rumor. I've learned more about them from talking to you than I've heard the whole rest of my life. Our land has been long removed from their doings; none of our folk have ever left Vaelonn-Marr. It is only our crones, spirit-women, who have seen the Aedolae's worlds, in visions and dreams. And no emissary of the Aedolae has ever come here. But I fear something has changed that, and that something must be you."

There was no accusation in Graham's eyes, only a penetrating focus, as if he were reading her heart.

"I don't want to put your people in danger," Ellie said. "I'm sure they've come for me. Because now I know who I am."

Graham frowned as he sat down. She knew the expression: dissatisfaction that his pupil was being illogical.

"I know," she acknowledged. "I didn't know who I was until last night and of course they were already here."

"You are right. They've been here some time, and they are taking the time to build a bridge, which means they feel no urgency. My theory is the rakshasa went to the Aedolae when his game with you began to unravel."

"When I started gathering too many clues."

"Exactly."

"But that would mean—"

"—the rakshasa is headed back to them right now," Graham concluded, "and after hearing his newest account they will pick up their pace. Their bridge was already nearing completion."

"How far away is the Va'e?"

"A day's hard ride at least. It would take an army several days. They have siege engines with them—"

"Siege engines!" Ellie wanted to both cry and laugh. She looked down at her thin young body. "But it's just me!"

"They must think you are a worthy opponent. From what we've read, it would be a logical precaution." Graham smiled, but she noticed a new character in his voice. Perhaps even Graham, so steady and calm, had become nervous around her. His fragile young pupil was a notorious renegade and killer.

"However they lost you last time," Graham added, "they are not going to let it happen again."

"What do I do?" She wanted to cry.

Graham put down the staff and rummaged in his pockets, pulling out a slender coil of well-woven rope, a loaf of bread, several apples, and a wheel of cheese. "There's also a ladder back there in the armory."

"You carried a ladder out here for me." She laughed.

"I did, and it was no easy task."

"Thank you."

"I don't think my escape tools are going to be all that useful, not until you've got your Eterokoni. We must find them. We have several days so you do have time to eat." He must have seen her ravenous gaze. "But how do we find them? You've been all over the castle already, and only found the Sundial. Have you read the end of the story yet?"

"No," Ellie said with her mouth full of bread. She had never been so famished. "I found the book about Siana's real name being Ellie and then I fainted."

"Well, let's go find the last book. Perhaps it will explain where your Eterokoni ended up." He stood and placed his hand on her shoulder. It seemed in the end her being Siana, warrior, brigand, didn't matter to Graham. He gathered up the rope and food and they walked slowly to the library, as Ellie stuffed her mouth with the apples and cheese he passed to her. At one point he even walked with his arm around her. His kindness was the most beautiful thing she could remember.

The upper floor of the library was weird without the familiar bas reliefs of Siana. On their right as they climbed up were the shelves the rakshasa had raided. On their left were two shelves, the shelf that held blank books and the shelf from which she had plucked the book describing Siana leaving Mercair's seashore retreat and returning to Forgotten Town, that first day in the library.

That seemed so long ago.

She led Graham left. Her eye alit upon that same book, recognizing its distinct green hue. She pulled out the book next to it: the first dreambook she had found. She was sure it hadn't been on this shelf before.

As Graham moved in to glance over her shoulder, his foot struck a book on the floor. Ellie bent to pick it up and glanced at the first page.

"Kadesh reached Paris before me, just as her grip failed. Once again she was borne aloft by his taloned hands, as lines of blood from his claws ran down her back."

"I think this is it," Ellie said. So Paris hadn't fallen to her death!

Graham had gone past her, to the shelf of blank books.

"That is wonderful," he commented, "but you need to see this." He held out an open book toward her. She tucked her find under her arm and walked over. The left-hand page of Graham's book sported Siana's familiar script but the right-hand page had only a single line of handwriting at the top.

To her amazement, as she watched, a second line of handwriting faded into view.

"I walked over to Graham to see what he had found, a book from the leftmost shelf..."

She pressed her palm to her forehead. "My God, someone's writing down my life as it happens."

"Even so," Graham smiled. "Quite a marvelous place, your castle."

"You picked up that book on your own."

"Yes, I can see it all now, just about."

She took his book and leafed back a few pages. A line caught her eye:

"Then I agree with your sweet Paris," the rakshasa said, "that you have a funny way of going about it."

"This is a book about today!" she exclaimed, "and it's written from my perspective. But how can the book speak for me? I didn't write it!" A storm of confused thoughts blustered through her head.

"Maybe not, but somehow this library records everything that happens to you, and it purports to capture your thoughts and feelings."

"Then this shelf must be about my time in the castle," Ellie said, overwhelmed. "I could find out what really happened, those first days I barely remember."

"Yes, we could," Graham said, with his constant reassuring use of the word *we*, "but let's start with the book you found, we've got time. Read it to me."

Sitting down in a small nook between the two shelves, Ellie did.

THE ATTACK ON KADESH

February 2010, 1015th Year of the Detheros

K adesh reached Paris before me, just as her grip failed. Once
again she was borne aloft by his taloned hands, as lines of
blood from his claws ran down her back. With a lazy thump of
dragon wings, Kadesh glided over my army and landed on the
deck of an Orsian sky ship. Even at this distance I saw it shudder
beneath his weight.

Achthroi, thousands to our hundreds, advanced on my
saboteurs with a rush of sound, beginning to encircle us. From
their rear, on the elevated rim of the Sky Island, I could easily
see the field of battle. Neikolan barked orders at their head. The
sun of Mihali flashed on a hundred blades. Estringites strode
through—and over—the army to reach the front line of battle,
hoisting huge chunks of the island's gray crumbly stone.

But there was little hope.

I had seen Ilanit's power revealed in the piazza below her
palace. Despite the brightness of the day I could see the arcs
of power radiating from her fingertips, settling around and
incinerating my warriors. I had seen Kadesh's power unveiled in
the Traverse of Stones. And I knew that Ghislain was here, on
the leftmost ship of the line, and I feared him more than all the
rest.

I couldn't despair. Hope rested with me and me alone. If
there was any chance at all, it would come from me.

I had practiced this in Mercair's World, during my retreat
there, knowing there would be need. I remembered the cool
beach air, the sand beneath my shapechanging feet as I molded

the power of the Eterokoni to my vision, combining all their energies for the first time. I remembered the thrum of that power.

I called on that feeling now, letting the same throbbing energy build behind my eyes. I directed it down the lines of my body and grew six-fold in size. My skin became a steely carapace stronger than any armor. Then I extended the carapace down my right arm, enclosing my vambraces, joining with the hilt of the Glass Sword. The Sword grew and become a bladed extension of my shell.

And then I disappeared.

The center skyship saw nothing when I smashed into its hull blade-first. They didn't see my head burst through the deck, only the spray of timbers. I slashed out with my sword-arm, throwing Orsians aside, cutting the lines to the balloons. The ship listed to one side, and fell, and the tilting deck pitched its screaming defenders onto the plain below. I seized one of the masts for balance and it broke free. So I perched instead on the port rail as the ship fell. I tensed my armored kangaroo legs and sprung down into the midst of the Achthroi host.

I hit the ground, crushing Achthroi, as the Orsian vessel struck behind me with thunder. The beetle clicks of the Achthroin army surrounded me and I had to shut my mind to the Star's frenetic attempt to translate all their alien, twisted thoughts. I focused instead on the Bracelet, encased in the steel armor of my wrist, and set it to constantly release its deadly energy in a wide circle. I smashed into stone Achthroi with twin weapons—the broken-off mast and the Glass Sword—whirling in a circle and propelling fragments of petrified flesh everywhere.

Half of their army was gone in five minutes. The remaining four sky ships turned, aiming their prows at me.

I was their real problem and they knew it. I redoubled my attack. By the time they reached me the Achthroi would be gone. My army would be free from certain destruction at the hands of that immense host.

Though the Aedolae might prove army enough.

The innermost two ships were flanking me now.

And then things went wrong.

My first clue was the clank of a porcupine warrior's crossbow bolt against the steel of my body. Up to now, in the chaos of being attacked by a deadly, gigantic and completely invisible foe, my foes hadn't struck me at all. But now the Glove must be failing, as it had in Kadesh's presence before, in a way that allowed more than Kadesh to see me.

My next clue was Achthroi refusing to be petrified. The Glass Sword decimated them all the same, but I had never known the Bracelet to fail.

The third and fourth ships were at my rear now, the four forming a loose diamond around me.

There was a weakness, a *shift* in my body, a diminution. My eyes fell from their fleshy perch thirty feet in the air to their normal place five feet above the ground. The Achthroi became a clicking wall of mottled flesh and grotesque features and many now towered above me. Talons scraped the ringmail of my back. The Torc had failed. The Achthroi in front of me backed away to avoid the dismembering slashes of my blade. At least there was that.

And then the Glass Sword shattered.

I reached for Daevon's blade, but not in time. The sizeable cudgel of a tall Achthron caught my chin and knocked me off my feet. His fan-shaped foot, webbed and taloned, pinned me to the sandy soil. Another Achthron pressed its wooden javelin to my throat, crudely made but sharpened to a fine point and more than capable of killing me.

I needed to see above the crowding forms, but I could not sense the Eye's power and I dared not reach for it. Had it too failed?

The Achthroi grew still, held at bay by some silent command.

My mind raced to explain what transpired. The Torc had failed in Ghislain's presence, the Glass Sword and Star had failed in the presence of the Twins, and Kadesh had seen through my invisibility above the Prismatic Pool. All four were here now, massed on purpose to negate my power.

Why hadn't I reflected more on the failure of the Eterokoni in the presence of the Aedolae? Each Aedolae seemed to have power over one of my artifacts. Singly they could do little. But the need to defeat me had united them at last in a common purpose. As the Twins had said, floating above the piazza, before Dreamslayer pierced my chest. Of course I didn't *expect* to be faced with four in one place today. But my lack of reflection was folly. I had let myself become the mortal weakness of my army.

I had time for another despairing thought: the Bracelet and the Eye had also failed. I reached the inescapable conclusion: *six* Aedolae were here.

The circle of Achthroi parted to let Iakovos through. He had Dreamslayer, with a fresh bolt, leveled at my head.

"Release her," he commanded. "She will obey."

He kept the weapon aimed at my back as I left the circle. Ilanit waited to escort me onto the nearest ship. She took my hand in her pale, cool fingers with grace. So small this Aedolae, just my height, in form an ordinary woman save her face was impossibly perfect, statue carved. A flowing white dress clung to her slender figure, stirred by the breeze. But her petulant beauty was gone, replaced with ice.

There were blood-red strands in the corn silk of her hair.

Ghislain waited on the ship. His mirror eyes hid behind smoky lenses. Iakovos bid me to climb up alone. On board were a few Orsian sailors and two of Ghislain's ice titans, the Glacii, but all kept their distance, leaving the deck a bare stage on which Ghislain and I would enact our play.

As we had done before on the surface on Cylindrax.

He had placed a high-backed chair for me at the center of that stage, upholstered in rich red velvet.

"Have a seat, Miss Grey," Ghislain purred.

"I'd rather stand."

I measured the scene, weighing my peril.

The other three sky ships were close by, hovering twenty feet above my carnage which bled *en masse* as it reverted to flesh. A vast shadow, disconcerting, pooled in the blue sky above the ruined palace of the Twins and its exoskeleton of scaffolding. Lightning flashed within that darkness.

The Spaerodont. So He was here too.

I spotted Isabiel on the leftmost ship, and tall Daphne, enshrouded in black, on the rightmost. All *seven* Aedolae were here.

"Oh, please sit," Ghislain urged. "Your war is done. There is nothing left but to witness our show. And I have courteously provided you a comfortable seat. It is the least I can do to honor your accomplishments."

He pointed with his ruby-topped walking stick, but I stood defiant.

"Sit, or I will have the Gnish cut her throat," he hissed. I scanned the scene in alarm.

On the furthest ship Lyaven, a furred female Gnish from my army, held a huge knife to Paris' throat.

"*Lyaven!*" I shouted.

Kadesh, no longer a dragon, stood behind Lyaven. Lyaven had betrayed us. I hadn't seen her in the Traverse. Had she joined Ghislain during the attack on Kadesh? She must have revealed our strategy and accompanied him here ahead of us. And yet the Aedolae must have been assembling this force at Mihali for some time.

So Ghislain, through Lyaven, had known my plan to use the Traverse of Stones and knew where it led. He had readied the Achthroin army and the sky ships against us. But I didn't know *how*. It was impossible. The Aedolae were subject to the spatial organization of the demesnes they created, bound to travel the Aedol Via in slow time while I used the Kalimba as a shortcut. But Ghislain, Lyaven and two Glacii, at least, had gone from Kadesh to Mihali in less time than we took in the Traverse.

"That is right," Ghislain spoke quietly at my side. "We have your precious darling. I know all about your love."

Was there anything this Aedolae didn't know?

"Kadesh is fond of her, but not so fond he would choose her over taming you. So do as I say, or she will die. Do not use that trinket"—he pointed at the Kalimba—"or we will kill her."

None of the Aedolae had power over the Kalimba. There were only seven of them to the twelve Eterokoni. Though once there had been more.

"So, renegade dreamer, for once you will do as I say, and I am asking you to sit."

So sit I did, in a ringside seat, to witness unfolding of my doom.

The battle below had stilled since my capture, the Achthroi held at bay and my remaining saboteurs holding position, knowing numbers were against them.

Ghislain directed his ship to climb over the field of battle, and the other three ships maintained a close semicircle to keep my power negated. But truly the threat against Paris was enough. I wouldn't have her die, not for my war, and not for my salvation or my escape.

I pleaded, "You have me. Let my people go. Keep Paris, if you must, to insure my good behavior. But let the rest go."

The Master of Cylindrax stood before me, a foot from the edge of the deck, at a division in the rail. It would be so easy to push him off. Or would it?

"Ah, I like that tone," he said, stroking the trim triangle of his beard. "I have heard so little complaisance from you in the past. If you beg me, perhaps I will spare *this* one too."

We were passing over the front lines of my saboteurs. Ghislain extended his arm. With a snap and an acrid smell, a line of light connected a figure below to Ghislain's ruby. Ghislain raised him until he was level with us a hundred feet away.

It was Neikolan.

"Or perhaps not," Ghislain sneered.

He thrust his walking stick forward and Neikolan went flying out over the edge of Mihali. To fall forever in that boundless nothingness.

I couldn't stop it or another would die, my innocent Paris.

Ghislain raised his walking stick over his head. In response Iavokos yelled commands on the field, renewing his army's attack. With a sparkle of light, a weight in my hand, the Glass Sword renewed itself, for I had still held the hilt. Either Iakovos or Ilanit had canceled its power but their power now lay too far below.

Ghislain laughed.

"Ah, choices," he said. "I love choices. Now you don't have to acquiesce to failure."

I stood.

"Go ahead. Slay me. See what happens. Your lady will die. Perhaps you save some of your warriors. But the other arrangements I have made for you remain intact."

"What arrangements?"

"Do you really want to know? Or can I surprise you?" Ghislain laughed again.

"Tell me." I touched the point of the sword to his chest.

He clacked his stick against it. "No need to threaten me. I tried to explain it to you three years ago, before your inconvenient escape. Now you give me another chance. I take pride in my work." Something like a grin but far too inhuman crossed his face.

My Brigandrie fell with screams and shouts before the onslaught of a host still far beyond their numbers.

"I did not tell you then about your brother's fate," Ghislain said. "That was stingy of me. But you know anyway, you have always *known*. The scourge we unleashed on dreamers a thousand years ago is no secret."

"The Coethyphys." I said.

"Of course. But the arrangement always had an Achilles Heel. Coethyphys become unruly when they consume a dreamer and find he is not available to eat again. Paucity of prey broke our amicable relationship with the dreamflesh eaters, centuries ago. Their priests tried to solve the problem with the ritual of the Aliment. But that solution failed, for there is no dreambody to regenerate if the dreamer refuses to dream again. But an innovation occurred to me a hundred years ago. And I had begun to miss the Coethyphys. My thought was: *What if a dreamer couldn't wake up?'*

Indeed, Bierce and I had figured as much, but not knowing for sure had left room for doubt.

Room for my War.

"And Timothy was your guinea pig," I said.

Ghislain smiled that mirthless smile again.

"So where is he now?" I screamed, leveling the Sword at him again.

"Oh, Siana. I so thought you were following me. Must you ask? Is it so hard for your human brain to think the thought? He is with the Coethyphys, in their castle, where he has been all these years, the first six years of a Feast of *Millennia*."

"Of course I know that, you fuck. I meant was *where is that?* Where are the Coethyphys?" I tried not to think of what my brother had been suffering. The unthinkable.

"I don't need to tell you," Ghislain laughed. "You'll be joining him soon enough."

How are distances reckoned in the worlds of the Aedolae? How many miles is it from the boundary of the aery demesne of the Twins to where the Sky Island of Mihali hangs at its center? From where the oceans of Zoorn give way to aether, the Sky Island is a tiny speck to the naked eye. Yet this vast space was crossed in a few minutes by the Thing that came for me.

An hour before It passed the Veil of Zoorn and soared over the Graveyard of Ships, moving in a succession of *shifts* and sonic booms. Adherents of the Zoorn cult had wailed and cringed in their temple at this black flashing comet that sucked in the daylight. It passed the ocean and flapped up into the aether, toward the island speck that lurched closer with every shift.

The end of my War was a winter's day in Mihali, bright and not cold. A robin's egg blue framed the sun-blasted rock of the Twins' abode, rocky plains above, dry pines clinging to fissures and valleys below, dangling tendrils that mixed roots and rock down into the Void. The Thing saw no movement, heard no sound, for these were still lost in the vastness of the scene. It did not know a war raged and an army was being lost. It only knew its quarry.

But as It flew, Achthroi swarmed my host, heedless of their own injury, driven by the Aedolae's command. Every Achthron is different, making them a difficult foe. Dwarf Achthroi scampered under my brigands' legs, slicing and biting at ankles and tendons, grappling with the Tzi who tried to commandeer the sun-magnifying spheres from the ship I'd destroyed. Titan Achthroi, grotesque with many-jointed arms, grappled with my Estringites, slashing at them with talons, spires, pincers, whatever random digits topped their contorted arms. And through the fray ranged Iakovos with his two-handed blade and Ilanit with her blasts of radiant power, untouchable in their rage.

I espied Paris across forty feet open air. Her shoulders were torn and bleeding from Kadesh's claws. This was the fate she had long feared, both of us in the grip of my enemies, watching my saboteurs die.

There was a flash of blinding light on the battlefield and then the flash arced across the plain and was among the ships. A beam of magnified sun struck the ship to my left, Daphne's vessel, setting its prow smoking. There was a flash from a different quarter, and another beam burnt a hole in its hull. The ship began to drop.

The Tzi had succeeded in using the magnifying spheres.

Ghislain's ship jolted, and a shudder rippled through the timbers beneath my feet. Vines wrapped themselves around the railing, time-lapse photography of a growing plant. An Estringite — Nao—hoisted himself onto the deck. Ghislain moved with an uncanny speed, a blur of motion, cracking Nao in the face with his walking stick. Ghislain ripped the smoky glasses from own face. A Tzi sunbeam settled on our ship's balloons.

There was a click like a giant match being struck and a hiss as air exhaled from the damaged balloons. Nao hung to the railing despite Ghislain's blow but suddenly he was on fire too, for Ghislain had reflected onto Nao a portion of the beam's energy with his mirrored eyes.

Burning fabric flapped like flags. The ship tilted violently and fell. I grabbed an iron ring set in the deck before I was thrown off. Ghislain lashed his arms around the rail and his discarded glasses skittered over the edge. As we tilted, I saw Talmei climbing the ship below Nao, punching holes in the hull with massive fists.

The ship fell with a crash on top of them, pitching Ghislain and me onto the rock. I rolled away, and looked back to find the ship a raging inferno. There was no sign of my Estringites.

Ghislain was over me faster than I thought possible, holding me at bay with his walking stick, his clothes smoking from the heat of the sunbeam weapon, but his flesh unsinged and pale. Daphne's ship crashed a moment later. Kadesh's vessel was down already, but had remained level, its balloons burning in a pile nearby. Kadesh, Lyaven and Paris still stood on deck. All the ships had come down at island's edge, a hundred feet from the Void.

The Tzi's attacks had achieved nothing. Nao and Talmei had been crushed under the whole weight of the Orsian vessel, a mercy since it now incinerated above them. The Aedolae still crowded about me. Isabiel's ship landed on its own volition to my left. The Spaerodont hovered overhead, casting us in a pool of shadow. I got to my feet, keeping my movements slow so that Ghislain knew I meant no violence. My army was completely surrounded and the Tzi's spheres had been shattered.

Iakovos and Ilanit were approaching from the field of battle. And then my dream ended.

• • • ● • ● • • •

I woke in a dark place, a circular tower of old stone. My head ached and my arm burned. My vision was fuzzy, but I saw a man nearby, back turned, dressed in dark, shapeless clothes. This wasn't my bedroom, what was I doing here?

Then I remembered: the bus from Seattle to Issaquah, the walk to the old farmhouse, the dinner party. John slamming a needle in my arm. That must be John here now. Why? What was this place? I staggered to my feet. I still wore the linen dress I'd worn to bed—a gift from a coworker I didn't like that I used as a nightgown. My bare legs were scratched and smudged with dirt and moss. I was woozy from whatever was in the needle and I ached with cold.

John heard me and spun around.

With all the accuracy and force I could muster I slugged him in the chest. Perhaps he was expecting me an easy victim, but I had trained for war, in both the waking world and the world of dreams. He stumbled back but as he righted himself a cruel and vengeful expression crossed his face. He threw his full weight at me and John is a big man. In a less drugged state I would have evaded him but he was able to shove me backwards. I expected to strike the interior wall of the tower, but instead found myself pitched through a hole in the masonry, a doorway into black night.

I fell into open air.

There was no bottom.

What I fell into was no ordinary darkness. A dreamer's instinct told me that at once. It was a nothingness between worlds. And I fell not as Siana, dreamer, but as Ellie, my waking world body swallowed up and extinguished. All that remained was my consciousness, which raced across the Fringe, over Nathnang, Ivilstuen, the Prismatic Jungle, over the Detheros and the Edoi Sea, in search of the dreambody that was now its only home.

The truth congealed in my mind, as I soared through a mad rush of dreamworld images. This was what they had done to Timothy.

· · · ● ●· ● ● ● · ·

The next moment I was at Mihali, Ghislain beside me, Spaerodont overhead. I shivered in the breeze. I was wearing my nightgown and the Eterokoni were nowhere to be seen.

Seeing the nightdress, Ghislain laughed. He knew.

"May all who stand here," he announced, turning slowly and raising one hand, "both friend and foe of the Aedolae, behold what this Siana, sojourner and Brigand, really is: a girl, just a little girl."

THE COMING OF THE FOOL

I would have fumed at his insult, but I was too disoriented from my disembodiment and flight to react. Being fully Within for the first time was different, in a way I can't define or describe, save to say I felt *vulnerable*, and not just because I had lost my Eterokoni and the trappings of war.

"Before you are taken to the Coethyphys, I would have you see the end of your Brigandrie, and the utter ruin of your designs," Ghislain whispered.

He nodded to Iakovos who turned and signaled his army. They were going to destroy all who remained.

But a warmth at my back cast a long shadow from my body onto the plain before me, fringed in a rainbow of color. My skin tingled.

Isabiel hissed.

Kadesh laughed, his hearty sardonic laugh.

"Leave him to me," Ghislain said to his fellows, his voice quiet, ice cold.

I turned to see.

At first I was blinded. Something more brilliant than the sun blazed in the void beyond Mihali. A distant figure traversed that riot of color, and as my eye focused on him, the swirl of fantastic colors around him began to make sense. A man, walking down a rainbow-floored avenue that began far off in the aether and touched the island's edge. Flanking this rainbow was a city of tinted ice and spun sugar, refracting the sun of Mihali in a thousand shimmering hues. It felt like Christmas morning, crisp and wintry, a dazzling beauty.

A strange thing to be surrounded by the Lords of the Night.

The man came closer and his movement was hard to track, something between walking and gliding. It took him a long time to approach, yet the Aedolae did not stir, and captivated by the glory of the amazing city, I noticed nothing else. We all waited in silence, until the man was close enough for me to discern the circular straw hat, the black dress clothes, the hooked cane, and the kindly face of my savior, my Mercair.

He was the last thing I expected.

As Mercair stepped onto the sands of Mihali the fantastic avenue of his arrival vanished. The silence was now immense, as if that glory of color had concealed a sound pitched below the ken of human hearing, and now that sound was gone.

Ghislain broke this silence with triumph in his voice. "We have lured the fool from his lair at last."

"So you have," Mercair replied calmly, walking slowly toward the Aedolae, showing no fear. His shiny black shoes crunched the soil. He appeared to gaze past the Aedolae to the legions of Achthroi beyond. He raised his walking stick, just perceptibly, in their direction. All the noise of the Achthroi—clicks and buzzes—ceased. They turned, every last one, toward Mercair, antennae bristling. But I had no chance to ponder the meaning of this, or Mercair's power over them.

"You have come to your destruction," Kadesh thundered and leapt from his ship's deck, a javelin in his right hand.

"Hold, brother." Ghislain raised his hand without turning Kadesh's way. "I am interested to discover what Mercair believes he is here to do. Bring the dancer." Kadesh climbed back up and took Paris from Lyaven, swinging her over his shoulder as if her weight was nothing. Lyaven followed him down the ropes.

"I have come to take Siana from you." Mercair stopped an arm's length away from Ghislain and leaned on his cane. "You had no right to do to her brother, or her, what you have done."

Isabiel hissed. Ghislain spoke slowly, containing a seething anger.

"Do we not rule here? Do you question this? She is a thief, taking away our property." He nodded toward Paris, who again had Lyaven's knife at her throat. "As such Siana is subject to our law and our retribution."

"I do not question the *fact* that you rule, but I question your *right* to rule, and the fashion in which you do. The Shekinah—"

"—is long since vanished, dead, extinguished," Kadesh interrupted with a growl. "The Shekinah's edicts are without value."

"All the same, I have come to appropriate this dreamer," Mercair concluded, with no hint of ire. His equanimity amazed me.

"You fool, it is far too late for that," Ghislain spat and pointed toward Zoorn.

With a distant rumble and a spark of pale lightning, the Thing that came for me *shifted* into Mihalian space, a Shadow from below and between the worlds of the Aedolae.

Mercair shrugged as if unimpressed.

"Come with me." He proffered his hand as if inviting me to walk along his beach.

"Do you think I—we—are so impotent as to let you take her—" Ghislain began with a uncharacteristic high-pitched fury.

"No matter, I will not go," I broke in. "I *can't* go with you."

For the first time, something other than calm stole across Mercair's face.

"These people," I said, pointing toward my saboteurs, whom I could no longer see for the decimation of their numbers and the black throng hemming them in, "are here only because of me. I will not leave them. And I will not leave her."

Paris was there because she loved me too much to be parted from me. She had no taste for violence, no skill as a warrior. Paris had always waited for me in Forgotten Town, providing the counterbalance to my war. She should never have been *here*.

"Siana, go!" Paris cried. "Don't die for me. Please!" Tears coursed down her face.

"Siana," Mercair spoke, drawing my gaze. I was surprised Aedolae had not lifted so much as a finger against him. What was he, to intimidate them so, to stand here at ease and coolly debate with them while surrounded by their power? "Staying is not one of your choices. You either leave with me or you leave with *that.*"

The Shadow was lurching its way across the remaining space. The distance was hard to judge against the backdrop of sky, but I knew it was too close.

All of a sudden I could not see.

Something overshadowed my vision, a whirling vortex of grey and white color. I realized the vortex was not out there; it was in my mind, an image so strong focusing on the external world was hard. The sensation was someone peering in on my thoughts and sharing the space within my brain. Through the haze of this vision I could see Mercair staring at me, compelling me to understand. He was the source of the vortex. But what did it mean?

There was a weight in my hands, and I opened my palm to find there the Sundial, the Eterokon of Time.

The first of my Eterokoni to return.

Its power coursed in me, a sense of communication with the device I had sought in vain a hundred times. At his estate, Mercair had feigned ignorance of its use. But now his vortex enabled me to activate it for the first time. To become at last my childhood demigoddess.

Time Princess.

Ghislain was first to sense what was happening. He swiped at the tiny Eterokon, but his fingers went through it to strike my palm.

"Who is the fool now?" Mercair said, with uncharacteristic mockery. "You know better than that."

And then Ghislain froze, hand partially retracted, mouth agape.

Isabiel's head was cocked at a bizarre angle, unmoving. Paris' tears were chips of ice on her cheeks, not falling. Behind her, the torn sails and balloons of the sky ship had frozen in mid-flap. There was no breeze. There was no sound. The battlefield was a still life.

And the Shadow was frozen in the sky a hundred feet away.

I had stopped Time. Or stepped outside of it. Perhaps there was no difference.

"I can kill them all," I said out loud, overwhelmed by the thought.

"There isn't time," a voice said behind me.

I wheeled about and found the Glass Sword in my other hand. Mercair's face was an inch from his tip, but his face registered no alarm.

"What? Why?" I blurted.

"You have exempted me from the Sundial's power," he said simply.

"I have?"

"Yes," he said. "Now is our only chance."

I wasn't watching Mercair anymore. I was watching the Shadow. As if popping from a mold, it extricated itself from the time freeze, one cloak-like wing at a time. With an audible click it zagged twenty feet closer before the power of my Eterokon glued it to the sky again.

"They are time shifters too," Mercair warned. "You are not experienced enough to hold it. It will be upon you."

"I don't care," I said, turning away from him. "I can't leave her here." I walked toward Paris.

"If you end up with the Coethyphys you will never save Timothy, only die forever at his side."

"Ghislain will kill her," I cried in anguish, not knowing what to do, unwilling that any who had loved me should die. I rushed toward Paris.

Lyaven was before me, a full head taller than Paris.

With a clean stroke of the Glass Sword I took off the Gnish's head.

There was no blood and no sound as her head struck the ground. But she didn't fall and her arms, stronger than mine, still held Paris like iron in the rigidity of time stop. I couldn't pry Paris loose for fear of Lyaven's blade slicing her throat.

"Oh fuck!" I cursed in frustration, kicking out at Isabiel, who fell over like a statue.

There was a crack of thunder at my back. I spun. The Shadow was free, descending on me with lazy strokes of its wings. Mercair threw himself in front of it, spreading his arms protectively around me. With an explosion of golden light, he disappeared from view, and I was enveloped in a warm presence, arms pinned to my sides.

Time resumed.

The Gnish's neck erupted with a spray of blood, and her body released Paris, collapsing in a heap. Isabiel shrieked. Ghislain startled, not finding me where I had been a second before.

And then the Thing ploughed into us, enfolding me in dark energy.

Or it attempted to. In a violent chiaroscuro the gold enveloping me fought off the infernal energy of the Shadow. Paris screamed but I could no longer see her.

With a rumbling growl beneath my feet, I was lifted by a prickling stabbing energy. I stood on top of the Shadow, which was rising from the ground like a manta ray. My arms were still pinned to my side by the golden haze. Through this haze I could now see Paris, with wide eyes reaching her hands ineffectually toward me.

"I have subdued it," a voice said from behind my left ear. It sounded like Mercair and yet not. "I will get you out of here."

"Don't!" I yelled, my eyes locked on Paris, but my words were muffled and lost.

"Kill the dancer," Ghislain commanded with venom.

No! Paris couldn't die now. She had made it through the whole battle, and survived her fall from the ropes.

There was a sickening chill as the Shadow shifted forwards through space. I was thrown backward against the force that held me against my will. It wasn't exactly physical, a warm pliant surface like a honey-filled mold.

I craned my neck to see what was happening behind. Paris was running after me, and Kadesh broke ranks and raised high his great javelin. It was the last time I saw her. The Shadow banked and my eyes were pulled heavenward. Paris screamed in agony, a scream of death.

By the time I could look again, the Aedolae were but tiny figures upon the plain and I could discern nothing.

I now saw a golden thread ran past my hip and leashed the Shadow's blunt head. Mercair—it must be he—tugged on the leash, pulling it to the right. But lightning cracked directly in front of us, and Mercair was forced to bank left. The sky darkened as the vast overarching expanse of the Spaerodont descended. And then lightning surrounded us, driving us fast over the desolate surface of Mihali toward the City of the Twins. The scaffolding over the ruined palace loomed ahead. As we barely cleared the alabaster walls of Mihali the Spaerodont's bolts crashed against them. The Shadow ploughed through scaffolding, shattering timbers and steel rods, but the destruction didn't touch me, enveloped in the golden nimbus of Mercair's power. I could only faintly hear the crash of metal and wood and the cries of workmen pitched onto the piazza below.

Mercair pulled hard on the leash, forcing the Shadow to bank over the City and head out toward the Void. I could feel the Shadow struggling against his dominance as we made a fierce oval toward the former location of Mercair's phantom rainbow city. There was motion inside the golden cocoon, Mercair raising his cane, which shone with the same golden light. We rose higher and struck an invisible barrier, like reaching the bottom of an escalator and finding one's feet want to keep moving. But in this case the Shadow was the escalator, and it imploded against the unseen barrier with a stentorious buzz. It screamed in defiance with deep subsonic tones but was consumed and obliterated all the same. As its momentum consumed it, we were pitched off its back, *through* the barrier, into a weird place of swirling mist.

I hung in mid-air in the dim nothingness, and Mercair hung beside me.

"Welcome to another of my secrets, my *in-between* place," he said, breathing heavily and adjusting his hat, as if trying to restore his gentleman's image. No chance of that. I was about to bark a protest but was interrupted by a clicking sound.

A giant mirror floated in the air, reflecting the streamers of mist at an odd angle.

It moved.

Mercair's usually placid face registered alarm. The mirror had grown arms and legs and was paddled through the mists toward us.

"Your folly has blinded you," Ghislain's voice said from within the mirrored thing his body had become. "I have known about—and traveled—your web for some time."

This was how he reached Mihali ahead of us.

"You will not have her," Mercair countered. A golden nimbus silhouetted his figure. The mirrored thing that was Ghislain raised one arm, thin as a sheet of paper and mirrored on both sides. It still gripped his walking stick, now massive as the bole of a tree, a pillar of ice lit from within by a red luminance. Mercair raised his cane in response, and superimposed upon it, in that dim and confusing place, was the silhouette of a great staff.

Red power launched from Ghislain's ruby. Mercair's weapon blocked the energy and held it, deflecting it back. Ghislain let the burst strike the rippling mirror of his torso, which sent a red cloud of refracted energy arcing wildly in all directions.

The arcs struck me where I floated. I expected pain but instead my eyesight went black. When I regained sight, the scene had grown hazier and I couldn't focus. All I could see clearly was Mercair's brilliant aura.

Which moved toward me, surrounding me again.

Mercair made no counter-attack. Rather he enveloped me in the same warm viscosity and propelled us forward. We picked up speed and air currents of varying coolness buffeted my face. Despite the openness of the place I still had the sense that we tunneled, following a burrowing spider's twisted web.

Without warning we burst forth into a high place of blinding sun. The archipelago of the Summer Isles drowsed a dizzying distance below, jade jewels set in a sapphire sea. But Ghislain was immediately beside us, a bird whose feathers were steel spikes and whose every surface was fulgent with sunlight.

Mercair banked to avoid him. Something circular whirred close and struck me in the head. My vision darkened again and Ghislain spoke in my mind.

"Fight him, resist him, sojourner. He carries you against your will."

Mercair took us into the *in-between* place again.

We tunneled again through the mist-boundaried strands of Mercair's web. But Ghislain was there in an instant, hounding us, flinging more of the psychic energy at my head. Each darkened my vision, left it cloudier than before, and filled my aching consciousness with surreal thoughts. Ghislain was my enemy; he had just tried to barter my dreambody to the Coethyphys. But he assaulted my confidence all the same.

Mercair is taking you for his own evil purposes. He stole you away from Paris when you cried to stay. Because of him, Paris is dead.

I tried to raise my arms, block my ears, but I couldn't move.

Let go of me! I screamed at Mercair, but the nightmare wouldn't end. I had no sense of his presence anymore, only that I was bound tight and hurtled through the void. *If she is dead, I want to die too!*

I was nothing, only a dream shade whose hope was destroyed, fought over by two powers that cared nothing for my soul.

We burst into the sky above Zoorn. The Veil, shimmering wall of Daphne's power, was in front of us, and we grazed its surface as we tore through the air. Mercair must have hoped Ghislain would strike it, unable to maneuver away. No such luck. I could sense, more than I could see, the Aedolae's presence right beside us, undeterred.

And then we were back inside. Our speed flagged. Something grabbed at my shoulder, trying to pull me from Mercair's grasp. This sent us into a spiral.

We tore out of the web a last time, into the sky of a place called Vaelonn-Marr.

The Va'e River glinted in wintry afternoon sun. We swooped down at a fierce angle over a landscape of heath and hills, crossing miles of terrain. Ghislain dropped out of the web behind us, sped forward to overshadow us and crushed us to the ground, bringing our long forward impetus to an abrupt and bracing halt. I was suffocated against wet soil, those two great powers on top of me, struggling for dominance.

I was pulled upwards as Mercair disengaged himself from Ghislain and stood, with me crushed to his chest as surely as if he had physical arms about me.

Ghislain was before us, three dimensional again, a shining cyborg of a man. His face, a metallic faceted mockery of a face, contorted in anger.

"I have had enough of your insolent resistance."

He swept his ruby-tipped weapon across his torso and aimed it at me. The air burned with the same acrid smell. This time I felt the power in my body, turning my flesh to water. I was lifted from Mercair's viscous aura and thrown to the side with a flick of Ghislain's hand. My body became a single giant bruise.

I crumpled to the ground.

Mercair's glowing amber hands closed on empty air. He turned on Ghislain.

"What you have done with her?"

Could he no longer see me? I tried to speak, but I had no voice. I tried to sit up but had no limbs. I craned my neck to see my body, but couldn't find myself at all. A sick feeling swept my consciousness.

Above me, Ghislain pummeled Mercair in mad fury.

Mercair was a golden demigod, bearing a grand staff, but as Ghislain's blows struck him, he faded to a dim silhouette. Only a man left inside. The man who had rescued me from the prison of my bower, who had escorted me along the beaches of his seaside estate. The person aside from Paris who had shown me the most kindness in the world of dreams.

No longer a savior, but a man, on his knees in agony, his cane and hat blasted away. I reached for the power of the Sundial, to stop time and save him, but I couldn't sense the Eterokoni either. I had become invisible, in a deeper way than the invisibility of the Glove. Invisible even to myself, reduced to an aching, shattered consciousness.

And then that too was gone.

IDENTITY

Ten months in the Castle

E llie closed the book.
"So that is what happened to me. I'm here because Ghislain's attack did...well, whatever it did. Made me invisible to Mercair, and Ghislain couldn't see me either. Else I'd be with one or the other."

She managed a feeble laugh and then what she'd read struck deeper.

Paris was dead.

Her eyes welled with tears. One of the buttresses of her fragile identity was shifting and falling away.

"The book makes sense," Graham said simply, "logical sense, that is. If it weren't also the most outlandish thing I've ever heard."

Ellie leaned against Graham for support. He put an arm around her waist.

"Paris is dead," she sputtered, unable to see his face through her flood of tears. She sobbed. "But what *is* this castle then? The book says nothing about it."

"I have an idea," Graham answered. "The story said the rakshasa fashioned a whole cityscape in Ampizand, in form a cityscape from your world—from your memories. So the rakshasa must have made this place from the material of your mind; hence in the end his creation turned against him and helped you find yourself."

"But why did I have a vision of Siana on the heath, shredded into ribbons and cast onto the library walls? That's not how this book says it was."

"I don't know, but perhaps that's how it felt, to have your last shred of identity taken away. It represented the violence done to your mind as the rakshasa fashioned this prison around you."

"Why weren't Ghislain and Mercair in the vision?"

"The vision must have been of a later time, after you had regained visible form. The rakshasa spotted you and did what he did," Graham answered. "Grant you, I'm not sure."

"You're good, don't apologize. I don't think what happened was all the rakshasa's doing. He built this place, but what happened to my mind was from Ghislain's attack." She paused. "Do you think he destroyed Mercair?" The possibility disgusted her.

"We can't know, but you were left at the rakshasa's mercy, and the book's last description of Mercair—well, neither bode well for his survival." He took the book from her hand and placed it back on the shelf.

Ellie sighed deeply. "I've got to get Timothy and get us out of this world as fast as possible. There is nothing left for me, and no help. Mercair dead, Paris dead."

"You don't know Mercair died—" Graham protested.

"I'm not going to hope. I can't afford it. Besides, Mercair didn't do what I begged him to do."

Graham frowned. "The Coethyphys would have you if it weren't for him."

"I've distracted myself from my responsibility for too long," Ellie continued, ignoring the issue of Mercair, "unable to bear the truth that Siana—*that I*—knew all along. My brother has suffered"—she could hardly bear to think about it—"for six years, and no matter what comes of it, I must find him or die trying. My vengeance was the pride and fury of a fool. That Siana must be no more. All of her hopes and loves and plans must be gone. There is only saving my brother and leaving this world behind."

They were both silent for a minute.

"Graham, I'm scared out of my mind."

Later that afternoon, Graham and Ellie sat in the Time Room, bundled in their cloaks. Her whole body ached, from a long walk through the castle prying at tiles and picture frames, and from stress. She held the Sundial in her hands, turning it over and over. Its workmanship was beautiful, as the books described.

"I wonder who made these?" she mused aloud.

"Try to use it," Graham prodded.

Ellie's head jerked up.

"Well, you are the Princess of Time," Graham chuckled.

She turned it over again in her palm and frowned. She had no sense of connection like the books described.

"What do I do?"

"Stop talking for starters," Graham urged. "Search inside."

She closed her eyes, feeling the weight of the Sundial in her hand. The books always described how Siana—how *she* (she corrected herself for the hundredth time that day)—felt a throb of energy, a presence, a mental corresponding weight. She tried to imagine the whirling grey and white vortex the last book described.

Nothing.

If I don't feel it, I'll have to conjure it.

To her frustration the images that came to mind were culled from the TV screen—news programs about tornadoes, satellite maps of storms.

"I'm pathetic." She opened her eyes. She wanted to hurl the Eterokon away but dared not. "I've lost everything. I found out who I am in time to realize it's not me. We can't find the other Eterokoni, and I can't use the one I have. I'm doomed."

Graham looked annoyed, but he spoke with his usual equilibrium. "Would it be safe to say, Elizabeth, that you're not known for your patience in the waking world?"

She smiled despite herself, a shy smile. "Yes. You're right as usual. But I *am* known for my stubbornness."

"Well and good," Graham said. "God gives us gifts to balance our failings. Let's make sure you use them."

"But we're running out of time," Ellie said, placing the Sundial on the pew with a clank. She started to pace. Graham stayed seated, as if to defy her impatience. "What's going to happen if they kill me now?"

"I don't recall Ghislain was all that interested in killing dreamers. He was more interested in feeding them to the Coethyphys."

"Don't *say* that," Ellie shouted.

"Hiding from the truth isn't going to help. It didn't help you before and it never does."

She huffed, "You're right, you're right. Are you ever not right?"

"Ask my wife that," Graham laughed. "Your question what would happen if they killed you now is actually a good one." She smiled at his obvious change in tone, a signal he was about to be didactic. "We can conclude from the books your dreamself is still anchored in the hermetus, and the hermetus is in Mercair's World—"

"But if Mercair is dead?"

"Then we don't know what would happen to his estate or the things in it. But surely the hermetus is *somewhere*, and would benefit you by performing its function again."

"But if I am captured and given to the Coethyphys, and they rooted my dreamself in their castle," Ellie reasoned, thinking of what Siana—*what she*—and Bierce had found in the Library of the Ancients, "my dreambody would be anchored in two places. What happens *then*, if I die?" She couldn't bring herself to say *eaten*.

"Another good question," Graham concluded, "which unfortunately neither of us has a prayer of answering. Let's hope you have no cause to find out."

"OK, Mr. Logician," Ellie said, pacing, "that was a fine circle of talk. We're back where we started, with me still a pathetic shadow of what I was."

Graham stood, glancing at the sky through the massive hole that had replaced the skylight. A furtive glance, but she caught it. He leaned on the amazing staff with its concentric circles of color.

"Do not despair. You are wiser, and that is worth all sorts of power. We know how things turned out for the powerful Siana. You will get your power back and you will use it with more wisdom this time. I have faith in you."

He grinned. She didn't deserve his kindness. She thought of Daevon and Paris, the tenderness of her lost lovers.

All I've done is let people down.

As if reading her mind, Graham replied, "Humility is the beginning of wisdom."

"It's late," she said. "We've done enough for today. I'll try to be patient. I'm just scared. Why don't you head home? Can you come back in the morning?"

"I will, God willing, little Ellie," he said, looking grateful for her encouragement that he go, "but I will leave you the ladder and the rope all the same."

"You wouldn't want to carry it back anyway," she teased.

Night descended on the castle. As the sky, visible in so many places above the castle now, faded to sullen purple, a new kind of darkness fell with deep shadows. The castle had always had a ghostly glow at night but not now. She realized with irritation that soon the only light would be from the stars. She bumbled around the familiar parts of the castle, still searching, the quest becoming increasingly pointless as her pace slowed, her aches intensified to a point of intolerance and the fading day left her blind. She sensed no menace from the empty rooms around her, but an intense loneliness and creeping anxiety more than made up for it. It was intensely silent, so silent she imagined the stars made a soft silvery noise as they twinkled high above. Around midnight a chill wind began to blow, whistling and howling through the darkness.

She didn't dare explore beyond her familiar boundaries in this gelid shadow, though that had been her original plan. She should reason like Graham, using her mind instead of her numb fingers, but fatigue slowed her thoughts to a crawl.

She collapsed on a stone bench in the amphitheater, exhausted and defeated.

She looked down at the ladder Graham had propped against the dais, faint white in the dark. She had said goodbye to Graham there, clinging to him despite her resolve to let him go. Why had she thought she would not see him again? She knew his word was good and he would return on the morrow.

She must have slept for next she knew it was even colder and a moon hung in the circle of sky framed by the hole in the amphitheater ceiling. The wind had subsided. A pure light filled the bowl-shaped room, casting eerie shadows between the tiers. A palpable urgency galvanized her sleepy brain. Reason no longer mattered. Ellie wanted to go, Eterokoni or not. There could never be enough time to search even a fraction of the massive compound she had viewed from the roof. She *had* to get out of the castle now.

She hefted the ladder and tucked it under one arm. It was long and unbalanced and dragged against the floor. She considered carrying it to the balcony where she had accessed the roof, but that was very far away to her tired body. She sized up the sloping walls of the amphitheater. The ladder was long but not that long. Ellie put it down, in a patch of moonlight, on the third tier from the top and huffed. The moonlight revealed the ladder could be expanded to twice its current length. She would give it a try.

It took her a long time to position it securely on both ends. The ladder was old and bowed slightly inwards where the two sections joined. The climb up to the hole in the convex roof appeared long and perilous in the darkness. She remembered her last sojourn to the castle roof and went back to the dais to retrieve Graham's rope. She could tie it to something on the roof just in case.

She coiled the rope about her shoulder and set one foot to the rungs when a howling breeze shot up, racing through open doors. Its ferocity pushed her sideways against a stone bench. With a crack the ladder's two sections snapped free of each other, and the whole apparatus fell with a crash.

Ellie swore. The damage was unfixable. Now the ladder was far too short.

The castle still fought her for her freedom.

Just as it had helped her rediscover herself.

Which was true? Was this a remnant of the rakshasa's power? Was the castle made from his power or her memories?

Both, I suppose.

Ellie set off with one of the remaining ladder pieces for the balcony below the armory. It might be long enough. When she was most of the way there, bruised from multiple encounters with things she couldn't see, she remembered that the roof of the balcony, defying the laws of physics, was thirty feet above the castle roof and she needed the rope, which she had absentmindedly left in the amphitheater.

I am too tired for this, I can't do it. If I persist in this I am going to make some other, more fatal, error.

The dread urgency still gnawed, but reason resurfaced. She was so tired that she curled up on the floor in her cloak and slept.

RAFF

E llie awoke with the sense she'd heard some noise, but it didn't repeat. She was a few rooms shy of the Time Room. She was less tired but sore from her uncomfortable resting place. She sat up and listened a long time. The ceiling here was intact but dawn was beginning to steal through adjoining rooms. After satisfying herself that she was alone, she rubbed the sleep out of her eyes and stood up. There was something in the periphery of her vision.

Like many in the castle, the room was an unfurnished square with door-less arches. But in a niche to her left, a trio of garments hung from a gleaming metal rod over an oval table of polished white stone. Ellie knew the items had never been here before. She approached them with a prickling sense of familiarity.

In the center hung a stiff vest armored in tiny steel rings, polished and sparkling even in the dim light of dawn. Below the vest, tied to the hanger by its drawstrings, was a pair of black breeches. From its thigh pockets protruded the hilts of small daggers. On the left hanger was a hooded cloak, thick and warm, short and with ¾ sleeves to accommodate combat. On the right hanger was a black tunic and a knapsack.

These were Siana's clothes—*her clothes*.

A spark of hope kindled in Ellie's breast.

She examined the items on the table. Her steel-paneled vambraces. Two belts, the brass-buckled one Paris had complained about and the wider belt with its myriad pockets for the Eterokoni. A pair of grey woolen socks. Close fitting leather gloves. A familiar comb and brush. Two small feathers from Mercair's birds, one purple, one scarlet.

Ellie laughed.

Beside the feathers were red silk underpants and a matching red bra inset with diamonds. These had come from Paris' room ring. She had asked Paris why she had, among her thousands of garments, a bra several cup sizes too small for her. Paris had shrugged and said something about ignorant admirers. She had gifted Siana with this elegantly wrought underwear. She had worn them, honoring the gift, but all the same she was very glad they were hidden beneath her trademark black.

Ellie's eyes went wide. She had *remembered*, remembered something concrete from her dreamlife within the Detheros! Something the books never revealed. This brought a deeper thrill of hope, a lightening of her spirit.

And with it sadness, in the juxtaposing of this sweet memory with the tragedy of the last book. Sadness she could not conjure an image of Paris' face.

Next to the underwear was a pendant on a very fine chain, with impossibly tiny white gems set in a ruby heart that spelled the letters "PCD". *Paris Christianne de Na-vaylah.* Another gift from my sweet Paris.

Will it all come back, all those memories? Do I even want to remember Paris?

The last item was Timothy's journal. Inside was his fine careful handwriting, so unlike her wide irregular hand. She clutched it to her chest and burst into tears.

The tears left her lightened but not exactly happy. She couldn't have described her feelings, but she definitely was more alive than she ever had. Energized. Washed by emotion.

She put down the journal and picked up the brush. As the daylight waxed, she spent a long time untangling her matted hair, then smoothed it out with the comb. Liberated from tangles it was far longer, falling to her collarbone. She sighed with pleasure.

An impulse struck her. She ran to the Time Room and broke the ice in the basin. She threw off her cloak and tore at her dress, rending it and leaving it a pathetic heap on the floor.

I spent months in a dress I always hated.

She clenched her teeth and forced herself into the freezing water, splashing it against her face. She shrieked at the cold, and shrieked again, beginning to laugh. She could only stand it for a couple minutes but felt clean, refreshed and awake when she slipped out.

Trying to savor the moment, she went back to her clothes. They were still there. (The thought crossed her mind in the bath that it had been stupid to be so careless with her dress.) She was reaching for the silk underwear but was interrupted by a noise from the niche in front of her. She knew at once this was the same noise that had awakened her.

The mailed vest rocked on its hanger, and muffled noises came from inside a zippered pocket. Some small thing was struggling inside. A mouse? But she thought she heard a voice.

She took a dagger from the breeches and gingerly hooked it in the zipper pull, keeping her distance best she could. She drew the zipper aside, opening the pocket.

She watched in fascination as a small hand and arm reached out and locked around the outside of the pocket. With a tiny grunt, the arm leveraged the rest of the torso into view. A miniature of a man balanced precariously on the zipper, suited in a black garment that showed only his shining eyes. Those eyes swept the length of her body, head to toe, quite a distance for him. She was so spellbound she forgot that she was nude and cold, wet and dripping.

A gasp came from the hooded mouth. A small but undeniably masculine voice rang out.

"You are more beautiful than I could have dreamt, my liege."

"Your what?" Ellie stammered.

"My liege. I am Raff, pledged Legionnaire of the Orange Guard of the Sojourners. And you are my liege, whom I am sworn to serve and protect."

"What??"

"Surely a sojourner of your reputation must know of the famed Orange Guard?"—he sounded hurt—"but it is of no matter. I will serve you faithfully, my lady, and die for you if need requires."

Raff bowed deeply, almost falling from his ringmail link perch.

"But you're only four inches tall," Ellie said.

Doubtless she was being rude. But she couldn't fathom any of this.

Raff snorted. "It seems I must demonstrate my skills to my liege."

He crouched and launched himself into a triple somersault before plunging toward the stone table. As he spun he pulled a narrow blade from the folds of his linen clothing, to her little more than a needle. All very impressive until he landed in one cup of Paris' bra and slipped on the silk which bunched up before his feet. The garment collapsed around him.

Ellie covered her mouth as she laughed. When Raff poked out his head out she burst out laughing again. With his hood knocked askew she could now see the small man's face; his skin was a strange DayGlo orange and a Fu Manchu moustache surrounded his firmly set mouth. His irises appeared to be yellow. He did not seem to be amused by his graceless landing.

He disengaged himself and stood up. Vivid confusion wafted across his face.

"It is not supposed to happen like that. None of this is right at all."

"How *is* it supposed to happen?" Ellie asked innocently, still smiling. "Uh, could you turn your head? I need to get dressed, I'm freezing." Her request wiped his face of confusion. He appeared relieved to have been given a command, and nodded and bowed with great seriousness. He turned his back.

She took the bra, almost pitching him off the table, for one of his feet was still on it.

"I'm sorry!" she exclaimed.

She adjusted the bra around her breasts. Soon clad in breeches and tunic she informed Raff he could turn around.

"You didn't answer my question," she said. He was appraising her again. She crouched down to meet his eye. Somehow, he seemed bigger than before and it wasn't just the angle.

"I was waiting for you to give me leave—and to finish dressing, my lady," Raff said.

"You don't need my leave to speak, Raff. I always told my commanders," she said, surprised at her words, "to be frank and straightforward with me and not to treat me as a superior. Please start at the beginning and tell me everything."

"I'd rather give you a *proper* demonstration of my skills," Raff countered.

"Well, okay," Ellie consented. Raff adjusted his hood and nodded, launching into a flawless series of spins, jumps and backflips. Through it all, his needle-like blade wove a flashing silver aura about his dark form. She winced, sure he would slice off a limb. His precision and skill were astounding but the demonstration was comical all the same.

She would be well protected if the Aedolae brought an army of rats.

Raff placed his blade in its well-hidden scabbard and stood, his palms pressed together at his chest. Ellie applauded. Raff nodded again and let down his hood. Indeed his skin was neon orange, and slightly translucent, for she could see the network of veins beneath. His face was sturdy and handsome. A shock of black hair was gathered in a topknot.

"Do I please you, my liege?"

His voice now was earnest, and polite, but definitely not obsequious.

"Very much, but now for my answer. I'm still freezing. I'll finish dressing while you answer." She took the mailed vest from its hanger, settling it on her shoulders. It was very heavy. "I have been told that I was a great swordswoman once."

"Once?" Raff looked puzzled. "Your reputation is huge, my lady—"

"Call me Ell—" she started to say then corrected herself, "you can call me Siana."

The name was still strange, as strange as the ringmail about her thin shoulders. "I don't really remember any of it."

"That is not good, my la—"—he frowned—"Siana. But now you have me. In the old days, many dreamers were not warriors, and the Orange Guard fought for them."

"Why have you found me only now?" she asked. She buckled both belts about her waist. She pulled the steel vambraces onto her forearms. They felt good despite the weight. She felt less vulnerable with the vambraces and mail. As Raff talked she pulled on the socks and she discovered her boots beneath the cloak. The thick soles lifted her a couple inches higher.

She was starting to feel like Siana, like herself again.

She worked on the myriad laces of the boots.

"My species are the Jicinti," Raff was explaining, "selected by the Shekinah to serve your kind before the Detheros isolated the worlds. She granted us our power of diminution. The Jicinti served with unfaltering honor through the Coethyphys' dark assault on sojourners and many of us perished. In that day, the Shekinah paired sojourners with their Jicinti guards, and the system broke down when she disappeared. That is why I could not find you. But an Orange Guard feels the call in his soul and cannot rest until he serves his liege. I am at peace now I have found you."

Raff's explanation seemed too brief. She suspected he omitted certain details but she did not mistrust him. She settled the war cloak about her, as warm as her present from Graham, yet easier to move in. She tucked Timothy's journal in its familiar place inside her vest.

Something else I remember.

"Who is the Shekinah?" Ellie asked. The necklace with Paris' initials now rested in her palm. "Mercair mentioned her in the last book."

"She was the Illumination of all these worlds, before the Aedolae grew in power," Raff replied, sounding sad.

She was curious, but her sense of impatience discouraged her from pressing further. She put the necklace about her neck and tucked the pendant inside her shirt, after gazing at the inscription *PCD* one more time, sifting through the mix of feelings it engendered. She drew on the gloves. Now she was completely armored.

Sudden movement jerked her head up from the gloves. Raff's blade was out, striking at her left hand—and then something metallic came up from her right and blocked the attack.

"What?" she exclaimed, then realized what had blocked Raff's attack: the dagger in her hand. She had not thought at all, only reacted.

Raff laughed heartily, sounding genuinely pleased for the first time.

He leapt off the table at her, blade high. Another dagger was in her left hand, swatting his blade and crashing him backwards. Her right hand dagger flew and pinned him by his clothing to the table.

Raff threw down his sword with a clatter. This time he applauded.

"Now disengage me and put me in your pocket," Raff said.

"What?"

"Well, I am a pocket ninja"—Raff laughed—"that is what the Jicinti are. We live in pockets."

She pulled her dagger free, and twirled both daggers in her hands before replacing them in her breeches. She hadn't forgotten everything.

"A ninja girl and her pocket ninja," she mused, picking up Raff. He jumped into her tunic pocket—the same out of which he'd come.

"We are the sojourner's secret weapon." His masculine but diminutive voice was funny coming from below her chin. "Eventually my diminution will be negated when I jump out to give battle. But in the beginning, when I first find my liege, it is like this."

"You're not stuck being this small?" He was squirming around above the softness of her left breast. His foot jabbed her in the nipple. "Um, ow, Raff."

"I am so sorry, my lady," he apologized. "I am not yet used to my new abode." (Did a sojourner's relationship with her Jicinti imply this kind of intimacy?) "Do not worry; the problem with my size is only temporary."

"I'm glad for that"—she craned her neck to see his head—"because as impressed as I am, you wouldn't do much good like that. How did you get into my pocket anyway?"

"I was poking about outside your castle and next thing I was inside the pocket."

"The castle sucked you in," Ellie concluded. "It's a pretty weird castle, I've found."

"Must be," Raff agreed. "I couldn't find a door." Why did he and Graham experience the castle's façade so differently?

"How much do you know about my predicament?" she asked

"There is an army less than a day's march away, and they are after you," he said, sounding nonchalant.

"*Less than a day?*" Ellie hissed. Graham had estimated otherwise. But she knew it was the truth, for she had known it, last night, in her gut. "OK, let's cut to the chase. I may be Siana, but I have only one Eterokon, and I don't know how to get out, any more than you could figure how to get in. I don't trust this damned building to pop me out in a timely fashion. We're both screwed if some part of that dismal summary doesn't change. My fine outfit and renewed skill with daggers notwithstanding."

"I thought the Eterokoni were inseparable from the sojourner who possesses them."

"So say the books in the library here, but the castle is still hiding them from me. It's the rakshasa's doing, I think, because the castle was formed by him too. I wish the castle would hurry up decaying and be done with it."

"Would killing this *rakshasa* help?" Raff sounded excited.

"Maybe," Ellie mused, "but he ran off yesterday."

An hour later Ellie and Raff were in the ballroom. The treks from room to room seemed to take less and less time, though there was no diminishing in the size of the chambers or their number. Her weakness had made the route of her daily wanderings take so long.

Sunlight blazed through the Siana window, and through a fresh hole in the ceiling. The orphaned staircase, scored as if by acid, still terminated in the air a long jump from the ruined doorframe of her gallery. Ellie fingered the Sundial in her belt pocket and contemplated the stained-glass image of herself.

"All dressed up with nowhere to go," she said out loud. "At least a girl can go to her doom well-dressed."

"Siana," said Raff, "cut the doom crap and tell me where the windows are."

"These are the only two," she answered, liking his attitude. "This big beautiful one of me, and the little one up past that doorway. It seems a shame to break the big one."

"Well, let's try the little one." Raff said. She had hauled both ladder pieces to the ballroom. With one she made a bridge between the top stair and the gallery. It bowed under her weight but held. Being back in the little room was strange. The floor was free of dust, but the window as begrimed as ever. She stomped on top of her dirty pallet in purposeful anger and then heaved the knight's helmet, stolen from the armory, at the panes of her little window. It gave way with a satisfying explosion of glass. She cleared the remaining shards from the frame and poked her head through. She couldn't see the wall of the castle beneath her, but she could see the ground. A gelid breeze struck her face as she cursed.

"I can't jump that far and I can't see the wall," she reported to Raff.

The rope! But what would they tie it to?

She went back to the amphitheater. No rope. She had seen it there last night, but the amphitheater was totally empty. She hunted for a few minutes, but she could *feel* that it was gone.

"The castle traded me rope for my garments—and you, Raff," she said. "It's not letting go of me easily."

"You'll have to lower yourself out and see if you can find a foothold," Raff suggested.

"*That* sounds like fun," Ellie said, but knew she'd try it all the same. She had butterflies in her stomach. Time was slipping away from them. They went back to the gallery. She expected, from the nervousness in her bones, to see the Aedolae's army cresting gently sloping hills in the distance, but the landscape was empty of all but the litter of wrecked houses.

She lifted herself out the window backwards, gripping the window frame. The sensation of dangling feet and trembling arm muscles was not pleasant. She couldn't feel any wall below and her eyes were squished against rough stone. It took all her strength to pull herself back up. As she crunched her way over the window frame Raff dragged across the stone beneath her chest, a lump in her pocket.

"Are you okay?" she worried, falling on her pallet with a thud.

"Fine," he said. "I'm tougher than that. Besides, it is part of our nature that nothing can harm us in the Pocket." She smiled at how he said *The Pocket*.

"What now?"

"There is one more window to break. Perhaps the castle wall is navigable there."

"And perhaps not," Ellie argued.

"That window doesn't look like you anyway," Raff said. "Let's break it."

She fancied she could hear his smirk.

"OK," Ellie said, and left her gallery for the last time.

Down on the ballroom floor she hefted a piece of leg armor, also purloined from the armory, and flung it with all her might at the center of the stained-glass goddess.

The ensuing eruption was a flock of glass bats. The colored shards and filaments of melted lead in between didn't just shatter, but swooped down and around her, falling in such a way that the entire window rushed past her and crashed onto the floor of the ballroom in a totally unnatural way. She screamed and held up her mailed arms to shield her eyes as the fragments smacked against her. When it was silent, she dared to peer out between her fingers. She expected to feel pain, see blood from cuts, but she was unscathed.

She stood in between the goddess' legs and the entire window lay on the floor behind her, the myriad panels separated and the lead work broken, but the overall design and appearance of her alter ego completely intact. Though now the image of Siana was spread apart and bloated.

Ellie noticed the Glass Sword first. It lay next to a glass hand severed at the wrist. It wasn't a flat panel of clear glass resembling the Glass Sword of the books. Sunlight glinted off a beveled surface. There was a hilt, wrought in three dimensions and largely translucent She reached for it. It felt perfect in her grip, made for her. She hoisted it aloft.

This was no stained-glass panel. This *was* the Glass Sword and the Siana in the window had been holding it all along.

Ellie whooped in triumph. Raff leapt the huge distance from her pocket to the floor without injury and ran in between the shards, which lay like jewels in the sun. He scavenged one from the wreck of the Siana-image's face, struggling with its girth. It was the Eye, freed from its prison upon the image's brow. She took it and rested it in her palm, a thin wafer of marvelous workmanship. A countless number of tiny gems were fused and, in places, melted together to depict an eye surrounded by whorled patterns of a myriad colors—itself a miniature stained glass, impossibly precise, impossibly beautiful.

It felt too good to be true, but it was true. She had found the Eterokoni after all!

The Glove was encased in a thin veneer of clear glass, easy enough to smash free. The Beetle was a brass marvel about the image's neck, and above it were the Kalimba and Torc. Ellie clasped the Torc about her neck with reverence, surprised by an immediate whisper of power. It had been one of her first discoveries. The Kalimba was a light cold touch on her neck below the Torc, virtually weightless on its fine chain.

Raff found the Bracelet, thrown a little farther toward the wall opposite her gallery. She placed it in her belt. Ellie soon found the Star, and latched it to its chain in her belt exactly where the image in the window had secreted it. All nine of her Eterokoni, settled on her person once again, after such long absence. She didn't know which to try to use first.

The pocket ninja was straining to lift a large panel of glass from Siana's torso. Underneath were two sheaths: one empty and gleaming—the Glass Sword's.

The other held Daevon's blade.

She knelt down and pulled them free. Raff dropped the panel and it cracked across the center. She sat on her knees with Daevon's blade in her lap and stared. She slid it from the scabbard. Tears welled in her eyes.

"Well, now I'm complete," Ellie said, holding the sword and touching Paris' pendant inside her shirt. "I may not remember much about them now, but this is proof of the books. These are my memories, the dreams I shared with them, for better or for ill."

She re-sheathed the blade and brushed away tears.

She stood and strapped the double sheaths across her back. She felt both weak and strong at the same time; the surprising physical weight of swords, belts and ringmail dragged on her body, but they also granted her energy, confidence, lift. The Ellie of the castle was gone at last.

She dug in her pockets, found a scarlet ribbon and tied back her hair. Despite the Eterokoni tugging at her mind, despite the cold of the day, despite the urgency in the pit of her stomach, she patiently threaded the stray wisps of her hair into tiny braids and wove in the two feathers, harvested from another pocket.

"Now I'm ready."

Raff had disappeared. Her eyes found him up on the broad window ledge.

"Good thing," he answered grimly, "for the army has arrived."

DREAMBINDER

1015th Year of the Detheros

E llie raced to the open window frame. The army of the Aedolae crested the low hills a half mile off. Black siege towers jutted a hundred feet into the air. Sunlight glinted on glass spheres. *Like the ones at Mihali.* Despite her terror, her eyes roved the scene with military instinct.

Between the towers mammoth sand barges crawled, drawn by oxen. She had seen such craft in the desert beyond Kadesh. A flock of green birds circled the towers—small at this distance but indubitably Kadesh's eagle guard. At the head of the advancing line was a smaller sandcraft fitted with a thousand flashing mirrors. The line of metal poles along its deck pricked her memory, akin to those in the waters of Cylindrax. She knew each pole would be topped with the symbol of Ghislain's realm: cross atop a half circle.

All of this informed her sinking heart that Ghislain was here.

The books couldn't really describe the fear. Siana had not always been courageous, and had admitted her fears and frustrations—increasingly so as the narrative had progressed. But reading the stories did nothing to prepare Ellie's heart for the experience she had now.

I am Siana, I have the Eterokoni. I am alive, they've never taken me and they aren't going to now. I have a job to do.

"My lady, they advance." Raff himself sounded none too sure. "What is our strategy?"

A strange calm settled in her, a frozen clarity. There was little noise as yet from the huge throng threading its way between the wrecks of fallen houses. The wintry day was beautiful and calm, a strange beauty amid the pulsing expectancy of coming battle. Her last thought resonated. *I have a job to do. I have to rescue Timothy.* She had told Graham the proud Siana must be gone.

"We flee," she told Raff and took the Kalimba down from its clasp. The tiny fan-like instrument rested in her hand. The books said a small button was hidden on its back to activate its power. She turned it over and quested for the button.

A shadow fell across them from the hole in the ballroom ceiling.

Ellie raised her eyes to witness a perfect facsimile of her childhood home crash down directly on top of her.

When she awoke Ellie had no sense of how long she had been knocked out. The day was still bright, and all was silent. Raff was nowhere in sight. She lay amid a fractured wreck of her childhood living room. Drywall dust coated everything. Through the shattered bay window (which once looked out on unkempt yard and busy road) she saw the familiar wall between amphitheater and ballroom. She realized with the weird clarity of dreams that *all* those falling houses, during the whole time of her imprisonment, were replicas of her childhood home. But for the first time one had landed inside the castle walls. She couldn't fathom why the impact hadn't killed her, and why she now sat inside the house instead of lying crushed beneath it. She stood up. Nearby was the mirror from the upstairs bathroom, fallen through the ceiling, and her eye was drawn to that same crack in its surface.

Seeing the crack woke her to full attention.

The army.

The Glass Sword was out of its scabbard and in her grip in an instant. She had been holding the Kalimba when the house struck, but now it was gone and its chain at her throat was empty. *I guess it will be back*, Ellie thought, not really understanding that aspect of the Eterokoni's workings. *And where is Raff?*

There was whump nearby, a room or so away. She tiptoed into the shadow of a closet door, where it hung askew on destroyed hinges and peered through a broken side window toward the hall that led to the Vicious Room. A rusty gutter had fallen across that doorway. Beyond something big and orange moved from left to right. She crouched down.

There was another whump, much closer. Something was in the ballroom, beyond the ruined kitchen. The kitchen windows were smaller, and from where she crouched in the living room they didn't afford any useful view.

Nails clicked on the ballroom floor.

She was barely hidden, for there were multiple fissures in the drywall and the windows were all blasted out. The noise sounded familiar, the same sound her cat's nails made on the old wood floor of her bedroom, waking her up on school days. Only this must be a much larger cat.

The clicking paced a semicircle around the living room and stopped below the side window facing the Vicious Room. Whatever it was was no more than three feet away, on the other side of the wall.

It began to purr, a deep throaty purr that vibrated the floorboards.

A shock of orange fur poked through a fissure in the wall. A memory burst to mind: Benjamine, crushed by the ship's mast, eyes blankly staring as he slid into the icy water.

During the attack of the cyclopean cats.

Ellie started to reach for the Glove then thought better. Cats smell too well. She couldn't think what to do. The clarity she'd had before the falling house was gone. Her simple resolve to flee had been blasted aside, and now she didn't know where the Kalimba was or how soon it would return.

Another whump. At least three cats.

She reached for the Bracelet of Petrifaction and strapped it to her wrist. She closed her eyes and tried to feel something. She was surprised to find its thrum of power, stronger than the Torc.

She *gathered* the power in her mind and then concentrated on releasing it in a wide circle. Old instincts were coming back.

With a cracking sound the purring abruptly ceased.

Well, that still works, she smiled and stood. The nearest cat had become a gray statue below the windowsill.

While a very lively orange cat perched on the jagged edge of the hole in the ceiling. Ellie ducked as an shockwave of radiant energy slammed through the wall. She smelt burnt wood.

She touched the Torc at her throat. She felt a questioning prick, as if a sentience within the Torc were querying her about something. Her mental response was aimless, panicked. Immediately she grew in size, feeling a buoyancy in her limbs. Her head cracked against the ceiling and instinctively she armored the top of her body, thickening her skin.

Ellie burst out of the damaged house fifty feet tall. Two thousand pounds of screaming feline leapt at her, but she backhanded it with a gloved fist and sent it spinning out over the amphitheater.

She could see three other petrified cats below her as she grew. The air about her flashed orange as six more cats were literally catapulted onto the castle roof. Her defensive swing of the Glass Sword was careless, but nonetheless it sliced open four of the beasts and took out a majority of the outer wall of the ballroom. She was now a hundred feet tall, the Torc's power coursing unchecked through her flesh. She was looking down on the castle roof, her feet rooted in the wreck of the northeastern end of the building. On either side of her peripheral vision was the impossible spread of the castle, her nine month prison, fanning out 180 degrees to fill all the world. But she had no time to see.

The remaining two cats sprung at her midriff, beating their bat's wings. She cracked one with a vambrace while the other one reached her belly, hanging by its claws. She ripped it loose, letting it dangle snarling between thumb and forefinger while she surveyed the scene.

The army of the Aedolae was an ant hive of activity at the base of the castle. The cats had been flung by catapults stationed at the rear of the force; two let loose more giant felines as she watched. The sparkle of mirrors showed Ghislain's sandcraft was hanging back, still a half mile away. But the other craft was against the walls, dropping a ramp into the gap her sword had cleared.

She flung the dangling cat at the nearest catapult, hearing its body crunch against the woodwork. More cats struck the ring-mailed expanse of her chest, which was now a hundred feet across, and she swept them away, down onto the black mass below. She was still growing; she couldn't stop the Torc.

A tiny voice at ground level yelled commands, and the army loosed a black cloud of arrows. A thousand struck her, some glancing off her armor but hundreds sticking into the flesh of her legs and upper arms like a welter of bee stings. Pain flooded her mind and she felt a shift in the power of the Torc, a disorienting deflation.

A thirty foot timber from one of the ruined houses, thrown by a trebuchet atop a black tower, socked her jaw and knocked her off balance. Her shin caught on the lip of the hole in the ballroom ceiling and she fell over the edge of the castle.

When she struck the sand barge below she was a hundred feet tall and shrinking. The barge split beneath her and the Eye filled her mind with a crazed susurrus of Achthroin thoughts as her weight crushed a hundred of them.

When she regained her feet she was normal size.

She stood between the halves of the barge, which groaned and settled, and amid a wreck of Achthroin bodies. Behind her was the curve of castle wall and before her the gap in the barge was quickly filling with enemies. Ellie was outside the castle, *Outside* for the first time in her memory. But she had no time to feel liberated.

She touched the Torc, but no power answered.

Four Achthroi rushed her. One, ten feet tall, wielded a metal-tipped staff. Two, small and beetle-like, held wooden crossbows. The fourth lumbered awkwardly on three legs and sported a rusty knife.

She drew on the Glove. She sidestepped right to avoid the tall Achthron. He clicked in confusion, misshapen head swiveling. The beetle-like ones somehow tracked her movement and aimed their weapons. A crossbow bolt grazed her ear and the second caught her in the shoulder but only bruised, deflected by the mail.

She slashed left with the Sword and sliced a leg from the tall one. Wielding her blade was natural, like falling into memory. The Achthron went down with a fury of clicks, dropping his staff. The fourth stood and stared stupidly. She rushed the beetle-like Achthroi, unsheathing Daevon's blade with her left as she ran. She had trained for this, and her skills were returning below the level of thought, dragging Ellie back into the lethal dreams of her past.

Wielding both blades she was a translucent shadow, taking them down.

The fourth Achthron seemed to have spotted her again. Her invisibility was incomplete or failing. More Achthroi entered the wreck of the barge, a closing dark circle, though they kept their distance, confused by what they saw. Not this one. He grinned from a lopsided, lipless mouth and circled her, blade extended. Ellie struck with the Glass Sword but the stroke didn't fall where she intended, and cleaved his knife not his arm.

She was already tired.

The Achthron dropped the remainder of his blade and in a movement too canny for such an awkward creature seized the staff of his dying comrade, bringing it around in the same arc of motion to smack her hand. Daevon's blade fell from her grip.

She sliced out with the Glass Sword, cutting through his left arm and across his chest to bisect the staff. He fell with a gurgling howl.

She spun about, sensing motion at her back. A blur of Achthroin limbs and faces closed in, ten feet off. She shook the Bracelet and watched a grey pallor rush across the features of her attackers. The front row toppled toward her, pushed by the continuing momentum of Achthroi behind.

With a rush of air a javelin pierced the fabric of her cloak beneath her left armpit. The javelin stuck in the ground, pinning her. She ripped free of it, but stumbled as one of the green eagles descended on her, talons first. She landed on her butt on a crushed corpse and raised her left vambrace to block the claws, which scraped on steel and found no purchase. But the bird's descending weight followed, knocking her backwards. She slashed desperately upwards and took off the eagle's left wing. It jumped backwards screaming, but its rider leapt over its head and landed with a mailed boot on Ellie's right shin. Ellie screamed and the warrior's response was to ground her heel into Ellie's flesh harder.

The woman was six feet tall and pulled a broadsword from the scabbard at her back. Ellie raised the Glass Sword in defense but was too weak and in pain to strike out. Her opponent seemed shocked when her gleaming steel parted on the translucent surface of the Eterokon. The woman threw down the useless hilt and stepped back, taking her foot off Ellie's shin.

Ellie forced herself to get up, at first afraid her leg had been broken. It didn't seem to be. The warrior removed her helm, waves of blonde hair streaming out. The beauty of her hair was incongruent and mesmerizing; Ellie stared until the amazon threw her massive helm at her face. It caught her in the temple, ringing her head with a fresh shock of pain and clouding her vision.

When her vision cleared the amazon had closed in on her with a pair of long daggers. Ellie shook the Bracelet and the warrior froze.

An eruption of dirt and grass to her left.

She had begun to feel sick and horrified and exhausted. Several cats perched atop the broken barge, cyclopean eyes glowing crimson. A second later the turf all around her was exploding.

She had never read about Siana wishing for more Eterokoni, but Ellie wished for more now. Something to block the pain of her damaged shin, or something to let her fly directly up.

She dodged as best she could, but couldn't do more. She couldn't get out of that narrow space and away, nor could she do anything to attack. She still wore the Glove, but it wasn't helping much.

Her face was pelted with pellets of stone as the cats' rays struck and shattered the petrified Achthroi. Hundreds of arrows, shrunk by the Torc to toothpick size, still tormented her skin, causing fresh waves of pain as she ran. And with every step, her shin and ankle lanced her mind with agony. The air was thick with dust and bright red light.

It was soon obvious they weren't trying to kill her. She would have been dead by now.

A huge fragment of fallen house was catapulted into the gap between the halves of the barge. On the side facing her she saw the window of her childhood bedroom. Another strange and incongruent sight. She was now boundaried on every front, by castle, barge and house. More cats were landing, flapping their wings. She petrified most as they alit. The tops of siege ladders appeared on the roof of the house, and archers rained down arrows—now full size and lethal. One glanced off her right vambrace. Soon all the cats were jumping down at her, heedless of the petrifaction, and the archers purposefully set the barge alight. Green eagles were landing on the castle wall behind the barge.

She touched the Torc again. Still nothing. She recalled from the books how Ghislain's presence had negated its power. He then, at least, must be here.

Ellie swept her braceleted wrist across the snarling scene in front of her, petrifying the current wave of orange felines. She had frozen most of the cats now, but the petrifaction would wear off if she didn't kill them soon. She ran toward the nearest, while her leg protested red agony.

A burning arrow swept past and lit her breeches on fire. She dropped the Glass Sword in surprise. She beat at her clothes ineffectually and was forced to drop and roll.

A net was cast over her. She sat up and found it was woven of tiny but resilient strands, a weave so close that it blocked half of her vision. She couldn't see her swords. She reached for her thigh daggers, but eagles landed on the net on all sides, pushing it down and restricting her movement. A javelin smacked her wrist as she prepared to use the Bracelet. Its power could be independent of her motion; the book said it acted on the Vinna birds without her consent during Paris' dance. But it did nothing now, and soon she was pinned mercilessly by huge stones dropped from the eagles' backs onto the net in a halo about her body. A thicket of javelins pricked through the net and settled inside her mailed vest above her heart.

Eagle guards dismounted and held her arms as others cut the net away. One held a blade to her throat as they hauled her to her feet. A Gnish parted the line of eagles, more vivid and ugly with his face-splitting maw than she could have imagined from the books. He held something reflective, a pair of steel vambraces linked by a silver chain.

Keeping the blade to her throat and javelins aimed at her chest, the guards stripped away her scabbards and vest and then ripped open her shirt from throat to belly. They tore off her belts, took the Eye from her brow, pulled vambraces, Glove and Bracelet from her wrists, and slashed at her breeches, dislodging the toothpick arrows, slicing her skin further, sending rills of blood down her legs.

They wrenched her arms behind her back and the Gnish stepped behind her. Cold steel enclosed her forearms; the thing he held was a sort of manacle. The host of javelins and the blade at her throat were removed as the metal snapped shut. The crowd of enemies stepped back. There were hot tears on her bruised cheeks. Her torn clothes and Eterokoni lay in a pile at her feet.

"Kneel"—the Gnish fixed his cruel eyes on her—"before the true Master of these Realms". Tears blocked her vision. She trembled with exhaustion and fear. Cooling sweat and the cold November wind raised goose bumps on her arms. Smoke from the burning barges choked her and made her cough. Paris' bra, torn into two, dangled uselessly from her shoulders. They had cut away her jeweled underpants along with her breeches and she felt all their eyes on her naked flesh, humiliating her. They had left her only her boots.

And Paris' pendant, still hanging between her breasts.

She raised her filthy tear-streaked face and met the Gnish's eyes.

"I will not kneel."

She had imagined her voice would come out strong and defiant, but to her own ears it sounded small and terrified. It had all gone wrong. She was Mistress of the Eterokoni, the books said, but they had all failed her. She tried to move her arms, but they were bound by the short chain between the manacles, and could only separate an inch. She knew they could not really take her Eterokoni from her, yet there was nothing when she reached for them with her mind. Why had she thought she could singlehandedly challenge these powers?

I can't even use my namesake weapon.

She was knocked from behind by some blunt weapon, forced to her knees.

A door opened in the ruined house that had been catapulted into the gap. A figure stepped through, a man, yet a halo of power surrounded him, a mirror which passed through his body left to right, ear to ear, bisecting him. Or so it appeared. The man walked toward her, holding the walking stick that he obviously did not need for support. Its haft was gleaming ice and the jewel on top a shining fire.

She felt queasy, and the world begin to spin. All of the minions of Ghislain blurred into a revolving circle of colors, until Ellie was alone on a patch of sunlit ground in the eye of a tornado. The roar of the flames hushed to a whisper, and all at once he was before her, her nemesis, or so the books said.

She did not remember him.

He chucked her chin with the enormous ruby atop his walking stick, and forced her head upwards to meet his eyes. His eyes were unveiled and a tiny, naked version of herself reflected in each. During her reading, she had imagined his mirror eyes as flat, but she saw that they were shaped like eyes, their curvature distorting the small Ellies that looked back at her.

She could not tear away her gaze.

The cold ruby moved down her neck, past her collarbone, and stopped over her heart. His eyes were expanding, filling her frame of vision, and the sunlight was going away. There were no longer Ellie reflections there, but pinpricks of darkness that grew to fill the mirrors, even as the mirrors expanded to fill the world. Her mind was awash in darkness and she lost consciousness.

THE DREAM ENDS

Waking World Calendar: November 11, 2010

When I open my eyes, I'm lying on a faded couch in my Seattle apartment. The clock says it's nine. I don't remember anything about the day or why I dozed. It must be nine PM because the windows are dark.

I decide to go to a tavern down the street. I don't exactly decide. There is a sense of necessity, as if I have lived this day before and know already this is what I decide to do. This compulsion reminds me of my first dreams, before I mastered my dreamself and began to dream with purpose. And yet I'm in my apartment, I'm awake, and I'm not dreaming.

Right?

It's chilly outside but the tavern exhales warmth. It must be a weekday because it's mostly empty. I choose a booth, where the light is dim. One of the bar's occupants stands out. I can't see his face, but his long, heavy coat is familiar. The fur-lined hood is drawn up and the coat is overly warm for a Seattle winter. But the strangest thing is the basket of unfolded laundry on the floor next to his seat at the bar. The basket is bright white plastic, and outshines every other color in the place.

I don't remember ordering but there is a beer in front of me. I look up from my beer and find the hooded figure and his laundry gone. Now there is absolutely no one in sight, though I hear sounds from bartenders, cooks, and waitresses bustling about elsewhere in the establishment. My seat faces the street and front door.

The door opens.

The woman who steps inside has very long brunette hair. Her eyes cast about before finding me, then she smiles and waves. Her blue jeans are brand new and her clingy, gauzy top bares both her belly and her cleavage. Her shoes, tall heels with thick soles, clack on the wood floor. She sits down opposite me. She smells of cinnamon, a comfortable smell. Her plentiful jewelry is vividly beautiful, but around her neck hangs a large and ugly medallion of flattened metal. It combines a circle and a cross. It nags at my mind but I can't place it.

The girl reaches across and touches my hand. Minutes tick by. We seem to be talking but I have no sense of what we say. I wonder if I have drank too much, yet the beer in front of me is hardly touched.

After a while, the girl excuses herself, presumably to the rest room. While she is gone, I notice a man alone at a far table, elegantly dressed in a Spanish style. He sips at a drink in a tall glass. The girl's return interrupts my surveillance and this time she slides into my side of the booth. Her jeans rub against my thigh and the raw feel of their texture makes me glance down. To my surprise I am not wearing anything and wonder if I left my apartment this way. But I remember hulking down in my coat to stay warm during my brief walk here.

The girl only smiles and shrugs, unconcerned. She rests her head on my shoulder—I am a bit taller—and places her left hand on my belly. I can feel the bite of her rings on my skin. She kisses my neck and her hand slides beneath my breast. I am no longer worried about being naked; it feels fine and natural because she isn't worried about it.

Her lips pause mid kiss. She sits bolt upright and says something, words I can't hear.

She has found the vicious scar along my ribcage, but I don't remember anything about it. Her eyes are full of concern. They are grey, beautifully shaped with long dark lashes. I shrug and she tries to smile. I notice her lips at rest form an unusual triangle shape. She puckers them for a kiss, which hides this, and then we are kissing for a long time.

More time passes in a dreamy haze. Light fills the windows of the tavern, but it can't be morning yet, as bars don't stay open all night in this city. The girl and I are on opposite sides of the booth again and I am picking at the label on my beer where it is coming loose. There are six or seven empty beer bottles on the table now, pushed to the side. I don't drink that much and neither does my friend, so this strikes me as odd. I worry the label off the bottle and glance at it as it falls to the tabletop. Another duo of shapes: cross and semicircle. It reminds me of the girl's incongruent necklace. If they were printed letters, they would be all the same font.

As the light grows, her words are coherent for the first time.

"Let's ride the ferry," she says.

I don't remember answering but soon we are beside the door. The tavern is empty and silent. The chairs have been placed atop the tables, the lights are off, and as the sun breaks through the skyline it cuts a yellow path through a thousand dust particles in the air. On an antique hat-rack by the door hangs a plethora of clothes. I am still naked, save for combat boots that are ridiculous in my otherwise unclothed state. There are a host of scratches on my legs, but the girl doesn't notice. She picks out a dress for me to wear, long and sleek with a big bow at the back. I have a dim memory of the two of us dressing up in an immense wardrobe whose only lighting was an effervescent red glow.

"You have the perfect figure and the perfect face and hair," the girl says as I put it on. "You can slip on a dress and be beautiful, no bra, no makeup. I'd look all saggy and tousled."

I sputter some protest but she pulls me by my arm, out into resplendent sunshine. Impossibly the sun is already at its zenith. I grab her wrist to read her digital watch, which I remember buying for her. She has bedazzled its perimeter with fake diamonds. It reads 2 AM.

The temperature is perfect. There are parked cars but no one else in sight. At only one intersection are there other people, huddled around a black mass in the street. They pay us no heed. Through the jumble of arms and legs I make out a bat with tattered wings prostrate on grey concrete, as big as a truck. My friend has no interest and pulls me toward the piers. She wants to walk hand in hand, and keeps admiring me in the dress. Her mood is as bright as the morning, but something feels wrong. It is 2 AM and the sun is out. I was naked in a bar but no one cared. I can't remember the date or what I did yesterday. Yesterday was winter and now a thin dress is warm enough.

I also know that while this girl is as dear as a sister, she has never been in my Seattle before.

I glance toward the Space Needle, or where it should be, but instead there is a black spire with wicked hook-like projections.

Down at the piers are a few more people, and a ferry is boarding for a morning commute that shouldn't yet be happening. We rush across the pedestrian ladder, barely on time. Inside, the small number of foot passengers is swallowed up by the immensity of the craft. We sit in a booth near the front, our seats sticky mustard-colored vinyl. The windows are bright but badly in need of cleaning. I watch the water moving away from the ferry's sides. It always seems at first that the world is moving, not the ferry.

The girl excuses herself to the bathroom and I watch the sway of her hips in her blue jeans as she walks. She is exquisitely graceful. She has pulled her tresses into twin pigtails but even still her hair falls quite a ways down her back.

She doesn't come back.

I wait, enjoying the sun and the view of forested coastlines dotted with houses, but the feeling that something has been wrong with the entire day grows, shattering my reverie. I don't want to lose her on the ship by leaving the booth, but it feels like an hour has passed, way too long. I get up and begin to explore. There are no longer people on board. I go into the women's bathroom on that level and it is empty. I check every stall.

When I leave the bathroom the day has changed. The water is choppy and the color of steel. The ferry is in open ocean with no land in sight. I run to every window frantically to verify this.

Through the windows I can see the sun has retreated behind high thin clouds.

I try the other levels but they are all empty and she is nowhere to be found. The doors to the outside decks are locked.

I spend another hour checking the ferry top to bottom. My stomach is a knot of anxiety. I think the ferry is still moving but with the featureless sea surrounding it is hard to be sure. I return to the booth, hoping against the knot in my stomach that somehow she will be waiting for me.

The booth is empty.

A footfall behind me. I spin.

The girl is fifty feet away, near the empty café, running.

"Elizabeth, go!" she yells, waving me away, though the gesture makes no sense in this enclosed, locked space. "I don't want you to die for me. Please!"

I can't even begin to understand what she is saying. Tears course down her face. She clutches her chest and skids and falls to her knees, all in the same motion. Bright red wells from between her fingers.

A strangled syllable is forced through my lips. I run to her. Blood pumps down the front of her gauzy shirt and her hands fall limp. I can see no reason for the blood from her chest. Her eyes are wide with shock and her lips are parted in agony as I cradle her in my arms and watch her die.

When her precious blood has coated her body and my legs and pooled on the floor all around us, and her body has gone lifeless in my arms, I scream and scream, and at last stand up with fists clenched. The empty ferry mocks me with echoes.

The girl's body is gone, floor clean. I shake my head in bafflement. My brain has been dredged by emotion.

One of the deck doors is now propped open and I rush through, expecting a rush of wind but there is none. Only severe cold. The door shuts behind me on its own. I find I'm naked again, with just my chunky shoes and a red pendant I haven't noticed before hanging above my heart. I am shivering immediately.

There is a footfall behind me. I turn. It is the man in the greatcoat from the tavern. His face is lean and feral, and at his throat is a large tiger's head amulet. His hands are gloved.

"Come here, my prize"—he beckons, but I trust him not at all—"you see now you cannot drive me out, you cannot run from me, and the only ending is you shall be mine."

My rush surprises him.

I headbutt him like a football player, knocking him aside. I make it through the door but the swish of his coat follows me. I run twenty more feet then I slip in the pool of blood that was gone five minutes before. I land awkwardly but manage to turn to face my pursuer.

There is someone else. In a booth is the other man from the tavern, elegantly dressed in a Spanish fashion, sitting at ease with one leg propped on the opposite knee. He holds out his walking stick, horizontal to the ground. A line of light, brilliant and precise, a razorblade through the fabric of reality, spurts from its ruby tip, crossing the interior of the ferry. My pursuer's momentum carries him into it and I see it etch a red line across his belly.

He falls in two pieces next to me.

The elegantly dressed man stands, leaning on his stick.

"Foolish being," he addresses the corpse as its eyes glass over, "did you really think you could defy an Aedolae?"

About his throat hangs the same symbol I saw on the beer label. My body tenses at the word Aedolae. I know he is evil.

The man smiles at me. He seems unconcerned about my possible escape.

I run.

I take the nearest door, the men's restroom. But instead of finding a restroom I step out into Seattle, into the preternatural morning sun the ferry left behind.

There is only a brick wall behind me.

The street is shadowed by the concrete track of the monorail, up on pylons. Even though there is no sign of the door I came through, I am panicked and need to get away. I run up the staircase to the monorail station. It seems the best way to put distance between the man and me, for I know he is coming after me, doorway or no.

The monorail comes at once and I slip inside. Through the scratched windows I watch familiar Seattle slip by, then all at once the cityscape drops away and we are out over a sparkling blue ocean. The monorail track stretches on ahead, and the concrete pylons rise out of the ocean. There is an archipelago of tropical islands ahead.

The overhead display in the monorail changes from "Seattle Center" to "Aedol Via". The name rings a bell. It is the same root word the man mentioned as he gloated over my slain pursuer. It is evil.

I get up to pace the empty car but there is no point. There is nothing but water on all sides and nothing but to follow the track wherever it takes me. So I sit.

The speed is prodigious for we are between two of the islands in a moment. One is wild jungle and the other has a dotting of buildings, docks and quays. Men prepare their fishing nets and gear, and curiously their skin is black as jet.

Next we travel through a host of smaller islands, jade gems set in a glassy sea.

And then the monorail track tilts, pylons lengthening until they are hundreds and soon thousands of feet in height, lifting us into wide open sky. Soon I can't see the bottom of the pylons ahead nor can I see any sea or land. Everything below is hazy white nothingness. We pass floating chunks of rock, growing to the size of islands. I know this isn't possible, not in a world of ferries and taverns and Seattle streets, but I have been somewhere that it *is* possible, where I have seen all these things before.

The largest of the floating islands is ahead. The monorail slows. Tall evergreens grow in long vertical clefts, sheltered from the sun, and men and women navigate complicated network of ladders and rope bridges. As the monorail track rounds the curve of the island I espy a high white-walled city, whose buildings are a checkerboard of black and white stone.

And on the rock plain beyond a battle rages.

The monorail track descends onto the plain, and the pylons, once again a plausible earthbound, divide the battlefield. We slow to a crawl so I can see the litter of fallen bodies, many strange and inhuman. The wrecks of seagoing vessels dot the plain, anomalous in this waterless scene. Ahead, where the monorail pylons forsake floating island for sky, a group of figures huddle on the lip of the rock.

A Shadow in the sky descends toward the huddle, winking on and off as it approaches. It comes from the opposite direction as the monorail, and much faster. It collides with a pair of figures at the center of the huddle in a nimbus of black and gold.

The group is now on my left. My heart leaps when I spot—alive—my girl from the tavern and ferry. She is dressed like a soldier which is strange. A headless body lays in the dust behind her.

We begin to pass up the scene, and the whirring cloud of black and gold slows, separates. A woman is revealed standing on the Shadow, a horizontal hovering blackness. Her stance is awkward, as if her limbs have been pinned by an unseen force field.

I remember the scene, a scene from my War.

I am looking at myself.

I am pulled from the scene, out into the aether beyond the isle. I run to the back of the monorail car to see what is happening. The Shadow, bat-like, or more like a manta ray, is flapping away, with me still riding, and gold haloes my retreating form. The girl—Paris—reaches for me and begins to run. A huge barbarian of a man—Kadesh—raises his javelin and hurls it at her back. It rockets through the air in slow motion.

And then the monorail dips and my angle of vision is raised ten degrees. Ahead is blue sky and I see nothing more of Mihali.

I pound my fist on the thick glass. I need to see. The force of the javelin was about to tear through her body. Her chest would erupt in blood as it did on the ferry, in that precise place. Did I really want to see my friend's death again? No, but yes. If it had to happen, I wanted to see it, to experience that dreadfulness, the last moment of her life.

The monorail ploughs through the aether and then descends over a jungled realm.

Kadesh.

Wakened by the battlefield scene on Mihali, my mind is clear of the hazy timelessness of my night with Paris. She has never been in Seattle, in my world, so I must be dreaming or hallucinating. I am bombarded by a disordered collage of images from my lives Within and Without. I feel like I've dreamt a rich dream and I'm gradually rising toward the surface of the world of sleep as morning comes.

The monorail runs out over a cold sea, thirty feet above choppy waves. A faint upright hexagon shimmers on the grey horizon. We make for it with prodigious dreamworld velocity and pass through as if using the Kalimba. The monorail now runs on the ground like a train. The barren landscape is encircled by low, spiky mountains sporting neither vegetation nor snow. Within that ring is no sign of life or growing thing. Only the plain, flat, featureless, and ugly.

A black hemispherical structure lies at its center, dead ahead.

Dread grips me. It snaps my mind to rigid attention, locks my eyes.

Nothing about it at this distance should affect me so. Is it because it is *almost* a perfect hemisphere and yet not, as if designed to irritate the mind's expectation of uniformity?

Or is it the cloud of Shadow things above, black forms snapping in and out of the time stream?

Or the Abyss it straddles, a void sucking light from the sky?

Whatever it is, I don't want to go there.

Inside the car I race from side to side. I entered through a door, but there is none now. The windows are embedded in steel. There is no way out. I need to wake up.

The structure looms closer. It is pierced by a black spire, hundreds of feet in height leaning *just* slightly to one side. The spire is familiar: it replaced the Space Needle in our sunlit 2 AM walk. Occasionally Shadows dive past the car's windows, arcing their electricity across the glass. I realize these things are what Ghislain summoned to take me at Mihali. What he must have summoned to carry my brother from Ebon to this accursed place.

How can I be seeing this place? I have never been here. Everything else in this dream has reflected my waking life, my adventures, or the books in the library. Not this.

The surface of the structure is not in fact smooth, but a disordered mélange of turrets, spires, bulbous chambers, and twisted stone buttresses, all quarried from night black stone. All a mockery of the crenellations and ornaments of medieval structure, all slightly askew, as if a cathedral melted in the sun and cooled off kilter. The whole shape of it makes me queasy. My breath comes faster in my throat, rasping in the ashy silence of the car.

The bulbous growths move, *open*. Stone lids retract from stone eyes, all a different size but the largest a hundred feet across, swiveling to espy my train's approach. The irises are not stone but smoky glass, hiding deep within a spectral red glow. Some of the eyes nestle beneath arcs of stone resembling inverted horns.

Memories flood my mind. Firsthand memories of what I have lived. The Coethyphys attacking Orsian ships, and the nightmare being that gifted me the Sundial. Both had eyes framed in mantles of horn.

Why have I never marked this before?

The being who gave me the Sundial was a priest of the Coethyphys, about whom Bierce and I read. Who called the Aedolae his brothers.

And now at last I see his castle.

I am doing more than see it. The monorail passes over the Abyss on a stone causeway shaped like a dragon's foreleg. Ahead is a portcullis of dark metal, to either side gleaming black poles skewering towers of human—and not so human—skulls. The smoky eyes glare down on me, unblinking, hateful. The portcullis grinds open.

The monorail passes inside.

I enter a vast hall. A cheerless white light is filtered by a roof mostly open to the sky, a vast ribcage of curved stone beams. The largest of these supports the base of the black spire. Charcoal grey tiles form the floor, each larger than me. Between the tiles, in place of grout, is a grid of red liquid. This tracery of blood is the only color in the place.

The monorail stops shy of the hall's center and its sides and ceiling open like the carapace of a beetle preparing for flight. I sit frozen, for shapes, *huge* shapes, are moving along the periphery of the room, where doors open on blackness and the hundred foot walls curve inward at the top to create unnatural shadow.

Before me is a square area marked off by four metal spires. Sheets of translucent lightning, a force field, shimmer between the spires. Two wildly spiraling stone staircases wind down into this protected square from the base of the black tower far above, like haphazardly stretched coils of spring with no visible means of support. Inside the force field are four metal slabs. Two are empty and bloodstained, but bodies occupy the other two.

The nearer body is female and her black hair splays over the edge of the slab and reaches the floor in a beautiful wave. But her flesh is gray and cold, and her chest is torn asunder, ribs forced open and apart. I am grateful her face is turned away from me. It is hard to tell through the force field but I think a different color shimmering hovers above her ruined torso.

Two beings stand over the other body, their features hidden beneath hoods and flowing capes. This body is pink and decorated with blood, blood that runs down its arms and legs and trails off the slab, feeding the grid of blood running between the tiles. A sickness pervades my being. I know what I am witnessing. The priests of the Coethyphys preparing their *aliment*. The shapes move out of the shadows, becoming the cross-shaped heads of Coethyphys on long saurian necks, red eyes flashing with hunger. They take no notice of me or the monorail, but crowd in on the slabs, jockeying for position, sparking the force field when they get too close. The priests bend over the pink flesh of their victim and throw gobbets of that flesh onto the bloody floor without, where the Coethyphys seize them, spearing the pieces with their tusks, raising their heads to swallow.

I have never been this close to Coethyphys before.

The scene has mesmerized me and I don't notice the Coethyphys next to the monorail until its head, three feet across, descends into the car and stops a foot before my face. All three eyes glow red, and the middle eye—this eye alone free of a veneer of bony protuberances—fixes on me. The iris is scarlet and disturbingly human. It doesn't blink. I can read no emotion in that noseless, mouthless face (its maw is below, hard to see behind the tusks). I hold my breath as that horrible eye draws closer, with its brilliant iris and conjunctiva that resembles spoilt milk. I can see the texture of the horns over its other two eyes; I can see the veins pulse beneath its mottled skin. It is unnaturally quiet; there is no indication that it breathes.

It pulls its head away and races after a piece of flesh. Could it see me, in this strange vision? While it was inches from me, I thought how it would soon be my turn to lie on those cold slabs, vivisected by the knives of its priests.

A black curtain falls on my sight. The hard plastic of the monorail seat is no longer at my back. I am lying on hard ground, and my mind is flooded with tangible sensation: pain from bruises and cuts, the scrape of frozen soil against my bare skin, the bite of a cold wind. I am being rolled over, and sun blinds me as my eyelids flutter open. I wake from my vision into another dream.

The dream in which I am trapped.

· · · ● · ● · ● · · ·

I see blue sky through a guttering haze of smoke. I roll onto my side to find my nose against the feathered and taloned feet of Kadesh's eagles.

I remember where I am, who I am. Elizabeth, Ellie, *Siana*. Defeated and bound.

"Grab this creature," a voice barks with cold authority. There is a scuffling behind me. I struggle to sit up against with the cold metal of the manacles binding my arms. The Gnish and two of the eagle guard are restraining the person that rolled me over and woke me up. His whiskers bristle with anger, and his green eyes blaze. The rakshasa. He squirms in their grasp then quiets himself, as if he perceives such is below him. He stares past me to Ghislain.

"I will not let you have her," the rakshasa says. He doesn't look as scared as I would be, telling Ghislain that.

"Let me?"—Ghislain laughs coolly, tapping the ground with his stick—"and I didn't think rakshasas were known for their sense of humor. What, my friend, were you thinking, when you came to me for assistance with your recalcitrant prize? Siana has been my prize from the beginning, and you are but a dallier in stolen goods."

The rakshasa makes no response but disappears in a black fog. His captors startle.

Ghislain raises his walking stick. The prehistoric bird that attacked me in the Time Room coalesces out of the air, followed by a flashing succession of the shapes—tiger skeleton, feral dog—as the rakshasa struggles to find a form free of Ghislain's binding.

Ghislain slashes his stick from left to right with a laugh and bisects the rakshasa—and all three of his captors—with the same razor edge of light I saw in my vision. Six corpses hit the ground.

"Foolish being," Ghislain addresses the rakshasa's glassing over eyes, tiger-like again in death, "did you really think you could defy an Aedolae?"

The same words from my vision.

An earthquake of sound follows Ghislain's words. At the end of the corridor framed by the broken barge, a spider web of cracks has beset the faceless wall of my castle. Masonry begins to tumble and crash, all its remaining rooflines, parapets, towers, and domes.

In the beginning only I could see the castle and Graham could see nothing. During this last month of my awakening, how it appeared to me and how it appeared to everyone else came into line.

Now it is disintegrating in a great wash of noise, shaking the ground. Ghislain's soldiers hold their ears and edge back from the walls, but I make no move and neither does the Aedolae. In fact he looks singularly unimpressed.

And I have nothing left to lose.

Such a monstrously huge edifice should take up a third of its normal size, even in its total wreck. But not this castle, this blending of my mind and the rakshasa's power. As the wall in front of me comes apart, the pieces disappear from view, as if swallowed by the ground. In ten minutes there is nothing left but bare heath and hills.

All that time I had longed to find a way out and now I wish I were safely within its walls again.

I struggle to my feet. My balance is unsteady and I am shivering. My legs are bleeding from the myriad pinpricks of tiny arrows. I turn from Ghislain, glancing behind me. Fires rip through the halves of the barge, and the fallen house still blocks the space between them. The houses are one part of the dream I can take sole credit for.

I turn back toward Ghislain. Ahead, where the castle was, is a gap in the thronging presence of my enemies, a wide open expanse.

Ghislain catches my furtive glance. He appears a man, but his presence radiates power like a tangible heat.

"Siana, Master Dreamer," he intones quietly. I don't want to stare into his mirrored eyes again, but I don't want to be craven either. I can't decide which is the more prideful—to meet his gaze or not. His voice is smooth, hypnotic, one might say it is beautiful. "I am sorry that my mind took you on a vision quest. I did not intend to, not this time. But what did you see there, dreamer?"

He sounds solicitous but of course I do not trust this. I know cruelty lies below. But I see no reason not to answer him.

"I was back in Seattle and I saw Paris, though I didn't know it was she. And then I traveled along the Aedol Via, and I saw their castle, the castle of the dreamflesh eaters."

"Ah," Ghislain says, voice still low and mellifluous. "You have seen your destiny at last. And how does that feel?"

"Are you that stupid?" I retort, finding my defiance at last, meeting his gaze. "I stand here freezing my ass off, I just had my friend die in my arms, and I have been to the place where the Coethyphys are slicing my brother to pieces, again and again, year after year, and you ask me that fucking stupid question? Cut the gentlemanly crap. You are nothing more than a hateful life-destroying bully."

My words, spit out despite chattering teeth, destroy Ghislain's façade of gentleness.

"You could have stayed where I put you—" he hisses.

"In the Gardens?"

"Yes, in the Gardens, where I gave you dreams of eternal pleasure. I can take your mind back there, free you from the suffering that is to come—"

"If you're going to give them my body, then I want to suffer with my brother. I want to be there with him, no matter what. That's where I should have been all along." I am crying now, but I don't care.

Ghislain is struck silent. He replaces his smoky-lensed glasses, hiding the eyes that betray nothing anyway.

"You see," I babble through my tears, "you don't understand us at all. You don't feel, you don't care, and that is why you are unfit to rule over anything. You're a phantom nothingness."

"You try my tolerance, dreamer. Twice I have offered you this kindness, an escape from the pain that will define your reality, day after day, for an eternity of dreaming. But I offer it no longer, impertinent girl. I hope you have enjoyed your dreams, because now they are done."

"My Eterokoni will be back," I sputter. But my defiant spirit has left me.

"Spare your breath, Miss Grey," Ghislain says. "I suppose you did not read of the Q' Or-Endokoni, but you experienced one of them, *Dreamslayer*, first hand. You are now bound by another, *Dreambinder*. You cannot escape it and it not only holds your arms but also bars the Eterokoni from you."

"Then Mercair will come for me, again," I say, reaching.

"Mercair," Ghislain purrs, as if pondering the name. "You think Mercair cares so much for you?"

I notice that Ghislain speaks in the present tense, acknowledging he did not destroy my savior after all. Ghislain's thin lips curve in a crooked smile.

"Mercair," he continues, as if musing to himself, "Mercair of the Third Demesne. Mercair of the Circle, Cross and Moon. Mercair of the Third Key upon the Kalimba Eterokon, whose Demesne is ever hidden beneath a veneer of Memory. Mercair, by whose command the Achthroi cease their attacking."

"What are you saying?" I breathe. A shiver moves up my spine and it isn't the cold.

"Mercair, who cares so much for his Siana," Ghislain continues in his honeyed, sardonic tone, "who rescued her from a place of peace, sweet dreams and contentment only to plunge her into a dreamscape of violence and war. Mercair, who cares so much for his Siana, but took her from her Paris against her protestations."

"You liar. Like you would have let me stay with her." I am trying to shield myself from his words, from the sick suspicion stealing through my body.

"You have accused my kind of not caring, not feeling"—Ghislain forges on undeterred—"so why is it that you think that Mercair cares so much for you? I don't know what game he is playing, but it isn't yours."

"You're not going to turn me against him, Ghislain," I sputter feebly.

"Did not Mercair hint to you that he has lived within the Detheros for many lifetimes of dreams? Did he not *tell* you that each key on your Eterokon represents a different demesne of the Aedolae? How then does one of those keys lead to *his* world? *And did not Mercair remind you of me?* He does so because he is my brother, Siana. Mercair is one of *our* kind. He is an Aedolae."

"No, he isn't, he can't be," I argue, but I know it is the truth.

Epilogue

It is deep night in Vaelonn-Marr, and I am completely exhausted but I can't sleep. I was huddling under the roughly hewn but blissfully warm blanket they gave me but began to feel suffocated, so now with my head out I am lying on my back studying the stars. I remember when I was a child, and had a fever, my dreams would be so vivid, the colors rich and sparkling, lurid in their brilliance. My mom would tell me it was just the sickness. But I don't think the sickness ever left me, for once I had tasted those dreams, I wanted more, I kept searching the strange world Within until I found places where dreams were like that all the time.

Is it fever now that makes the stars so uncannily bright in the heavens? They twinkle violently, flashing silver, and I fancy I hear their jangling whispers. Is it fever that makes the moon, full and glorious, cast its light so fiercely on the river nearby? I thought my life in the world Without was brutal. I lost my brother, I lost my mom. But now, here Within, my body is feverish with cold, and a fatigue more severe than any I have ever known, and my soul is feverish with Loss. I have fashioned for myself a whole empire of Loss. And I am beyond tears. A succession of memories, names and faces, flit across my febrile consciousness, hanging in the star-kissed air above my head.

Benjamine, lost in the attack near Cylindrax.

Assav, killed at Mihali while sounding the alarm.

Daevon, slain defending me against the swords of Ghislain's mercenaries.

Mr. Bierce, irreconcilably bitter that his beloved servant was lost.

Talmei, Nao, ever faithful, strange beings of this world, crushed beneath an Orsian ship.

Neikolan, my stalwart captain, flung away like chaff.

Paris, sweet, loquacious, and graceful, who gave me tenderness and regard I didn't deserve, selflessly sharing with me her vivacity and beauty, slain by Kadesh.

Raff, who made me laugh and named me liege. I presume he too is gone, crushed by a falling house created from my own memories.

Parson Graham. At least his kindness did not prove fatal.

And Mercair, who lied to me all along.

I must have slept, for the stars are gone and I inhabit a world of cold grey twilight—the first hint of dawn. The moon has set and clouds have blown in, covering the sky. Frost crusts my eyelashes and my lips feel frozen in place. My body aches everywhere, from marching many miles in bitter cold, dressed in nothing but my boots, surrounded by the forces of the Aedolae. Yesterday, they showed my frail body no pity. My feet blistered horribly but at least the exertion kept me slightly warm and alive. They threw me to the ground amid their tents and retired to the warmth within. They left me without guard, assured that Dreambinder would keep me complacent. I assume they wanted me to feel utterly forsaken, miserable and alone. I saw no more of Ghislain. A few hours after nightfall, someone had tossed me the blanket, and I managed to roll myself up in it. I would have died from exposure otherwise.

I feel less feverish now, though no less miserable. I recall the night's whispering stars, and it is like remembering a dream of some totally other place. Something kisses my cheek, cold and wet. In the dim light, I can't see them, but I can feel the snowflakes beginning to fall. I must not be dead because my skin is still warm enough to melt them.

The phantoms of the night are gone. The faces, the names of those I loved, and who loved me. Now in this early morning grey my heart is still at last and my mind lingers only on the last part of Ghislain's vision, seeing again that dark castle and its Abyss. It floats before my eyes, threatening to overshadow the wintry scene. Between the black tents of Ghislain's army lumber shadowy forms of Coethyphys, gathering for their feast. They set down on their haunches like giant dogs, gruesome heads pillowed on massive paws, forming an expectant circle about me. Waiting for their Masters to ordain the feast.

The light of dawn waxes and I can see the spiraling snowflakes, big and puffy and tremendously beautiful. I remember how a rare Washington snowstorm would take all the litter in my backyard, the tires, the rotting furniture, the beer bottles, the muddy ruts in the driveway, and blanket it all in sameness, an even carpet of beautiful white. For a day, my ugly little world would seem lovely, pure and clean, and I would feel lovely inside.

The snow is piling on top of the tents, and the Coethyphys are revealed as bags and trunks and chariots. All these accoutrements of war slowly accumulate a film of snow that makes them beautiful too. I must still be feverish to have imagined dreamflesh eaters in the camp.

None of the army is awake, and a pure and holy silence dominates the scene, matching the singular elegance of the snow. I can't say I am happy to be alive, for my mind pictures the long hall beneath its stone ribcage and its floor crisscrossed with blood, an image that forestalls any hope. It is where I go now, to die and die again.

But the snow is beautiful and my heart still thrills with the magic of this moment. I know this magic is as fleeting as the snow days of my youth, for the next day the rain would return and wash away the beauty, uncovering those same ugly things, baring again the despair, the boredom, the hopelessness.

But that doesn't change the fact that for right now, for this singular, short moment in time, the world in which my consciousness dwells is surpassingly lovely.

I am still imagining. I must be, for a woman threads her way through the piles of gear I mistook for Coethyphys. She shines like an angel, shedding a rosy halo onto the snow at her feet.

I roll onto my side to better see her. She is oblivious to the cold, barefoot, dressed in a simply cut dress of resplendent satin. Her hair is free and falls about her shoulders, past her waist. She is kneeling beside me and her fingers gently stroke my face. The snow is beautiful, but she is far lovelier, with all the solidity and humanity that nature lacks. She is the love, the beauty that I long for, something less evanescent than the snow, something that would change my life forever and not just for a day.

She lays down beside me, on top of my blanket, and puts her hand on my blanketed shoulder. Her face is inches from mine. She touches her outspread palm to my chest, resting her hand above my heart and my angel, my Paris, says to me:

"I will never leave you, for I am here."

Then she snuggles up against me in the cold and puts her arms around me.

And I close my eyes to sleep again, leaving the barrenness of my dreams behind.

About the Author

Charles McCrone has been writing stories about alternate realities since elementary school. Two of his oldest characters are Siana and Mercair, who first appeared in the weightily titled _Advent Ingnaritatis_ when he was 13.

Charles lives in the Seattle area with wife Malena and runs Kaleidoscope School of Music, teaching guitar, bass, ukulele and rock band skills to students of all ages. When not playing music, he hikes, doodles, watches sci-fi, and daydreams about crossing the Detheros to behold the wonders Within.

https://charlesmccroneauthor.com

Made in the USA
Columbia, SC
07 November 2023